SISTER

KJELL OLA DAHL
Translated by Don Bartlett

ORENDA
BOOKS

Orenda Books
16 Carson Road
West Dulwich
London SE21 8HU
www.orendabooks.co.uk

First published in the United Kingdom by Orenda Books, 2020
First published in Norwegian as *Søsteren* by Gyldendal, 2018
Copyright © Kjell Ola Dahl, 2018
English translation copyright © Don Bartlett, 2020

A catalogue record for this book is available from the British Library.

This book has been translated with financial support from NORLA

NORLA
NORWEGIAN LITERATURE ABROAD

ISBN 978-1-913193-02-7
eISBN 978-1-913193-03-4

Typeset in Garamond by www.typesetter.org.uk
Printed and bound by CPI Group (UK) Ltd, Croydon CR0 4YY

For sales and distribution, please contact *info@orendabooks.co.uk*
or visit *www.orendabooks.co.uk*.

SISTER

PRAISE FOR KJELL OLA DAHL

'A triumph of skill, invention and edge-of-the-seat storytelling. As always, not to be missed!' Denzil Meyrick

'Kjell Ola Dahl's novels are superb. If you haven't read one, you need to – right now' William Ryan

'Dahl ratchets up the tension from the first pages and never lets go' *The Times*

'More than gripping' European Literature Network

'Utterly convincing' *Publishers Weekly*

'If you have never sampled Dahl, now is the time to try' *Daily Mail*

'Impossible to put down' *Guardian*

'The perfect example of why Nordic Noir has become such a popular genre' *Reader's Digest*

'Skilful blend of police procedural and psychological insight' Crime Fiction Lover

'Fiercely powerful and convincing' LoveReading

'Further cements Dahl as the Godfather of Nordic Noir, reminding readers why they fell in love with the genre in the first place' Culture Fly

'Kjell Ola Dahl's fine style and intricate plotting are superb. He keeps firm hold of the story, never letting go of the tension ... a dark and complex story, and convincing characters presented in excellent prose' Crime Review

'Dahl is such a talented writer whose writing is powerful and so convincing ... The only fault being the crime gets solved and life moves on!' *New Books Magazine*

'Suspenseful, beautifully and clearly written, with a sure-footed plot, this is a book that thrills' Live and Deadly

'Dahl writes wonderfully and it's clear why he is regarded so highly'
Have Books Will Read

'This is a dark, emotive and twisty mystery that has been tightly
woven, full of surprises and lovable characters – such a fab treat for
fans of Nordic Noir!' Chillers, Killers & Thrillers

'Twisty and incredibly well-written story, full of suspense and
intrigue and it had me glued to the pages!' Novel Deelights

'Full of plot, twists and tales, this kept me intrigued from the first
to the last page ... Clever, twisty' Harry's Book Club

'Extremely gripping ... fast paced and exceptionally tense'
Misti Moo Book Reviews

'If you like novels where the story is gripping and the writing is so
good that you actually feel like you are in the place it is set then I
would highly recommend Kjell Ola Dahl' A Crime Reader's Blog

'A gripping story with an unexpected outcome. Highly
recommend' Gemma's Book Review

'I found myself burning through the pages to the highly satisfying
conclusion. Highly Recommended' Bookie Wookie

'This is good old-fashioned storytelling at its best ... Excellent'
Beverley Has Read

'Kjell Ola Dahl has once again gripped me from start to finish,
hooking me whole-heartedly with his beautiful writing and
complex plot' Ronnie Turner

'Kjell Ola's writing is amazing as it keeps you tense throughout and
you just never know where it is going to end'
The Secret World of a Book Blogger

'The aspect of this novel I found most compelling was the author's
style of writing. I could hear his voice clearly and I loved it'
Books, Life and Everything

'A fast-paced, well-plotted story ... Each move is planned, no loose ends are left to ponder over, and the intimacy between the characters and the reader makes you want to come back for more' Cheryll MM's Book Blog

'Kjell's style of writing is relaxed and allows you to get to know the characters, but don't be fooled, it had my heart pumping ... I promise you will be hooked!' Wrong Side of Forty

'A compelling and complex book that will have you chomping down on your nails, waiting to see what happens ... Brilliant stuff' Jen Med's Book Review

'A complex, tightly plotted noir crime book, full of tension, suspense, twists and atmosphere' Emma's Bookish Corner

'I can most certainly see why this author is considered one of the godfathers of Nordic Noir. He spins his tale with ease and keeps you guessing up until the very end. Intricately plotted ... with a satisfying ending' Where the Reader Grows

'I was gripped' Portable Magic

'The author's style of writing and pace is very easy to read ... If you are a fan of Nordic Noir or like intriguing crime mysteries then you will love this' Over the Rainbow Book Blog

'An engrossing and beautifully crafted novel ... it is a book that captivated me from the very first page through to the startling finale. Highly recommended' Hair Past a Freckle

'Thrilling and complex ... an enthralling read' The Quiet Knitter

'I loved the plot in this book and the writing style was excellent! ... A thorough enjoyable read' Donna's Book Blog

'I thought Dahl got the pacing of the novel just right, hooking me into the story from the very first page' My Bookish Blogspot

A number was nailed to the corner of the house wall. He slowed down, leaned forward and glanced to the side and up as he drove past. There was no light in the windows or any other sign of life. He carried on. Rounded first one bend, then another. A place to turn came into sight. A tractor trail leading into the woods. Frank Frølich braked, reversed into it a few metres, pulled out and drove back, past the house again. This time he noticed the gable of another building behind the main house. He continued for a short distance, still unsure how he should go about this, and came level with a wider turning area beside the remains of a brick construction. It looked like a disused petrol station. He pulled off the road and stopped. Made up his mind. Did a U-turn and drove back. Came to a halt by the bus stop near the drive of what appeared to be an abandoned smallholding. He switched off the ignition. Opened the door and got out. There was complete silence. No traffic. A line of trees along the road screened the property. Through the trees, he could see no neighbouring houses. The deserted house stood about twenty metres from the road, in front of a dilapidated outbuilding. He strolled up the narrow drive. The house was chalet style, with one and a half floors, old and run-down. The white paint was flaking off and there were green stains down the wood panelling. Two upper-floor windows were boarded up. The original front door had been replaced with a newer type. The posts supporting the porch roof were rotten at the bottom, where they rested on a concrete plinth. No name-plate on the door, but the number on the house wall didn't lie.

He couldn't see a doorbell anywhere. But a sheep bell hung from a blue nylon cord beside the door.

He rang it.

No response.

He rang the bell again. Pressed his fingers against the door. Locked.

He turned away from the front door and stared at the tumble-down outbuilding. It looked as though a gigantic thumb had pushed the roof down in the middle. One end-wall was bulging under the pressure. Presumably the stanchions had started to give way. Tiles had fallen off. Some of the gaps in the roof had been repaired with corrugated-iron sheets. An optimist had attached a ratchet strap between a post in the entrance and a telephone mast. Probably as a kind of preventative measure against the increasing tilt on one side. An opening in the longer wall was covered with a green tarpaulin. It hung like a huge curtain, with a plank nailed fast lengthwise under the eaves.

He crossed the yard, lifted a corner of the tarpaulin and pulled it aside. The opening was revealed; it was dark inside. He stepped in. The tarpaulin fell back. He stood waiting for his eyes to become accustomed to the dim light. There were stacks of beer crates and several cardboard boxes. He had found what he was looking for: beer and cigarettes. He took some photographs with his mobile phone. The pictures would probably be evidence enough for his employer – a food wholesaler. The works manager suspected the driver who lived here of siphoning off goods. This stock suggested she was right.

He crouched down under the tarpaulin again, ambled back to the car, got in and drove towards Moss to find the motorway back to Oslo. This job had been easier than he had imagined. Quick, not much effort involved. All he had to do now was write a report and attach the photographs.

By the slip road onto the motorway there was a shopping centre. He followed an impulse, braked, headed down to the centre and found a place to park. For ages he had been planning to swim a couple of times a week. But to do that he needed a swimming costume, and now he had the time to buy one.

The broad glass doors slid open. It was early in the day. Not many customers. He walked down the main avenue with shops on both sides. Passed a café. Green eyes behind heavy eyelids checked him over as he walked past. She was in her thirties and wore her red hair in a bob, like a helmet.

It turned out to be too early in the year for swimwear. The assistant in the sports shop tried to sell him some running tights instead. Frølich politely declined.

He walked back the same way and made eye contact with the woman in the café from a distance. She started tidying up behind the counter, so as to appear busier than she actually was, he imagined. A thought struck him. People usually say, when planning a holiday in a big town: if you are choosing somewhere to eat you should go for a place where there are already lots of customers. No one was sitting in this café.

She had finely drawn lips and a hint of a cleft chin. A young Catherine Deneuve maybe. The top of a tattoo licked at her neck.

He stood at the counter and asked what the menu of the day was. She recommended a tapas salad, which she could make up using whatever ingredients she had at her disposal in the kitchen. She assured him that she was good and smiled self-ironically, revealing shiny white teeth in a broad mouth, which made him want to see the smile again. He said: 'I'll try that then.' Immediately she left to make the salad. There was a languorous sensuality about her body. She moved from the counter to a fridge and back again, rhythmically, lissomly, as though dancing. Since there was no one else in the café he saw no reason not to start a conversation. He told her that in fact he had come to buy a swimming costume, but the sports shop didn't have its summer stock in yet; did she know anywhere else that sold swimwear?

She looked up with Mona Lisa eyes and almost imperceptibly shook her head. After another sashay she told him she was a naturist, and with that she channelled the conversation into an intimate zone, one where he felt unsure of himself; he wondered whether she was trying to kill off the conversation. But after serving a salad consisting of cherry tomatoes, cos lettuce, salami, roasted pine kernels and slices of parmesan with freshly baked bread, she came over to his table and asked if everything was alright. He said, as was indeed the truth, that it was the best meal he had eaten for a long time. She asked him where he was from. He answered, and gradually they moved on to more personal topics, with the result that, as he was driving to Oslo, she was on his mind and he caught himself coming up with new questions he would have liked to ask her. The conversation had rattled along with no longueurs. What a shame she lived so far away.

*

That evening he sat with a laptop on his knees, trying to write a report to the works manager at the food wholesaler's while studying the photographs on his mobile. The majority of the shots he had taken of the stolen goods were dark and grainy. He put aside the laptop, fetched a beer and hunkered down in front of a serial on TV, having decided that he would repeat the trip the following day. This time he would be able to make use of the digital Canon and flash he had invested in when he started up his business, but which he hadn't taken many photographs with so far.

2

The next day he knew where to go and headed out on the E6 south of Oslo. He maintained a good speed and came off at Vestby, took the Oslo road to Hølen and continued to the slip road onto the R120, where he turned off and drove in the direction of the small-holding. There weren't any cars in the yard today, either. The house seemed just as abandoned. He parked by the bus stop, walked up to the house, stood at the front door and, to be on the safe side, rang the bell. Pushed at the door. Locked. Then he slipped under the tarpaulin covering the opening in the tilting barn. He took some pictures with the proper camera and flash this time. Checked the display to make sure the quality of the photographs was good enough, then got back in the car and drove to the shopping centre.

As soon as he was through the automatic doors he feared he was on a wild-goose chase. The café was packed, and she was nowhere to be seen. But as he turned to leave she appeared behind him and said:

'Hi. Back again, are you? That's nice.'

He asked her straight out whether she was doing anything that evening. She was. Presumably she read the disappointment in his eyes because she hastened to ask if he had found the swimming costume he was after. He shook his head. Then she flashed him a smile and said he could go swimming with her at the weekend.

A swim at the beginning of March, he thought, and nodded. Perhaps she was an ice swimmer. He asked where he should pick her up.

'Just a mo,' she said, went back to the counter, dealt with a couple of customers and returned a few minutes later with a map she had drawn. She was renting a house in Skjeberg.

'By the way, my name's Matilde.'

'Frank,' he said, choosing not to mention that most people called him Frankie.

He was keen to hear how she pronounced his name, if they ever got as far as calling each other by their first names, that is.

3

On Saturday the rain was falling in sheets. A sombre atmosphere lay over the countryside as he drove his Mini Cooper south. Black tarmac and black ploughed fields stole the light, and the rain collected in small lakes on the biggest of them. Bare branches were outlined against the sky. The ground hadn't started to send up green shoots, either.

He was going to Skjeberg Bay, not far from Høysand. There were plenty of summer cabins and older detached houses between the rocks. Matilde lived in one of the smallest. It nestled there, with a drive and a handkerchief of a garden behind a white picket fence. As he turned in to park in front of the cabin, the worst of the rain had passed. She was sitting on the terrace in front of the door, barefoot, wearing jeans and a loose sweater. In one hand she held an umbrella, in the other a lit cigarette. Beside her sat a border collie, which meekly stood up to be stroked when he mounted the steps.

They stood smiling at each other for a few seconds.

'Crap weather,' he said.

She said nothing, just went in and held the door open.

It was like walking into a room from the 1950s. The sofa looked as if it had been bought from the furniture catalogues of the time, and there was kitsch on the walls: flea-market art – a gipsy girl stretched out on a divan beside a seaman in a sou'wester with a crooked pipe in the corner of his mouth. Above the dining table was a retro wall light with a miniature bulb shining from behind a heart-shaped lampshade. The most modern object in the room was a small Bluetooth speaker on the teak table in front of the sofa. From it came muted country-and-western music. The room had an open kitchen and Matilde was already sashaying between the fridge and the hotplates. The dog sat in front of the wood burner, watching him as he crouched down beside her record collection. Vinyl albums, most of them classics from the golden age. *Every One of Us* by Eric Burdon and the Animals, *Trilogy* by Emerson, Lake & Palmer, B.B. King's *Live at the Regal* and, further along, gems such as *Exile on Main Street, Wave, Spectrum* and *Heavy Weather*. The LPs were wedged onto a shelf beside a Tandberg Sølvsuper 10, with inbuilt speakers in a wooden cabinet, and a record-player with a strobe light on the side of the turntable.

He could feel he liked her tastes and the contrasts they created. In addition, he was happy she hadn't broached the subject of swimming. And he appreciated the way they didn't have to say everything to each other, which was the same feeling he'd had when they spoke for the first time in the café.

A photograph on the wall showed two ungainly figures on skis, both wearing jeans and anoraks. Both were covered in snow, as if they'd just had a fall.

Matilde turned away from the stove. 'That's me and my mum. Neither of us is very good at skiing, but we have such a lot of fun together.'

He sat down on the low sofa.

'What's your dog's name?'

'Petter,' she said. 'It's actually my mother's dog, but she has a new partner and he's allergic.'

Petter rose to his feet and pinned back his ears when he heard his name. Matilde knelt down and stroked him. 'So that's why he lives with me.' She looked up. 'Hope you're not allergic to dogs.'

They exchanged glances with an energy that was fuelled by all the layers of the question. 'No, I'm not,' he said. 'Not as far as I know.'

She came over and sat beside him. 'There's some coffee on the go,' she said. 'Just have to wait a bit.'

The dog laid his head on the floor and looked up at them. Frank leaned back with his eyes closed and took in all the sounds of the room. Water boiling, the noise of the kitchen extractor fan and the faint quiver of a pan lid, the muted C&W music, the crackling of logs in the stove.

He opened his eyes and gazed straight at her, she was resting her head on the back of the sofa, too. They sat looking into each other's faces. Matilde smiled gently as he took her hand and her sweater crackled with electricity as she moved closer.

4

He visited Matilde the following weekend as well. And the following one, and the one after that. The fourth weekend she caught a train to Oslo. They went out in the city centre and she stayed over until Monday morning.

Matilde thought it was good that he had stopped working for the police. She was unwilling to say why, but considered it absolutely fine that he was working as a private investigator. The reason came out on the last day of May. They were sitting in garden chairs on her terrace in the sun. Matilde's mobile was quietly playing Lyle Lovett on the portable speaker. She said she had loved books about Nancy Drew when she was a child. She had dreamed about becoming a detective herself.

'Then I got myself a detective buddy instead.'

'The question is: how long will it last?'

She sat bolt upright.

'The work, I mean,' he added quickly. 'I haven't got any commissions at the moment and I'm living off savings. When they come to an end, I'll have to get a different job.'

Matilde stretched for the Marlboro pack on the floor, tapped out a cigarette and lit it using a white lighter. She inhaled deeply and said she had a friend who needed a detective.

'Her name's Guri, and she works at a refugee centre in Hobøl. What's the matter with you?'

'She *needs* a private investigator?'

'Someone's gone missing, from what I can gather. I'm not absolutely sure. I wasn't really following when she was talking about it. But when I told her the guy I was dating was a detective she went wild.'

'OK,' he said, closing his eyes again and continuing to enjoy the atmosphere, the mild weather and all the post-coital peace.

Later, when the sun disappeared behind the trees and it became cooler, Matilde went in and fetched two blankets. After a while she asked him if he felt up to driving her somewhere.

'Of course.'

∗

It wasn't a long trip. They drove away from the holiday cottages and turned north onto the motorway. Came off by Moss, continued along the R120 eastward and after a while took the Dillingøy exit. Here they drove on muddy gravel tracks as Matilde fed him instructions:

'Right here … carry straight on … There,' she said, pointing to a padlocked, ramshackle shed. 'I've got a summer car.'

Matilde smiled mischievously as she inserted the key into the lock. The hinges creaked as she opened one broad door.

'Same model as the one Thelma and Louise drove around in. It's even the same colour.'

As the crooked doors revealed metre after metre of chrome and steel, he was reminded of something from a film. The flashy convertible was turquoise and had white leather seats. The wings were incorporated into the bodywork. The wheels had whitewall tyres and the long bonnet set off associations with the spaceship in *Star Trek*.

'Ford Thunderbird, 1966, convertible,' Matilde said, unable now to hold back the smile. 'Whenever I say that, it sounds as unreal as ever.'

She got in, adjusted levers. Moved the column gear shift back and forth. Then pulled another lever. The bonnet opened a few centimetres. She clambered out again. Lifted the bonnet, bent over the engine. 'We need some electricity,' she mumbled and attached the earth cable to the battery, dropped the bonnet and climbed back in. Waved another key and said: 'Cover your ears.'

It sounded like a landslide as the V8 engine started up. It almost choked. She put her foot on the accelerator. The engine roared and grey exhaust fumes filled the space between the timber walls. 'It's a bit out of sorts at the moment,' she shouted.

He could barely see the car through the fumes. But when she finally eased the pressure on the accelerator the engine idled comfortably.

He asked her how she had managed to land such a treasure and was told she and an ex had been on holiday in the US. They had bought the T-bird when they had to drive from San Francisco to New York. On reaching the east coast her ex wanted to sell the car, but Matilde had grown to love it. So she costed the price of transport to Norway. It was freighted across the Atlantic in a container ship. When the relationship finished she bought his share of the car.

'It runs on ninety-eight octane leaded petrol. I have to put lead substitute in the tank whenever I fill up.'

There was one downside though, she said. There was a faint smell of mould inside the car. Matilde put the smell down to the hard winter and the poor state of the garage. The soft-top over the car couldn't keep out the damp on its own, she said. But a good run-out would help. The smell would go with the fresh air and the heating system working.

'It was the same problem last summer, but it resolved itself.'

5

If Matilde was a competent cook she was at least as competent a mechanic, he quickly gathered. At the back of the garage there was a socket set and some flexible box wrenches. On their way back they drove in convoy and popped into a Biltema warehouse. The oil, filters and antifreeze had to be changed. At home she had new fan belts and other parts that frequently needed replacing. The rest of the weekend they spent getting the T-bird ready, punctuated only by bouts of passion in Matilde's double bed.

To suppress the smell of mould they went to work with two rounds of water, soap and disinfectant. And still they had to hang four Wunderbaum air fresheners to dull the odour when on Sunday they went on a kind of maiden voyage and cruised north-wards to Moss, turned down through the town and crossed the channel to the island of Jeløya. They went past the Sjøhaug naturist centre, which didn't appear to have opened for the summer. Matilde told him that she and her mother had gone on holiday there every summer, in a caravan. She remained a naturist herself, but had dropped the caravan holiday.

'It's too crowded when you can hear your neighbour fart in the morning as he gets up. Not to mention all the rest.'

They continued towards Refsnes Gods hotel. Matilde said she had worked there in the summer as a waitress.

They walked down to the shore. The sea was dead calm and the sun hung high in the sky. One of the Bastøy ferries was on its way over.

The beach was full of tiny pebbles. Matilde picked the ones that she considered appealing, either because they felt good in her hand or because they had nice patterns.

Frank sat down and watched the sea absorb the light from the sky. He suddenly thought about his father. Saw him in his mind's eye with his shirt-sleeves rolled up, walking in the mountains.

'What are you thinking about?' Matilde said, sitting down beside him.

'My father.'

'I've never seen mine,' she said. 'He and my mother lived together before they had me. That's all I know.'

'Did they split up?'

'I don't know. My mother doesn't like to talk about him.'

'Why not?'

'I don't know.'

'Haven't you ever had any contact with him?'

'I have a few letters and a couple of photographs.'

At the end of the beach a boy in an anorak and windproof trousers was walking with a spinning rod in his hand. He jumped up onto a sea-smoothed rock and began to cast his line.

This sight reminded Frank of his own boyhood. Some summers his family had rented a cabin in Tjøme. When they weren't fishing from the rowing boat that came with the cabin, he used to cast a line from a hill behind the outside toilet, hoping to catch mackerel and small saithe.

He watched the boy as he set one foot behind the other, brought the rod back, threw, and let go of the finger holding the line. Heard the sound of the line spinning out of the reel and the little plop as the lure broke the surface of the water. The boy stood still, waiting for the lure to sink before he reeled in.

After the third or fourth throw, the rod bent in classic fashion.

The fish tossed around. It might have been a sea trout. They were usually pretty frisky when they bit.

Frank lay back, felt a breath of wind caress his eyelashes and heard the undulating drone of a passenger plane in the distance.

Matilde's mobile rang. She answered it. He opened his eyes and watched her.

'Of course,' she said, put down her phone and looked at him. 'Do you remember me talking about Guri?'

Frank didn't.

'The woman who works at the refugee centre and needs a detective.'

He nodded.

She put the phone to her ear again. 'We'll be there in an hour.'

She rang off and stood up. 'Let's get going,' she said. 'It's quite a drive.'

'A missing person, wasn't that the story?'

'A woman from the Middle East. She's searching for her sister. Apparently this girl travelled to Norway because her sister had travelled ahead of her several years before. The detective's job is to find the sister.'

He fell silent, concerned.

'What's the matter?' Matilde said. 'Are you going to turn down work?'

'I fear this lady may not necessarily have any money to pay with.'

Matilde didn't say anything for a while.

'You could talk to her, couldn't you?' she said, slightly disgruntled.

Frank was still silent.

'I can give you some money. I get paid on Wednesday.'

'Out of the question.'

'What's wrong with my money?'

'Forget it,' he said. 'I'll talk to her and you're not paying for anything.'

Matilde stretched out a hand and squeezed his forearm.

'The main thing is you listen to what she has to say. They don't have an easy time of it, these poor people, and this girl's sister means everything to her.'

6

Matilde said she had met Guri for the first time after a gig at the Down on the Farm festival in Halden four years before. They had been travelling on the same train home when it hit an elk, which affected the electricity supply and left them stuck between two stations. It had been the last train that day, so NSB had organised buses instead. She and Guri had struck up a conversation as they stood waiting for a bus that showed no signs of ever appearing. Then Guri had rung her brother and he had come to drive them home. Afterwards they had often been together. Guri was a trained psychiatric nurse. She was crazy about everything to do with horses and had long had her own horse stabled on a farm not far from Svinndal. There she used to practise showjumping. But the previous winter the horse had baulked at a fence. Guri had dug in her heels, but this startled the stallion; it kicked out its rear legs, or something like that, and Guri fell off.

'An Arab. It must've been on edge.'

Guri had fallen badly. Fortunately she had been wearing a helmet, but it didn't protect her back. So, no more showjumping for a good while. However, the prognosis was better than expected. She had retrained her body by paddling a kayak.

As they approached Spydeberg they turned off the main road and continued towards Lyseren. Matilde drove right down to a grassy slope, which must have been a kind of beach, and parked beneath a huge pine tree. She texted a message and received an answer at once. They strolled down to the water's edge to wait.

Frank sat down on a stump and gazed across as Matilde took off her sandals, folded up her trousers and waded in. A swarm of midges danced above her head; they looked like a little cloud.

After a while a kayak approached at great speed. The sun glinted on the paddle blades with every stroke that Guri took. The kayak glided up onto the grass, then she lifted herself out: a lithe woman in her thirties, wearing a wetsuit down to mid-thigh, long, blonde hair in a plait over her shoulder.

She and Matilde hugged.

Afterwards she turned to him: a face with limpid blue eyes and a narrow, slightly crooked nose above attractive but vulnerable lips that made her seem shy when she smiled. Like now, as they exchanged looks, a 'hi' and a handshake.

*

Guri told him that the refugee centre where she worked had what
they called a 'dedicated area' for asylum seekers with psychological
or other illnesses requiring special treatment. This was where she
met the girl who was searching for her sister.

'She's in a bad way,' Guri said. 'The doctors can't agree on
whether this is post-traumatic stress syndrome or a deeper psychological issue. But she's had an awful time. She's fled from war and
abuse into more abuse here in the west. And now they've decided
she has to leave again. They're kicking her out on her arse. The
bloody government. It's so cynical. She can barely look after herself,
but out she goes. She has one last hope: her sister, who travelled
the same road a few years ago. Her sister came here, to Norway.
But no one has a clue where she's living or what she's doing. Now
Aisha's stuck in the refugee centre and desperately needs to be
reunited with her sister while the police just can't wait to fly her to
Turkey. She'll never stand it. If she's sent to Istanbul she'll die or
take her own life, I'm sure of that.'

Guri's kayak must have been very light because she carried it
under her arm, to a red Volvo estate parked under the trees, and
hoisted it onto the roof. She took a couple of rollers with straps
from the car and attached the kayak firmly, with sharp yanks,
glanced across at Frølich and said: 'Turn around.'

He didn't understand what she meant. 'I'm going to change my
clothes,' she said.

He wandered down to the water as the women sorted out Guri's
outfit. On his return Guri was wearing a flowery top, light-blue
jeans and sandals.

They got into their cars. Guri led the way while they followed
in the convertible. Guri's Volvo had only one rear light working.

7

It wasn't a long journey. Soon they were driving into the refugee centre by Elvestad. Guri parked by what appeared to be the main building. Matilde pulled up beside her.

The doors slammed as they got out.

'This is where I work,' Guri said.

'One of your rear lights isn't working,' Frank said.

'He used to be in the police,' Matilde said.

'Good job you aren't anymore,' Guri said. 'There's a lot more than the rear lights that doesn't work on the car.'

A group of tall, lean Africans were playing basketball on a court. They waved to Guri, who showed Frank and Matilde the way in.

The place felt like an institution. The residents sat in small groups, chatting, playing cards or Chinese chequers, or simply trying to kill time.

A man in jeans and a sweater grabbed Guri. All three of them stopped. Guri gave him a quick hug and asked him, in English, to fetch Aisha. But the man said Guri should come with him, so she showed Frank and Matilde into a small room and said, 'Wait here and I'll bring her to you.'

The waiting room also smacked of an institution. Second-hand tables, second-hand chairs and by the windows hung stiff, yellow curtains that could well have been the originals from the time when the house was built many decades before.

The woman who followed Guri into the room a few minutes later seemed very young. She wore brown trousers and an acrylic sweater with a roll neck, probably a survivor of the 1970s. Her black hair was gathered in a thick ponytail. It was clear from her facial features that she was unwell. When she talked, there was a white streak of saliva at the corner of her mouth, and she sat with a rigid, crooked grimace on her lips as her eyes flickered nervously between Frølich, Matilde, Guri and the interpreter, a buxom woman in a dark dress, her hair covered by a white hijab. She introduced herself as Havin and told them in good Norwegian that she had lived in the country since the early nineties.

The woman spoke to the interpreter, who spoke to Frølich. The woman's name was Aisha. The interpreter took the trouble to explain that Aisha was also the name of the prophet's youngest wife.

Aisha said that her sister had left Iraq in the autumn of 2005 and had come to Norway. The family had been in touch via the telephone. She had been working and had earned money and was happy.

Frølich remembered the time of the Bush administration's bombing raids on what they called the Axis of Evil. He remembered the immense anti-war demonstration in Oslo in which he'd taken part.

He asked Aisha what her sister's name was.

'Sheyma.'

'When was she born?'

The young woman hesitated. Said something.

The interpreter said that Aisha thought her sister was eighteen when she fled.

'So she must be around thirty now,' Frank said, appraising Aisha, who could barely be eighteen.

'You can't have been very old when your sister fled?'

Aisha didn't answer.

'Why did she flee?'

The young woman shook her head. 'No understand.'

'She doesn't understand,' the interpreter said.

He took a deep breath and waited, wanting to give her time.

There was nothing else forthcoming.

'What kind of work did your sister do in Norway?'

The interpreter translated: 'Hotel work. She tidied rooms and made beds and cleaned at a hotel.'

'You don't know which one?'

The interpreter asked.

The woman shook her head again. 'A hotel in Oslo. She made beds, cleaned.'

'When did you lose contact?'

'No understand.'

'You said your sister rang home. When was that?'

'Two years later, in 2007,' the interpreter said.

'Has she contacted you since then?'

Aisha shook her head.

Frank turned to Guri. 'But you've tried to trace her?'

'We have. But we can't find her name. She must've changed it.'

'Why would she do that?'

Guri shrugged. 'Aisha's sure she's alive and living in Norway.'

The interpreter translated. Aisha nodded energetically and said something.

'"I can feel she's here",' the interpreter translated. '"I know Sheyma's in Norway."'

'She made a long journey to get here?'

Aisha nodded.

'Was there any special reason for her choosing Norway specifically?'

Aisha sat thinking after the interpreter had explained. 'No understand.'

'I mean, did she know anyone here? Why did she choose to come to Norway instead of Sweden or Germany, for example?'

Aisha glanced anxiously from one to the other and finally shrugged her shoulders.

'Did she ring home many times?'

'Once. She was so happy.' Aisha smiled. 'Happy to be in Europe.'

'Did your sister travel alone?'

The young woman eyed him as the interpreter translated, and she gave a curt answer.

'She doesn't know,' the interpreter said.

'Surely she must know whether her sister fled alone or with others.'

The interpreter sent him a kind look. 'She doesn't know. If she doesn't know, she doesn't know.'

Frank leaned back on his chair. Trying to make eye contact with the young woman, which appeared to be nigh on impossible. Aisha looked down and away, as though not willing to meet his gaze. An air of helplessness seemed to surround her, but also a vulnerability, which emphasised how lonely she must be. However, none of this made the task any easier.

He glanced at Guri and Matilde for help, thinking they must see how hopeless this all was, but their attention was focused on the young woman on the chair.

'Help me, sir. Please help me to find my sister,' Aisha pleaded in English, leaning across the table.

Matilde nodded authoritatively.

Frank realised that everyone else in the room was looking at him, as though he were the main protagonist, someone they expected a few timely words from.

'I assume you've checked other refugee centres to see if she's there?' he said to Guri.

She nodded.

'I need a pic, a photo,' he said. 'Something to show people.'

The interpreter translated.

Aisha still appeared confused. She said a name.

Guri intervened. 'Shamal?' She turned to Frølich. 'Shamal. He's in this section. He can lay his hands on the picture.'

Guri went to the door. The same man in jeans and a sweater appeared and was gone again. 'Shamal's off to get the photo,' Guri said, and closed the door.

8

Half an hour later Frank was standing by Matilde's car examining a tatty photograph of a girl wearing a long, flowery dress, her hair hidden by a light-blue headscarf. Clean features. Large, dark eyes and finely drawn eyebrows. Full lips and a mole on her right cheek. Quite different from the sister in the dedicated area in the centre. According to Guri, one of the doctors visiting the centre thought Aisha had a personality disorder. Another doctor considered it a variant of PTSS. A gang rape and other abuse during her escape from Iraq had traumatised her.

A cruel fate, Frank reflected, re-examining the faded photograph of Sheyma. And wondered what she looked like now. Was she still alive? If she was eighteen when she left she would be thirty or thirty-one. If she still lived in Norway she might be integrated, employed, with her hair uncovered, the mother of small children, with the appearance of someone who had undergone all the changes family life can impose. Or she might be married to a Muslim of the conservative variety; perhaps she lived in a marriage that didn't allow her to be seen outside. The photograph he was holding in his hand might be completely worthless.

If Aisha's sister had a residence permit it ought to be possible to trace her. She might even have Norwegian nationality. But she could also have been deported from Norway, transported back to some transit country. She might be stuck in some refugee camp in Greece or Hungary, or indeed anywhere. Perhaps she was living illegally in Italy or Germany. On the other hand, all the years without a sign of life could just as well mean she was dead.

The sad fates of asylum seekers were only one side of this business. Naturally, Frank felt sorry for Aisha, because she was a victim. She had fled the war, lost her family and been exposed to abuse and mistreatment, and now she had to live an undignified transit life. If he could alleviate some of the girl's suffering by searching for her sister he would happily try. But he was unsure whether Guri or Aisha understood how pointless the whole thing was. Had he made it clear enough to them? Or was he creating un-realistic expectations by agreeing to this job? Would it be more honest to spell it out? *Forget your sister. It's a waste of time trying to locate her.* But how cynical was that approach? The poor girl was alone in a strange part of the world. She was on the threshold of a good life in Norway while the sands of time were running out. The machinery of power was about to close the door on her. *Out you go, back to broken dreams.* It could happen tomorrow, or in a week's time. No wonder Aisha was desperate.

Yes, he told himself. You know people at Kripos and Oslo Police. You're bound to be able to pull in a favour.

The front door of the red building slammed. Matilde and Guri came out, stopped and talked. Matilde said goodbye to Guri, who waved to him, turned and went back inside.

He stuffed the photograph into the breast pocket of his shirt.

'Thank you so much for doing this,' Matilde said as they got into the car. 'I can feel it,' she said. 'I can feel your energy and aura. I know this is going to be a success.'

9

Later that evening, driving towards Oslo, he mulled over the strange meeting at the refugee centre. It wasn't only the futility of the enterprise that bothered him. If he was to have a sniff of a chance of achieving some kind of result he needed more information. But it wasn't only that, there was something about Guri's involvement. What made her hire a private investigator on behalf of someone in the refugee centre? Sure it was a shame about Aisha, but it was a shame about anyone fleeing a country. And people who worked with refugees ought to be trained to keep a professional distance. The first commandment in that line of work was not to get involved personally. Why did Guri feel so strongly about Aisha's fate?

Another thing he should check more thoroughly was Guri Sekkelsten's family. He had recently completed an investigative assignment involving another Sekkelsten. The driver who stole beer and cigarettes from his employer. Ivar Sekkelsten had had to go to prison because he already had a conditional sentence. After producing visual evidence against Ivar Sekkelsten, Frølich had also testified against the man at the trial. It was his evidence that had sent Sekkelsten to the slammer.

Could Guri and Ivar be related? If they were, might that be a problem? Should he reject the job?

Well, he thought at once, this was a favour to a friend. Locating

Aisha's sister seemed pretty futile anyway. What he could do was go through the national registers, talk to the right people and have his assumption confirmed: finding Sheyma Bashur in Norway today is mission impossible.

*

After returning home, he started on precisely that. He tried a few electronic searches for Sheyma Bashur without getting a nibble. That offered three possibilities: she had left the country; she was still living in Norway but had changed her surname, possibly her first name as well; or she could be dead and had died here in Norway. Matilde, Guri and Aisha insisted she was still alive and in this country. They had no basis for this assumption. But if he was going to work on this hypothesis he was looking for a woman with a different name from Sheyma Bashur.

*

He started the next working day with nothing to tax his brain apart from the photograph in his breast pocket. In other words, he had no employment that offered any prospect of earning an income. He refrained from checking his bank account, but knew from earlier checks that he would have enough for his rent and other necessities for at least a month. The smartest move now would be to sit down and write job applications. With his police experience he would be in with a chance at the biggest security agencies. Looking for work, however, required the kind of motivation he didn't possess at present.

He rang NOAS, the Norwegian organisation for asylum seekers. Frølich introduced himself and presented the case. A woman fleeing Iraq – reportedly in 2005 – and coming to Norway – possibly in 2006, perhaps later. Which countries she had passed through was unknown, but presumably included Turkey, Greece, Italy and Germany, because that route was supposed to have been used a lot at the time. But no one with this particular person's name existed in the national registers Frølich had been able to peruse. If she had taken Norwegian nationality or had a residence permit for Norway, she was not registered anywhere under her real name. Nor was she registered at any refugee centre. She had left Iraq in November 2005. Two years later, in late autumn 2007, she rang home from Oslo. She told her family that she was working as a cleaner in a hotel in Norway, in Oslo. She was fine. Thereafter, silence. No one knew why.

'I've checked the missing-persons register at Kripos. No hits.'

The man on the telephone asked if she had travelled from Iraq on her own.

'I don't know.'

'How old was she when she left her home country?'

'About eighteen, apparently.'

'It seems rather unlikely that she'd travel alone then. As a woman, she was vulnerable. Presumably she did travel with someone. One other thing: if she's been in Norway without an official residence permit there are not many jobs she could have taken. She must've looked for illegal work, and in the environments frequented by people from the Middle East it is usually the men who get the few jobs there are. As a refugee from Iraq she came from a strongly gender-segregated society. A male society.'

'Her family insists she worked here in Norway.'

'Are you sure you have the correct name, then? If she was employed it suggests there was a residence permit.'

'I had her name spelt to me by a member of the family.'

'Sure it's spelt correctly?'

'Yes.'

'As I said, paid work suggests a residence permit. Some women fleeing alone can be forced into prostitution or taken care of by someone who either protects or exploits them. Are you sure she wasn't travelling with a man?'

Frank Frølich hesitated. 'I don't know.'

'Why did she flee?'

'I don't know that, either.'

'What ethnicity? Kurd, Armenian, Turkmen, Sabaean…'

Frank smiled with embarrassment at his reflection in the window and said in all honesty: 'I don't know that, either.'

'She's a Muslim, not a Christian Syrian?'

'Her sister's named after the prophet's youngest wife – Aisha.'

'Shia or Sunni?'

'I don't know.'

'The reason I ask is that there have been, and still are, tensions between these branches of Islam in Iraq, as I'm sure you're aware. But it seems improbable that a woman would flee alone. To escape from a country requires preparation and money. It's often organised, usually by the family. They collect money. A young woman on her own ... Are you sure she set out with the family's blessing?'

After the conversation Frank sat studying his notes. On the piece of paper were a number of logical questions. They made him wonder why he hadn't been more persistent with Aisha? Why hadn't he questioned her in more detail?

Because he hadn't prepared for the meeting.

He knew nothing at all about refugees. All he had to go on was an old photograph and some hearsay that the sister had worked at a hotel in Oslo. He had gone with Matilde to Lyseren to be accommodating. He'd met Guri to be accommodating and joined them at the refugee centre for the same reason. Deep down, though, he hadn't taken this assignment seriously.

As he had taken on the job now, it was obvious he would have to talk to Aisha again. And ask the right questions.

It would have to be another day. But he couldn't let the day go without doing *something*. The best thing he could do was make a start.

10

Over the last ten to twelve years the hotel business had seen many changes. The acquisition of hotels to form chains was only one side. Several of today's commercially run establishments didn't exist when Sheyma Bashur rang home. Travel and tourism were industries that had grown in the capital. If Sheyma had worked in a hotel in Oslo, there was no guarantee the place was still in business.

A woman of around twenty, in transit, with years behind her as a refugee, presumably had to live from hand to mouth, had to deal with people smugglers and border police, possibly without a legal permit to stay in the country, but she still got work as a cleaner, someone who tidied and cleaned up after others travelling through. There was a substantial dose of irony in that. If Aisha's sister had worked illegally, it would have been in a less luxurious hotel, he reasoned. As though a hotel's size and standards would tell us anything about its relationship with the tax authorities, he thought afterwards, but he did what he had decided nonetheless. He started at the bottom of the price range, with the youth hostel in Sinsen, continued fruitlessly through Oslo centre, with pension houses and B&Bs. Then he went to work on smaller well-known hotels in the Oslo 'pot'. On the occasions he met hotel managers, most of them tried to convince him that they didn't employ illegal staff. However, they had agreements with sub-contractors and couldn't guarantee what *they* got up to. Frølich nodded understandingly and asked if he could talk with someone on the cleaning side. Many hotels had delegated this service to agencies. Frølich made the effort anyway to question them. Most of the cleaners he met were of foreign origin. There were Russian women, there were Ukrainian women, Lithuanians, Filipinas, Polish, Somalian, Nigerian, Eritrean, Iraqi, Thai women wearing plastic gloves on their hands pushing vacuum cleaners or trolleys equipped with detergents, cloths, soaps, kitchen scourers and mops. They straightened up, blew strands of hair from their mouths, looked at the photograph, shook their heads and passed it back. He felt like a fisherman with one pathetic rod faced by an enormous sea with only one fish that was worth reeling in. He had, however, been smart enough to collate a list of hotels and overnight accommodation in Oslo and the region. He crossed off the places he had visited and started on the next. The plan lacked much ambition. He set himself a target of getting through the list, only so that he could sit back with a clear conscience – he had no hopes of actually getting a bite.

*

When evening came he tried to work out how he could write a report for Guri about his lack of success – but without seeming too negative.

Matilde rang a little before midnight. She had got hold of a CD by a German indie band who had released two records before they went their separate ways in the nineties. She was excited and asked him to listen while she turned up the volume. He said he would rather be with her and listen to the music there, which was the truth. She agreed and asked him how he had got on 'with his search for the sister'.

He had to be honest. It had gone badly. But he added that he was planning another trip to Elvestad to talk to Aisha again. Some additional information would focus his search better.

Matilde said she would ask Guri to call him.

11

Next day he carried on with the list of overnight accommodation. And after another series of wasted trips he got what appeared to be a nibble. It was at a hotel near Bankplassen. A chain with a low-budget profile. The clientele seemed to be predominantly backpackers, most of them with their noses buried in their mobile phones or iPads. One person stood at the check-in desk in front of shelves of soft drinks and peanuts. The other end of the lobby was fitted out as a breakfast bar. He showed the photograph of Sheyma to a Thai-looking woman who was clearing the breakfast tables. She removed her disposable gloves and studied the picture. Then she took it with her and disappeared through a swing door. Frølich followed her. He found her again, in a kitchen with a line of sinks and dishwashers. She was standing and talking animatedly with a thin African-looking woman in a tight, grey, ankle-length dress. The Thai woman pointed at Frølich and gesticulated. Both women turned their backs on him. Eventually the Thai woman came back, passed him the photograph and said in English:

'Sorry, we don't know this woman.'

But she wasn't so sure, Frølich thought. What gave rise to the uncertainty? And why did she have to confer with the other woman before she could make up her mind?

They stood eyeing each other. The woman seemed suddenly uneasy. She started putting her gloves back on. On her chest she wore a badge bearing her name: Gamon. She turned away from him.

'Gamon.'

She turned back.

He rummaged in his wallet and handed her his business card.

She read the card and looked at him enquiringly.

'Keep it,' he said. 'If you should happen to remember something or see her, I'd be grateful if you got in touch.'

She turned on her heel and left.

He walked out and trudged in the direction of his office. Bought a couple of newspapers on the way at one of the kiosks down in Kirkeristen and continued to Storgata. His stomach told him he was hungry, so he turned into Oslo's last outpost of the old-style, dimly lit, café bar: Dovrehallen. He found some of the regulars were already in position: carefully combed grey hair above ruddy-cheeked faces staring pensively into the day's first and perhaps Oslo's cheapest beer. He nodded to the familiar faces and sat at a window table in a partitioned stall completely to himself. He ordered a fry-up from the faded beauty who brought the menus. She recognised him and asked what he wanted to drink. He was tempted to order a Pils, but went for iced water and coffee. After all, it was the middle of the day and he had convinced himself he was working on an assignment. This didn't stop him musing on the fiasco that was Frank Frølich while he waited for the food. He had left the police in what some might call disgrace. And now he resembled the parody of a failed private detective, someone who wasted his time on an absolutely pointless assignment without getting paid, and on top of that had managed to slip into this place without even a second thought: Dovrehallen, which a hundred years ago had been a theatre and revue venue with enough excitement to entertain both the working class in the stalls and the champagne-sipping middle class in the boxes. What remained after fires, innumerable conversions and bankruptcies was the long railway carriage of a restaurant with chandeliers hanging from the ceiling, pictures of old film stars on the walls, the cloakroom adorned by unused clothes hangers and a ballroom for the old guard: retired tramway employees, former taxi drivers, lift installers and brewery workers and not least the women they had once been aroused to great passion by. The interior was originally of heavy wood. The historical patina gleamed on the walls, and Frølich could easily imagine the place was haunted by the revue queen Hansy Petra, who might let her hair down after the doors were closed. He was served his two fried eggs, potato wedges and crispy bacon, ate with a hearty appetite, flicked through the newspapers and savoured how much he appreciated exactly this: home-made food, the peace and aura of the place, the fact that in Oslo there were still oases where you could escape from American-style urban hustle-and-bustle, from the noise, the pace of life and boiling-hot drinks in paper cups. Once he was full and pushed the plate aside, the waitress appeared, unbidden, with coffee in a porcelain cup, which was so delectable that he was able to repress all his self-contempt and continue reading the papers.

12

At home he had access to the net and all digital conveniences. He was accessible via his mobile at all times of day and night. All his work could be done on site, so to speak. So renting an office was probably one of the most stupid decisions he had taken when he started up. He knew that, but still he set great store by being able to walk there. It was like a continuation of an earlier existence. In a way, having a workplace to go to seemed therapeutic. The office was a symbol, confirmation that he was in charge of his life as a self-employed businessman. He had felt important when he put his name on the board on the ground floor, as important as when he bought the desk from a widow in Smestad. But it cost an arm and a leg to rent an office, even in the cheapest parts of Oslo. The rent was so painful that every time it fell due he had to confront the decision of whether to continue or not. And every time he realised that the expense stung because his income was so poor. And every time he told himself that business would soon pick up. So he deferred the decision, like the master of self-deception that he was.

His office was in the corner block at the crossroads between Storgata and Brugata, with an entrance in Storgata. It was at this corner, in Frank Frølich's view, that middle-class Oslo finished and multi-ethnic Oslo started. His office was on the second storey, above a dentist's surgery that infected the whole floor with the smell of dental care and sterilisation. From the west-facing window he could look down on the city's most hardened drug addicts performing self-destructive acts and related business activities on the corner beside the entrance. If he lifted his head he could make out the Folketeater building, beside it the opera passage where Marc Quinn's sculpture of Kate Moss projected a western art aesthetic on an eastern yoga position. If he got up from the desk, went to the other window and peered down, he could observe Brugata, where international phone-call kiosks and hawala money transfer bureaus served Somalis, Afghans and others who in this way bypassed inefficient infrastructure in their home countries.

In the corridor outside the office the owner of the block had provided a kind of kitchenette with a sink, a cupboard filled with cups, a worktop, and on top a modern coffee machine and a dish containing two packets of Marie biscuits. Beside the kitchenette was a chair. It was Frank's chair. It had been placed there in a moment of optimism when the office was being furnished and he imagined there could possibly be more than one client at a time. The chair was considered a waiting room.

Now something unusual must have happened, because someone was sitting on it.

When there were three metres left between Frank and the waiting-room chair and office door, the man stood up. He was a slight figure in his late forties, dressed in red cords and a light-green shirt. The man was somewhat smaller than Frank. His fair hair was short, but long enough to reveal suggestions of a curl at the nape and on top. He was carrying a leather shoulder bag.

'Are you Frølich?'

Frank nodded and rummaged in his pocket for the keys.

The man extended a hand. 'Fredrik Andersen.'

Frank shook his hand and mumbled a greeting, then unlocked the door and held it open. The air inside was stuffy and stale. The office stank of dust and inactivity. The sense increased as the man entered the room and Frank imagined what he must smell. Frank went straight to the window facing Storgata and managed, after struggling with a stubborn handle, to push the window ajar.

'What can I do for you, Andersen?'

'I'm a writer.'

There was a well-camouflaged melody to his intonation. Trondheim, Frølich thought, refined standard Norwegian. A genuine Trondheimer of the finer sort, he concluded, sitting down behind his desk. He watched his guest, who stayed on his feet, in a state Frank interpreted as unease.

He stood up again and made for the door. 'May I offer you something? Coffee perhaps?'

'No, thank you.'

He plumped back down on his chair. It rolled backwards, collided with the wall and came to a halt. This was his routine. He stretched out a foot as usual, hooked the tip of his shoe under the drawer handle, pulled out the bottom drawer of the desk and rested his foot on the edge.

He pointed to the chair in the corner. 'Won't you sit down?'

The writer remained where he was, in the middle of the room.

'Among other things I've written a book about the *Sea Breeze* disaster, which happened in 1988. Have you read it?'

'No,' Frank Frølich said. 'But I've heard about it. Well, not about your book – the disaster.'

'There are lots of people with ties to the police who don't like the book.'

'Oh, yes?'

'I find fault with the police investigation and their conclusions, and also criticise their working methods and the culture in the Oslo Police. I demonstrate how the police have overlooked evidence and as a consequence the killers have gone free.'

'How can I help you in this regard?'

'I know that you used to be a policeman.'

There was nothing he could say to that.

'And that you fell out with the force and left.'

Frølich still had nothing to say. It was interesting that this man had investigated his background. It wasn't against the law. And if the guy had come to hire him for a job, it wasn't at all strange either. The only thing that slightly rankled was the talk about police incompetence. As though the writer were suggesting a kind of common cause between them.

'I've come here for a completely different reason though,' Andersen said. 'I'm working on a new book, about immigration – legal and illegal – especially the grey area between, and people smuggling.'

The writer walked towards the open window. He looked out, as though the words he was searching for were to be found there.

'People smuggling organised from departure countries and the networks across Europe and here in Norway. The book I'm working on is based on a number of cases.'

He turned from the window and stared straight at Frølich. 'It's come to my ears that you're searching for someone who figures in one of my cases.'

'Is that so?'

'You visited a hotel in town, presented a photo and asked after this someone.'

Sheyma is alive, Frølich thought. *She is in Norway.* Had he not had some practice in concealing his reactions, he might have got up and waltzed around the floor. Instead he concentrated on not smiling.

Fredrik Andersen approached the desk, placed both hands on top, leaned forward and looked Frank in the eye.

Frank met his gaze.

'Let me put it like this,' Fredrik Andersen said in great earnest. 'The woman you're looking for is very vulnerable. Both she and I would like to know why you're asking after her.'

She is *here, in Norway*, Frank thought. *Aisha's right. Her sister is alive and living here.* Success. Bull's eye, jackpot and eight score draws on the pools.

He said: 'I don't talk about my assignments with strangers. I'm sure you understand.'

'I wouldn't have visited you unless this was important. This woman fears for her own safety.'

'Can you expand?'

Fredrik Andersen straightened up. 'This is about the life of a vulnerable person,' he said.

Frølich waited for him to continue. He didn't. Andersen just looked at him.

'Then I suggest you try to convince me,' Frølich said. 'Tell me what threats you're talking about, so that perhaps we can have a dialogue.'

Andersen cleared his throat. 'You'll get twenty thousand kroner if you tell me who's asked you to trace this person.'

'Are you trying to bribe me?'

'Did you hear what I said? We're talking twenty thousand!'

Frølich shook his head again.

'What's your price?'

Frølich took a deep breath. 'Try to digest the following: I don't give the names of my employers whatever money you slap on the table. The answer's no.'

'You don't enter a hornet's nest without an agenda,' Andersen countered.

'A hornet's nest?'

'The place you're heading isn't very welcoming. We're talking about an unparalleled cynicism. About people smugglers, pimps and fortune hunters who make filthy lucre from the trials and tribulations of others. We're talking about people who have had to drop whatever they're holding to escape barrages of bombs. They've walked for mile after mile through war zones; some of them have bought a place on unseaworthy, overcrowded rafts to cross strips of water, knowing the chances of drowning are much greater than landing safely. Those who reach a western country are thrown out; they live in a kind of hiatus then try again. They live hand to mouth for year after year. Dante's descent into hell is nothing compared with what some of these people go through or have gone through. But not even in Norway can they breathe freely. However, so far they've been able to content themselves with the fact that Norwegians are happy to observe what's going on and only draw a conclusion when there are elections. For the moment Norwegian businesses haven't entered this market in order to make money from other people's suffering. The appearance of your profession in this cynical killing game would be unflattering in a book, Frølich.'

Frank couldn't repress a smile.

'What's so funny?'

'Your version of reality. Isn't business interested in the politics of asylum seeking? Norwegian refugee centres are private concerns and have been for years. The whole logistics of refugees and asylum seekers in Norway is a big money-spinner. You say you're going to write a book about this. So you're going to profit from these people's suffering, too. Let me be honest with you: I have no agenda, other than to reassure a very anxious individual. I haven't decided yet, but I doubt I'm going to demand a fee when this job's done. It's you who is the cynic here, not me.'

Andersen continued to send Frank grave looks. 'Perhaps you

imagine you know what this is about,' he said in a low voice. 'Believe me, you have no idea. I've researched this shadowland for years. You imagine you have a perspective and control. You imagine the person who commissioned you is an honest soul. Even in that you've revealed your naivety.'

'I represent someone whose desire to be reunited with the person you want to protect is sincere – transparently so. Why can't we meet each other halfway? Show me your cards and I'll show you mine. The result will probably be two happy people.'

Andersen heaved a deep sigh and shook his head, desperate. 'You may think this client of yours is open and sincere. You may not think this person has a hidden agenda. Unfortunately you're showing all too clearly where you come from. At one time you might've considered yourself a good policeman. But on this pitch, in this game, you're an amateur. You know nothing, Frølich.'

'How come this woman's identity is so secret if she's going to be in your book?'

'I anonymise all my cases.'

Andersen picked up his shoulder bag from the floor, opened it and placed an envelope on the table. 'Have you got a pen?'

Frølich walked the swivel chair, and himself, back to the desk. Opened the top drawer and rooted for a pen. Considered making a witticism about writers who had nothing to write with, but thought better of it. In the drawer was a blue Bic. He tried it out on the margin of an old newspaper that lay on the desk.

'Here you are.'

Fredrik Andersen took the biro and scribbled something on the envelope. Then he made for the door, leaving the envelope where it was.

'And what's that?' Frank asked.

'An advance,' Andersen said. 'I'm hiring you to find out what your client's actual agenda is. You'll get double that when the job's done.'

With that he was gone.

13

Frank looked down at the envelope. Picked it up. It had once been addressed to Fredrik Andersen. Under the address Andersen had written a telephone number.

He opened the envelope. There was a little wad of blue notes inside.

'Hey, wait.'

He got up, crossed the floor and tore open the door. Fredrik Andersen was nowhere to be seen. Frank strode down the corridor, holding the envelope in his hand. The lift was on its way down. He broke into a run. And reached the bottom at the same time as the lift.

A heavily made-up woman came out. Where was the writer? Outside, Storgata was packed with people. He stepped onto the pavement and looked in both directions. No Fredrik Andersen.

He turned and took the steps up to the reception desk on the first floor. No writer there. He carried on up to the second. Walked back to the office and stopped inside the door.

He opened the envelope and counted the notes. Twenty thousand kroner. That was the fee for a lot of hours' work. It covered the rent for his home and office for quite a while. But he wasn't going to take this man's assignment. What sort of a person was he actually? Giving him money to conspire against his client? The whole thing was ridiculous.

He took a deep breath and picked up his phone. Keyed in the number the writer had scribbled on the envelope. The phone rang four times before the voicemail kicked in.

'Hi, this is Fredrik. I'm busy at the moment. Just leave a message and I'll consider getting back to you.'

The answer tone peeped.

'This is Frølich. I'm not taking the assignment in this way. We don't have an agreement. You can come back and collect the money.'

Then he ended the call. Put the phone down on the desk. Stared at it. This wasn't right. He shouldn't be dependent on people calling back.

He raised his head and looked out. In the offices behind the glass wall on the opposite side of the street sat a line of successful young people in front of their screens, deep in concentration. They were links in some value chain. As for himself, he felt like an idiot. An angry idiot, but one who didn't intend to let Fredrik Andersen get away with this easily. After all, Andersen was the person who knew where Aisha's sister was. The smart move now would be to have another chat with the writer. He grabbed his phone and rang again. And once more reached Andersen's voicemail.

'You don't need to come here to collect the money,' he said. 'I'll go to yours. Now.'

14

The writer's address was on the envelope. He stuffed the banknotes into his pocket, took the key of his Mini Cooper and left. The car was in Spektrum multi-storey car park in Christian Krohgs gate. In the streets the air was warm, a breath of summer. Two pencil-thin boys in hoodies and drop-crotch pants skated past. One performed a jump onto the pavement, rotated the skateboard and landed back on it. The second boy cheered and almost fell flat on his face.

Frank had already begun to sweat, so he was happy to feel the cool air in the car park. From here it wasn't far to Gamlebyen and up the mountainside to Holtet, an attractive area with fruit trees, birches wrapped in green veils of leaves, spiraea bushes and other bourgeois idylls along the picket fences.

Fredrik Andersen lived in a west-facing detached house with a garden. The house didn't have a view of the sea, though he could probably still bask in the long sunsets he'd get up here. It was a yellow building slightly set back from the road, typically functional – no doubt with a square living area, flat roof and small windows.

He parked by the fence, walked through a low, wrought-iron gate and onto a tarmac path to a double garage and a set of steps leading up to a teak front door. He rang the bell. Heard some noise inside, but no one opened the door. He rang again. Walked back down the steps and looked up. He saw a curtain twitch on the floor above and the outline of someone backing away. He rang again. No reaction. Well, sooner or later the person would come out or someone else would go in. He decided to wait. Walked back to the gate, closed it behind him and got into his car.

Time passed interminably slowly. Nothing happened around the house. But eventually a car did appear. A Toyota RAV4 with darkened windows. The car drove up at a crawl, braked by the entrance to Andersen's house and stood idling for a long time.

He watched the car in his side mirror, but resisted the desire to get out and ask what the problem was. He glanced over at the house. The same curtain twitched. As though the fluttering material was a sign, the car moved off, indicated right onto Solveien and disappeared.

He made a note of the registration number and went back to his mobile and social media.

Then the door opened.

An elderly woman came out. She turned, rattled a bunch of keys, locked the door and carefully walked down the steps.

Her grey hair was fastened in a bun at the back. She walked with a stoop and wore light-blue trousers and a grey jacket. Over her arm she carried a handbag.

She made for the gate, opened it and walked out.

Here, she turned back to the house. She waved to someone inside, turned and continued down the road, away from Frølich's car.

And who might she be? Frank wondered. A house help? Andersen's grandmother or a tenant?

He looked in the mirror at the figure toddling into the distance. Took a decision and got out of the car. He went after her.

She shot a glance over her shoulder when she heard his footsteps.

'Yes?' she asked, and stopped. She had a body that age refused to straighten. Her pale face was wrinkled, and the eyes that met his were ones that had seen most things.

'My name's Frølich,' he said. 'Frank Frølich. I was hoping to talk to Fredrik Andersen. I rang the bell.'

She eyed him in silence.

He nodded towards the house. 'But no one answered the door.'

'Sorry,' she said. 'I probably didn't hear. That's how it is with age. Getting old is a tragedy. One thing is you don't hear so well. Fredrik won't be home until late tonight. His days are busy.'

Then she turned away from him and carried on.

He walked back to the car. Got in. What should he do? Wait or do something more sensible?

He chose to stay. After a long wait he could see in the side mirror that the car was on its way back. The same Toyota that stopped and waited with the engine idling. The minutes dragged by.

Now he concentrated on the first-floor window. At last the curtain twitched. He could no longer control his curiosity. He opened the car door, got out and walked towards the Toyota, which revved up and drove off so suddenly that he had to jump to the side to avoid being knocked down. An instinct made him get in his own car and drive after it, onto Solveien, left onto Kongsveien, over the tramlines and straight on.

Frank was doing 110 km/h without gaining any ground on the Toyota. It wasn't much slower down Mount Ekeberg. The tyres screeched on the bends. He registered oncoming cyclists as shadows.

What am I doing? he asked himself, and slowed down. He let the Toyota go.

At that moment his phone rang. A number he didn't recognise appeared on the display. He put the phone to his ear.

'Hi, this is Guri. I was with you and Matilde at the refugee centre. Matilde asked me to call you.'

'Hi, Guri,' he said, and looked around. He was in Gamlebyen. He pulled into the kerb.

She was wondering how things were going. Had he started his investigation?

Yes, he had.

'Just wanted to know,' she said. 'Matilde said you wanted to talk to Aisha again. I'm not sure if that'll be possible. The police came last night. They moved Aisha and some other women to the centre in Trandum – the prison, that is. It means she could be deported at any moment. We're pretty desperate. The immigration police are bloody Nazis. They put her in a security cell without letting her talk to her solicitor. They claim she's lying about her age and bluffing about her health. She only found out at five o'clock in the morning that her appeal against being rejected asylum had been turned down. One of the Nazi bastards told her. Her solicitor knows nothing. So she has no information about what rights she has. Then it was off to Trandum. Her solicitor has only been informed just now that she's in a cell. If I wasn't so angry, I'd be ashamed of my own country. We're behaving almost worse than the regime she escaped from.'

Frank didn't know how to answer. He had heard similar stories before. However, the police were only the musicians in this concert; after all, they had a job to do, even if it was a shit one.

'I've had confirmation that her sister is in Norway,' he said.

'What?'

The joy in Guri's voice immediately made him regret what he had said.

'Tell me more,' she shouted down the phone. 'No, wait,' she added. 'Where are you?'

He craned his neck. 'In Oslo, by Ruinparken, in Konows gate.'

'I'm outside Sentrum police station,' she said. 'In Hammersborggata. Shall we meet for a coffee?'

15

Twenty minutes later he found Guri at one of the tables in a café bar in Byporten. She was drinking from a cup that looked more like a soup bowl. Her blonde hair billowed becomingly around her face. She was not unlike Agnetha of Abba fame.

He took a seat and told her the little information he had. He hadn't got a lead from visiting Oslo's hotels, but someone must have reacted and informed the central actors in this drama that he was looking for Sheyma – because a writer had come to his office and confirmed that Sheyma was alive, but in hiding.

'It seems as though she has taken precautions so that she can't be traced.'

Guri put the cup down on the table. 'What writer?'

'You gave me this job. You have to let me do it. I can't have any interference from my client. That's not how this works.'

'But this means everything to Aisha. We can contact the Foreign Office and tell them she really does have a sister in the country and that their rejection of a family reunion is based on false premises. It means she and her sister can be reunited.'

'Give me a bit more time.'

'But this is urgent. Aisha's in Trandum Prison. She might be on her way out of the country now, at this very minute.'

'You'll have to get her solicitor to enter another appeal against the rejection or find some ploy. We need more time.'

'That's no good. She's used up all the appeals.'

They sat looking at each other in silence for a few seconds. Until he decided to ask what had been on his mind for the last twenty-four hours:

'There's something I'm wondering about, Guri. Why are you so committed to this woman?'

Guri was clearly unsettled by this question. She lowered her gaze and fidgeted with her coffee cup on the table.

No answer was forthcoming, and he suddenly felt embarrassed as well. 'I mean, there are lots of people in distress,' he said. 'You work with so many people in this situation every day. I'm sure all of them have a tragic story behind them. Have you set up any other investigations?'

'No.'

He waited for her to carry on. She still seemed ill at ease. In the end she raised her head and met his gaze. 'You saw her. You saw how unbelievably helpless Aisha is.'

She searched for more to say. But was apparently unable to find anything else.

She was right, Frank thought. Aisha was incredibly helpless. But could that be the whole answer? He wasn't convinced it was.

'There's so much at stake now,' Guri said. 'They're on the point of kicking her out. If that happens, she'll die. I know she will. I can feel it in my bones. And now we know her sister's alive and living in Norway. The finishing line's in sight. Don't you understand what that means?'

She gripped his forearm in her agitation. Then she looked down at her hand and let go.

'Yes, I do,' Frank said. 'But Sheyma's in hiding and doesn't want to be found by anyone. I was following this up when you rang. Let me carry on with my work, let me finish the job.'

'Surely you can tell me which writer told you about her? I'm just curious.'

'His name's Fredrik Andersen.'

When she raised both eyebrows in enquiry they took on the form of outspread bird wings. 'Who's that?'

'He writes books. That's all I know.'

Suddenly he had a sense that sitting and chatting here with Guri was wasting valuable time. 'Now I'll carry on from where I left off when you rang. You'll be hearing from me.'

He stood up. She followed suit.

'Frank.'

He turned towards her.

'Thank you very much,' she said, stood on the tips of her toes and gave him a hug. Then she headed in the direction of the railway lines.

He stood watching her. A breath of fresh air, a blonde woman full of well-meant commitment and solidarity with her fellow creatures. Someone to cherish.

As though she could feel the energy of these thoughts she turned right round, waved to him again and walked backwards for a few metres, smiling, then disappeared around the corner.

Frank thought about the meeting with Fredrik Andersen in his office. One thing at any rate was certain: Andersen was way off target with his conspiracies and Frank could feel nothing but irritation at not being able to get in touch with the guy to return the money.

16

He made his way back to his office. Logged onto the net and checked the registration number of the car he had seen outside Andersen's house.

The Toyota belonged to an ex-colleague: Bjørn Thyness.

So the police were carrying out surveillance on Andersen. Or at least Thyness was. But why? He knew Bjørn a little. It wouldn't hurt to ask. He had Bjørn's number on his phone.

He plugged his mobile in to charge and rang Thyness.

'Hello.'

'Frank Frølich here.'

'Hi.'

'I saw your car in Holtet a couple of hours ago.'

'Oh, you did, did you?'

'Did you see me?'

Bjørn didn't answer at once. And when he did it was in a measured tone.

'What is it you actually want?'

'You were outside the house of a guy called Fredrik Andersen. I was just wondering if you have a case on the go involving him. You see, Andersen's part of one I'm working on.'

He stopped there. Waited with his ear to the phone. But Bjørn didn't answer. The phone was dead. Had he rung off?

He called again. A message said the phone had been switched off.

He sat back, thinking. Even when they had been working together Bjørn and he hadn't been good friends. The fact was that he had once shared a bed with Gøril, Bjørn's partner. It had been a passionate but extremely short relationship and had all happened a long time before Gøril and Bjørn got together.

Nevertheless he wondered if that could be the reason for Bjørn's dismissive attitude. Had the guy been walking around for years nourishing a sense of slighted manhood?

There was no point speculating.

Instead he took his phone and rang Andersen. Once again he went through to voicemail. He left a message:

'Hi, Frølich here again. I've rung you several times now and I've been to your house, all without success. It's important we talk. You can call me whenever.'

17

He sat for a while longer, pondering what to do. And concluded he would have to leave the writer in peace. Sooner or later Fredrik Andersen would come to his senses and contact him. He got to his feet, went to the window and peered out, bereft of ideas as to his next step. The phone on the desk rang. He shuffled over and picked it up.

It was Matilde. She was excited. Guri had been talking to her. 'I knew you'd crack it,' she shouted down the phone. 'I knew it!'

'I haven't cracked it yet,' he answered and regretted telling Guri everything. Now the cat was out of the bag it would be hopeless trying to put it back in.

Matilde asked where he was.

'At the office.'

'Have you got any time?'

If there was one thing he had enough of, it was time.

'I can be with you in ten minutes,' she said. 'In the T-bird. Would be good if you could meet me outside. It's hard to find parking spots there.'

After ringing off he stood deliberating. He had rung Andersen several times. He had been to his house. He had waited for ages without catching a glimpse of him. Aisha's case was urgent, yes.

But he wouldn't get any further unless Andersen decided to call him.

He went outside. He didn't have to wait long on the pavement before the turquoise convertible floated up in front of a tram. The car stopped. The tram had to stop, too. The tram driver clearly wasn't best pleased. She splayed a palm in desperation, tapped her forehead at him, then gestured with her arms to Frølich, as though he were sitting behind the wheel and could move the car. The tram driver hooted his horn.

A man with a shaven head clambered out of the passenger seat. He was wearing a T-shirt and military fatigues.

'This is Harry,' Matilde said.

Harry and Frank shook hands.

The tram driver leaned on the horn. Matilde took no notice.

'Harry's got an appointment with his psychiatrist,' she said. 'Good luck,' she said to Harry and squeezed his hand.

Harry set off down Storgata.

Frank got in and looked around at the rear seat.

'Where's the dog?'

'At my mother's. She's helping me out.'

She pushed the automatic gear lever and moved off. 'Harry's an Afghanistan war veteran,' she said. 'He freaked out, but I'm not sure if that happened over there or afterwards – him losing it, I mean. Harry and his comrades were in a column making for Meymaneh, and a vehicle in front of them was blown up by a landmine. Metal and rags and body parts rained down over them. It was his best friend. And Harry was jumpy enough before, sitting there with his machine gun, scouring the mountainsides for armed Taliban and ISIS loonies and God knows what. Then there's a bang and he has bits of his best friend falling on his head, right. So that's probably the reason, the shock, I think. But maybe he didn't go properly crazy until he came home. They had moved his post box. Bit special. Nothing ever happens in the tiny village of Ise, does it. He was stationed in Afghanistan for years and years. And when he returned home everything was as it had been. The

same woman with curlers in her hair looking out of the window
and checking to see who came out of the shop, and the local paper
dropping into his post box. He had his on a metal stand, like a
lot of the neighbours. And the pole had always been on the right-
hand side of the path, for him coming out, that is, past the bus
stop. But then along came the Highways Agency and moved the
post box to the other side of the road, by the actual bus stop. They
did this so that the postwoman would be able to park without
being run over by a juggernaut or suchlike as she put the post in
the boxes. But Harry hadn't realised that. The safety argument, I
mean. He had been in Afghanistan and was suffering from PTSS.
When he came home and had to search for the post box he lost it
completely, mounted a pallet fork on his tractor, lifted all the post
boxes and stands and tipped them in the river. All the bills and
love letters and short lyrical poems, etc, floating downstream. That
was when he started to attend therapy classes. What are you
thinking about?'

'I was thinking post should go into digital boxes,' he said.

'Harry wouldn't have been able to destroy that,' Matilde said.
'He would've wrecked the computer instead.'

They passed the bus terminal and she queued to go onto the E6
towards Bjørvika.

'Where are we going?' he asked.

'Thought we could go to yours,' Matilde said with a grin. 'We'll
find something or other to do.'

18

It wasn't yet morning when she shook him awake. 'A bell's ringing,'
she said. 'And it won't stop.'

With that he realised what the annoying racket was and opened
his eyes. She was right. The doorbell was ringing.

Matilde wasn't ready for this noise. She buried herself deeper
under the duvet.

He sat up. Swung his legs to the floor. Stood up. Teetered.

Walked around the bed. No clothes. The bell rang again. Now whoever it was wasn't taking their finger off the bell.

He opened the bedroom door and stumbled through the sitting room to the intercom in the hall. 'Hello?'

'It's me.'

He recognised the voice. But hearing it confused him. Besides, he was thirsty. Strangely enough, his voice carried when he spoke.

'What are you doing here?'

'Let me in.'

He pressed the intercom buzzer. Heard the front door open in the receiver. Hung up.

He walked into the kitchen and drank two glasses of water in quick succession.

'What's going on?' Matilde stood in the bedroom doorway with the duvet wrapped around her body. 'Who was it?'

He found his trousers and pulled them on. 'Someone I know.'

'Who?'

'A cop.'

A hollow thud told him that the lift door had closed. Seconds later the bell rang. Matilde backed into the bedroom and closed the door behind her.

Frank looked around him in panic. An empty bottle of wine on the floor. He put it on the table. Went to the front door and opened it. 'Apologies for the mess,' he said. 'But you woke me up.'

He turned, found his T-shirt on the sofa. He pulled it over his head.

Gunnarstranda bent down and picked up the wine bottle, read the label and placed it back on the table. 'Fredrik Andersen,' he stated sharply.

'What about him?'

'He's dead.'

'Dead?'

'Come on, Frølich. If I say a man's dead, he's dead.'

Frank slumped down onto the sofa.

'Killed by an unknown perpetrator,' Gunnarstranda said. He

stood in the middle of the room with his hands buried in his coat pockets.

Gunnarstranda turned to the closed bedroom door. 'Late night?'

Frank didn't answer. He was thinking about Fredrik Andersen. Dead. That was definitely unreal.

Gunnarstranda turned back. 'Your car was seen outside his place yesterday afternoon. Now he's been murdered and you have something to tell me.'

Frank didn't answer at once. He formed a mental image of Fredrik Andersen on the chair outside his office. The well-spoken Trondheimer with the shoulder bag and the tenacious commitment.

As he tried to digest the tragic event he felt the smart of a growing annoyance. Andersen had sprung up from nowhere and into his office. The writer had known what Frølich had been doing. Now Gunnarstranda had come through the door and he knew what Frank had been doing. As though he were a chess piece being moved around, watched by an invisible audience.

Gunnarstranda sat on the chair opposite the sofa. They sat eyeing each other. Frank noticed Gunnarstranda had given up on ties. The top button of his shirt was open. There were red patches on the skin around his Adam's apple. It moved.

'Something's happened to your mug.'

Involuntarily, Frank ran a hand over his chin. 'Am I bleeding?'

Gunnarstranda shook his head.

Frølich twigged. 'I shaved off my beard.'

Gunnarstranda produced a wan smile. 'So that's what you look like.'

He cleared his throat before Gunnarstranda could say any more: 'I was there about an assignment. Andersen hired me for a job.'

'What kind of job?'

'Oath of confidentiality.'

'Are you being funny?'

'I earn my bread from this. I don't joke about the source of my existence.'

'Frølich. The man was killed.'

'How?'

Gunnarstranda gave a wry smile. 'Why was your car outside his house?'

'He came to my office and told me he was working on a book. For some reason he thought I could help him with it and wanted to hire me.'

'To do what?'

'This assignment is between me and my client.'

'This client's dead.'

'Then I'll deal with his heirs.'

Another wan smile from Gunnarstranda. 'Andersen hires you to do a job and you decide to drive to his house and spy on him?'

'I was waiting for him. Others were spying on him.'

'And what do you mean by that?'

'Bjørn Thyness. He had Andersen under surveillance. I went there because I had to turn down the job. I wanted to make that clear and return the advance he'd given me. That was why I was sitting in my car.'

'Did he turn up?'

'No. But I waited there from two till four. And I saw Thyness stop outside the house twice in that time.'

Gunnarstranda was silent.

'Has that given you food for thought?'

Gunnarstranda shook his head. 'Bjørn Thyness works in the immigration unit. What he or the immigration police were doing outside Fredrik Andersen's house yesterday I have no idea, but I doubt it was surveillance of Andersen. I would've known.'

'Immigration? When did he start there?'

'Six months ago – maybe more like a year. I don't remember. But you're digressing. Did you try to contact Andersen in any other way?'

'I rang him. But I got his voicemail. That happened every time I called. By the way, he's written a book about the *Sea Breeze*. The fire on board the ferry.'

'I know. I've read it. Crap, if you ask me.'

'Why?'

'Conspiracy theories and a load of hot air about how incompetent the police are. Crap and always has been.'

'Were you on the case at the time?'

'I interviewed some survivors, yes. It was a massive job. It wore people down. It used all the resources we had for months. A hundred and fifty people died.'

'What do you reckon? Was the case solved?'

Gunnarstranda shook his head. 'Don't know.'

'You don't know?'

'It's possible. But the chief of police was a clown and the DPP never had any direct dealings with the work that was done. This happened half a lifetime ago, though, and I don't give a shit about the case. You're digressing again. You used to have a gun. A Heckler & Koch P30.'

'Don't have it anymore.'

'What happened to it?'

'I sold it.'

'You did what?'

'Relax. The guy who bought it had all the right papers.'

'The guy? Why won't you say his name?'

'You didn't ask. And I still can't see what relevance it has to your case.'

Gunnarstranda sat watching him without speaking.

'Yes?'

'Time for the question we've both been waiting for: Where were you between midnight and two o'clock last night?'

Frølich smacked the table.

'You were on the table?'

He nodded.

'What were you doing there?'

'Would you believe me if I told you?'

'Try me.'

'I was pretending to be a lion tamer.'

Gunnarstranda got up and made for the door.

Frølich watched him go. 'Was Andersen shot?'

Gunnarstranda turned. 'Funny old situation we've ended up in,' he said. 'Don't you think?'

Frank nodded.

Gunnarstranda gripped the handle and pulled the door open.

'Let me put this the way they do in the films you like,' he said. 'Don't leave town. The police will need to question you again. Many times.'

Then he was gone. The door slammed behind him.

He waited until he heard the lift start up. Only then did he struggle to his feet and go to the window.

In the reflection he saw the bedroom door open. Matilde came out, without the duvet this time.

'You'll catch a cold,' he said.

She didn't answer.

Gunnarstranda appeared on the pavement in front of the block. Bald, lean and stooped. His coat tails flapped. He resembled a miserable bird of prey flapping its wings.

'Who's he?'

'Someone I worked with for many years.'

'What did you do?'

'We caught crooks. Now he's probably thinking I'm one of them.'

'Does that matter?'

He turned to her. It struck him that Guri would be upset when she heard what had happened. Aisha, too. The hopes that Guri had for her had probably gone with Andersen.

'Not sure,' Frank said. 'This situation's new for both of us.'

19

While Matilde was in the shower, he went online. The various websites presented the case in very similar ways. A man in his forties had been found dead in his home by the police and medics between two and three o'clock in the morning. A neighbour had heard some noise in the house and rung emergency services. Some news sites focused on a potential scandal about response times. The ambulance had arrived two hours after the neighbour rang. The man had been dead when the ambulance staff finally reached the place. The cause of death wasn't given, but police assumed it was murder. So, he mused, Andersen must have been stabbed or shot. Gunnarstranda asking about his Heckler & Koch suggested shot. But if he had been, neighbours would surely have reacted to the sound, it wouldn't have been just *some noise in the house.*

Found in his home.

There had only been one name under the doorbell. Did Fredrik Andersen live alone? The way the news was being reported suggested he did. But someone had been in the house while he was waiting in the car outside. An elderly woman had come out. Furthermore, someone else had remained inside. The woman had turned and waved to them. Who was she? And who had she waved to? Andersen? A partner or a guest?

Matilde came out of the bathroom wearing jeans and a black bra. Water dripped from her hair onto his shoulder as she stood behind him, reading.

'Is the dead man the one who knew about Aisha's sister?'

He nodded.

'Did he have any family?'

'Dunno. Doesn't say anything about one.'

'Did that guy who came here say anything about how it happened?'

'Gunnarstranda? No.'

'Did you ask?'

'No. He wouldn't have told me a thing anyway.'

'Why did he come here?'

'They're sure Andersen was killed and I was in contact with him yesterday.'

He entered Andersen's name on the Yellow Pages website and discovered that only one person lived in the house: Fredrik Andersen.

'He lived alone,' he said. 'Of course he may have children or they might live somewhere else. With their mother, for example.'

Matilde went onto the veranda and lit up a cigarette.

He stayed where he was. Recalling the previous day. Visualising Andersen's house, the fence, the narrow path with spiraea bushes and the rubbish bins by the drives.

Bjørn Thyness from the immigration unit was carrying out surveillance on a writer who had criticised the police in a book. A book about a tragedy at sea.

He Googled *Sea Breeze*. The screen was filled with photographs of the ferry on fire, pictures he had seen in newspapers countless times over the years. He Googled the ferry again, but combined with Andersen's name. Bookshop advertisements and a couple of hits came up. He skimmed the articles. The blaze aboard the boat happened in 1988. Arson on a ferry from Oslo to Copenhagen. It had started in the middle of the night while the passengers were asleep; 159 people died. A mass killing. The investigation was carried out by the fire department at Oslo Police Headquarters, as it was known then. There were photographs of the main investigator. Frølich knew that the man was dead now. There were photographs of the puffed-up Tromsø chief of police, who promised the public that the case had been cleared up. He was also dead now. There were photographs of the then assistant DPP, who dismissed the case against the man the Oslo chief of police singled out as the arsonist. The assistant DPP was now Norway's DPP. There were photographs of the man the police identified as the culprit. A young Dane who died in the fire. Oslo Police thought he had tried to chat up a few women on the trip between Oslo and Copenhagen, had been rejected and stormed into a rage. So he had set fire to some rubbish in a corridor and then went to his cabin to sleep. Odd behaviour. Everyone thought so. And the conspiracy theories grew from there. Someone else had set fire to the boat. Someone cashed in big time on the insurance. Financiers. Mafia.

Andersen's book must have had some impact on the public as Oslo Police had been ordered to re-investigate the case two years earlier. He knew about the new investigation, now that he came to think about it. But he had never taken much interest. These specialist groups in the police soon became full of themselves. This particular one had come to the same conclusion that the police had put forward in 1988. The police rejected the notion that there had been criminal goings-on after the ship had been evacuated. Actually they hadn't found any evidence against the alleged perpetrator either, but they still didn't want to acquit him.

Andersen had obviously had a different opinion from the police. The publisher's promotion highlighted Andersen's assertion in the book that there was no evidence against the man the police identified in 1988. Furthermore, Andersen named members of the crew he believed were involved in the onboard sabotage. Andersen maintained that they pumped great quantities of diesel from their tanks around the ship. The fuel was allowed to burn for hours and in this way caused immense destruction. This damage guaranteed the payment of a huge insurance sum to the owners. Andersen had followed the money trail. In his opinion, the ferry had been sold by one company to another for an artificially inflated price. So the insurance pay-out was disproportionately high. The knock-on effect for the seller, an American shipping company, which at that point still held insurance rights, was that it reaped the rewards. The police had never been interested in facts such as these, he claimed.

Fine, but what sort of proof did Andersen have that the police had overlooked? Frank continued to Google without finding an answer. However, he did turn up the fact that the Norwegian Parliament had set up a committee to carry out an inquiry at the same time as the police's second investigation. This committee came to the same conclusion as the police: no sabotage activity on board the ferry.

The parliamentary committee's view was that there was a natural explanation for how the blaze had developed.

So, he thought to himself: the *Sea Breeze* case had been shelved, filed away and assigned to oblivion. Twice it had been dropped by the police, and once by a parliamentary committee. Andersen's book had stirred up a storm, but in the end was just baying at the moon.

But why would the police be keeping an eye on Andersen now?

Bjørn Thyness worked in the immigration unit and Andersen had said he was working on a book about refugees in Norway. Writing a book wasn't a crime, though. At least not in Norway. There were two possible reasons for the surveillance on Andersen: either he had committed a criminal act during his research into refugees in Norway, or the surveillance team had gone too far and done something that didn't bear scrutiny.

Matilde was behind him again. On the screen was a picture of the ferry in flames.

'What's so special about that boat?'

'Apparently Andersen wrote a book about it. The fire on the passenger ferry.'

'I've heard about it,' Matilde said. 'A neighbour of my mother's lost a twelve-year-old daughter. She was going on holiday to Denmark with a friend.'

They concentrated on the text, both of them.

'Let's eat,' Matilde said. 'I'm meeting Guri in a couple of hours. If she remembers.'

20

After Matilde had left, Frank prepared to leave for the office. As he came out of his flat he found himself staring at Bergersen, who was sporting a pair of shorts. The sight was so unusual and Bergersen's legs were so parchment-white that he felt he had to say something. 'Nice out today,' he said, opening the door of the lift when it stopped in front of them.

·'Not half,' Bergersen said. 'Lovely out today.'

They stood in silence as the lift descended to the ground floor. He let Bergersen leave first. Shot him a glance as he unlocked and checked his post box. He and Bergersen had been neighbours for at least eight years. And this was perhaps the third time they had spoken to each other.

No post. He locked the box and left.

At that moment a taxi pulled up by the entrance. He stepped aside to let it pass. An elderly man was sitting on the back seat.

The man waved.

Frank nodded back and walked on as a car door opened behind him.

'Frølich?'

The elderly man was attempting to haul himself out of the taxi. He had a crown of wild, grey hair. His beard was as hoary as his hair, and his mouth shone with gold fillings as he grimaced with his exertions.

'It is Frølich, isn't it?'

He nodded to the man, who was probably in his seventies, wearing mustard-yellow trousers and a blue shirt under a light-grey jacket. He struggled out of the back seat with an elbow crutch in his hand. The driver passed him a receipt and his change, and the man switched the crutch to his other hand.

Frølich moved back as the taxi set off down the drive. The man was leaning on his crutch.

'Jørgen Svinland,' the man said, extending a hand. 'Fredrik Andersen was my nephew.'

He shook the man's hand. 'My condolences,' Frank said, not quite knowing how to handle this situation.

They were both silent. Svinland was clearly moved. It was as if he were burning to say something.

'Can we find somewhere to sit?' he said at length, raised his crutch and patted his hip with his free hand.

'Arthritis.'

Frølich cast around. There were no benches in Havreveien despite all the lawns.

'Let's go up to my flat.'

21

He held the door open for Svinland and led the way to the lift, which they found waiting for them. He let the old boy go in first. The man was sucking a pastille. A smell of camphor spread through the lift, which stopped on the first floor. A small girl with pigtails and wearing a summer dress came in. She stood staring at the wall in embarrassment as the lift ascended. No one said a word.

The lift stopped and Frank held the door open for the man, who hobbled out.

Frank unlocked his flat and held open the front door. 'Excuse the mess. I live on my own.'

Frank noticed an empty beer can beside the record-player. He stuffed it into his jacket pocket and turned to his guest.

'I understand you've heard what happened last night,' Svinland said.

His eyes were moist.

'I know that Fredrik Andersen died,' Frølich said warily. 'But I don't know any more than is on the net.'

'Fredrik's mother, Katinka, is my sister,' Svinland said, sitting down in the armchair in front of the television.

Frølich sat on the sofa.

An embarrassed silence overtook them both. Frank cleared his throat. 'So his parents are still alive?'

'My sister is. His father was spared this terrible business.'

Svinland shook his head sadly and became lost in thought, then he continued: 'Fredrik had just turned forty-eight. No children. Thirty years younger than me. What can you say? How meaningless is something like this?'

'Do you know what happened?'

Svinland shook his head. 'He was attacked at home. Someone must've been in the house. An intruder perhaps. No one knows.'

'Who told you this?'

'Katinka. His mother. She was informed by the police this morning and called me afterwards.'

'Was she told what happened? How he was killed?'

'No.'

There was another silence.

'You're a private investigator,' Svinland said.

'That's correct.'

Svinland studied him with steel-grey eyes from under bushy eyebrows. 'Last time I spoke to Fredrik he mentioned your name. He wrote a book in which the Oslo police came in for some harsh criticism, I understand. He said you had a past in the police and were given the boot.'

'Did he now?'

What the man was really saying was that Andersen had not only researched his background, he had also talked to others about it. That at any rate was interesting.

'Fredrik said you were a good man. Trustworthy. You know I don't trust the police to handle this case satisfactorily, Frølich. I don't think they'll make a good job of it.'

'Why wouldn't they?'

'Fredrik was afraid of the police. He was frightened they'd do something like this.'

'Kill him, you mean? Did Fredrik think a police officer would hurt him?'

The man didn't answer at once. They ended up eyeing each other for a few eloquent seconds.

Frank wasn't sure if he liked the thoughts that were beginning to form in his flat.

'The police do a lot of strange things, but they don't kill people,' he said. The old man kept shtum.

'You're on a wild goose chase, Svinland.'

'Have you read Fredrik's book – about the *Sea Breeze* disaster?'

He shook his head.

'My daughter died on board the *Sea Breeze*,' Svinland said. 'My only child.'

'My condolences,' Frank said, for lack of anything better to say.

'She would've been fifty this year if she'd lived. We might've had grandchildren. Well, what you don't know can't hurt you, we try to think. However, my wife can't think like that. She hasn't been herself for thirty years.'

Svinland paused. Obviously moved, he was searching for words.

'Fredrik used to write novels. I remember telling him he'd be better off sticking to reality instead of fantasy. Reality throws up more sensations. A few years passed. Then he made the move to reality and with a vengeance. The police don't come out of his book well. Nor the crew, nor the shipowners.'

Svinland searched for words again. 'Fredrik had found an eyewitness.'

Frølich hoped the man would soon come to the point. He coughed.

'I can see you're becoming impatient,' Svinland said. 'I'll get straight to the point. You're a private investigator. I want to hire you for a job.'

22

Frank reacted by throwing his arms in the air. He had no idea what this man was imagining he'd say, nor where this conversation was going. But he hoped the proposed job had nothing to do with what they had been discussing. He was on the point of mentioning his reservations when Svinland explained:

'I want to hire you to find the person who was with Fredrik last night.'

'Someone was with him?'

'Yes.'

'Don't you think the police are better qualified than me to do this work?'

'As I said, I don't trust the police in this instance. You see, I'm fairly sure the man who was with Fredrik last night was the eyewitness on the *Sea Breeze*.'

'And how can you know that?'

'I'm a hundred per cent certain. What do you know about the ferry disaster?'

'Very little.'

'What actually killed the people were the gases that developed as the paint on the corridor walls caught fire. It was all over in a few minutes. The paint burned, formed hydrogen cyanide and they died. One of the great mysteries surrounding the tragedy is how the ship kept burning for hours – although there was no combustible material that could go up in smoke. Everyone who has lit a fire in a hearth knows you have to throw on more wood to keep it going.'

'Are you saying that someone on board must've been throwing wood on the fire?'

Svinland nodded and took a deep breath. 'The answer's in Fredrik's book. What kept the fire burning was diesel. It was pumped up from the ship's tanks and into the cabin corridors. Members of the crew were behind the sabotage. They rigged up some pipes and pumps so that the diesel could burn in the passenger areas.'

'I know that's what he wrote,' Frank said. 'I had a look on the net. But it's not only the police who refuse to listen to Fredrik's claims. A parliamentary inquiry views the sabotage claims as nonsense.'

'The parliamentary committee commissioned several reports from experts. One of them confirmed Fredrik's revelations. But the committee made a political decision. When they received this report confirming sabotage, they quickly ordered a new one. It was obvious they wanted a different outcome. That was what they got. The new report was commissioned and drew the conclusions they wanted. So the committee could lean on the experts' report and sweep all the dirt under the carpet. You can search the company the committee used on the internet. You can examine the company's areas of expertise. It doesn't have any competence in fires at sea. In other words, the parliamentary inquiry's report is a political commission which is worth zero. Parliament was playing to the gallery. The state machinery of power wanted to put a lid on the case and presided over a show in which the police and politicians played roles. But despatching scandals into oblivion is nothing new in Norwegian politics. I only have to mention the trials of the Nazis or the surveillance of communists during the cold war. Or the surveillance of the political radicals in the 1970s, or the Alexander Kielland oil-rig disaster. I could go on. But there's no point. I haven't come here to discuss political science with you. The point is that the man who was with Fredrik last night wasn't evacuated from the *Sea Breeze*. He was on board until the ship was towed to land in Sweden. He was an eyewitness. And he's sitting on the truth of what actually happened.'

'Why was he on board?'

'I don't know,' Svinland said. 'But the fact is that he was there. This man watched the crew sabotaging the boat.'

'It's the same old story,' Frank Frølich said.

'As I said, this man's an eyewitness. One of the things he can say something about is lifeboat number nine.'

'Lifeboat number nine?'

Svinland nodded. 'I know that Fredrik was supposed to meet the man last night. This man was ready to spill the beans.'

'What about this lifeboat?'

'It disappeared.'

'How is that relevant to the case?'

'There's one thing I'd like to find out. And there's one man who knows. The man who was on board and met Fredrik last night, who saw what happened – Fredrik called him Ole Berg. I want to hire you to find this man – Ole Berg.'

'A man who's a rumour? This sounds like part of a conspiracy theory, Svinland.'

Svinland shook his head. 'Ole Berg's real. And he was with Fredrik last night. I know it.'

'OK, let's say this man was with Fredrik last night, but why is it so important for you to find him?'

'I lost my only child thirty years ago, Frølich. She had just turned twenty. She was travelling with her best friend. They went to bed at around midnight. My daughter couldn't sleep. Witnesses have told me she came back up to the bar, without waking Karin, her friend. Half an hour later the fire alarm went off. At first my daughter ran up to the deck, apparently. Then she ran back into the ship. I'm sure she wanted to wake Karin and save her life. My daughter was found kneeling with her forehead against the wall outside the cabin. She had fallen to her knees and died in that position, in a sea of flames, alone with her mortal dread. Have you got any children?'

23

No, Frølich didn't have any children.

'Nothing feels worse to a mother or a father than the inability to alleviate a child's suffering,' Svinland said, breathing in deeply. 'Whether it's fear or pain. You spend every day for year after year of your life wondering: What could I have done if I'd been there? How could I have stopped it? Why did she die and not me? I can see it in your face. You think I'm going to say some rubbish about losing the apple of my eye. I won't bother you with that. I'll just list a few objective facts. Vilda was a great pleasure to her parents for as long as she was allowed to live. The sound of her light footsteps in the morning gave our lives meaning. Apart from that she was a talent. She liked am-dram. Cared about everyone, friends and family. But her goodness isn't where the pain lies. Nor the joy she spread around her. These are hooks my wife and I have been left with. Hooks we can hang our memories on. What's more important to me is that I was meant to leave Vilda behind me on earth. She was taken away from me by the ship of death, the *Sea Breeze*. She was killed by cynics who did dirty work for money. But those who killed her didn't just remove Vilda from the face of the earth. They destroyed much more – they also destroyed living people. My wife's still woken at night by Vilda's screams of pain. This has scarred her and it has scarred me. Our memories of our child and the dreams we had for her have been destroyed – and all we're left with are the shattered remains. We've been stripped of all that was good in our lives by bastards who never gave us a thought. But Lise and I are only two of a large number of victims. These arseholes killed more than a hundred and fifty people. They wiped out whole families. And they destroyed the lives of parents and children who survived. There are victims all over the country. Now they've taken Fredrik from us, too. I want to hire you because I have to do something about this. For thirty years I've watched the police stick their heads in the sand when it comes to the *Sea Breeze*. I'm bloody sick of it. I believe – no, I know that the police won't find out who killed Fredrik and ensure that he gets his just deserts.'

'I know the man running the investigation,' Frølich said. 'He'll find the answer.'

'I understand your naivety in this matter. After all, you worked in the police for a long time. But I'll still do everything I can. For Fredrik's sake. Fredrik talked to me about most things. He thought the police were out to get him. He thought you were also being manipulated – part of the police's game.'

'Me?'

'I know Fredrik paid you an advance to do a job. Now he's dead. You can't work for him anymore. The job he gave you is irrelevant now. But I'm here to ask you to do something for me instead. I want you to find Fredrik's eyewitness. Ole Berg's sitting on the truth about what happened. Not only about who killed my daughter. Ole Berg also knows what happened to Fredrik last night. I want you to find him before the police do. So that we can be sure the truth comes out.'

Frølich leaned back in his chair. Was this something he should rack his brains over? Was this something he should spend any time on? Trespass on Gunnarstranda's territory? Every single cell of the nerves in his spine screamed in unison: *no*.

On the other hand…

He lowered his gaze, self-critically. What about the other hand? A man comes to your office. He says he knows something you want to know. He wants information from you, but doesn't get it. He puts twenty thousand in an envelope and leaves. He avoids you, doesn't pick up when you ring, despite the fact that he must know why you are ringing, despite actually wanting to talk to you to get information.

Then he is killed.

He got up, walked to the window and looked out.

'Will you take the job?'

He turned back to Svinland. 'You say this eyewitness was with Andersen last night. Do you think their meeting has anything to do with Andersen's murder?'

Jørgen Svinland inclined his head in silence.

'Have you any idea?'

Svinland took a deep breath. 'Will you take the job, Frølich?'

He stood by the window, weighing up the matter. His spine was still screaming no. But he also had other things to take into account. He owed Andersen twenty grand. He could give the money back to Andersen's mother. Or he could make himself useful. He could spend the money on doing something sensible for Andersen. *Something sensible?* His spine jeered at him, but he repressed the feeling and turned back to Svinland.

'What about this lifeboat that went missing?'

Svinland took a deep breath. 'In the mayhem, when the passengers were leaving the ferry in lifeboats, there was one on the starboard side that got stuck. It hung alongside the ferry for quite a long time and the passengers in it panicked. There were forty of them in a boat that wouldn't go up or down, you know. Hanging there, they see another lifeboat further aft being lowered into the sea. In this lifeboat there are only two people – two uniformed crew members. The passengers in the lifeboat stuck on the side of the boat cry for help. But the two crewmen don't take any notice. They just start the engine and make for the horizon. There are close on forty survivors who say the same thing. In the middle of the chaos the two crewmen flee the burning ferry. Ole Berg has an explanation for why it happened. What is it?'

This assignment seemed innocuous enough: locate a person who had dinner with Fredrik Andersen last night.

'Actually I owe Andersen a job,' he said.

Jørgen Svinland stretched out a hand. 'Now you're working for me. Let's shake hands on it.'

Frank ignored the feeling in his spine and took his hand. A strong, dry hand.

'Ole Berg was the cover name Fredrik gave him. When Fredrik and I discussed the events he was always referred to as Ole Berg. I doubt it's his real name.'

Was that all Svinland had to say? 'You have to give me more than that,' Frølich said. 'An Ole Berg who doesn't exist in the national register isn't a lot to go on.'

'There is one thing,' Svinland said. 'Fredrik talked about a crewman, a Rolf Myhre. This Myhre's supposed to be connected to Berg in some way or other, although I don't know how.'

Rolf Myhre, Frølich thought. He had come across that name not so long ago, but where?

The man hobbled towards the door.

Frank stayed where he was, by the window. He searched his memory while the man opened the door, turned and sent him a look. 'Let me know when Fredrik's advance is used up. I'll transfer more money immediately.'

'Have you got a telephone number?'

The man leaned on the crutch and one hand bored into the inside pocket of his jacket. 'Here,' he said, passing him a business card.

Frølich crossed the floor and took it.

'I'll send you a contract. Sign it and return it to me,' he said, and added: 'All the formalities are covered now.'

Svinland nodded.

'How's the girlfriend?'

'Which girlfriend?'

'Your daughter's.'

'Karin? She survived. She managed to escape from the cabin just before Vilda went back.'

24

He drove to the city centre in case he needed his car later. Found a bay free in Oslo City multi-storey car park. Shortly afterwards he unlocked the door to his office. Repeated the routine with his chair, which rolled against the wall with a bang. Sat down and went through what happened here a day ago. Andersen scribbled down a telephone number on an envelope containing twenty thousand kroner. Andersen put it on the table and left. He followed him, came back, stuffed the notes in his pocket and drove to Andersen's flat.

The envelope? Where had he put it?

The waste-paper basket was empty. So the cleaner had been in. He walked out of the office and down the stairs. Located the cellar door. Opened it. Switched on the light. Nothing. No refuse room. He walked back and into the backyard. There were some green plastic containers here. One was for paper recycling. He opened the lid. It was half full, but he could barely reach in. He sighed. There was nothing for it. He went back up the stairs and fetched the chair from beside the office door. Placed it in front of the container, opened the lid, climbed up on the chair and started rummaging through the pile of used newspapers and shredded letters. Ten minutes later he found it. The envelope was addressed to Fredrik Andersen. Two stamps with a picture of a Norwegian mountain plateau. With a postmark.

In the top left-hand corner of the envelope was the sender's name. A company logo. *Rolf Myhre. Timepieces bought and sold.* The address was Porfyrveien 7b.

*

Frank got into his car and turned onto the inner ring road and up Tråkka to Oslo West.

As he swung into Stasjonsveien, Matilde rang. She seemed uneasy. She said she had gone to where they had agreed to meet, but Guri hadn't appeared.

'I can't get hold of her.'

There was an anxious edge to Matilde's voice. He wasn't sure how to respond, apart from trying to calm her nerves.

'She's bound to show up.'

'But we'd agreed the time and place. I don't like this. Now that writer's been killed.'

'Have you rung her?'

'Several times. She isn't answering.'

'She has to show up. There might be something at work preventing her from getting to a phone.'

'I've rung there, too. She's not at work. This is her day off and that was why we were going to meet, of course.'

'Give it a little while yet, anyway.'

'Where are you?'

'In my car on my way to Røa. Have to talk to a guy, find out more.'

'Where?'

'It might take a bit.'

'I can wait. I'll go there.'

'Porfyrveien 7b. Can you find it?'

'Yes, I'm on my way now.'

'You'll see my car. Call me if you get bored waiting.'

25

The posh West End of Oslo was not only posh. Rolf Myhre lived in a sleepy area at the foot of the Ullernåsen hills, in a three-storey block of flats beside a road that led down to a river valley that gave the area an attractive, child-friendly quality. The greyish-white concrete blocks stood in a line along the road and on the slope above, all with pointed roofs, and verandas that protruded from the facades like pouting lower lips. 7b turned out to be the lowest block of the three along the road. Myhre lived in the corner flat on the ground floor and opened up after three rings of the bell. He was a stocky, elderly man with a muscular face, a big nose and a broad mouth. He had combed his grey hair back in a way that was reminiscent of the sixties and the regulars at Dovrehallen. This was also true of his shoes, which were black, pointed and shiny.

'Myhre?'

'Rolf,' Myhre said, holding the door open. 'Tick-Tock Rolf,' he said, extending his hands as if he wanted to be clapped in irons. His shirt sleeves rode up. He had a formidable watch around each wrist. 'I'm known as just Tick-Tock Rolf. Because I'm unusually interested in timepieces. If you're after a Rolex, you'll have to ring and book an appointment.'

'I'm a private investigator,' Frølich said, and explained that he was searching for a person called Ole Berg and a reliable source had told him that Rolf Myhre knew him.

Tick-Tock Rolf's mouth fell open.

Frølich explained that he had been hired by a relative of Fredrik Andersen's after he died.

The name Fredrik Andersen seemed to function like a password.

'Is Fredrik dead?'

'There's something about it on the net. A man killed in Holtet last night.'

Tick-Tock Rolf stared at him in amazement.

'I've spoken to the policeman responsible for the investigation. The victim is the writer Fredrik Andersen. There's no doubt about it.'

'Come in,' Rolf said, and walked into the flat. He stopped in the living room, in front of a low leather suite and a glass table.

They stood here while Tick-Tock Rolf talked about his business with an absent-minded expression on his face. He bought and sold second-hand wristwatches, principally valuable Swiss items he acquired on eBay and the like. These watches he sold on to vain Norwegian men. Once he'd organised a sale in Bygdøy allé, but after being robbed three times in a week and five times in a month, he moved his stock to a secret address and operated his business from his flat while displaying his goods on social media.

'Bloody Norwegian police. Can't trust them. No bloody use at all. But with my business at home, clients have to ring in advance and make an appointment. If you'd been considering robbing me now, good luck to you; you won't find any watches here. I can't take this in though. Fredrik Andersen dead! He was the salt of the earth. And not even fifty years old. He had a fancy IWC by the way.'

'A what?'

'A wristwatch. One he'd inherited from his father.'

The walls of Myhre's flat were dominated by pictures of sea-going craft. The biggest was of a white three-masted warship being towed by a paddle-wheeled tugboat.

'That's the *Temeraire*,' Myhre said. 'She's being taken to be broken up. By a steamboat. Symbolic stuff. I used to be a seaman, you know.'

The kitchen was furnished in a modern style. The window looked out on the river valley. They perched on two bar stools by a window sill. Myhre fetched two porcelain cups with a golden border around the rim. He made espresso by putting small green capsules in a machine that groaned away while a thin, brown liquid trickled into the cups.

'I didn't know Andersen that well,' Tick-Tock Rolf said as he passed Frank a cup and wriggled up onto the stool. 'But murder. That's mind-boggling.'

'The police say they're keeping all lines of enquiry open. That means the murder may have some connection with the book he wrote.'

'The one about the *Sea Breeze*?'

'Yes.'

'I worked on the *Sea Breeze*, as first mate.'

'Do you know anything about a man on board called Ole Berg?'

'A passenger?'

'Don't know. But what I've been told suggests that he was crew.'

The man shook his head. 'I would've known.'

'Ole Berg's supposed to be an alias. It's what Andersen called him. This Ole Berg's supposed to have information about the missing lifeboat.'

'A missing lifeboat?'

'A lifeboat with two men on board. Two officers who left the burning vessel for land without taking anyone with them.'

Tick-Tock Rolf shook his head. 'Absolute rubbish. I've heard a similar rumour, but it just shows how far from reality such speculation can take you. Remember: I was on board. The ship was on fire, wasn't it. People were running for their lives and boarded lifeboats higgledy-piggledy. And two men were supposed to have taken a lifeboat and shoved off without taking anyone else? It's nonsense.'

'What happened?'

Tick-Tock Rolf sipped his coffee. 'We left Oslo four hours late. It was a Friday, an Easter exodus, and absolute chaos packing vehicles on the car deck. That was my responsibility, by the way. Organising the vehicles. But everyone was new on the boat. She had only come into operation five days earlier. The shipowners had chartered an Italian ship for a few months as a stopgap, and when that boat had to go back to Sardinia, the *Sea Breeze* was commissioned at once. It was a lovely ferry, nice to manoeuvre, but passenger accommodation was a total nightmare. They had been booked into cabins on the Italian boat, of course. So people were allotted cabins that didn't exist and the chaos was complete. Fortunately, this was nothing to do with me. I was first mate, wasn't I. We slipped our moorings at around ten in the evening. We'd passed Færder lighthouse and were on our way into the Skagerrak. I was on mid-to-four watch and alone on the bridge. The captain had gone to his cabin. Then a seaman ran into the wheelhouse shouting that a fire had broken out in a cabin on deck four. The man said it had been put out. I called the captain. He arrived in seconds and took the helm. I belted down to find out what was going on. It turned out there'd been a fire in some linen on the corridor floor, on the port side of deck four. It'd been put out by a passenger. But there was a bit of a to-do outside the cabin. The passengers were het up, and no wonder. They'd just put out a fire. In some linen on the floor, right. It had to be the work of an arsonist. It took me all my time to calm them down, then I had to run to the wheelhouse and report back to the captain. I didn't get a chance because when I opened the door to the bridge all hell had broken loose. A second fire – on the deck beneath the first one – had caught hold of the walls. The paint on the bulkheads was burning like petrol. On the bridge we saw the control panel light up, so we had no choice but to set off the alarms and activate the fire doors. But the fire spread faster than we could close the doors. In very few minutes every bloody cabin corridor was alight.'

Tick-Tock Rolf sat immersed in thought before continuing:

'The captain sent a Mayday message and we started evacuating the boat. That, too, was chaotic. The passengers who made it to the open air survived. Many of the poor devils who had retired to their beds died. Families with children, right. Children had crawled under the beds to get air. Mothers with children had fled into the shower rooms. They died hugging each other on the floor.'

Tick-Tock Rolf rubbed his face. It was obvious that he got no pleasure from recalling that night. He sighed and cursed.

'Are you still in touch with anyone from the boat?'

'No.'

The answer came back like a whip. He looked at his watch demonstratively.

'Any idea who it was Fredrik referred to as Ole Berg?'

'Nope.'

Tick-Tock had his eyes closed. 'You come here and pursue the *Sea Breeze* tragedy as if it were a footnote in a humorous book you've read. But those of us who went through that living hell never forget. However we try. Every bloody day we try. You don't understand. You're obsessed by some trivial detail I can't help you with. A lifeboat? A missing lifeboat? It's just rubbish. Andersen must've known there was nothing to his story. I presume he found time to talk to this person you call Ole Berg because he was wondering if the man had other, more far-reaching information up his sleeve. Fredrik was like that. He knew the *Sea Breeze* tragedy was big, so immense that the police were never even close to finding out what really happened. But a lifeboat that goes missing? That's plain ridiculous.'

He cast a fleeting glance at the watch on his left wrist. 'And now I have stuff to do. I'm sorry.'

'I can drive you.'

'Drive?'

'If you want to go somewhere.'

'I'm not going anywhere. Goodbye.'

26

Frank almost collided with a young boy on his bike as he came out of the building. He jinked to the side and walked back to the car.

Rolf Myhre was upset. But no more than that. The outcome for Frank was that he hadn't got any closer to solving the riddle of Ole Berg.

He sat behind the wheel unsure what to do next. Then the passenger door opened. Matilde got in with a serious look on her face. She brought with her a waft of fresh citrus and summer.

'What's new?' she asked.

'Nothing. I've just been speaking to a guy in connection with an assignment, and I don't quite know where to start.'

'I must've rung Guri eleven times. She doesn't pick up. That's never happened before.'

'Perhaps she's found a man.'

Matilde didn't answer. Instead she stroked his neck.

A front door slammed.

'Him,' he said.

It was Tick-Tock Rolf on his way out. The man had changed into green Bermudas and a red-and-yellow Hawaiian shirt. He was still wearing black, pointed shoes and white ankle socks.

Matilde whistled softly.

'What is that?'

'I like his style.'

They watched him. He walked with a heavy gait and a stoop.

His destination turned out to be a cycle rack. He bent over the front wheel of a bike to open the lock.

Perhaps Tick-Tock was only going to the shops. Perhaps he was going to visit his sick mother. But Frank's visit had upset him. And this could be a sort of reaction. And Frank had no pressing engagements.

'Feel like helping me?'

'Of course,' she said.

27

When Rolf trundled past on his modern mountain bike Matilde was already out of the car. Frank sat watching the first mate cycle past.

He twisted the ignition key and drove after him at a leisurely speed, but stopped now and then to keep a suitable distance between them.

Rolf sat back in the saddle. He held the handlebars with straight arms while pedalling slowly and calmly up the incline. It soon became obvious the man was making for the metro station. They passed a three-storey brick building that turned out to be Huseby School. Here, Rolf turned left onto a path. Frank had to continue along the road and therefore lost sight of the bike, but at the lights he saw Rolf locking up his bike outside Hovseter station. The man checked the lock with a quick tug, then went down to the platform.

Frank made for a Co-op on the other side of the rails. Found a spot in the customers' car park, got out of his car and locked it. The train was just pulling in. He headed for the station and hoped Rolf wouldn't spot him among the people on the platform. The odds of being seen were high as it was a quieter time of day.

He waited until Rolf was on the train. Then he made a move, got into the next carriage and found a seat right at the back. Through the windows between the cars he could see Rolf's colourful shirt.

But Matilde was nowhere to be seen.

The man in the Hawaiian shirt sat still all the way to Nationaltheatret station. Then he stood up and got off.

The man walked without a backward look, past the peacock fountain and on under the trees by Spikersuppa pool. He disappeared into the Paleet shopping arcade and took the escalator up to the first floor.

Matilde rang as Frank was doing a round of the shops to see where Rolf had gone.

'Where are you?'

'Behind you.'

He turned, but couldn't see her. 'You're good, you are. Carry on like this and I'll hire you.'

He caught a glimpse of a Hawaiian shirt in a clothes shop. Soon the man was out again and descending to the ground floor and back onto the street. They walked along Karl Johans gate. Frank stayed fifty metres behind. They crossed Egertorget square. A silver living statue stood on a plinth beside a guitar-strumming street singer on a chair, accompanied by a rhythm box. Once again Rolf went into a shop.

Frank walked past the store, and nipped into the greengrocer's in Kirkeristen to wait. Soon Rolf came out again, still empty-handed. Now the man was making a beeline for the greengrocer's.

Frank grabbed a *Verdens Gang* from the display stand as Rolf approached.

'My goodness, you here too,' Rolf said and came up close to him. 'What a bloody small world it is.'

'Indeed it is,' Frank said, feeling a complete fool.

'Why don't you just ask where I'm going instead of buggering about like this?'

'Where are you going?'

'To meet some pals. Were you ever in the police?'

Frank nodded.

'Thought so. Ever since the *Sea Breeze* I've wondered what it is with people like you. You ring doorbells. Ask questions. Get answers. But for some reason that's not good enough. You traipse after me – as if I've got a better answer in the back of my pants. You're just like the fools who investigated the *Sea Breeze* case. They stick their noses in everywhere and what do they find out? Sweet F.A. I hope this is the last time I see you. Bye,' Rolf said and walked on.

Frank stood watching the broad figure disappearing into the distance. He looked around for Matilde, but couldn't see her.

He turned and trudged back to the metro to recover his car.

28

Later that afternoon, as Frank let himself into Brugata 1, he saw a small padded envelope in the post rack. He turned it over. No sender's name. The envelope contained a memory stick, but there was no accompanying letter. He took the stairs to his office. Once inside he fired up his laptop. Put the stick into a USB. The stick was full of PDF files, which turned out to be police documents: the interviews with survivors after the lethal fire on board *MS Sea Breeze*.

Who would feed him information about this case? And anonymously.

Never mind. He could investigate the donor's motive later.

He treated himself to a ten-minute read, after which he felt like he had been shipwrecked on the open sea. The survivors described what they had experienced, what they had seen and what they had done. All of them, one after the other. But the stick was also full of technical documents, drawings of the ship and an overview of the security systems. He had no idea what to do with this material. Furthermore, he realised that to gain a perspective on all this information, to be able to differentiate between what was important and what wasn't, would be an almost impossible task.

He searched the files for the name Ole Berg. No hits.

Then his phone rang.

'Hello, this is Nicolai Smith Falck.'

'Hi,' Frank said. He remembered the guy. However, he wasn't sure how enthusiastic he was about being called by this particular journalist.

'It's Frølich, isn't it, the ex-policeman?'

'It is.'

'I'm covering the murder of Fredrik Andersen.'

'For which newspaper?'

'I'm a freelancer. But this is for *Verdens Gang*. My understanding is that you had contact with Andersen just before he was found dead.'

'I think you've called the wrong person. Have a nice day.'

'Wait.'

'Mhm?'

'I've interviewed you once before,' Falck said. 'A couple of years ago, regarding some aggravated rapes.'

'No, you haven't. The interview was about an alleged suicide in Bygdøy. A woman was killed by a juggernaut going round the Bygdøy roundabout. Turned out that she hadn't jumped of her own volition.'

'Ah, yes, that was the one.'

'Have a nice day.'

Frank rang off and wondered how the journalist had been tipped off. It could have been anyone. But he doubted it was Gunnarstranda.

He pounded away on his laptop again. Went online. Googled Nicolai Smith Falck. There were news items, recent and older articles in *Verdens Gang*, *Dagbladet*, *Nettavisen* and a local Østfold paper. Falck lived in Grünerløkka. He was thirty-seven years old.

A number of photographs of Falck came up. The journalist looked as he remembered him, the spitting image of Alfred E. Neumann, the *MAD* magazine mascot, a guy with a round head, protruding ears, a fringe above sleepy eyes and a scampish smile. But he knew for certain that in his case appearances deceived. Nicolai Smith Falck had a poison pen if he was in the mood.

Frank scrolled down the screen. The *Sea Breeze* came up. A lot. Article after article after article. They had been written about a year ago. *Dagbladet* had run a long series about the catastrophe. All the articles were signed by Nicolai Smith Falck.

Perhaps I was too dismissive with this journalist, Frank mused. Falck knew the case well. So there was a good chance he had also known Fredrik Andersen.

He looked up as the door opened.

29

In the doorway was Matilde. She was holding an ice-cream cornet in each hand.

'Nougat or chocolate sprinkles?'

'Chocolate.'

'I knew it.'

The cornet with chocolate sprinkles was wrapped in a serviette. She handed it to him and sat on the edge of the desk. 'Do you know how I knew?'

'No idea.'

'You're a Capricorn. And when I called you earlier today I was in Bergkristallen, the street in Lambertseter. And then I remembered that the right crystals or minerals for your sign are quartz and onyx. Quartz can sparkle in a variety of colours. But the onyx colour is like chocolate.'

'You're good,' he said, leaning back. 'I didn't see you once.'

'You didn't know I was good?' she said, gripping the muzzle-loader pistol that functioned as a paperweight.

'Actually I like strawberry sprinkles best,' she said and pointed the pistol at the office workers across the street. 'There's something about artifice that floats my boat. Artificial silk, artificial fur, artificial sweets. But they only had nougat.'

'Put it down,' Frank said, pointing to a woman in an office across the street. She had got to her feet and was peering nervously in their direction. 'They don't know it's sealed with lead.'

Matilde put down the pistol and waved to the woman in the window.

'So, tell me more,' he said. 'Where did Rolf Myhre go?'

'He went for a walk – from Bjørvika, along the docks, past Vippetangen peninsula and the fishermen on Akershus quay – he stopped and exchanged a few words with some of the men on the sailing boats there. He knew several of them. At any rate, he greeted them. He continued back to City Hall quay. There he caught the boat to Gressholmen island.'

'What did he do there?'

'Went in the restaurant, Gressholmen kro. He had a mug of beer and talked to a guy I'd guess was the owner. A big, fat man. Afterwards he caught another boat. To Nakholmen. He visited a man in a cabin there. A man who looks like Frank Sinatra and whose name is Bernt Weddevåg.'

'How did you find out his name?'

'It was on a sign.'

'What did they do in the cabin?'

'They patted each other on the back like old pals. Sat down on the veranda to chat. By that time I'd lost interest and caught the boat back and bought ice creams for us.'

Her phone rang.

'It's Guri,' she said excitedly and put the phone to her ear. 'Hi, where've you been?' She left the room.

Shortly afterwards she poked her head in again – with the phone held to her chest.

'I'm off to meet Guri. I'll ring you.'

With that she was gone.

30

Frank made a note of the name – Bernt Weddevåg.

He ate the rest of the ice cream. Then he lifted his phone. Rang the last number and got an answer at once. 'Nicolai Smith Falck here.'

'Hi Nicolai. Frank Frølich.'

'Hi there.'

'I Googled you and saw that you'd written quite a bit about the *Sea Breeze* in a newspaper series, a while back.'

'Yes, I did. *Dagbladet* even presented it at an investigative journalism conference.'

'Did you interview Fredrik Andersen in this regard?'

'In this regard he and I were competitors.'

'And what do you mean by that?'

'He wrote about the case. I wrote about the case. I assume we used the same sources.'

'Did you reach the same conclusions?'

'I doubt it.'

'What do you mean by that?'

'I think he allowed himself to be led by conspiracy theories more than I did.'

'As an ex-policeman I ought to be flattered. It's not often that the tabloid press bats for the state machinery.'

'To be honest, I have no idea what Andersen's conclusions were. I never read his book. But what can you say about the murder?'

'Nothing more than I've read in the papers. You probably know more than me.'

'It's rumoured someone hired you to carry out surveillance on Andersen. Have you any comment to make?'

'Before I answer I'd like to know who said what.'

There was a brief silence. He could hear the journalist thinking and weighing the odds before he answered: 'I was tipped off by an ex-colleague of yours.'

'Who?'

This time the silence was longer, and Frank was about to abandon the conversation when the journalist cleared his throat and said:

'Bjørn Thyness. What can you give me in return?'

The answer nettled him. He had never had a very high opinion of Nicolai Smith Falck, but he hadn't imagined he would serve up the name of a source on a silver platter. Thyness also annoyed him – the fact that he had voluntarily talked about Frank and Andersen to the journo, but didn't want to talk to him.

'Still there?' the journalist said. 'What can you give me in return?'

'No one hired me to do surveillance on Andersen. Andersen himself came to me and hired me for an assignment.'

'What kind of assignment?'

'I can't say any more about that case.'

'Surely you can give me a hint? After all, I blew my source.'

'It's about asylum seekers. Andersen was writing a book about immigrants.'

'OK.' Falck suddenly seemed excited. 'Bjørn works in the immigration unit. Is there a connection – between Andersen and the unit?'

The journo and Thyness were on first-name terms, Frank thought, and said:

'I have no idea. The person who might be able to answer that question is Bjørn Thyness.'

After he rang off he sat thinking. Bjørn Thyness manipulated and schemed, as though Frank were a piece in some game.

Was this a kick in the bollocks for an ex-colleague who had once had a relationship with his partner?

Bjørn had never been a good guy, but the idea still seemed unlikely.

He hadn't seen either Bjørn or Gøril for at least a year. Then you make a short phone call. And this drops on you.

There was only one thing to do. He would have to talk to Bjørn again.

He took a deep breath and found Bjørn's number. It rang for an eternity.

He put down the phone. Who could he ask then? Not a word would pass Gunnarstranda's lips, there was no doubt about that. But there were others. He seemed to remember that Bjørn and Lena Stigersand had worked together quite a lot.

31

Half an hour later Frank walked through the door of Grand Pizza in Brugata, Lena Stigersand's first choice for fast food. She hadn't arrived yet. He was the only customer and stood watching the man behind the counter filling a pitta bread with meat, vegetables and a sauce, then Frank helped himself to a Coke from the display fridge, found a plastic fork on the counter, wriggled up onto a stool by the window and began to eat. The pitta bread was freshly toasted with a nice crust, and the meat was juicy. He could understand why this place was Lena's first choice.

A few minutes later she was leaning against the counter. She appeared to have come from a fitness session, wearing leggings, a pale sweater and yellow trainers. She ordered the same kebab as he had.

He had swallowed the last bite when she sat down on the stool next to him.

'I've just finished,' Frank said.

'Have a coffee,' Lena said, tucking in.

He stood up, but the man behind the counter had overheard the conversation. 'Turkish coffee?'

'Cortado, please.'

He sat down again.

'How's business?' Lena asked, and sipped her Coke.

'I take one day at a time.'

'Bit delicate, you being a witness in the Fredrik Andersen case,' she said.

'Gunnarstranda doesn't like it?'

She shrugged. 'Never easy to say what he likes or doesn't like. But he's annoyed that you don't want to say what kind of assignment it was that Andersen gave you.'

'Hardly know myself. I told him all I know.'

The man came with the coffee.

Lena waited until the man had returned to his position behind the counter. 'Why did you want to meet?'

'I'd like to ask you a favour.'

'What sort?' she said quickly, with a suspicious frown.

'And I was wondering if it was you who put a memory stick in my post box.'

'No. Why would I?'

'There were police documents in it.'

'New or old?'

'1988.'

'My guess is they weren't confidential. You can find them in the Public Records Office.'

'How's the Andersen case going?'

Lena chewed without answering.

'You're on the team, aren't you?'

'For as long as it lasts. I'm writing job applications at the moment.'

'You're unhappy there?'

'I've applied for several posts. They've chosen a man every time. I'm at least as well or better qualified. I'm pretty fed up.'

'What are you applying for now?'

'There's a job going in Kripos.'

'You'll get it.'

'You can't say that. I'm still a woman.'

'But you've got the best CV. Are there any other applicants?'

'Bound to be. But if they choose someone else too, I'll do what you did and stop.'

They sat in silence for a while. Lena finished her kebab. Frank drained his coffee.

She pushed her plate away and regarded him with an expectant expression.

'Did Gunnarstranda tell you I saw Bjørn Thyness keeping Andersen's place under surveillance?'

She nodded. 'So far that's off the record.'

'Why?'

'It comes from you and you haven't made a formal statement.'

'Was there a case against Andersen?'

Lena drank her Coke. Put down the bottle. 'We're keeping our minds open, as they say. What I *can* tell you is that Bjørn's alleged surveillance isn't our most interesting line of enquiry.'

He waited for her to carry on. But she didn't.

'I still think Andersen must've had something on Thyness,' he said.

Lena shook her head. 'You don't know what line we're pursuing, and in any case I can't tell you.'

'OK. These are my thoughts: Probably no one in-house was working against Andersen. However, the fact is that Thyness was spying on the man. I saw that with my own eyes. Why would he do that if he hadn't had a report or a tip-off?'

'Because the immigration unit has its own life to lead and works on cases the rest of us are neither interested in or know about.'

'I ring Bjørn and he doesn't pick up.'

'If you were messing about with his partner, that's not altogether surprising.'

'Who says I was messing about with his partner?'

'It's a rumour I've heard.'

Lena sent him an angled look, with an almost gloating smile on her lips.

'Gøril and I finished long before those two got together,' Frank said. 'And I never "messed about" with her.'

Lena was still smiling. 'That's the way Bjørn is,' she said. 'He's VERY jealous.'

'I was called by a journo. He asked me about my relationship with Andersen. He knew about things I've only told the police. I've worked out who his source is. It's Bjørn Thyness. But he doesn't answer the phone to me.'

'Things are pretty turbulent between him and Gøril at the moment. Apparently they were rowing and Gøril said something nice about you to rub a little salt into his macho-man wound. My guess is it's that simple.'

Frank gave this some thought. Could it be so simple? Or was it connected with Andersen?

Lena watched him again. 'Why are you asking me of all people about this?'

'I thought you knew Bjørn.'

She shrugged. 'I don't know Bjørn any better than I know you.'

She sat in silence, gazing out of the window as she finished chewing. At length she rolled up her serviette. 'If Bjørn's pissing you about and you're wondering why, I think you'll have to go and ask him.'

'But he doesn't want to talk to me.'

'Nothing I can do about that.'

Lena gathered her things ready to leave.

'I only need to know where I can find him,' Frank said.

'The immigration unit's in Økern. You'll find him there, I reckon.'

'I'd prefer not to go there. It's too official.'

'Go to his house then. If you're lucky you'll find Gøril alone there.'

'Very droll.'

Lena slid down off the stool. 'I have to go to Økern anyway. But not to talk to Bjørn.'

She left.

Frank stayed where he was, watching people stream past the windows. He had two assignments and they had both come to a standstill. He hadn't the slightest idea how to proceed with either of them.

32

Frank spent the evening watching a couple of episodes of *Breaking Bad*. By the end he realised he had seen both of them before. Switched off the television when it was almost midnight. Not much else to do but go to bed.

Lena rang as he was about to clean his teeth.

He abandoned his dental ablutions, got dressed again and went out to his Mini Cooper.

It was still light outside, even if it was past midnight. He went through the lights in Alexander Kiellands plass at just before one.

Found a parking spot at the bottom of Waldemar Thranes gate opposite Tranen bakery and the asylum-seekers centre. Tipped his seat back and prepared to wait.

He dropped off. But he never slept soundly sitting upright. So he quickly came to when the procession roared past.

He got out of his car and watched.

Bearing in mind the intensity, the speed and the pounding of feet, you could be forgiven for thinking a heavily armed Mafia Don was being arrested. But the targets were children. He caught a brief glimpse of Bjørn's tall figure and crew cut on the way into the main entrance. Frølich followed and had to go past a skinny, semi-naked boy who was trembling as if he had just fallen through ice: cowering, bent forward, with a cuddly toy in his hand, a pink cloth pig. A uniformed woman dragged the boy and lifted him into one of the police cars along with a shabby wheelie bag. The boy was still wearing only pyjama trousers and his chest was bare.

Presumably this kind of action suited Bjørn down to the ground. He got an adrenaline kick if all the external symbols harmonised with the superiority he felt when exercising power over the weak.

Then the tall figure came back and down the stairs. Bjørn was speaking on a walkie-talkie; he rang off and slipped it onto his belt.

'Bjørn!'

Bjørn turned. 'What are you doing here?'

'You won't take my calls.'

'Can't you see I'm busy?'

'They're children. They won't be upset if you and I talk for two minutes.'

'They're not children. They lie about their ages, they lie about their identities, they lie about not having parents, they lie—'

'This is about Fredrik Andersen. I was wondering what you and the immigration unit have on him.'

'And why were you wondering?'

'I have the feeling you're freelancing.'

'Freelancing? That's what you do. I don't do any freelancing.'

'Why do you ring journalists and tell them rubbish about me and Andersen?'

Thyness stopped for two seconds. Eyed Frølich, at a loss for words, then turned his back on him and was gone. The next moment two male officers dragged a girl each out of the door. They couldn't have been more than ten years old. They were struggling and screaming with fear. They still had nighties on under their jackets.

Frølich followed Bjørn to the lead car.

'Fine,' he said. 'I don't know what your agenda is with respect to me and Andersen. But I'll find out.'

Bjørn shook his head and grinned.

'I'd like to ask you a favour anyway.'

'No chance.'

'Aisha Bashur.'

Thyness stopped and turned to him.

'Who's that?'

'An asylum seeker you picked up from a centre in Hobøl the other day. She was taken to Trandum. Slightly built girl from Iraq – maybe eighteen, nineteen years old.'

'Sure of the name?'

'Yes. Aisha Bashur.'

'What about her?'

'I need to talk to her.'

'Why?'

'It's confidential.'

Bjørn Thyness sneered. 'Shame about that. The girls who were taken from the Hobøl centre were deported today. That would apply to the one you call Aisha Bashur. If I'd known where to, I would've told you, just to get rid of you.'

Thyness walked on.

Frølich followed.

Thyness turned on his heel. 'You still here?'

Frølich could feel himself getting irritated by Thyness's arrogance. He said:

'You were one of the last people to see Andersen alive.'

A searchlight behind Bjørn's back made it difficult for Frølich to read his face.

'Bloody hell, you're deafer than I thought.'

Bjørn's face came closer. 'I've never been any more interested in Fredrik Andersen than I am in your mother-in-law, if you have one. Go home and don't bother your little head with things you don't understand.' He opened a car door.

'Say hi to Gøril from me. For some strange reason I've been thinking about her more and more recently.'

It was childish. However, it was Bjørn, after all, who had ratcheted up the aggro.

Bjørn was already in the car. Frølich leaned in to speak. Bjørn slapped his face and quickly closed the door.

The reaction was comical. But Frølich wasn't smiling as the cars left. The lead car was now the last in the procession of three. They turned into the road.

They were gone, leaving behind them night and silence. Their operation was over.

On the front steps sat a lone figure in a yellow hi-vis vest.

She had her face buried in her hands.

Frank Frølich walked up to her.

She raised her head. She looked Norwegian, was in her sixties and wore glasses. Her face was grimy with tears. 'You saw what happened,' she said. 'You saw what they did to the children.'

Frank didn't reply.

The woman was sobbing. Her body rocked to and fro.

Frank turned and walked to his car.

It was almost three o'clock in the morning. The police had carried out what they would probably call a successful operation. As for Frank, he was no further on. At that moment his phone rang.

33

'Hi Frank. Guri Sekkelsten here.'

'Hi.'

'I'm so glad you answered. I was afraid you were in bed, asleep.'

She gave a short, somewhat embarrassed chuckle. 'Or were you? Did I wake you?'

'No, I wasn't. It's fine.'

'Sorry if this is inconvenient. I wouldn't have rung if it wasn't important,' she said.

'Right.'

'I managed to contact the writer, Fredrik Andersen.'

He let the information sink in, thinking: *I should never have told her his name. Never.*

'He and I met that evening.'

'You met Andersen?'

'Yes.'

'You did. OK,' he said, thinking: *She was with Andersen shortly before he was killed.*

'Along with Sheyma,' she said.

'The sister?'

'Something's not right there.'

'OK, let me get this clear. You, Andersen and Sheyma, the woman I was meant to find, you three met that evening?'

'Yes.'

'Where?'

'At a restaurant, some tarted-up place. She wanted to go there, Sheyma. It's her style. But what's so crazy is that she denies knowing Aisha. She says Aisha's lying, that the whole story is a figment of her imagination.'

'What's more important,' Frank said, 'is that Andersen was killed afterwards. You're one of the last people to see the man alive.'

'I think about that all the time. I'm afraid. And I reckon I have good reason to be.'

'Why?'

There was a silence. Frank waited for a reply. None came. He said:

'You have to talk to the police.'

'No.'

'Why not?'

'I don't want to talk to the police.'

'But why not?'

Again there was a silence, longer this time.

'Can we meet?' she said at length. 'It's easier to explain things when you can see who you're talking to.'

'When?'

'Preferably as soon as possible.'

'Where are you?'

'I'm out of town, but I've got a car. I have to pop back home. I daren't sleep there anymore. After what's happened to Andersen, I've been staying with an aunt. But I have to go home to pick up some clothes.'

'We can meet there,' he said. 'At your place. What's the address?'

34

Frank got into his car and started to tap Guri's address into the satnav.

The address came up automatically. That made him think twice. He had put in the address once before. Ivar Sekkelsten and Guri Sekkelsten. She had the same address as the small-time crook who pinched beer and cigarettes from his employer. Matilde hadn't told him Guri was married. So Ivar and Guri *were* related – brother and sister.

Well, there wasn't much he could do about that. He put his car into gear. Then the phone rang again.

It was Gunnarstranda.

'We have to talk. Where are you?'

'Do you know what time it is?'

There was a silence and then Gunnarstranda gave a low curse. 'Sorry,' he mumbled. 'I didn't realise it was so late. Did I wake you?'

'No, I'm out on a job.'

'When can you be here? At police HQ?'

Frølich hesitated. 'As I said, I'm busy right now. I'll be a few hours.'

He cast a quick glance at his watch. It was about seventy kilometres to where Guri lived. A good hour's drive each way, he calculated. Add an hour, plus a bit more on the way back because of the rush hour. How long would he and Guri talk for? Half an hour? An hour?

Actually he ought to open up to Gunnarstranda here and now and leave Guri to him. However, he had promised her not to get the police involved. He looked at his watch again.

'Police HQ? I'd guess between seven and eight.'

'See you then. Report to reception,' Gunnarstranda said and rang off.

35

On the E6 Frank kept his foot down. It was a summer's night and there was barely any traffic. He met the occasional semi-trailer and overtook various other vehicles. At Råde he turned off and continued on smaller roads towards Missingmyr. The light was soft and clear, and he had the sense that he owned the road, driving alone along the straight stretches through the forest. It was only when he went around the bends beside Lake Sæby that there was any oncoming traffic. He saw a Volvo estate and it seemed to be red. It passed him. Involuntarily, he slowed down. He watched the car disappearing in his rear-view mirror. The Volvo had only one rear light working. It had to be Guri's car. He cast a glance at the satnav. There were fewer than five kilometres to her house. Within a radius of five kilometres how many red Volvos are there on the road at four in the morning? With only one rear light working?

Well, they had made an arrangement. If she had wanted to cancel it, she would have rung. After all, she knew he was coming.

He carried on and stopped in the same place he had parked the car twice earlier, at the bus stop by the drive. He got out of the car and peered between the trees.

He closed the car door. It sounded like an immense bang in the night stillness.

This was a much more verdant time of the year than his last visit. But the smallholding was the same. The main house still had two windows boarded up and green stains on the wood panelling. The crooked barn was still tethered to a telephone mast by a ratchet strap.

He checked his watch. A quarter to four. The morning was lighter now. The edge of the sky almost purple. At least in one of the windows in the house there was light.

He walked slowly up to it.

The land on the smallholding was overgrown with weeds and small wisps of sallow, alder and birch, which in a few years would form impenetrable scrub on rich soil. There was a little greenhouse next to the main house. The door was open. There were three or four potted tomato plants inside. A kind of pavilion had been rigged up on the veranda, a party tent with a few garden chairs in front of a globe-shaped cooking grill.

Against the house wall was a kayak he had seen before. But Guri's car was nowhere to be seen.

Guri had said she had a car when she rang. He thought about the Volvo he had passed a few minutes ago. He didn't like the gut feeling he was getting.

Had she asked him to come all this way out here only to leave before he had arrived?

He walked over to the front door. Still no proper bell. Only the same sheep bell hanging from a cord by the door. He rang. Nothing happened.

He rang again.

Then the door slipped open a few centimetres. It wasn't locked. And the spring on the handle must have been broken because it was hanging loose.

'Hello? Guri?'

No answer.

He knocked on the door. There was still total silence except for something that sounded like a distant wheeze. He listened carefully.

Could she have dropped by to collect her clothes and then driven off without waiting for him?

Wouldn't she have locked the door after her?

The low whistle continued unabated.

He pushed open the front door and entered.

The light was on in the hallway. There were several pairs of shoes on the floor. Women's shoes with high heels. The whistling sound was getting louder. He pushed open the door leading to the kitchen. The light was off here. Blue cabinet doors and a white worktop. A stove with a ceramic hob. On it an old-fashioned kettle was boiling. That was where the whistling was coming from. Steam was coming through the spout. Condensation had begun to settle on the window. Frank took the kettle off the hob. It weighed very little in his hand; there was almost no water left. The whistling stopped. He switched off the stove.

One door led further into the house. He knocked without getting any response. He entered a small square room and pressed the light switch by the door. A wooden chandelier lit up. The person who lived here had very similar taste to Matilde. A vinyl record collection. A gramophone. Furniture that was evocative of another time. Only the ticking of an old-fashioned alarm clock on the windowsill could be heard.

A door led into another small room. Here the light was on, a white globe lamp hanging from the ceiling. There was a flat screen on the wall. Two speakers on either side. A window blind drawn. This was a home cinema. A sofa and a table, bowls with the remains of crisps and some Twist chocolates. No DVDs anywhere. A router with two aerials flashed from the windowsill.

He heard a thud somewhere else in the house. As though a door had slammed.

He stood motionless and listened. But heard nothing else.

He opened another door and was back in the little hallway. That was the ground floor covered.

Which door had slammed?

He gazed at the front door. Then he looked up the stairs leading to the first floor.

He cleared his throat. 'Hello?'

Not a sound.

'Guri?'

The same silence.

He gripped the handle, opened the front door a few centimetres and stared out. Everything was as it had been a few minutes ago. If someone had been in the house and had left, they had vanished.

Could the sound have come from the floor above?

He closed the door and turned to the stairs. Peered up. All he could see was the staircase and the banisters. He grasped the handrail and set off.

36

A step groaned as he pressed down his foot. He stopped and listened. Feeling like a burglar, he clung closer to the wall and tried to tread lightly. But it wasn't possible to make no sound. The stairs creaked with every movement he made.

At the top he stopped.

He found himself at the end of a corridor with four doors. One was open and led into a bathroom. He glanced in. A bath with a shower curtain, toilet, sink and a washing machine. A shelf crammed with shampoos and creams. The tap over the sink dripped.

He knocked on the adjacent door.

No reaction.

He opened the door.

The room was decorated in a feminine way. The sloping ceiling made the room feel small and intimate. A dressing table with an embroidered cloth and small framed pictures. Guri in a bikini. Guri and a dark-haired man arm in arm. Guri on a horse.

There was an electric alarm clock on the bedside table. The second hand was slowly passing the figure seven.

A window was ajar. The opening must have made a draught, Frank thought.

There was a broad bed under the window. On the opposite wall was a wardrobe. Three doors, one with a mirror. He walked over and opened the wardrobe. Dresses on hangers inside, a wetsuit he recognised. There was also a section of drawers filled with nylons, tops and underwear.

He left the room and went into the next. It had to be some kind of guest room. There was a bed with a bare mattress. The dresser by the wall had four empty drawers. A wardrobe with no clothes in. Only loose clothes hangers. The window was covered with plywood.

He went out and turned to the last door. Hesitated in front of it. He knocked, but there was no reaction. He shoved the door open. A smell of after-shave hung in the air. A bed hugged one sloping wall. On it a duvet. By the bed on the floor there were two dumbbells. A desk with no drawers was placed against one wall. Someone had slept here not too long ago.

A clinking sound made him spin round.

He left the room and stopped by the bathroom door. The shower curtain. It was moving slightly. He coughed. No response. He broke into a sweat. Forced himself to cross the threshold and step in.

He stared at the curtain, which was perfectly still now.

He stretched out an arm. Not wishing to go too close. He glanced quickly over his shoulder. Stepped to the side. Made a lunge and pulled the curtain back. Simultaneously ducking.

He looked down into an empty bath.

Then there was another thud. A door being closed on the floor below. That had to be someone.

'Hello,' he said, feeling stupid when no one answered.

He went to the small bathroom window and looked out.

There was no one to be seen. The only difference was the light. A bright morning sun hung low in the sky, making the leaves on the trees glisten. He allowed his eyes to wander across to the crooked barn with the bulging wooden cladding.

What were the sounds he had heard? A cellar door banging in the wind?

He went downstairs. Stood in the little hallway looking into the kitchen. Under the kitchen table there was a trapdoor in the floor.

37

He went in, pulled the table to one side and lifted the trapdoor, which had hinges at one end. A wooden staircase led down into the darkness. Holding the door with one hand, he crouched down, rummaged for his phone and switched on the torch function. He could make out an earthen floor and the supports for some shelving down below. Attached under the trapdoor was a loose purpose-made bar to keep it open. He fiddled with it and got the trap door to stay upright. Frank straightened up and went backwards down the ladder. It was a rickety affair and swayed under his weight. He stretched out a leg so that his foot could search for the next step. Found it and placed his weight on it. Then the step broke. Panic-stricken, he wafted his hands around to find something to hold onto and pulled down the bar. The trapdoor slammed shut. He fell on his back, knocking the air out of his lungs. He gasped. It was pitch-black inside. He couldn't see a thing. Panicked. Imagining rats and snakes on the earthen floor. Jumped to his feet, hitting his head hard. He fell back down again, but struggled up. He fumbled in his pockets for his phone. Couldn't find it. Either he had lost it in the fall or it was on the kitchen floor.

He stood still, listening in the darkness. No sounds. He lifted his hands and groped around him.

His hands found a wall, a shelf. He felt his way along the shelf. Found the ladder. Searched with his hands and found the broken step. Lifted his foot and felt a step that held. Dragged himself up. Pushed at the trapdoor, which refused to budge. He pushed. But the trapdoor didn't give.

He was sweating. Hyperventilating. Was someone standing on the trapdoor? Someone who wanted to keep him down here?

He pushed again. It was like pushing a concrete block. The trapdoor didn't move.

He blinked the sweat out of his eyes and fumbled around to find the cracks between the door and the floor. Found them and finally realised what he had been doing wrong. He had been pushing the floor and not the door. He took a new grip. The trapdoor opened with a bang.

The phone was nearby on the kitchen floor.

Seconds later he was up. Brushed the dust and dead insects off his clothes, closed the trapdoor, pushed the table back to its original position and couldn't get out of the house fast enough.

On the front doorstep he stood gasping for air.

The place seemed as abandoned as before. Although he had actually heard a door bang.

He tried closing the front door behind him to compare that with the sound he had heard in the house.

Closed it once again. It might have been the sound he had heard. He tried the door handle. The spring was weak. The strike plate from the lock was embedded in the lock-case. It could have been the wind playing with the door.

Even if Guri's car still wasn't anywhere to be seen, the kettle on the hob meant that she wasn't far away.

He set off from the front door and crossed the yard towards the barn. Observed the tarpaulin covering the opening in the wall. It was moving slightly.

Could be the wind.

He stopped. Moistened his index finger in his mouth and held it in the air. A slight chill on his finger told him there was a light wind from the west. He looked at the tarpaulin again. Now it was completely still.

Must be the wind.

38

He walked over to the barn, took hold of the tarpaulin and moved it aside. Went in. There was a rustle as the tarpaulin slipped back and covered the opening behind him.

It wasn't completely dark inside. The dim light was created by narrow gaps between the boards in the cladding. There were no boxes of goods stored here anymore. The large space was almost empty. There were three rectangular bales of hay in one corner. An axe was lodged in a chopping block. Some logs lay around on the floor.

He stood still again and listened. What was that noise? It sounded like a plank creaking. But it didn't come from this room. On the wall opposite the tarpaulin was a low opening in the cobwork. He went to the opening, bent down and wriggled through. Straightened up again.

All the walls here were cogged timber.

He heard the sound again. A soft creaking.

He stood still, all his senses sharpened. Suddenly wishing he hadn't left the axe in the chopping block behind him.

Why did he wish that? There was nothing unusual to be seen in this large space. An aluminium ladder, the length of one wall. In the corner, an old-fashioned cart with two immense wooden wheels.

He felt something wet drip onto his hair.

Another droplet fell on him.

He raised his hand and smelt the moisture, looked at his finger. A colourless liquid.

He leaned back. Looked up. And found himself staring at two bare feet. A drop fell from one foot and landed on his forehead.

He didn't move, he observed and listened. It was her body that was making the noise. It was swinging gently from the beam where a rope was tied. What was dripping from her feet had to be urine.

He took his phone. Switched on the torch function again. Shone the light upward.

The tip of her tongue was blue and protruded from between

equally blue lips. She was hanging by her neck from a thin rope. She was barefoot, but was wearing jeans and a T-shirt. Like a huge lamp she hung from a supporting beam of what was the access ramp into the upper part of the barn. The rope had cut into the skin of her neck. Her eyes were matt, like two marbles.

This woman would never paddle a kayak again.

If you want to commit suicide you do not boil water in a kettle first.

Someone had done this to her and it couldn't have been very long ago.

As he shone the torch he seemed to sense that he wasn't alone. It felt as if someone was standing right behind him.

The axe, he thought. Whoever it was had the axe.

He slowly craned his head round.

No one.

Then he heard something outside. It was the sound of footsteps.

39

Stiffly, he walked back the same way he had come, but misjudged where the opening was, hit his head on a crossbeam, fell on his face, his head reeling, crawled on all fours, still giddy, managed to stand up, but hit his head again, fell, groped his way through the hole in the wall and struggled to his feet. Turned and glanced over his shoulder with every step he took. No one was there. Sweat coursing down him, he ran the last few metres to the tarpaulin, which he hit with full force. It wrapped its arms around him. It enveloped him. He completely lost his senses and grappled with the tarpaulin to find a way out. In the end, he just leaned against it, fell forward and was free.

On his knees on the ground, he hyperventilated. Stood up. Told himself to get a grip.

No one around anywhere.

Were these noises he heard just his imagination? He stood still, listening, but heard only his own panting.

This was nothing to do with him. Nothing he should vex his brain and emotions over. If not doing so was at all possible.

A Volvo estate had driven away from here.

Her car. She had come here in her car. A kettle had been boiling on the hob. How could he find out who had taken her car?

Guri's phone.

Was it in her pocket?

He was reluctant to go back into the barn. The phone could be in the house anyway.

He hurried back to the farmhouse. Pushed open the door and went in.

He went into the kitchen, telling himself he should leave this to the police. He ignored his inner voice. Stood scanning the room. It couldn't be here. He repeated the same procedure in the sitting room and the TV room. No phone anywhere. Could it be in a pocket or some other item of clothing? He went into the hall. No outdoor clothes.

He took out his own phone and called. Listened. The phone was ringing, but there wasn't a sound to be heard in the house.

So it had to be in her jeans pocket. He was on his way through the door when the display showed that someone had received the call.

'Hello,' he said.

The someone didn't reply.

He could clearly hear the sound of a moving car.

'Who are you?' he said, with no hope of receiving an answer. All he could hear was the drone of an engine.

Then a sombre voice came through: 'I'll find you.'

The line was cut.

For a few seconds he gazed at his phone. His blood froze.

What was that? *I'll find you.* The driver of the car had killed her. This individual was now out to get him.

The clock on his phone told him that he had no chance of keeping his appointment with Gunnarstranda. Perhaps it was just as well that Gunnarstranda would be coming here anyway.

*

After ringing him, he put his phone in his trouser pocket. He looked down at his hands. They were trembling. He couldn't stay here. He felt a need to move, went out and back to the barn. Stopped in front of the tarpaulin. His feet itched to go in, examine the ramp, search, try to find clues, try to read the crime scene, form a picture of what might have happened. But it wasn't his job to investigate. Presumably he had destroyed enough clues already, inside the farmhouse.

He stuffed his hands in his pockets and thought about Guri. This lovely woman, so committed to her cause. Now she was gone. Killed by a man as yet unknown. He thought about Ivar Sekkelsten. Where was he right now? What was actually going on?

40

Frank was waiting in exactly the same place when a white Passat with yellow and black stripes swerved into the drive and braked sharply in front of him.

Police District East, he thought. A woman in uniform and a man in civvies stepped out. He recognised the man. They had been on the same course at police college years before. The man had also worked in Oslo. Arnfinn Brede was an arrogant Nordlander with long hair tied into a ponytail, a relic of the time when he worked on crime-crackdown patrols, looking like a rocker. The ponytail was beginning to look a bit thin now. A lack of growth on top had had consequences for the rest of the hirsute embellishment.

Brede must have recognised him as well because he nodded.

Frølich nodded back. 'In there,' he said, inclining his head towards the barn.

'She's hanging from a beam under the barn ramp.'

Neither of the two made a move.

Frølich decided to take the initiative. He went over to them. Shook hands. 'Frank Frølich,' he said to the female officer. 'I'm a private investigator.'

She curtsied, but caught herself as she did so, mumbled

something incomprehensible and turned to Brede. She was young, smooth-skinned, blonde, with her hair also in a ponytail. The dark-blue, short-sleeved uniform shirt revealed a tattooed wreath on her upper arm.

'A red Volvo V70 was leaving here as I was arriving,' Frølich said. 'You should set up a search for it.'

'Are you teaching me how to do my job?' Brede said, looking around. He was wearing a tight-fitting jacket and dark jeans. It wasn't yet five in the morning, but he smelt of eau de cologne.

'The ops centre received a message from Oslo. Why did you ring them and not us?'

Frølich's mind was on other matters. How much time had passed since the car left? How long had he been here? Twenty minutes? Half an hour?

Arnfin Brede seemed impatient. 'Why did you ring Oslo and not us?'

He had no real wish to apprise these two of Fredrik Andersen's story. So he shrugged his shoulders.

'They're kind of my family,' he confined himself to saying.

The female officer pushed the tarpaulin aside and peered in.

'Don't touch anything,' Brede barked.

'Perhaps you'd like to take my statement,' Frølich said. 'At least then we're doing something useful.'

41

Gunnarstranda was the last to arrive. He was driving his own car, a fairly new Prius hybrid, and he appeared exhausted, with dark bags under his eyes and his jaws slowly churning a piece of chewing gum. He made the effort to greet both the SOC officers and Arnfinn Brede before entering the tumbledown barn. Once inside, he was there for a good while, then suddenly appeared beside Frølich, his hands buried deep in his coat pockets.

'New car?' Frølich said, to take the edge off the unease that afflicted both of them.

'How can you know the woman was with Andersen the night he was killed?'

'She told me.'

'When?'

'On the phone last night.'

'Was this where you were going when I called you?'

'Yes.'

'Why didn't you say so?'

Frølich tried to think up a clever riposte, but failed and said nothing.

'You know we're investigating a murder, then you get a tip-off about a witness and you fail to inform me when I ring.'

'I didn't know if there was anything in what she said.'

'So you came here in the middle of the night to find out if there was any point telling the police about a witness? Do you know it's a punishable offence to impede a civil servant in the performance of his duties?'

Frank Frølich raised both hands in defence. 'Listen to what I'm saying. I didn't know if she was telling the truth or not.'

'Don't take that tone with me, Frølich. I haven't slept a wink and I've just driven seventy kilometres to listen to you talking rubbish. If you start messing me about, you're making a great mistake.'

'I couldn't know this would happen,' Frølich said, indicating the crooked barn with a hand. 'I came here to talk to her. She said she was frightened. But I had no idea what she was frightened of. She told me on the phone she was with Andersen on the night he died. I told her to contact the police, but she didn't want to. We agreed to meet here and talk, so I came here to do just that. My plan was to talk to her first and try and persuade her to go with me to talk to you.'

'What are you up to, Frølich?'

'I'm not up to anything. Andersen's dead. The woman in there is dead. What they perhaps have in common is that they were together that night. The most important thing to do now is to clear up where they were and who else they were both in contact with that night.'

'Why's that the most important thing?'

'Because it concerns me to a great degree.'

'But why, Frølich? What makes you, a private individual, think that you can interfere in police business?'

'I'm not interfering.'

'You get a tip-off from a witness in a murder case. You drive in the middle of the night to talk to her. You behave as if you're doing overtime in the force. But you're doing this as a private individual. So what are you up to?'

'You can believe what I'm saying or not, but this isn't my case,' he answered and began to move towards the drive.

'Not so fast,' Gunnarstranda said.

42

Frølich stopped and turned around slowly. They measured each other up for a few long seconds. It was Gunnarstranda who broke the silence:

'I've got a bone to pick with you, Frølich. We're trying to track Andersen's movements during the time before he was killed. We're aware that he was in a meeting with a publisher in the afternoon. He received a telephone call and broke off the meeting without giving any explanation. Where did he go? No one knows. According to you, though, he appeared in your office in Brugata. He was supposed to return to the publisher, but he didn't. That evening he and his friends had their monthly get-together, when they play chess and drink beer. Andersen never misses it, but this time he did. He didn't ring any of his pals to tell them he wasn't going. You say he chose to spend the evening with a woman from Østfold instead of with his pals. How long did they spend together? No one knows. All we know is that Andersen returned home sometime around midnight and was murdered. And in his pocket we found your business card.'

'My business card?'

'Don't interrupt.'

'But I never gave the guy my card.'

'And I want to know what made Andersen break off an important meeting to talk to you. I want to know why he was upset when he received a call about you. And don't you come with that oath of confidentiality crap to me. So far there's only one connection between the murder of Fredrik Andersen and the woman in the old barn, and it's standing in front of me.'

Gunnarstranda's forefinger poked Frølich in the chest.

'If you set off my bullshit detector again, you'll be back to Oslo in my car and in solitary for as long as I say. Have you got that?'

Frølich nodded.

'Now spit it out.'

'I didn't call Andersen when he was in a meeting. I'd never seen the man before he turned up at my office. He was waiting on a chair for me outside the door. He told me he was writing a book about Norwegian immigration politics. He reeled off the usual nonsense about people smuggling and cynical financiers. He wanted to commission me for a job to do with the book and gave me an advance of twenty thousand kroner, then left. I considered the assignment and decided against it. So I tried to ring him and ask him to take the money back. I got no further than his voicemail and he didn't call me back. My interpretation of this was that he chose not to. So I drove to his house to return the money. No one answered the door when I rang. I sat in the car waiting, but he didn't show up. The only thing that happened was that an elderly lady left the house.'

'An elderly lady?'

'Yes, between seventy-five and eighty. His mother or grandmother, for all I know. I didn't ask her who she was. I drove off, had dinner and shared a couple of bottles of wine with my partner. That night Andersen was killed. It was you who told me when you woke me in the morning and I was curious. You would've been, too, if you'd been in my shoes.'

'Why didn't you just leave the money in his post box? Why did you wait outside his house for such a long time?'

'It was a lot of money. I wanted him to know that I wasn't going to take the assignment. That's why I wanted to give him the money back face to face.'

'What was the job he gave you?' Gunnarstranda said.

'I can't see that has any relevance for your investigation.'

'No relevance?' Gunnarstranda tossed his head. 'Could it possibly have anything to do with the lady dangling from the beam over there? Why did she call you in particular and say she'd been with Andersen in the evening?'

'That,' Frank Frølich said, 'I cannot answer.'

'You're tripping the bullshit detector, Frølich. If what you've said now is true, this case has something to do with your job. You can do your civil duty and tell me what it was.'

'That job no longer exists.'

'And why not?'

'Because it was about a woman Bjørn Thyness ensured was deported from Trandum transit camp at some point over the last two days. I've asked Bjørn, but he won't give me the reason for her deportation or tell me where she was sent. He won't take my calls.'

This, thought Frank Frølich sadly, was the first time in all the years he had known him that the old fogey was lost for words.

'Put me in solitary by all means,' he continued, 'because I need to sleep. But for the sake of the case you'd better tell me first what you're charging me with.'

Gunnarstranda drew a deep breath. 'We haven't finished yet. Drop by and make a statement any time before four,' he said, spun on his heel and padded back to his car.

Before he got in, he turned around.

'Could Andersen have taken a business card when he was in your office?'

Frølich shook his head. 'I have a couple in my wallet and the rest in a drawer. He never got a card from me.'

'Any idea who could've given him the card?'

He didn't like lying to Gunnarstranda. So he just splayed his palms and walked to his car.

43

Frank brought his car to a halt behind the T-bird parked in the drive by the house. He switched off the engine, but didn't make a move. Presumably she was still asleep. The windows were dark. No growling from the dog, either. It was half past seven in the morning. He was fit to drop, but wondered how he was going to break the news. Closing his eyes, he leaned back.

He woke to Matilde banging on the car window.

'I have to go to work. You need to move your car.'

Her voice was muffled by the glass. She smiled.

He looked at his watch. He had been asleep for three quarters of an hour. The events of the night already seemed like a dream.

He pulled at the release handle and opened the door.

'What's the matter?' She held her hair in place with a hand on either side of her face. There was an expression of unease in her eyes.

'It's Guri,' he said.

Matilde straightened up. Took her phone from her back pocket and tapped in a number. She turned her back on him and he heard the phone ringing by her ear. Someone answered.

'Matilde here,' she said. 'I won't be at work today. I'm not feeling well.'

He got out of the car and closed the door.

She put the phone back in her pocket, turned and looked at him.

'When did you last see her?' he asked.

'Tell me what's happened to her.'

'Guri's dead.'

Matilde's face drained of colour.

'I'm sorry,' he said, only too aware of his impoverished vocabulary.

She walked ahead of him and inside the house.

The dog was here. It curled up, wagged its tail and wanted him to say hello. He patted it absent-mindedly.

They sat down on the sofa.

The dog settled in front of the wood burner and yawned with a long, creaking sound. It lay watching them from the floor.

It struck Frank that they were about to experience a moment that would etch itself in both their minds whatever happened from now on. And the memory would always be accompanied by the cold resonance that death brings with it.

'There's no doubt about what's happened. I've seen her.'

Matilde took a cigarette from the packet of Marlboro she was holding. The packet fell to the floor. The fingers holding the cigarette were trembling. She tried to flick the lighter into life and failed. He took it from her. Her fingers were cold. He rolled the spark wheel and held the flame to her. She seemed small and shrunken as she puffed the cigarette into life.

I have to do it, he told himself. *Then let's see where it leads.*

He cleared his throat.

She looked up.

'Matilde.'

'Yes?'

'I have to ask you something.'

'Not now,' she said and stubbed out the cigarette in the ashtray. 'We can talk later.'

44

He hovered in the borderland between sleeping and waking. Slowly his consciousness surfaced into the real world. He lay with his eyes closed.

The duvet rustled. He assumed she was raising herself onto her elbows. Her hair tickled. She ran a finger down the bridge of his nose. Eyes still closed, he asked:

'Have I been asleep long?'

'Half an hour maybe.'

'What did you and Guri talk about?'

'Yesterday?'

'When you met her.'

'She was completely different.'

'In what way?'

'Worked up. Jumpy. She'd panicked when she heard what had happened to the writer. She'd gone to stay with an aunt who lives on the Swedish border, in Ørje. She planned to stay there for a while. I asked her why. She said it was because she was sure no one would find her there. "Who's trying to find you," I asked. "Who are you frightened of? Who's after you?" But she pretended she hadn't heard me. All she said was that she'd met the sister you were supposed to be looking for.'

Frank opened his eyes.

A daddy-long-legs slowly moved up from the windowsill to the ceiling and towards the base of the lamp.

'She said the same to me on the phone,' he said with a deep intake of breath.

'What is it?'

Guri had apparently neglected to tell them some very important things, he thought. She had kept things back from him and Matilde. He cleared his throat:

'I should never have given her the writer's name.'

'Why?'

'Because she contacted him as a result. And now she's dead.'

Matilde sat up. 'I don't like you talking like that.'

She wrapped the duvet around her.

'Sorry,' he said. 'Did she say how she managed to get in touch with the writer?'

'He had a desk in the House of Literature.'

It was his turn to sit up. 'How did she find that out?'

'She went there to ask after him. He had office space there. It was pure luck. Guri had told him about Aisha, how they had to find her sister urgently because Aisha was in Trandum prison. The writer thought someone had been pulling the wool over her eyes though and that Aisha wasn't telling the truth. He'd been very arrogant and had told her to forget the whole business.'

The House of Literature, Frank mused. Why hadn't he thought of that himself?

'What did she do?'

'She caught a bus home. And while she was on the bus, her phone rang. It was the writer. He wanted to meet her again. Guri said: "I'm on the bus and I live quite a long way away." The writer said: "I'll buy you dinner. Come back to town." He said it was very important that they talked. So she got off the bus and caught another one back to Oslo. They met in a very fancy restaurant. Sheyma was there as well. She was waiting for them at the restaurant. It turned out that it had been Sheyma who'd made the writer arrange the meeting because she wanted to talk to Guri and find out more about Aisha. Sheyma had said she had several sisters. But not one called Aisha. And all her sisters were older than her. She and the writer were very keen to find out who Aisha was and where she could've got the story about a sister from. The writer wanted to know where he could find Aisha to talk to her. Guri said Aisha was in Trandum, so good luck, the walls there were higher than around Ullersmo prison. Guri was quite put out when Sheyma said she wasn't related to Aisha. Guri couldn't understand it.'

Matilde reached out for a cigarette on the bedside table.

Frank got up, stretched for the daddy-long-legs, held it in his hand, went to the window, opened it, and let the insect go.

'My lighter,' she said. 'Could you see if it's in the sitting room?'

Frank went out and fetched it. Lit her cigarette.

She smiled. 'Could you do me another favour?'

He nodded. Went back to the sitting room and brought an ashtray. Passed it to her.

He could see Fredrik Andersen sitting in his office that day. Telling Frank that his employer was lying to him. Had Andersen been right all along? Why would Aisha lie about her sister?

Matilde was staring at him with a smile playing on her lips.

'What's up?'

'Aren't you cold?'

He smiled back. 'I have to go back. And talk to the police.'

He started to get dressed. 'Was Guri a hundred per cent sure it was Sheyma she met?'

'Yes. She'd seen her picture, hadn't she. She was absolutely sure. But she didn't understand why Aisha would make up a story like this. It was one thing Aisha being desperate and wanting to stay in Norway. You can understand that she might've made up the idea of a family reunion. But this story must've come from somewhere. She must've found out Sheyma's name somehow. She even had a photo.'

'What did Guri think about all this? Where did she think Aisha could've got the story about the sister from?'

'I asked, but she didn't want to talk about it. She went all paranoid. Shut herself off. But the sister's name isn't Sheyma anymore. She's married and has taken another name.'

'What's she called now?'

'Guri didn't know. The whole business was creepy.'

'Someone's after her.'

'What do you mean?'

'Someone wants to find Sheyma. But she doesn't want to be found.'

They stared at each other for a long time. Lots of questions followed in the wake of this conclusion. But he didn't want to say them aloud. Not now. Why not? Because Fredrik Andersen had been killed by an unknown perpetrator. Because the same thing had happened to Guri. Because the person who killed her had threatened to come after him as well. This was a detail he didn't want Matilde to know, not yet at least, not until he knew more.

He turned away from her and looked outside.

A magpie jumped from the fence post down onto a rock. Here it hesitated, let a few seconds pass as if it wasn't bothered by his presence, then unfolded its wings and flew away.

Get out of this, he told himself. Leave it to Gunnarstranda and Arnfinn Brede.

But his spine protested.

Because the words the voice spoke on the phone were unmistakeable: *I'll find you.*

In response, his spinal reflex said one thing only: *Find him first.*

'What are you thinking about?' Matilde said.

'Did Guri contact anyone while you were together?'

'No. Maybe afterwards. I told her to contact you.'

'She did, but not until later in the night. When did you say goodbye?'

'Late yesterday evening. I wasn't looking at my watch. She said she had things to do.'

'Things to do?'

'Those are the words she used.'

'What do you think she meant by that – "things to do"?'

'No idea.'

'Did she ever say she was afraid of anyone in particular?'

Matilde shook her head.

'Guri didn't seem to be living on her own.'

'She lived with her brother. But he's in prison. He was on probation, but then was arrested again. He was stealing beer and fags from work and was caught. So he had to do time.'

'OK,' Frank Frølich said, suddenly unsure what would be the right thing to do. He ought to tell Matilde that he had played a not insignificant role in that story. But he couldn't bring himself to do it. Not now.

'I'll try and get hold of Ivar,' she said. 'He's alright really and deserves to know what's happened.'

45

As he was about to drive home he accidentally sat on his phone, which was on his seat. He raised himself and checked it. There were four unanswered calls. All from Nicolai Smith Falck. All during the last hour. He'd had more than enough of this journalist and decided not to call back. In the left-hand lane of the motorway and approaching Vestby, he felt another vibration in his pocket. He took out the phone and saw that it was Falck again. He let the phone ring.

It was approximately two in the afternoon when he found a parking spot not too far from his home. He had two hours before his promised appointment with Gunnarstranda. Just enough time to have a shower and get some food down him. He got out of the car. Nearby he heard another car door open and glanced over his shoulder. Out of a small white van stepped a man with a face that was the spitting image of the *MAD* magazine mascot.

Nicolai Smith Falck was not a tall man. He only reached Frølich's shoulders. But it is not only in the police that an ego compensates for a lack of height.

'Didn't you see I'd rung?' the journalist said. He seemed annoyed. 'Guri Sekkelsten,' he went on to say.

'Yes?'

'She's been found dead in her own home. According to my sources, you were the first person at the scene of the crime.'

'I'm a witness and have no comment to make.'

'The police say the death isn't considered suspicious.'

'So what are you after then?'

'Fredrik Andersen was killed a short time ago and now this woman's dead. Your name's been mentioned in both cases.'

'So?'

'You have experience as an investigator. You found the body. What do you think about the police verdict?'

'As I said, I have nothing to say.'

'According to my sources, the police believe the woman killed herself.'

He didn't answer.

'According to my sources, you saw things others didn't.'

'Oh?'

'Would you like to share your observations with our readers?'

'I can repeat what I've said. I don't wish to make a comment.'

'But off the record,' Falck said in a more conciliatory tone.

'Between you and me. What do you think about the police concluding that Guri Sekkelsten took her own life?'

'I don't think anything about it,' he answered and walked with an accelerated step to the front entrance, the journalist chasing after him.

'But this has echoes of the Bygdøy roundabout story,' Falck said. 'The case of the woman who was run over by the juggernaut was classified as suicide. However, you found the man who pushed her. Newspapers like such cases. We like police officers who swim against the tide.'

'I'm no longer employed by the police. I'm a private individual and I have no comment to make on the police investigation.'

Frank had the key in his hand, inserted it in the lock and twisted and was about to slip inside when Falck said:

'They've found her suicide note.'

'They've what?'

He turned to the journalist. Holding the door ajar. Nicolai Smith Falck revealed a crown in his upper jaw as he grinned. This roguish grin made the similarity with the *MAD* mascot complete.

'Police District East have Guri Sekkelsten's written farewell to the world.'

Frank continued to focus on the darkish crown in Falck's row of teeth.

'That got your interest, didn't it,' Falck said. 'Why can't we do what we always do? I give you a few snippets and then you give me a few.'

'Or,' he continued when no answer was forthcoming, 'what's your comment on the police discovery of a suicide note? Does that put what you observed in a new light?'

'You're a serious journalist, aren't you?'

Falck angled his head, indulgently.

'Then you're governed by ethics and really oughtn't to make news out of suicide,' Frølich said, slipped inside the door and left Nicolai Smith Falck outside.

He took the stairs up to the flat just to expend some energy.

Suicide note? Complete bollocks to the power of five. But who was Falck's source?

46

After a shower and a shave, he cracked a couple of eggs into a frying pan. Stood by the window, keeping an eye out for Falck's van while the eggs fried. He couldn't see it, but still wasn't convinced. He went to his Moccamaster and brewed enough coffee for two decent cups. Sat at the table and ate as the coffee trickled into the jug. Stood by the window again and kept watch as he sipped the coffee. What he really wanted to do was sleep. He would have to make do with dreaming about it.

When he left home for the metro station, Falck was still nowhere to be seen.

∗

Half an hour later he was sitting opposite Gunnarstranda in his office.

Gunnarstranda appeared to be aware of the irony of this situation too. He indulged himself in a wry smile as he produced a mini tape recorder and started it.

Frølich felt the onset of a faint headache as he spoke into the microphone on the table. He gave his name, date of birth, address, telephone number and email address.

Gunnarstranda asked him to talk about Fredrik Andersen. Frank Frølich repeated what he had told him before, to wit, that Andersen had turned up at his office wanting to hire him for an assignment. Andersen had given him some money, an advance, and left the office. Frølich realised he couldn't commit himself to this assignment. He called Andersen to inform him of his decision, but got no further than the voicemail. So he drove to Andersen's house to return the money personally. No one answered the door when he rang the bell. He sat in his car, waiting. Then he saw a car stop outside the entrance. A Toyota RAV4.

Gunnarstranda leaned forward and paused the tape recorder. He said: 'Is this car relevant to the case?'

'That's for you to decide.'

Gunnarstranda regarded him pensively. 'We don't think it's relevant to the case.'

'And I have no idea where your investigation's going. But I've been asked to make a statement. The Toyota's part of my statement.'

Gunnarstranda sighed. 'Of course.'

'While the tape recorder's off,' Frølich said, 'there's something I was wondering about.'

'Mhm?'

'I have a journo pursuing me. Nicolai Smith Falck.'

'I know who he is.'

'He knows a hell of a lot.'

'He always knows a lot. He's the kind of hack who thinks delving into crime is the meaning of life.'

'True, but now he knows a lot more about the state of the Guri Sekkelsten case than I do. Much more – even though it was me who found the body.'

'I'm not at all surprised.'

'He must have exceptionally good sources.'

'You know the game, Frølich. Someone owes Falck a favour.'

'Yes, but who?'

'God knows.'

'I think I do.'

Gunnarstranda leaned back in his chair, slightly more interested.

'Arnfinn Brede.'

47

Gunnarstranda waved a hand as if he were swatting a fly. 'This is horse-trading, Frølich. Falck's probably done a favour for Arnfinn. He wrote something Arnfinn wanted him to write or, at his behest, refrained from writing something – and Arnfinn gives him the odd tip-off. That's all there is to it.'

'Oh, there's more than that.'

'How so?'

'I passed her car – a Volvo V70 – driving away from the small-holding just before I found her. Someone left the crime scene. Without a shadow of doubt. I saw a kettle boiling on the hob in the farmhouse. I removed it and switched off the stove. The journo told me the officers investigating think she killed herself. So they must imagine I made up the bit about the hob. Also, they must think I'm lying about the car I saw. How can they?'

'They have a suicide note written by her.'

'That's what the journo said, yes. I don't believe in any final words by Guri Sekkelsten for a second. Do you?'

Gunnarstranda cleared his throat. 'Before I answer that, the question is whether you have an alternative theory.'

'I think so.'

'OK. Well, I'm sceptical about the suicide note.'

'Why?'

'It was a text to her employer.'

Frølich's face broke into a grin.

'What's so funny?'

'To her employer? Would you text the chief of police if you were going to top yourself?'

'I don't know. I'm not in the risk group.'

'Have they confirmed the message? Is it on her phone as well?'

'Haven't the foggiest.'

'When I found the body, I thought about the car I'd passed just before I arrived. It struck me she must've contacted the driver during the day. In other words, I got involved to some extent and wondered if her phone could tell me anything. So I rang her number to see if I could hear where it was. Someone answered the call. I could tell from the sound that the man answering was in a car.'

'What did you talk about?'

'He threatened me.'

Gunnarstranda tilted his head, intrigued.

'At least I perceived it as a threat,' Frølich said and considered what the voice in his ear had growled. 'He said: "I'll find you." Can that be interpreted as anything other than a threat?'

Gunnarstranda didn't reply.

'The point is that this man had her phone. In other words, Guri Sekkelsten was boiling the water either for herself or for this man and herself. She never actually made the tea or coffee. This guy killed her, made the murder look like suicide by hanging, took her phone and drove away from the crime scene in her car. It's as obvious as saying if an apple falls from a tree it'll land on the ground.'

'Whether you were threatened or not, this is a police matter and you have to keep your paws off.'

Frølich heaved a heavy sigh. 'Paws off what? Off who? The guy who threatened me? Do you want me to report an unknown killer perhaps?'

Gunnarstranda deliberated. 'The threat should be in your statement.'

'And what good is that to me?'

Gunnarstranda didn't answer. Lost for words again, thought Frank, and decided to forget all talk of the threat. He said:

'The killer has Guri Sekkelsten's phone. He finds a number there, writes a text in her name and sends it.'

Gunnarstranda cleared his throat and said: 'OK, someone drove off with her phone, but that doesn't necessarily lend support to all your conclusions.'

Frølich sighed and shook his head.

'Hang on,' Gunnarstranda said. 'Before you came I spoke to the public prosecutor whose case this is. She thinks mobile phones have a code. If anyone other than Guri Sekkelsten sent the text they must've known about the code. That's very unlikely.'

'Not all mobile phones have a code,' Frølich said. 'But what do we actually know about what happened? She might've been threatened, forced to reveal the code or let the killer use her phone, or made to send the text herself. How can the police conclude anything when they don't have the phone or they don't know whether her phone has a code?'

Gunnarstranda threw his arms into the air. 'You have a point. But whether you like it or not, the public prosecutor and Police District East doubt your credibility. They say it could've been a random car you saw. There are loads of red Volvos in Østland. Arnfinn Brede said he asked you for the registration number. You didn't know. He asked you about the driver's appearance. You didn't know.'

'But this car had a defective rear light. I know that Guri's car had one, too. I saw the car four kilometres from the crime scene and it was half past three in the morning. I didn't meet any other cars.'

'Brede said at best the car was circumstantial evidence, and while he thinks like that, there's little you can do.'

'And what about the kettle?'

'Brede said you might well be right about that, but it's still only circumstantial evidence, which is trumped by the suicide text. He said you're a private investigator and you don't have a lot to do. He thinks you're pushing these things to get into the papers and raise your profile.'

'Do you share Brede's views?'

'No. But try for a moment to see this case from Brede's standpoint. What would the motive be for killing Guri Sekkelsten and making the murder look like a suicide? She was dressed. There are no signs of rape or any other injuries apart from strangling caused by the rope around her neck. There are no signs of a break-in. The door was unlocked and there were lots of valuables in the house. She didn't have any particles of skin under her fingernails. All Brede has is the clues they find at the crime scene and your statement. He has no motives to go on. What you and I think about Guri Sekkelsten's death makes no difference one way or the other.'

'Guri Sekkelsten rang me because she was frightened.'

'Brede's understanding is that she was desperate, needed someone to talk to, but killed herself before anyone – in this case you – could come and talk her out of it.'

'Arnfinn's mouth is bigger than his brain.'

'Such subjectivity doesn't make you any more credible, Frølich. Brede bases his judgement on the fact that Guri Sekkelsten has a history of psychiatric problems. Her boss at the refugee centre has confirmed that she was absent from work for psychological reasons, among others.'

'She fell off a horse. She was a showjumper and had to terminate her career. It wasn't at all surprising that she was depressed.'

'Nevertheless, Brede sees this as a history of problems. Can you say exactly what the time was when you found the body?'

Frank Frølich shrugged. 'I can say to plus or minus ten minutes.'

'Ten minutes is a long time, Frølich. Arnfinn Brede has your statement. The text message was sent *before* you say you found her body.'

Frank Frølich shook his head. 'What is this? Do you believe that prat rather than me?'

Gunnarstranda dismissed him with a sweep of the hand. 'You say a lot of strange things. For example, you claim you saw an elderly woman come out of Andersen's place when you were waiting for him outside. Are you sure?'

'Why on earth would you ask me about that?'

'Because the only person who's seen this woman is you.'

'I saw her. I don't make things up.'

The ensuing silence was long – so long, that Frank felt the need to repeat himself, stressing every single syllable: 'I do not make things up.'

48

They sat almost glowering at each other.

It was Gunnarstranda who finally broke the silence. He said:

'If the public prosecutor is of a mind to dismiss Guri Sekkelsten's death as suicide and not a punishable offence, there's nothing you or I can do.'

'If the body's sent for an autopsy, the pathologists will find her death is not consistent with suicide, I can guarantee you that.'

'The case has been cleared up. There won't be an autopsy.'

'Why not?'

'I don't know. But I assume the cause of death is thought to be obvious, so money needn't be spent on an expensive autopsy.'

'What about her car?'

'What about it?'

'Where is it?'

'Her car hasn't disappeared. It's parked at the refugee centre where she worked. According to Brede that's where it's usually parked, even when she's not there.'

'But how did she get home if her car was at the centre?'

'According to Brede, this is no mystery. She went to and from work like everyone else – caught a bus or got a lift from a colleague or a kind neighbour. You'll soon have to accept that your theory that Guri Sekkelsten was murdered is a lost cause.'

'She talked about the car when she rang me.'

'What did she say?'

'She said: "I've got a car."'

'I've got a car. Did she say which car? Did she specifically mention the Volvo?'

'No.'

Gunnarstranda turned his hands over, showing his palms.

'Have they been in touch with her aunt?'

'Why would they want to talk to an aunt?'

'Because Guri Sekkelsten was staying with her before she was killed. Furthermore, she'd said she was going to return there. Don't you think it strange that she killed herself after making such an arrangement? Why did she write a suicide text to her employer and not to someone close, for example to her aunt or her brother?'

'Her brother's in prison and has no access to a phone. We'll leave the aunt to Police District East. Anything else?'

'You know there's more. Guri Sekkelsten was with Fredrik Andersen just before he was killed.'

'Your assignment, Frølich. It's your turn to give us something. I want to know the exact wording of the job you were given by Andersen.'

'It was about an asylum seeker at the centre where Guri Sekkelsten worked. This asylum seeker wanted to find her sister. Her application to stay in Norway had been rejected, and her appeal too, so finding this sister might have helped. I was hired to find the sister this woman claimed lived in Norway. Suddenly, out of the blue, Andersen appears in my office. And he knows I'm looking for this woman. He says the people who hired me weren't being honest.'

'That explains the business card,' Gunnarstranda said. 'You gave the business card to someone who knows the woman you were searching for.'

'My own thoughts exactly.'

'What's the name of the woman?'

'Her name isn't listed anywhere. She's called Sheyma Bashur. That's all I know.'

'What did Andersen say when he visited you?'

'He thought the woman who gave me the assignment was bluffing. She had no relatives in Norway. He hired me to have this theory confirmed. As you can see, this assignment ran counter to the one I already had so I couldn't take it on – it wouldn't be ethical, or even practical. Now the woman I was going to work for is out of the country and the person who knows something about that is Bjørn Thyness.'

'Who did you give a business card to?'

'Someone who knew.'

'What's that supposed to mean?'

'I think I may've given one out at a hotel when I was walking around asking after this Sheyma. The woman I'm thinking about looks Thai. She was working at a hotel in the City Hall quarter. I don't have a full name. But I can probably locate her for you.'

Gunnarstranda grabbed the tape recorder on the table, clearly annoyed.

'We don't want any more interference from you regarding this case.'

49

Gunnarstranda pressed the button on the tape recorder. He coughed and said: 'You say Fredrik Andersen met Guri Sekkelsten a few hours before he was killed?'

'That was what she wanted to talk to me about last night. That was why I drove to her home.'

'Do you know where they met?'

'At a restaurant.'

'Which one?'

'I don't know. A sophisticated one, that's all I know.'

'Why was Guri Sekkelsten with Fredrik Andersen that evening?'

'She worked at a refugee centre in Hobøl. She had a close, confidential relationship with a special client, a female asylum seeker who wanted to be reunited with family because she'd had her application turned down. Fredrik Andersen knew the woman the asylum seeker claimed was her sister. That's all I know.'

'That's all you know. How come you know that Guri Sekkelsten and Fredrik Andersen were going to meet?'

'Because I told Guri Sekkelsten that Andersen knew the details of this family-reunion case. When she rang me last night she said she'd contacted Andersen about it personally. She'd spent an evening with him. The fact he was killed right after they parted had an enormous impact on her. She feared for her own safety and decided to stay in hiding.'

'Why did she fear for her own safety?'

'I don't know.'

'Where did she seek shelter?'

'With a relative. An aunt. When she rang me last night I had the impression she was sitting on vital information about Andersen's murder. I told her to go to the police and tell them everything she knew, but she refused. She also refused to tell me why she mistrusted the police. I offered to listen to what she had to say. We arranged to meet at her house. She was going there to pick up clothes before returning to her aunt. I drove to her place.'

Frølich paused.

Gunnarstranda gesticulated for him to go on. He sat without interrupting as Frølich once again described what happened when he found the body.

After finishing, Frank Frølich rummaged in his pocket for his phone and placed it on the table.

'I'm placing my phone on the table now so that the police can check this information.'

Gunnarstranda switched off the tape recorder.

'Show me the log.'

Frølich showed him the calls. 'This is Guri Sekkelsten phoning me last night. This is you ringing me afterwards. Here, I'm calling Guri's phone when the killer receives my call in the car and threatens me. The time's four thirty-two.'

Gunnarstranda made a note. 'You'd better drop by later and sign the interview sheet,' he said. 'I'll send a copy to Police District East.'

50

Standing on the stairs waiting for the lift, he felt once again the unease that crept over him when he was in the vicinity of his old workplace. He was exhausted and had little desire to bump into any ex-colleagues. The only officer he met was a guy in reception. A young man he had never seen before. He nodded to him anyway.

Frølich strode down the hill to Grønlandsleiret. Thinking about the pile of business cards he kept in his desk drawer in the office. He had only given away a single card that month. On his way to the metro station he rang the hotel where he had left the card.

A man answered the phone.

Frølich said he would like to talk to a woman who worked in the kitchen, by the name of Gamon. The receptionist was unable to put him through.

How long would Gamon be at work?

The receptionist told him when they changed shifts. It was quite a while yet.

Why was he bothering with this? he asked himself, after he had rung off. He knew the answer. It was all about understanding what was going on. Since he gave Gamon the business card, life had batted him around like a shuttlecock. It wasn't a feeling he enjoyed. It wasn't a game he wanted to continue.

51

He managed to doze off for an hour on the sofa before having to drive down to the hotel in time for the change of shift. It was sultry outside, overcast, with thicker, black blankets of cloud over the Nesodden peninsula and broken patches of grey over Holmenkollen.

He parked outside Oslo Stock Exchange to wait. It lay low, dark and heavy behind tall wrought-iron fences. He observed the building, which was reminiscent of L'église de la Madeleine in Paris. Both structures seemed somehow misplaced in their environments. The exchange had probably dominated the area with its classical features when it was built almost two hundred years ago, but now it was surrounded by modern high-rises that seemed to force it into the ground and jeer at it.

He glanced across at the hotel. Guests were going in and coming out. Dragging their wheelie-bags.

Ten minutes passed before Gamon came out. She was a slight figure, wearing tight trousers and a short leather jacket. But he recognised her face and the hair that was held in place with a sturdy slide. She walked with short, quick steps. Frølich got out of the car and caught up with her outside a strip bar.

'Gamon!'

She stopped, turned and looked at him, astonished.

'I was in the hotel a few days ago asking about a woman called Sheyma Bashur,' he said.

She still looked at him in amazement.

He repeated himself in English and added: 'I gave you a business card.'

He waved another card and pointed: 'One like this. I gave it to you and you gave it away.'

She shrugged and walked on. He stepped into the street to be able to keep up. A line of parked cars forced him to walk in the middle of the road. He shouted:

'You gave the card to Fredrik Andersen. You know her, don't you. You know Sheyma Bashur.'

Gamon broke into a run. Frølich jogged a few metres behind her until he realised he was behaving stupidly. He let her run and stopped. Allowed her to gain a head-start on him. She glanced over her shoulder to see if he was following her. Soon she was just one of many silhouettes in the crowd by the bus stops in Jernbanetorget.

He caught a glimpse of her as she pushed open the door to Oslo Central Station. When she was at the top of the escalator he was at the foot. She walked through the station, exited and took the stairs down to the Radisson Hotel and continued towards Grønland.

He kept a short distance behind her, out of sight. She was walking more slowly now that she thought she was rid of him. She continued across the Akerselva river. The small figure was lost in the crowds again. This time among all the people visiting the immigrant shops in Smalgangen. He walked slowly down the street, past the butcher's and the greengrocer's, unable to see her anywhere.

He turned into a clothes shop. Lifted sweaters and studied the price tags on shirts and waited.

A few minutes later she passed the shop windows with two bags full of vegetables. She was heading towards Motzfeldts gate and disappeared into a green block of flats in Tøyengata. So she was going home. Now he knew where she lived.

52

The plan was to nip into the office on the way back to the car. But when he came out of the lift on the second floor, he gave a start and realised this wouldn't be a short visit. It was evening and the building was closed and locked. Yet a man he didn't know was sitting on the chair outside his office. Even though the man's appearance was quite different from Andersen's, this felt like déjà vu. He was around forty, clean-shaven and tanned with short, fair hair and bright, blue eyes. When he stood up he revealed a tall, lean but supple body. He extended a hand.

'Frølich?'

They shook hands as the man introduced himself:

'Norheim, Snorre Norheim. I came in via the dentist's on the floor below, on the off-chance that you might come by.' He beamed a wry, charming smile. 'And you did. My good fortune.'

They went into Frølich's office.

Frølich walked over to the window and opened it a fraction. Looked out. It was still sultry and the cloud was thickening. Thunder on the way, he thought. Turned back from the window, performed his usual routine with the chair and drawer and looked at his visitor.

The man was standing erect in the middle of the room, dressed in dark trousers and a baggy jumper. Yet there was something military about him.

'Won't you take a seat?'

Norheim remained on his feet.

'What can I do for you, Norheim?'

'Last night a woman was found dead in her home in Våler, Østfold.'

Frølich ran his eyes over him again. This was special.

'I have reason to believe you know this woman.'

Frølich saw no reason to answer him.

'In the news the police said they aren't treating the death as suspicious.'

Snorre Norheim opened the briefcase he had been holding under his arm and placed a folded newspaper on the table. It was *Verdens Gang* and open at page six. There was a news story written by Nicolai Smith Falck. And Norheim was right. Falck wrote that the police didn't regard the case as suspicious.

'That would mean this woman died of natural causes,' Frølich said, looking up at his visitor again.

'I find that hard to believe.'

They looked each other in the eye for several long seconds. 'But why would you have an opinion about her death?' Frølich said at length.

'I simply can't believe it.'

Frølich leaned back in his chair and felt an unease he couldn't satisfactorily explain. It was something to do with the déjà vu experience. The re-enactment of a scene and the strangeness of his sudden popularity. He was being visited by one person after the other. They wanted something. Everyone wanted something from him. And now he was more nervous than excited about what this man actually wanted.

'Why can't you believe it?'

'I happen to know that this woman was with Fredrik Andersen a few hours before he was murdered. Now she's dead herself.'

The man straightened up and continued:

'I'm aware of your connection with Andersen. I'm also aware you used to be a police officer. I wish to hire you regarding this matter.'

What? Him too? Frølich thought. He cleared his throat and said: 'Hire me to do what?'

'This woman was young and strong. She cannot have died a natural death. Also, I cannot accept that she took her own life. I'd like to have my suspicions documented – that this woman was murdered.'

'But why?'

'That's my business.'

Actually Frank Frølich didn't care why people wanted to hire him. But this was special. He sat studying the man whose military background seemed to be coming to the fore with every moment. He had rolled up the sleeves of his sweater to his elbows and revealed two muscular forearms; one wrist was adorned with a paracord bracelet and the other a chunky watch. He held the briefcase in position with his elbow as though it were a uniform cap.

'For personal reasons you wish to find out if this woman was murdered?'

Frank could hear that the question had come out wrong; his intonation was too sardonic. However, Norheim stared back blankly without answering. The silence hung in the air until Frølich continued:

'Why don't you trust the police?'

'I can't believe what's in the newspaper. It's absurd.'

'Why do you wish to engage me in particular?'

'I spoke to Andersen the day before he was murdered. He'd spoken to you. He said he'd hired you. What was more, he'd been contacted by the woman who is now dead. He said he was going to meet this woman later the same evening.'

Frølich heard what the man said, but he was none the wiser. Andersen and this man had a common cause with regard to him. But why? He cleared his throat and said:

'And why did Andersen tell you this?'

'That's my business.'

'The conversation about me is also your business?'

The man continued to look him in the eye, unmoved. You couldn't fault his self-assurance. This was a man who was used to being obeyed. But there was also something a little childish about this obstinacy.

'I may be willing to double your usual fee,' Norheim said. 'Find out what happened to this woman. Find out what evidence the police have to draw the conclusions they do. If there's any other evidence, I'd like you to apprise me of it.'

'If I took on this job, the fee's the same as always.'

'Why wouldn't you take on this job?'

There was a provocation in the attitude that accompanied the question. As though Norheim were asking in order to challenge him. Frølich wondered: Why wouldn't he accept the job? Or, to be more precise, why would he? To understand what was happening? To find out what actually lay behind these events? Should he say yes or no to this assignment from this particular man? No, he thought. This was also about Guri Sekkelsten. He was angry that the police had shelved the crime, allowing a young woman to be murdered without performing the thorough investigation that was their civic duty. Or was he angry because the police hadn't taken his statement seriously. Or was he giving too much credence to his own conspiracy theories? Had he sunk so low that he suspected the shelving of the crime was not only down to poor police work but something else? Some corruption? What were the answers to these questions? He knew the only way to find an answer was to walk into the hornet's nest and see what made it buzz. And now a man was in his office offering him a fee to do this. That alone was the kind of act that could motivate him to do several investigations.

'The police are on the case. They've reached a conclusion. And you want me to find out things they haven't managed to clarify?'

Norheim didn't answer.

'What if the police evidence stands up?'

'We'll cross that bridge when we come to it.'

'Supposing I took on the job, who would I report to?'

'Me.'

'Have you got an email address?'

Norheim took a business card from his briefcase and held it out.

Frølich took the card. Armed Forces' logo. Akershus Fortress. The man was in the military. He hadn't been wrong there.

'I'll email you a contract, which you accept by signing and returning.'

Norheim nodded briefly, turned on his heel and left.

Frølich sat staring at the door while flicking the man's card between his fingers.

It was one thing to take on an assignment like this. Quite another to know how to set about it.

53

There was a din outside. The rain was pounding the window and the sill. Frank got up and looked out. People in Storgata were scampering for shelter, under awnings and into covered gateways. One woman was trying to keep her hair dry under her coat. A man was crossing the street with a carrier bag over his head. Frank thought about his car outside the hotel. He would have to go back and get it. May as well wait until the rain stopped.

While he was waiting he took out his phone and rang Matilde, who answered at once. He asked:

'What are you doing?'

'I was trying to read a book, but couldn't. I can't think about anything except Guri. Whoever did this must've made it look as if Guri hanged herself. Do you think she died while they were doing it or was she already dead?'

Frank Frølich had no answer to that question, nor did he know what difference his opinion on the matter would make. But he had to be honest.

'I don't know. An autopsy would've told us, but there wasn't one. The case has been closed and the body has been released. That means the next step's a funeral.'

'But that's terrible, isn't it? Don't the police want to know what happened?'

'They say they do know.'

Matilde went quiet.

He coughed.

'Yes?' she said.

'Are we going to see each other soon?'

'Yes.'

'There's one thing I should ask you, but it can wait.'

'Come on,' she said. 'Ask away.'

'I was wondering if Guri ever mentioned the name Snorre Norheim to you.'

'No.'

'Sure? You've never heard the name, even casually?'

'Very sure. Who is it?'

'Tall guy. Slim. Forty, maybe older. Blond crew cut. Blue eyes. Wedding ring. In the armed forces.'

'No, definitely don't know him. Why?'

'He's upset that she's dead. He came to my office and wants me to investigate her death.'

'That's good though,' Matilde said. 'That someone cares so much. What did you say the guy's name was?'

'Norheim. Snorre Norheim.'

54

Frank opened his eyes and looked up at the ceiling lamp that never worked. The light in the room stole in through the sitting-room door. So he was at home in his own bedroom. But it wasn't morning. He had fallen asleep on the bed, on top of the duvet, fully dressed. It had to be late. And the reason he woke up was in his pocket. His hands seemed to have no energy. But the phone wouldn't stop ringing. In the end, he summoned all his strength to lift his hand. It's always like this, he thought, when you go to sleep after you've been restless. You wake up and you have no idea where you are or why you are there.

He pulled out his phone. Not a number he recognised. He put down the phone and sat up. Rubbed his face and yawned. Finally the phone stopped ringing. He got up from the bed and went into the kitchen. Drank a glass of water. The clock showed it was just after midnight.

He put on a CD. Wanting to hear Johnny Cash and Joe Strummer singing 'Redemption Song'. It was music that fitted the time of night and his mood perfectly. He heard Johnny Cash sing the first verse and Joe Strummer had almost finished the second when the phone rang again. The same number. This time he answered, but without turning down the music.

'Jørgen Svinland here.'

Frølich couldn't place his name at first.

'Fredrik Andersen's uncle.'

He turned down the music. 'Oh, yes, hi,' he said, and sat down. He yawned.

Svinland was the man who wanted him to find the mysterious Ole Berg, the man with the unknown identity. The whole job had been buried under other events. But he couldn't say that out loud.

'I've only managed to do a little delving,' he said, and added: 'But I have to be honest with you. I think you're on the wrong track as regards what Fredrik Andersen was doing the night before he died.'

'Have you found Ole Berg?'

'Fredrik Andersen wasn't – as far as I've been able to establish – in contact with Ole Berg the night before he was killed. He was with two women, at a restaurant. Both women were connected with a book he was working on.'

There was a silence at the other end.

He could literally feel Svinland's disappointment streaming through the ether and out of the phone into his ear.

'As I said, Fredrik Andersen was working on a new book,' Frølich said. 'This book was about immigration. I've had confirmation that the person Fredrik was with on the last evening he was alive was a source he was going to use to write the book. Fredrik Andersen wasn't concerned with the *Sea Breeze* the night he died.'

There was still silence, and it persisted.

'Are you there?'

'I've become accustomed to disappointment, Frølich. But that doesn't mean I'm giving up. I know Fredrik was busy trying to bring Ole Berg's story to public attention. Naturally, I don't doubt that you're right when you say Fredrik was with other people on the night in question. But I know he'd established contact with the eyewitness, Ole Berg. I know he was preoccupied with finding out the truth about what happened on the *Sea Breeze*. I represent an undervalued group of people, Frølich. I'm someone society at large wishes to forget. When Fredrik told me about Ole Berg he sparked hope in me. That spark won't go out so easily. I've lived with dis-

appointment and political cowardice for thirty years. I don't want
to stop fighting now. I want you to keep going. What have you
found out so far?'

'I'm afraid I haven't found out very much. I've focused on es-
tablishing what Fredrik was doing in the hours before he died. But
I've spoken to the first mate on board the *Sea Breeze*, Rolf Myhre.
By the way, do you know someone called Bernt Weddevåg?'

'I don't know him, but he was one of Fredrik's sources for his
book. I'm sure about that.'

'He lives in a cabin on Nakholmen. I'm thinking of talking to
him tomorrow.'

'Did you get the papers?' Svinland asked.

'What papers?'

'A memory stick full of police interviews and so on.'

'Ah, was that you? Was it in my pigeon hole at the office?'

'Yes.'

'I've had a look, yes. But there's a lot of it, an enormous quantity
of documents.'

'That's Fredrik's source material. If he ever wrote anything down
about Ole Berg, it'll be there.'

Frank Frølich gave a deep sigh and hoped Svinland couldn't hear
his despair. Finding the eyewitness from the *Sea Breeze* was like
hunting for a fairy-tale character. Rumpelstiltskin or a dwarf from
the Blue Mountains.

'I feel obliged to say that I'm sure you can invest your money in
something more sensible than hiring me. I can put the twenty
thousand I received from Fredrik into your account tomorrow. I
think you can use the money in far better ways than getting me to
locate a person who may or may not be real.'

'I don't want that,' Svinland said. 'The money must be used to
pay for your work. I want you to find Ole Berg, Frølich. I want
you to do your best.'

Silence had them in its thrall again.

He didn't want to argue, at least not with a man in Svinland's
situation.

'OK,' he said. 'I'll do what I can.'

He sat for a few minutes after ringing off, brooding. One man wanted him to investigate Guri Sekkelsten's death, and another wanted him to find a person who possibly didn't exist. Which should he prioritise the following morning? He couldn't decide yet. It was late at night. He was still dog-tired. It was time for a hot shower, something to eat and bed.

55

The ferries that took people to the islands in Oslo fjord left from City Hall wharf. On the pier the queues to the various destinations were channelled and separated by fences. Hardly anyone was getting on board the Gressholmen ferry. The most popular trip was to Langøya, and the queue was wide and long. Kids stood holding fishing rods. Some also had flippers attached to their rucksacks. When the boat came it transpired that it went to all of the islands. The little ferry docked bow first, and people streamed through the gates onto the foredeck and on into the boat. Despite the number of passengers Frank was almost alone on the foredeck as the ferry backed away from the wharf. A mild föhn wind caressed his forehead as a flood of childhood memories of boat trips here in the fjord came back to him: trips to the islands of Hovedøya, Bleikøya and Langøya, which for some reason was always talked about in the plural – Langøyene. He tried to remember if he had ever set foot on Gressholmen. Probably not. If he took a ferry trip on the fjord in those days, it was usually organised by his school. If they had a teacher who wanted to show them the monastery ruins on Hovedøya, they caught the boat and examined the low remains of walls that indicated the position of the monks' cells around an ancient garden with curious herbs, which probably grew there because the seeds had survived in the ground for hundreds of years. And after a few dips in the sea they would run over the rocks and ogle the beautiful women sunbathing, try to catch their sultry gazes and think about what history and centuries do to people and civilisations, or what a monk might have thought about the sight of such thighs and mounds and crevices. Or they went to buy a hot dog at the kiosk, queued, surrounded by the scents of summer: sun cream, hot skin, the water the frankfurters were boiled in and the saccharine odour of sticky gum.

He turned, leaned back against the railing and watched the passengers – children going swimming, a young couple and a scattering of tourists, recognisable by the cameras most had hanging around their necks.

A couple with a pram were the only ones waiting to come on board when the ferry heaved to at Gressholmen. Frølich and some of the tourists stepped ashore.

He walked up the hill and into the wood. Gunnarstranda, he remembered, had talked about this island a few times with annoyance because the wild rabbits were eating the special flora that grew there. So Gunnarstranda was very excited when the local council had several rabbits shot to retain the biodiversity.

The island was a pure idyll – windless, a veil of birch leaves above green undergrowth.

The Gressholmen inn turned out to be a red, box-shaped house with a line of large windows across the front, under a sign in big, white letters. This is where Tick-Tock Rolf had met the owner and chatted to him.

Frølich entered the light summer restaurant with timber walls, small tables and spindle-back chairs.

The room was empty except for a young girl behind the counter. They served draught beer, wine, shrimps with French bread and aioli, marinated olives and filled baguettes wrapped in clingfilm.

He asked after the owner.

He wasn't there today. The girl behind the counter didn't know when he would be back. Could she pass on a message?

'Never mind,' he said, ordered a draught beer and sat down at a table outside. His forehead baked in the sun. But he was still the only customer. Chinese lanterns hung from the trees by the terrace. The view was of the factories in Sjursøya and Mosseveien on the mainland. Down on the beach a few children were jumping between rocks, taking photos of one another.

Once his half litre was drunk and as the owner still hadn't shown up, he strolled back to the quay. He had to wait for five minutes before the boat arrived. By then he had been joined by one of the tourists who had stepped ashore at the same time as him.

He and the tourist waited patiently as a group of kindergarten children accompanied by three adults came ashore. The children set off at a run and the adults shouted after them.

He boarded the ferry.

The ferry departed.

He went through the salon and up to the sun deck. Here he found a space on a bench and felt the wind ruffle his hair. It was still a lovely day; there wasn't a cloud in the sky and the gentle föhn wind was blowing the yachts along at a fair pace. The ferry stopped at Lindøya in two places, then set a course for the harbour on the opposite side of the sound. A skerry jeep roared past just before the ferry moored at Nakholmen. The small, low island was full of summer cabins. He followed Matilde's instructions and located the red cabin with a partly roofed terrace and a gravel path leading down to the water.

There wasn't a sound. The cabin seemed empty. He was about to turn back when he saw some strands of hair over a fence in front of some decking.

56

He opened the wrought-iron gate to the scream of hinges. The man on the terrace stood up.

He was in his sixties and corresponded to Matilde's description. There was a slight resemblance to Frank Sinatra. He was lean with an almost spherical head and thin hair teased forward in a charming comb-over. His eyes were kind and brown.

Frank raised an arm in greeting.

The man greeted him back.

'Are you Bernt Weddevåg?'

'Who's asking?' the man said.

'Frank Frølich. Private investigator.'

Weddevåg was dressed for summer: sandals, no socks, faded jeans and a T-shirt from the Hard Rock Café in Singapore. He smiled with teeth so white they had to be bleached.

'When I bought this cabin on the island people said I'd be bored stiff. Since then I've made a mockery of that particular prediction. Today, too. Come on up.'

Frølich walked up to the terrace. Beneath the half-roof there was a suite of wicker furniture around a low table with a glass top.

Suddenly the veranda door opened and a thin man with a bent back appeared.

'Right, Bernt,' said the stooped man in a squeaky voice. 'I'll be off then. Thanks for breakfast.'

The man stumped across the terrace and peered up at Frølich with the lifeless eyes of a serious drug addict.

'Take care of yourself, Rikard,' Bernt Weddevåg shouted after him.

The man called Rikard carefully walked down from the terrace, gripping the banister with a shaky hand.

Frølich watched him leave, convinced he had seen this person before. Must have been when I was a cop, he thought, on some patrol to pick up creatures of the night. The man was so skinny and his face so ravaged he resembled the living dead.

Both of them watched him slowly plod in the direction of the ferry quay.

'There goes a hard-working drudge,' Weddevåg said in a low voice so as not to be heard.

'Oh, yes,' Frølich said, not so convinced.

'Rikard was once a very competent studio musician,' Weddevåg said. 'He was multi-talented – played with all the greats. Until 1988. Then he had to bury his whole family. His wife, two daughters, his mother and both in-laws. They died on the *Sea Breeze*. Perhaps you remember it. The ferry catastrophe.'

'That's what I came here to talk to you about,' Frølich said.

The thin figure with the bent back above two pipe-cleaner legs was now out of sight.

'Since then Rikard has clung to life – with the help of drugs,' Weddevåg said. 'He has nothing else. No home. No family. When society wants something from him, it's to offer him a prison cell or detox. It's a miracle he's still hanging in there. Do you remember being twenty-eight?'

'I think so.'

'Imagine you're sitting in a church, the only surviving relative, with six coffins in the aisle. Everyone you care about has been snatched from you and you're left all on your own. That's no small challenge,' Weddevåg said. 'It's a miracle Rikard's still alive. Feel free,' he said, pointing to the suite.

On the glass table there was a tumbler with something green in it.

The man raised his glass. 'Fancy a taste?'

Frank shrugged. 'Why not?' he said, taking a seat.

Weddevåg went through the veranda door and returned with a shot glass and a bottle containing the green drink. He poured.

'*Skål.*'

It tasted sweet, bitter and sticky, all at the same time. Frølich was unable to control his grimaces and smacked his lips before putting down the glass.

'Had it before?'

'Don't think so.'

'Curaçao. A liqueur. Comes from the island of that name.'

Frank took another sip, but the taste was no better.

'I got to like it when I was at sea. In Willemstad. We took on water there. Water and booze. And you've come here to talk about the *Sea Breeze*? Why?'

'I was hired by Fredrik Andersen shortly before he was killed. Now I'm working for his uncle.'

'Fredrik Andersen, yes, tragic story,' the man said, peering into his tumbler. Looked up again with the suggestion of a grin playing on his lips. 'You wouldn't be the ex-cop who grilled Tick-Tock by any chance, would you?'

'That's very possible.'

Weddevåg's grin grew wider.

'I see he's good at telling stories.'

'You can imagine,' Weddevåg said, casting his eyes down. 'You can imagine how good he is. But if you want to know something about the *Sea Breeze*, in all modesty, you've hit the jackpot.'

'You know?'

'I sailed the seas for almost thirty years, first as an engineer and then as a chief engineer – on lots of passenger ferries too, even a sister-ship of the *Sea Breeze*, built at the same shipyard. So I know that boat inside out. After I signed off, I worked as a surveyor until I retired. I certified ships, everything from passenger ferries to supertankers, first for Veritas, the ship classification group, and afterwards for Lloyd's Register of Ships. So you can say I know quite a bit about fire, fire protection and safety at sea. The *Sea Breeze* was a terrible story. But the biggest problem was that the police didn't know what they were doing in their investigation. Since then everything they've done has been marked by their fear of having to go back on their conclusions.'

'And you were contacted by Fredrik Andersen?'

'Yes, fortunately for him.'

57

'Fortunately?'

Weddevåg nodded. 'Fredrik first rang me when he was writing the book about the catastrophe. You might say it was a useful strategy. It gave his book the tech-savvy lift it needed. Most of the technical detail in the book came from here.'

He tapped his chest.

Frank Frølich sipped some more of the green liquid and concluded once again that the bitter-sweet, green liqueur was not his favourite.

'Fredrik was already well under way with following the money, but after a while he realised he also had to focus on the technical side.'

'Was the other bit useful?'

'Which bit?'

'Following the money.'

Weddevåg shrugged. 'What he realised was that the *Sea Breeze* was a pawn in a scam.'

Weddevåg leaned forward as if to share a secret. 'The American shipping line sold the boat to a Danish shipping line for three times its market price.'

He held three fingers in the air. 'Three times. So the insurance fee was sky-high. But the buyer hadn't started paying at the time of the blaze. Therefore the seller was entitled to any pay-out there might be. Once the wrecked ship had burned out, solicitors from the three parties got round a table and negotiated a percentage pay-out. The insurance company then paid up. That's what I call a scam. They pretended it was a ship sale and the American shipping line earned millions.'

'And Fredrik Andersen believed this?'

'Did he believe it? The only people who refuse to see what happened is the police, because if they accept the evidence they'll be admitting they did everything wrong when they investigated the case thirty years ago. They refuse to do that.'

Weddevåg fell quiet when footsteps were heard on the gravel path.

They turned to the noise, both of them. A woman in a green bikini approached. She had her hair in dreads. A tattooed sun glittered on her stomach and a mobile phone was tucked inside the bikini elastic.

Weddevåg poured himself some more green liquid.

Frølich held a hand over his glass.

'That seems very speculative,' he said.

Actually he was more focused on the woman in the bikini than on Weddevåg or the *Sea Breeze*. She seemed to have slowed down.

She walked in a leisurely fashion; it was impossible not to follow her and her swinging hips with your eyes.

'A plot and mass murder for a pot of gold, as it were. Doesn't sound very likely.'

Frank studied the body in the green bikini. Weddevåg studied the green liquid in his glass.

'I don't think the plan had been to kill people,' Weddevåg said.

Frølich glanced over at him.

'In this instance I'm not speculating,' Weddevåg said in great earnest. 'I'm sticking exclusively to the facts, the laws of physics and the resultant conclusions.'

'Unlike Fredrik Andersen?'

Weddevåg shook his head. 'Fredrik did, too. He kept to physics and things that could be documented. Nothing else.'

58

Frank Frølich watched the woman in the green bikini again. She was almost past them now. She noticed his gaze, turned her head and looked him in the eye as she passed.

'Andersen found out that the American seller was in desperate need of money,' Weddevåg said. 'They owed huge amounts of tax – going back years – to the American authorities. In addition, they owed enormous sums in harbour charges in Miami. The American shipping line was on the verge of bankruptcy. To make things worse, they'd bought the ship purely to sell it on. And to buy it they'd taken out a sizeable loan. That debt added to all the money they already owed. You might say they had good reason to pump up the price. They needed the money. Fredrik Andersen thought, like me, that a gang of crew members – those who were on board and still worked for the American company – sabotaged the boat. They wanted to wreak as much destruction as possible so that their employer would hit the jackpot and get a gigantic insurance pay-out – but the damage to the ship needed to be serious enough.'

'But companies are always going bankrupt,' Frank Frølich said. 'Owners don't commit mass murder for that reason.'

'Of course not. But some can afford to go bankrupt – others can't. This seller was no normal shipping line, with grandad sitting on his Chesterfield, smoking cigars he bought with money salted away in Switzerland. This shipping line was financed by shady investors who used cruises in Miami to launder gambling money.'

Frølich cut a dubious grimace.

Weddevåg looked back at him, equally serious. 'The fact is that strange things happened on board after the fire broke out,' he said. 'And there's only one explanation for the ship burning for such a long time: someone was stoking the fires and starting new ones while unsuspecting firemen were doing what they could to extinguish them.'

Weddevåg poured himself some more green liquid.

'The ship is evacuated at half past three in the morning. One hour later, at half past four, firefighters are lowered to the deck from helicopters. They put out the remaining flames pretty quickly. While they're doing this, three crewmen who still work for the American company return to the ship. When these three board the wreck, the teams of firefighters suddenly find inexplicable conflagrations breaking out and blazing for hours.

'But the police reject that time line,' Weddevåg continued. 'They're sticking to their 1988 version and insist the boat is set alight by a drunken passenger and what happens over the following thirty-eight hours are "natural flare-ups" from an already existing fire. They say that the boat "burns by itself" for thirty-eight hours. That's absolute tosh. There's not enough combustible material in the corridors or the restaurant sections to keep the fire burning for longer than minutes. It's proven. What's worse is that Fredrik Andersen could've persuaded the police to change their minds, but now it's too late.'

'How could he have made the police do a U-turn?'

'With the help of Ole Berg.'

Frølich gazed at his host with renewed energy. 'Ole Berg?'

'Do you know him?' Weddevåg said.

'No. But I have an assignment concerning a person by the name of Ole Berg. I'd like to meet him.'

Weddevåg grinned. 'Join the queue.'

'What do you mean?'

'There are lots of us who'd like a word with Ole Berg.'

'Who is he?'

Weddevåg shrugged. 'A witness. I don't know the man's real name, but Fredrik did. He gave the man an alias: Ole Berg. According to Fredrik, this man was on board the whole time. Ole Berg saw everything. This guy read Fredrik's book and contacted him.'

'Why did he do that?'

'Because he was an eyewitness.'

'An eyewitness to what exactly?'

'That's something I and many others would love to know. Ole Berg was never interviewed by the police. There are many of us who want to know what he has to say. But Fredrik was killed before Ole Berg's story came out.'

Frølich was silent, thinking. Could the murder of Andersen be linked with the story of the *Sea Breeze*? Could Jørgen Svinland be right after all?

He got up and went to the veranda balustrade. He gripped the handrail and closed his eyes. Andersen had appeared from nowhere at his office. Afterwards Andersen had been visited by Guri Sekkelsten. Andersen had met Guri twice that day – first in the afternoon at the House of Literature and afterwards at the restaurant in the evening. Andersen had also spent his last evening with Guri and Sheyma Bashur. These events – the conversations and the meals – were all innocuous activities and it appeared highly unlikely that any motive for murder could be found there.

The other story, however – the mass murder, the huge sums of money, the fight for truth – that was a scenario with a lot at stake.

Jørgen Svinland might be right. Andersen's murder could be linked with the *Sea Breeze* mystery.

But if the murder of Andersen was connected with the *Sea Breeze*, what about the murder of Guri? Why would this thirty-year-old story about arson on a passenger ferry lead to her death? As far as he knew, there was no connection between Guri Sekkelsten and the *Sea Breeze*. If there was, it must have come to light when she met Andersen. But was that likely?

Guri had become nervous when she found out that Andersen was dead. But why had she panicked? It *had* to be something that happened the night they met. And that night was *not* linked with the *Sea Breeze* – as far as he could ascertain.

He inhaled. Told himself there were two distinct cases here.

He turned to Weddevåg, who was calmly surveying him.

'What do you think?' Frank Frølich asked. 'Why was Andersen killed?'

'I haven't a clue.'

'Do you think it has something to do with this case? The *Sea Breeze* and the secret witness, Ole Berg?'

'I don't know. But I'm ruling nothing out.'

Silence prevailed again.

'There's one thing I don't quite understand,' Frølich said at length: 'Why did Andersen invent a cover name for this source? Why call him Ole Berg instead of using the man's real name?'

59

Weddevåg shrugged his shoulders at first. 'It's hard to say why, but the most obvious reason is that Berg's testimony is dynamite. If Berg knows who's behind the mass murder on the *Sea Breeze*, his safety will clearly be jeopardised if it comes out.'

'Tell me more…'

'I think those behind the mass murder may be willing to go to great lengths not to be unmasked.'

'Murder, for example?'

'As I said, I rule nothing out. A hundred and fifty-nine people were killed on the ferry.'

They exchanged glances.

Frank Frølich thought: Was that likely?

Possibly, he concluded. Someone killed Andersen. No one knew why as yet. Someone killed Guri Sekkelsten. Assessing the probabilities wasn't going to resolve who committed these acts and why. Murder investigation wasn't a game of chess.

'Another possible reason for Andersen making up an alias for the witness is the press,' Weddevåg said. 'The *Sea Breeze* is a massive case and has always been like a magnet for them. But newspaper interest has good and bad sides. It's positive that the press hasn't dropped the case over the years. And negative that their interest is superficial. Editors are more interested in the number of readers the news attracts than the consequences the coverage has for the public. You have to remember that we don't know what Berg actually saw. It's not certain that he witnessed people lighting fires or sabotaging the ship. But he may've seen things that could cast some light on the facts of the case. Andersen knew that if a journalist got hold of Ole Berg, the information he was sitting on would be made public in seconds. *Verdens Gang* or *Dagbladet* would print Berg's statement in order to cause a sensation. And no one would be able to guarantee that the real impact Berg's testimony could have on the case would come out. And his information wouldn't be fact-checked before it was published. The news wouldn't be properly contextualised, either. In fact most of the coverage about the *Sea Breeze* case has been neither fact-checked nor properly contextualised over the years. So any statements that refute the police version of events can easily be dismissed as conspiracy theories.'

'Surely you can protect a source in other ways than giving the man a cover name?'

Weddevåg shrugged. 'I know that Fredrik wanted to keep his source secret until he was a hundred per cent sure of him. Then he wanted to use him in any way he saw fit.'

'Which way?'

'I don't know. I'm not a writer. But it's too late now anyway. Fredrik's gone. He can't do anything about the case anymore.'

'I've spoken to a journalist who's taken a lot of interest in the *Sea Breeze*. Nicolai Smith Falck.'

'Right,' Weddevåg said with a snort. 'He's also known as "Nick, Smile and Fake".'

'You know him?'

Weddevåg shook his head. 'He rang me, asked questions, did some digging and got what he wanted. But what he ended up writing was absolute rubbish. He's a crime reporter and wants to keep in with the police. He needs them as a source for other cases. That's why he chose to tread on eggshells on this one.'

Frank had to smile.

'What are you grinning about?'

'He might've wanted to write objectively, with subtlety, and not just be your mouthpiece.'

'Nicolai doesn't bother with subtleties. He's obsessed with himself and his career. That's why he adjusts to whichever way the wind blows, and in this particular case that means writing what the police want.'

60

Frank Frølich turned and looked out. The woman in the green bikini was nowhere to be seen. All he could see from the veranda was the trees above Lindøya, Oslo Harbour and the mountains around. Holmenkollen hill looked like an over-sized shoe with a stiletto heel, abandoned in the forest. Two Nesodden ferries met in front of the entrance to Frogner Bay, hiding the Kongen clubhouse for a few seconds. The ferries were like two dung beetles on a shiny surface. A flock of cormorants had settled on the islets in the sound towards Lindøya, one had stretched out its wings to dry.

'Fredrik spoke to Ole Berg and was killed immediately afterwards,' Weddevåg said.

'Fredrik Andersen spoke to a lot of people before he was killed,' Frølich said.

'He also spoke to me.'

Frank turned and stared at Weddevåg, who shrugged.

'What do you think?' Frølich asked. 'Does Ole Berg have anything to contribute regarding the *Sea Breeze*?'

'I know it was an insurance scam,' Weddevåg said. 'I don't need any Ole Berg to tell me that.'

'How can you claim that?'

'I found the diesel evidence. It's still there. Have you seen the photos of the victims?'

61

Frølich had to admit he hadn't.

'Some of them were cremated. Ashes were all that was left,' Weddevåg said. 'There weren't even any bones. Fossil fuel *must* have been added to create damage of that order. I doubt that the parliamentary inspectors were allowed to see the photos. If they'd seen body one hundred and fifty-one, for example … just a minute.' Weddevåg stood up and went through the veranda door.

Frank continued to gaze across to Oslo harbour as he listened to Weddevåg rummaging around in the cabin.

A cruise ship was on its way into the fjord. The boat resembled a layer cake. Storey upon storey of cabins, and every one with its own balcony. A few tourists had strolled out. They stood leaning against the railings looking down on the water and the world.

Weddevåg reappeared with a ring folder crammed with documents. He placed it on his lap. Flicked through, opened the file and passed him a piece of paper.

It was a photograph of a ruler showing thirty-five centimetres. Over the ruler were some black fragments. They looked like gravel.

'Count,' Weddevåg said.

'Count?'

'Count the pieces.'

Frank counted. He found twenty small pieces. 'Twenty,' he said.

'This is body number fifteen,' Weddevåg said. 'Twenty pieces of coal. That's all that's left of a man who weighed ninety kilos. Altogether these fragments weigh less than four hundred grams. Don't forget this was a person of your stature. For a human to combust to this degree, the body has to be exposed to extreme temperatures for hour after hour after hour. But these were found in a corridor where the fire had supposedly died out after fifteen minutes.'

Weddevåg stretched across and took the photograph back. 'No one can tell me this damage came from natural causes.'

Weddevåg passed Frank another photograph. It showed another charred body.

'This woman's lying on the floor of a cabin that was completely untouched by the fire,' Weddevåg said. 'Have the police tried to explain how it was possible for her body to be so charred? No. But the explanation's simple. She was lying on the floor, as I said. Right below her, in the corridor, so on the lower deck, the saboteurs had broken off a pipe at the joint. This fractured pipe was used to pump diesel into the corridor. That's in the fire crew's log. They had to fight blazing oil here – between passengers' cabins where there shouldn't be any fossil fuel. This victim was lying over where the pipe was broken. Between the floor she was lying on and the pipe joint below there was fire-resistant insulation. Yet her body is burnt to a char. Her skull shrank because of the heat. Inside a cabin that wasn't touched by fire!'

Weddevåg was angry. It was obvious. Frølich couldn't look at the photograph for long. He passed it back, but still had to ask:

'If what you say is true, if the sabotage was already proven by photos like these, why was Fredrik so keen to meet Ole Berg?'

'Because the police have had control of the narrative ever since they started fiddling with the case again. The police don't talk about the damage to the dead bodies. They never have. They consciously avoid the subject – because the police want to tell their own story. Both the police investigators and the parliamentary ones refuse to take account of the diesel evidence and the damage to the bodies. So, if Ole Berg's willing to show his face he'll be living proof the police won't be able to deny. A testimony from Berg will first and foremost smash the police lies. Next, his statement will explain how thoroughly rotten Norway's state machinery is – from the parliamentary inquiry via the public prosecutor and down to the lowest-ranking police officer.'

'Who do you think he is?' Frank Frølich asked. 'Ole Berg? What's his real name?'

'No idea,' Bernt Weddevåg said. 'All I know is that he's from Møre. Think he's got some connection with a shipyard or other.'

'Do you know which one?

Weddevåg shook his head.

'What are your thoughts about the Fredrik Andersen murder?' Frølich said.

'I have no illusions on that score,' Weddevåg said.

'And how should I interpret that?'

'Interpret it however you like.'

'Are you saying the police are involved in the murder?'

'I'm not saying anything. But I stopped being surprised by what the Norwegian police do or don't do a long time ago.'

62

When he left Weddevåg Frølich cast a quick glance at his watch. They had talked for a good hour. Presumably he would have to wait for the boat.

He strolled back to the ferry berth. Small holiday cabins were clustered around it. Nakholmen resembled a village of the allotment variety.

No passengers were waiting. He passed a red shelter and walked to the end of the embarkation area. Stared down into the water at the clumps of seaweed dancing in the current around the quay poles. He waited to catch a glimpse of a starfish clinging to the pole under the water, or perhaps snails, or the movements of a shrimp in the seaweed. But the city was probably too close by. The water wasn't that clean. Something flickered in his brain, a sense of how it was when he was a child: feeling the sun-warmed planks of the quay against his stomach as he watched the crabs advancing on the bait he had lowered on a piece of string into the water.

He turned on hearing footsteps. A man was sitting down on the bench to his right. He was one of the tourists who had stepped ashore with him.

This tourist is probably beginning to get a little hot in his jumper, Frank thought, and observed that he didn't have a camera, either.

As though the man were a mind-reader, he got up and started snapping the City Hall, Piper Bay and the fortress with his phone.

After a while he sat back down on the bench.

There was something familiar about the man's appearance, but he couldn't quite place him.

He looked to the right.

The man looked away.

Then he thought: *Perhaps this tourist just looks like someone I've met.*

Nevertheless, he couldn't help feeling some unease. The echo of a voice: *I'll find you.*

Could this be the voice on the phone?

He *had* seen the man on the bench before. But where? It was as though the right side of his body was aglow. He forced himself to stand still. Leaned back and gazed across the water. A pair of swans swam past the quay. They continued towards the sea-smoothed rocks where people from the cluster of cabins had found themselves spots to lie, sheltered from the wind. There were people around. There were witnesses. A man with a fishing rod was walking between the boats in the marina beside the ferry berth.

Frank Frølich coughed.

The man with the fishing rod glanced towards the berth before jumping down into a skerry jeep. He unhitched the mooring ropes and used a boat hook to manoeuvre his way out of the marina.

The ferry arrived. A young woman in a white blouse and black trousers was standing at the stern. The sight of her calmed Frølich's nerves. She leapt ashore and motioned for them to board.

He went up to the top deck. The tourist stayed below.

Frølich found himself a seat where he could keep an eye on the ladder protruding from the lower deck.

During the trip people came up to the top deck, but they were usually children and their parents. The tourist wasn't among them.

The return to the City Hall pier took just over half an hour. The passengers queued on the steps as the boat approached land. The tourist wasn't anywhere to be seen.

Frank trudged after a group of small boys and had almost crossed the City Hall square when once again he sensed the presence of the tourist from Nakholmen. There was something familiar about the shadow reflected in the display window of Hatte Holm. He glanced over his shoulder. It was the tourist, no doubt about it.

His legs suddenly felt heavy. This man was following him. What did he want?

He ambled up Rosenkrantz' gate, crossed on red, continued past Stortinget, the Norwegian Parliament, and on towards the law court. Again he glanced over his shoulder as he ascended the steps in Teatergata.

The man crossed the tramlines a hundred metres behind him. This area was uncomfortably deserted. Frølich started to sweat and increased his speed. He wanted to be surrounded by people. Jogged the last few metres to the lights in Akersgata. Had to wait for cars passing. Should he turn and check? There was a gap in the traffic. He ran across the street towards the government quarter and in the reflection of a large entrance door saw the man crossing the street behind him.

He took a left and turned into the portico of the Deichmanske Library, strode up the stairs and through the broad doors.

Inside, he stood gasping for breath. There were people here. He continued up the staircase to the first floor. Keeping an eye on the doors. They remained closed. He stood by the panoramic window and looked out. The man was standing in the square outside.

It was clear the man didn't want to come in. Instead he withdrew a few metres. A tall, thin guy dressed in jeans and a short jacket, with combed-back, dark hair, greying in places, a three-day beard and a little ring in one ear.

Frank still couldn't remember where he had seen him. At that moment the man looked up.

Eye contact.

The man averted his gaze. A solitary individual on a walkway where people were now rushing back and forth.

If Frank was going to react, now was the time. He descended the staircase. Continued out of the building and down the steps between the pillars and headed for the passageway over the inner ring road.

The man was nowhere to be seen.

He scanned the streets. The man had disappeared. What was this? Two people had been killed and someone was following him. How long had this been going on? Was the man watching him now, at this very moment?

He stood motionless, going over the previous day's events. The meeting with Bjørn Thyness, the drive south to Råde and from there to Våler. He had spent most of the night at Guri Sekkelsten's place. Then he visited Matilde before driving home and talking to the wearying journalist.

Could the man have been waiting for him at home, as Nicolai Smith Falck had done?

He didn't know. He had been too busy with the journalist to notice anything else. But when he caught the metro to Police HQ a bit later to make a statement? He'd had his eyes open for the journalist. Had he observed anyone else tailing him? He couldn't say. After Police HQ, he had gone home and had stayed there for a few hours before driving to the city centre to meet Gamon. Of course, someone might have followed him there. He wouldn't have noticed anything because he had been exclusively focused on the woman who worked at the hotel. Afterwards: his office and the meeting with Snorre Norheim.

A wild thought struck him. Could the man who was spying on him be working for Snorre Norheim?

The notion seemed inane as soon as it entered his head. The conclusion was actually clear. He had no idea who was spying on him, how long this had been going on or why it was happening.

He began to make for Brugata. This was a different kind of walk. He had pins and needles running down his spine, and he kept checking behind him.

63

Back in his office, at first he stood by the window, studying the streets below. A stream of people was passing on the pavements in Storgata and in the pedestrian area. The man wasn't to be seen. But that didn't necessarily mean he wasn't down there. He could be anywhere.

He realised there was little more he could do about his stalker, and he'd simply have to find a new lead. For lack of a better idea he sat down at his desk with the laptop. He inserted the memory stick containing Andersen's research material.

Bernt Weddevåg had said he thought Berg was from Møre and had some connection with a shipyard. So he started to search the stick for Møre, Sunnmøre and Romsdal counties. Lots of hits. He went online and searched for Norwegian shipyards. There were quite a few. He started at the top of the list. Found out where the shipyard was, then searched for the address. When he searched for a shipyard in the Ulstein group he got lots of hits. And when he searched for the town Ulsteinvik, he had several hits in which one name kept coming up. It belonged to a woman: Oda Borgersrud.

He looked at the list of hits. They were the same initials. Could Andersen's secret source be a woman?

Who was Oda Borgersrud?

He tried to search through the documents more systematically. There was no police interview with Borgersrud. So she couldn't have been a passenger on board the *Sea Breeze*. But her name appeared in a log signed by a Swedish firefighter – the section leader of the team extinguishing the fires on the ship.

The section leader wrote that the fire crews arrived on the burning ship by helicopter. They were lowered onto the mooring deck at the front. Afterwards they entered the ship to gain an overview of the situation. They moved towards the car deck and descended below. That was when they found Oda Borgersrud. She had survived the first few hours in a crew cabin. In the log she was referred to as a young woman. The leader wrote that she must have survived because she had been in the aft of the ship and at a level below where the first fire started.

He searched through more of Andersen's files and found her again. Oda Borgersrud had testified in the maritime inquiry. It appeared that she was twenty-four years old when the fire broke out on the *Sea Breeze*. She worked in the perfume section of the duty-free shop. When the fire alarms went off she was asleep in her cabin, but she wasn't woken up. The fire detector installed outside her cabin was defective. However, in the morning she was awoken by the smell of smoke. At first she had tried to leave her cabin, but wasn't able to beat a path up to the deck. The corridor outside her cabin was burning hot and thick with smoke. In her cabin, on the other hand, there was no smoke. She had backed into her cabin and stayed there. She had observed the evacuation of the ship from her cabin window and had seen people in lifeboats on the water, people being rescued by other boats, while she was imprisoned in her cabin. She had panicked and tried to smash the cabin window with any object she had to hand. At first she had tried a perfume bottle and afterwards a showerhead. Her attempts failed and she was sure she was going to die. But all of a sudden she heard voices from inside the ferry. Then she shouted for help. This was how she was found and rescued by the fire crews. They had taken her up to fresh air. That was all that the document said about her. Nothing about what she had seen while she was above deck – on the bridge.

What happened to her later? Why wasn't she interviewed by the police? The last question was impossible to answer. There were many important witnesses who weren't interviewed by the police in 1988. The fireman who wrote the log hadn't been interviewed, either. Frank Frølich began to understand why the police had been criticised over this case.

He went online and searched for Oda Borgersrud on the Yellow Pages website. There was only one hit. Someone living in Ulsteinvik. Presumably it was the same person. Now she would be between fifty and sixty years old. He sat looking at the telephone number. Should he ring?

He gripped the phone.

A woman's voice said 'Hello'.

'Is that Oda Borgersrud?'

'I don't do phone sales.'

'This is about Fredrik Andersen.'

Silence.

'My name's Frølich. I'm a private investigator. I assume you know the writer, Fredrik Andersen, is dead?'

More silence.

'I've been given an assignment by Andersen's family. I was wondering therefore if you're the Oda Borgersrud who was working on the *Sea Breeze* in 1988.'

Still no answer.

'I'd like to talk to you about Fredrik Andersen and the book he wrote.'

'How do I know you're who you say you are?'

'You can ring me. My company's registered in the Yellow Pages. Frølich. Private investigator.'

'I don't wish to talk to you. Goodbye.'

Frank stared at the silent phone. She had rung off.

He tapped in the number again. It rang. It continued to ring. She didn't answer.

64

He opened the door onto Storgata. Looked around for a few seconds, then made for Grønlands torg and the metro. As far as he could see, there was no one following him.

He was the only passenger to alight at Ryen station. He waited on the platform until the train had departed. Only then, when he was sure he was alone, did he set off. At first the sounds of his footsteps were drowned by the noise of the motorway, but they became clearer the closer he was to his block of flats. No one was waiting outside, it seemed.

He opened the front door and locked it behind him.

It was late. He was exhausted. He went straight to the bathroom and then to bed.

*

He slept so soundly that he didn't hear the door open. Nor did he hear any footsteps. He didn't notice the light from the sitting room that cast a stripe across the floor and his duvet. He didn't hear the sounds. Nor did he feel the mattress move or see the flash of light when a match was struck.

Nevertheless, deep in his slumbers, the smell of smoke made a nostril twitch – but it didn't wake him. He started dreaming about his father. About the stink of tobacco in his nostrils when he was sitting in the back of the car and they were going on holiday. About him opening a window and sticking his head out so as not to throw up.

Nor did he wake up when the duvet was lifted. He only woke up when he felt her hand.

'You have to open a window,' he whispered in a drowsy voice.

'Have done.'

'Good,' he said, observing Matilde's attractive face in the light from the door that was still ajar. Her eyes reflected the light and took on a reddish hue from the glow of the cigarette when she inhaled.

'You look French.'

'*Then she lit a cigarette*,' she whispered in English.

'I noticed.'

'*Don't let this put you off*,' she said.

'Is this where I say "*You want an apple?*"'

She lay down. 'Take the cigarette,' she whispered.

He took it from her mouth.

'Stub it out,' she said and held out the ashtray.

He did as she said.

65

Otis Taylor was on the stereo. The trumpet solo on the recording of 'Hey Joe'. Behind the music he could hear Matilde having a shower.

He turned up the volume. He loved this version: fiddle, guitars and brass.

When the song was over he switched off the stereo. The tap was running again in the bathroom. Teeth were being cleaned. The door opened.

'Why did you switch it off?'

'So that I can hear you better. Besides, it's late.'

She smiled. 'That guy.'

She stood in the doorway drying her hair.

'Which guy?'

'Snorre Norheim. The one who went to your office and said Guri couldn't have died a natural death.'

'What about him?'

'You said he was in the military.'

'It was on his business card – colonel.'

'I talked to Harry,' she said.

'Harry?'

'The guy whose friend landed on his head and who destroyed the post-box stand.'

'Ah, right.'

'Harry says Snorre Norheim's a veteran. He served in Iraq.'

She came in and spread the towel over the pillow. The mattress moved as she slipped under the duvet. 'MNF,' she said. 'Multi-National Force – a Norwegian contingent in a multi-national force in Iraq. I asked Harry to check. The Norheim guy was on lots of missions in Afghanistan and Iraq apparently. Among others, in Basra in 2004. That's why I thought of Aisha and Guri, and the story of the sister.'

'It's possible. In fact, it's possible you're on to something.'

'Fine,' Matilde said and switched off the light. The darkness was impenetrable.

Her mouth tasted of toothpaste. 'Are you coming to the funeral?' she whispered.

'When is it?'

'They haven't decided on the day yet.'

'Gotcha.' He sat up.

'What is it?' Matilde sat up as well.

He had remembered the face. Of the man who had been following him. He had seen him at the refugee centre. It was the man they'd met first. Guri had called him Shamal.

66

The middle classes start their working day, if they have one, at nine, he thought next morning, as he tiptoed out of the bathroom, so as not to wake Matilde. The working classes usually start at seven. If you are on the defence staff, you probably have the authority to start whenever you like. He brewed himself a cup of coffee in the kitchen and wrote her a Post-it. Stuck it to the mirror in the bathroom to be sure she would find it. It was a quarter past six. He cast a final glance into the bedroom. She was as sound asleep as before.

He walked out to the car and drove off. Keeping an eye on the rear-view mirror, though he doubted that anyone would actually be following him; he performed a little manoeuvre to check. Entered the motorway, came off again almost immediately – towards Manglerud, alone, as far as he could make out, went along Plogveien, Enebakkveien and into Sandstuveien to get back onto the E6, with no traffic behind him, then headed west.

Perhaps Colonel Snorre Norheim follows a duty roster. But his wife doesn't necessarily, he mused, as he parked his car under a maple tree in Stabekk. It was ten minutes to seven.

Snorre Norheim lived in a house set back from the road, detached and clad with vertical red panels. The pitched roof was covered with black glass tiles. The acute angle gave the house height and a distinctive appearance. A set of steps built with impregnated wood led to the front door. A dormer window protruding from the roof revealed that the house had two storeys. This was a house and garden at its ease, surrounded by a mellow Oslo West End aura, which suggested that it must have been built during the inter-war years or even earlier, when Bærum was more a country village than a suburb of the capital. Between the house and the road stood a broad, more recently constructed garage with two doors.

The paterfamilias himself was the first to emerge. Today Snorre Norheim was wearing a green uniform with military insignia and a sharp crease in his trousers. At almost half past seven he strode energetically down the steps and opened one garage door. A minute later he reversed out in a small electric car. The single-seater was so small it looked as though he had put it on over his uniform. Without closing the garage door he set off for the motorway.

Another half hour passed before the two children came out. Two girls. They were probably eight to ten years old and wore shorts and jumpers. One had a bow in her hair. They played hopscotch down the drive and tied a French-skipping rope to a tree beside the garage. One stood with the rope around her ankles. The other jumped, still wearing her satchel. When she made a mistake they swapped positions.

After another twenty minutes the door opened again. A slim, dark-haired woman rushed down the steps and over to the double garage. She was wearing jeans and a white blouse. She called the girls, who carried on skipping. There was a little disagreement about whose turn it was and what was fair.

The woman reversed a slightly larger family car from the garage. A Nissan Qashqai. She opened a rear door from inside and called again.

The girls sauntered to the car and scrambled in. Afterwards the mother jumped out and closed the garage doors. The car then rolled down the drive and sped away.

67

He followed her. It wasn't a long journey. The car went towards Bekkestua, along Gamle Ringeriksvei and across the railway tracks. She drove into a car park belonging to Stabekk School – two older brick buildings in front of park-like outdoor facilities. The girls were probably pupils here. Perhaps their mother worked at the school, too. Not improbable, he thought. It was such a short distance to the school the girls ought to be able to walk it alone. Going with Mama could be a practical solution. But he might be wrong. She might of course work elsewhere. He sat back to wait. The minutes dragged. There was no sign of the woman. And her car was still parked in the line of cars reserved for staff.

He took out his phone, went online and found the school website. The staff page. Found her under the heading 'Teaching Staff'. Her name was Alicia Norheim. So that was what she looked like close up. A dark-skinned *donna* with straight hair, large brown eyes, full lips and a pronounced mole on her right cheek.

Alicia was a new name in this case. Nevertheless, he took the photograph of Sheyma Bashur from the glove compartment to compare. Alicia Norheim's cheeks weren't as round. But his eyes were drawn automatically to the mole on Sheyma's cheek, and then moved to her eyes and mouth, as though these attractive features were only waiting to make their entrance.

If Alicia Norheim and Sheyma Bashur were one and the same person, that would explain how Snorre Norheim could know what he did. But it didn't explain why Norheim wanted to hire him to investigate Guri Sekkelsten's death.

He studied the pictures again. The similarity between the two faces was clearer now. Alicia Norheim was Sheyma Bashur.

Had she contacted the police? She should have done. She was

sitting on important information in a murder case. She was one of the last people to see Fredrik Andersen alive.

He sat looking at the photographs, unsure what to do next.

He made a decision and searched for the school telephone number on the net.

He waited until he heard the school bell ring and saw the pupils streaming out. Gave her two minutes to reach the staff room. Called. There was a switchboard. Asked to speak to Alicia Norheim.

'Just a moment.'

There were only two rings.

'Alicia Norheim here.'

Her voice was pleasantly soft with hardly any accent.

'I believe your real name is Sheyma?'

A shot in the dark. But had he hit bullseye or not?

No answer. For a long time. He could hear her breathing. 'Hello,' he said.

'Who is this?' said the voice, which was no longer pleasantly soft. But nervous now. 'Who is this? Who are you?'

For a few seconds he deliberated. Aisha had been deported. Guri Sekkelsten was dead. He no longer had an assignment that had any connection with Sheyma Bashur – he just wanted to satisfy his curiosity.

'My name's Frølich. I'm a private investigator. I'm sorry to bother you with this, but some time ago I was commissioned to locate a woman by the name of Sheyma Bashur.'

He paused.

'You're Sheyma Bashur,' he said.

He could hear her breathing.

'I'd like you to contact the police,' he said. 'You were one of the last people to see Fredrik Andersen alive. I can give you the phone number of...'

He paused. The dialling tone told him that she had already rung off.

He stared at the school. Should he call her again?

No. He had said what it was right to say.

The break was over and the small kids were trudging back in. Children in short trousers and summer dresses.

There was no point pressing Alicia Norheim any further. He was no longer employed by either Aisha or Guri. But he could give Alicia a few days. Sooner or later he would have to tell Gunnarstranda about her. But it would be best if she contacted the police herself. In that way, he would be kept out of it.

He switched on the ignition and drove off – towards Elvestad.

68

A good hour later he pulled into the car park in Elvestad where he and Matilde had found a place next to Guri's Volvo not so many days ago.

He was met by a group of sweaty, laughing African-looking men who had just finished the morning session on the sports pitch.

He went in and met a dark, young girl in reception. He asked to speak to someone in management.

The girl lifted a telephone receiver and rang.

She put it down and explained where the office was.

A tall, slim woman in her late thirties was waiting for him in a doorway at the end of the corridor. Her hair was dark and cut short. She was wearing a knee-length skirt and a light, white woollen cardigan over a beige top.

They shook hands.

Inside the office she had photographs of a man and children on the desk. On the wall behind the desk hung stick drawings with titles like 'To Mama' and 'The nicest mum in the world'. She had dimples in both cheeks and as she took a seat behind the desk she said she had already spoken to the police.

He told her he was a private investigator.

He stood with his hands behind his back and felt a little like a constable when he said that he had known the late Guri Sekkelsten, which was the truth. He had been doing a job for her, and in that connection he had been to the refugee centre almost a week before. He had met a man called Shamal and now he would like to talk to him again.

The woman behind the desk was taken aback.

'A man with a little ring in one ear and combed-back hair,' he said.

'Yes, I know who Shamal is. It's just that he no longer works here.'

'So where is he?'

She shrugged. 'As we said to the other lady, Shamal's packed his things and gone.'

'The other lady?'

69

'A woman was here asking after him.'

'Who?'

'She didn't say her name. She just asked after Shamal.'

'Ethnically Norwegian?'

'I'm not sure, but she spoke Norwegian anyway. Dark-skinned, maybe thirty-five? Sorry, but I didn't ask where she came from.'

'Did she have a mole here?' He pointed to his right cheek.

'Yes, in fact she did. Why do you ask?'

Frølich chose to ignore her question for the moment. 'But if I were to have any chance of finding Shamal, where should I look?'

She sent him a winning smile. 'I'm afraid I don't have the slightest idea.'

She took a deep breath and eyed him as if considering whether to betray a secret.

'Yes?' he said.

'I might not be playing by the book to say this, but I think I know why he took flight. You see, not so long ago, he had his final appeal turned down. He could be deported at any moment.'

Took flight, he thought. Shamal was a case for Bjørn Thyness.

'Where do you think he's hiding?'

'As I said, I've no idea.'

'In Oslo? He might have friends among other immigrants.'

'I'd assume so, but I don't know.'

'Is anyone in the centre close to him? Anyone I can talk to who might be able to give me a clue as to where he's hiding?'

'I shouldn't build up your hopes on that front. If Guri had still been here, I would've said you should talk to her. They worked together quite a bit.'

She stared into the middle distance. Serious now, and affected.

'Guri was very well liked and good at her job. What happened is a great loss, not only for us, but for everyone who knew her.'

He nodded.

'Tragic. That's the only word for it. Absolutely tragic.'

'What kind of relationship did Guri and Shamal have?'

'A good one. They liked each other and worked well together. They had conversation groups and some activity training.'

'Were they lovers?'

She smiled again. 'No,' she said, as though what he asked was foolish. 'I don't think so.' She considered the question for a few seconds. 'Well,' she said, 'if they did, I didn't know anything about it. I don't think so, though.'

He made a move to leave.

She coughed.

He stopped.

'That would be a breach of all our ethical principles,' she said.

'What would be?'

'Starting a relationship with a refugee. Guri wasn't the type.'

His question had clearly given her food for thought. But he chose not to pursue the topic. 'Have you tried to locate him?'

'We don't have the resources.'

'Surely you've tried ringing him though?'

'Yes, we have.'

'You have his phone number?'

She leaned back and examined him more closely. 'What's this actually about?'

He pulled the visitor's chair over and sat down. 'If only I knew,' he said glumly.

'Knew what?'

'What this was about. You had a woman here called Aisha. She wanted to be reunited with a sister.'

She nodded. There was a pile of letters on her desk. Addressed to an Anne Kari.

'Guri and Shamal, together, hired me to find Aisha's sister.'

She raised both eyebrows in astonishment.

'You didn't know?'

She shook her head.

'I think I've found her sister. But it's too late. From what I understand Aisha has been deported.'

Anne Kari nodded.

'Guri Sekkelsten's dead and I want to close the case. So I'd like to be able to contact Shamal, who helped and was involved.'

'You say you *think* you've found the sister?'

It was his turn to nod.

'Another tragic story with a tragic outcome,' she said. 'That's what we deal with in this business. Tragedies.'

She got up. 'I've got Shamal's phone number, the one we used when he was here. But no one picks up. It's probably a pay-as-you-go phone. I suppose he's changed the number or the SIM card or whatever they're called.'

'A phone number will be somewhere to start,' he said and watched as she took a ring-file from a cabinet behind the desk, leafed through and jotted down a number.

He took the note, thanked her, shook her hand and said goodbye.

The bird's flown, he thought, as he padded through the main entrance to his car.

Shamal had gone. Taken flight.

So why did the guy spend a whole day tailing me?

He sat for a while in his car before starting up. Going over what happened the day he had been here. Shamal and Guri saying hi as they came in. A little later Guri called Shamal over.

And what happened afterwards?

Aisha was forcibly deported. Guri Sekkelsten died. Shamal left the centre and started stalking him. Why?

70

It was afternoon when, once again, he left his car in the multistorey car park by Spektrum, the indoor arena. He was hungry. Considered checking what was today's menu at Dovrehallen, but chose fast food instead. Went to Grand Pizza in Grønland and bought a kebab in pitta bread. He grabbed a plastic fork and set to, straightaway in the street. Stood looking at a man without a head on a stool outside Teddys Softbar, playing guitar. The hat above the collar was floating in the air. At first, it was quite an impressive stunt, even if you realised the man must have hidden his head in his shirt. A lot of fuss for a relatively unprofitable act though, Frølich noticed, when he looked at the few coins there were in the guitar case on the ground. Private investigation was not the only industry where you had to toil for your supper. The hipsters sitting outside Teddys weren't impressed, either. They shouted to each other to be heard over the guitar. Frank ate his kebab and tried to make up his mind whether headless guitar-playing was an art it was worth rewarding or not. No, he concluded, there were limits. Turning to walk on, he looked up to the right. There was a light on in the window above the dentist's.

That was his office.

He walked slowly on.

He might have forgotten to switch off the light.

Or the cleaner might have forgotten.

It was probably the cleaner.

He rounded the corner and entered the hall with the lift and the staircase. Stared at the lift. Decided to take the stairs and was slightly out of breath when he pushed open the door leading to the corridor on the second floor. The chair beside the coffee machine was empty.

He went back to the Coke machine and inserted some coins. A can of Coke rumbled in the machine and fell. He took it. And managed, with the use of his elbow, to hold the kebab, the Coke and the pitta in one hand and the key in the other. Unlocked the door. Kicked the door open with his right foot. Went in.

For one second he caught the whiff of after-shave. The next he was in free fall towards the floor and as he fell he noticed the meat and Coke in mid-flight with him.

71

There was nothing to break his fall. He hit the floor like a sack of flour. His head banged down on the lino, temple first.

Everything went black. When he saw light again, his ears were buzzing. He tried to sit up. Another blow hit him across the back and he fell forward again. This time his chin hit the floor. His teeth crunched. Another blow rained down. And another. He thought: *I mustn't lose consciousness.*

He rolled over onto his back.

Snorre Norheim stood by the door weighing a baseball bat in his hand, ready to strike again.

'What are you doing?'

'You've been ringing my wife and pestering her.'

He didn't feel any pain. It must have been the shock. What he felt was numb. He tried to sit up.

'Don't move.'

Snorre Norheim's pose with the baseball bat was warning enough.

He lay motionless on the floor, but shouted: 'Take it easy. I just want to see if anything's broken.'

'Nothing's broken. You rang my wife. Why?'

'You asked me to find out if Guri Sekkelsten died of natural causes. To be able to say anything useful, I had to find out who she was with the night Andersen was killed. I had reason to believe one of the people she was with was your wife. I called her to have this confirmed, but she rang off before I could say anything.'

Snorre Norheim lowered the bat.

'From now on my home, wife and children are out of bounds to you. Have you got that?'

'I'm not very comfortable down here. Is it alright if I sit up? Then we can talk, calmly, like two sensible adults.'

'Have you got that?'

'Yes!'

Norheim took a step back, but held the bat ready to strike.

Frølich needed time. Now that he was getting over the shock, he was beginning to feel the pain. He struggled to his knees, went giddy and had to hold on to the desk and pull himself up. Nausea swirled in his chest. He took a deep breath and let it out again to gather himself. Turned to the determined man standing by the door. Once again he had his concept of idiocy incarnate confirmed: an angry man with a weapon in his hand.

He went dizzy again. Rubbed his neck. He had never been more fed up with his job than at this moment.

He shot a glance outside. No commotion in the windows across the street. Heads were dutifully bent over computer screens as always. Then he knew. He could be killed in his own office without anyone realising.

He staggered over to the window, supporting himself on the wall. Saw the pitiful remains of his meal on the floor.

The nausea trapped in his diaphragm was getting stronger. He swallowed, not that that did any good. He had to sit down and groaned with pain as the chair fell backward and hit the wall.

'Tell me what you've found out.'

'Guri Sekkelsten hired me on behalf of an asylum seeker – the aim was to trace your wife.'

'I know the story. Fantasies. A sister that doesn't exist.'

'If you'd let me finish.'

Norheim didn't answer.

'When I started searching, I met a woman who became nervous when I showed her a photo. I gave her my business card and asked her to contact me if anything occurred to her. She never did.

Instead I was contacted by Fredrik Andersen. He asked about my assignment and pumped me for information. I understood one thing from what he said, namely that the woman I was trying to trace – Sheyma – was alive and lived in Norway. But Andersen refused to tell me anything about her. After Andersen left here, I met Guri Sekkelsten. I told her about Andersen. She contacted him and wanted him to tell her what he knew. Andersen and your wife met Guri Sekkelsten that night.'

'How do you know that's true?'

'Guri told me on the phone.'

'She promised not to say anything.'

'Well, she broke her promise and she's dead. There's very little you can do about that.'

'Did she tell many other people?'

'I have no idea. I know Guri went into hiding after Andersen was killed. She contacted me about twenty-four hours later. We arranged to meet at her place. She got there before me. When I arrived I found she'd been killed.'

'Why do you say she was killed when the police reject that version of events?'

72

Why do I claim Guri was killed? he thought, as he waited for another wave of nausea to pass. It didn't. He had to swallow again. He said:

'Experience. I've investigated murder. Lots of murders. And I saw her car fleeing the scene before I found her. Someone must've been driving that car, and whoever it was must also have had a reason to want to leave the place. There was a kettle boiling on the hob when I went in. I don't think anyone about to commit suicide puts on coffee. She's supposed to have texted a final farewell to her employer. That stinks.'

'Why?'

'Because the person who drove off in her car also had her phone.

And if she'd sent a final message, she would've sent it to someone she cared about.'

'Who?'

'How should I know? Her mother? Father? I could've sent you all this in a report. Instead you turn up here and attack me with a baseball bat. I'd like you to leave now.'

Norheim eyed him, without moving.

'Well?'

'Have you told the police about all this?'

'Yes.'

'If you've explained to the police that it was murder, why do they see the case as suicide?'

'Don't know. But my guess is they don't consider my testimony credible enough.'

'Why not?'

'I'm not a mind-reader. I don't know.'

'Have they dropped the case?'

'I don't know.'

'Guri told my wife she occasionally had a guy living with her. An asylum seeker.'

'So?'

'If he was there that night it could've been him driving off in her car.'

'That,' Frølich said, inhaling deeply. 'That may well be right.'

'He may also be the person who killed her.'

'Of course, that is possible, too.'

'If you find the guy, you have the final proof.'

Snorre Norheim lifted the bat and tapped it lightly on his left hand. It was made of metal.

Norheim's face split into a good-natured smile. 'My apologies for the walloping I gave you. How much do I owe you so far?'

'Nothing.'

'Don't be afraid to say what I owe you.'

'I don't want anything to do with you. Please get out of my sight.'

'You work for me.'

'I don't wish to work for anyone who breaks into my office and tries to kill me.'

'I've apologised. I want you to carry on.'

'Why?'

Snorre Norheim held the metal bat under his elbow while he fished a thin wad of notes from his pocket.

'Why?' Frank Frølich repeated.

'Why what?'

'Why do you want to find out about these things?'

'Focus, Frølich. Your job is to find the man who lived with her.'

Norheim counted the notes.

'Look upon this as an advance,' he said and placed the wad of notes on the desk. 'When you've found the man who lived with Guri Sekkelsten, you'll get three times the amount.'

'What's your wife's real name?'

Snorre Norheim's eyes blackened again. He supported himself on the bat and leaned across the desk. 'As I said, focus on the job. My wife has no relevance for you. Is that understood?'

It wasn't difficult to nod in the affirmative.

Snorre Norheim tucked the bat under his arm and was gone. This situation reminded Frank of a previous one. But there was a difference. He didn't run after the man to return the money this time. He leaned his head against the wall and contemplated the money on the table. Filthy lucre. As filthy as the motives of all those who were circling around him and around the deceased: Fredrik Andersen and Guri Sekkelsten.

He asked himself: *Why don't you run after the man and give the money back?*

Because, he thought, *Snorre Norheim is playing his filthy game, and I'm sitting at the table and playing with him, whether I like it or not.*

And because, he told himself in the next breath, *I am or have been very close to the heart of all this.*

The nausea and the pain he could feel now were proof enough. He had been on to something. But what?

The conversation with Alicia Norheim. He had told her to report what she knew to the police. Why had her crazy husband come here, really? Was it because Frank had rung Alicia or was it because of what he had told her to do?

Alicia Norheim had been to the refugee centre and asked after Shamal. Did her husband know that?

Impossible to know. Frank hadn't asked.

Guri and Shamal had worked together, closely. It must have been Shamal who occasionally slept over at Guri's.

He thought back to the minutes when he had searched her house. The room where someone had obviously slept in the bed. The duvet and the smell of after-shave that still hung in the air.

Norheim had a point. Shamal was a potential killer. But what would his motive be for harming Guri?

She had been on her way home. She arrived at the house. Pulled up in front. Stopped and switched off the engine.

He tried to imagine what might have happened next. She got out of the car. Walked inside. Kicked off her shoes. Went into the kitchen. Put on the kettle. Left the kitchen. Met Shamal, who had got out of bed.

What sort of person was Shamal? The person who killed her had done it quickly. She hadn't been able to resist for long. And afterwards it was arranged to look like suicide. It seemed planned: the surprise and the orchestration. Had Shamal been lying in bed waiting for her; had he waited and planned what would happen? Had he heard her car drive up, got out of bed and made his preparations? If so, why? What was the motive?

He recalled the short telephone conversation that morning. The silence, the noise of the car in motion: *I'll find you.*

Could it have been Shamal who uttered those words? It was impossible to know.

Snorre Norheim wanted to pay him to locate Shamal. He wanted to get hold of Shamal as well. To question him. And somewhere out there this very Shamal might be wondering about him. From now on, it was perhaps simply better to sit on the fence.

He got up and looked around. The floor needed a wash. He pulled out a drawer and checked the calendar. The cleaner would be coming tomorrow. He grabbed the wad of notes and stuffed them into his pocket without bothering to count them. Ignored the mess on the floor and left.

73

There was a note from Matilde on the kitchen table. And lots of red hearts. She wrote that she had made an omelette with the last two eggs and she'd had to leave for work and she was sorry she hadn't had time to go shopping.

He went to the fridge. It was ominously empty. A carton of milk past its sell-by date, a bit of ham and cheese, and a lunch packet from Fjordland. A few dishes of dried-up leftovers, the composition of which he didn't even dare speculate on. He was embarrassed. Knowing Matilde didn't like a badly stocked fridge. But he was no great shakes at food shopping.

He took the lift down to the cellar and unlocked the door. Went to his storeroom. The padlock was on. No one had broken in trying to get to his bike. That was good news. The bike had become a bit dusty in the course of the winter and spring, but the tyres were hard. On the shelf there was a red can of oil. He lubricated the chain and tried the brakes. Everything was in order. He pushed the bike to the stairs and took it with him in the lift up to his flat. Here he found the cycle lock hanging on a hook in the hallway. He opened the wardrobe and found his cycling uniform: shorts, jersey, helmet and sunglasses. Inside the wardrobe was a rucksack, which he swung onto his back. He caught the lift back down. Cycled the eight or nine hundred metres to the Manglerud shopping centre. Locked the bike in the stand outside, but kept his helmet and sunglasses on as he went in. He took a shopping basket at the entrance to Meny supermarket and made a beeline for the freezer counters.

Then he caught sight of a familiar figure in an aisle between the shelves. A grey-haired old gentleman was leaning on a crutch and pushing a shopping trolley. It was his client – Jørgen Svinland, Fredrik Andersen's uncle. As Svinland was shopping here, he had to live close by.

He thought he should introduce himself and went over. But he pulled up short.

An elderly woman was walking towards Jørgen Svinland. She was carrying a packet from the meat counter. It was the sight of the woman that had made Frank waver.

She was wearing a blue dress and glasses. She was reading the information on the packet and talking about the best-before date, then put it in the trolley. The woman had to be Svinland's wife.

But Frank Frølich had seen this woman once before. She had come out of Fredrik Andersen's place while he was waiting in his car outside. She was no longer a mystery. He could ring Gunnarstranda and say that the mysterious woman was a relative of Andersen's.

If it was in his interest at all to assist the police with whatever they were doing.

He stood observing the couple. Svinland stopped by a shelf, took an item and read the data. A soup in a bag. The husband talked to his wife, who nodded and gave him a hand. There was an intimacy about the elderly couple shopping together; it was a kind of idyll. Then a young man came down the same aisle, carrying a cardboard box full of Coke cans. He stopped by the couple and put the box in the trolley. The woman said something and laughed out loud. The young man smiled. He was dark-haired and thin, with slightly severe, central-Asian features, which suggested he might be from Tibet or around there. His hair was black, thick and reached down to his shoulders. When he laughed, his face opened, he showed white teeth and became a good-looking young man. He was wearing a short-sleeved shirt and worn jeans and sandals without socks. He probably wasn't even twenty years old.

The three of them looked like a grandfather and grandmother shopping with a well-loved grandchild. But herr and fru Svinland didn't have any grandchildren, according to Svinland. They had lost their only daughter on the *Sea Breeze*.

Perhaps Svinland had a well-loved nephew? A nephew from Nepal?

The three of them came towards him. Frank Frølich removed his sunglasses.

'Well, hello there,' he said to Svinland, who stopped and regarded him for a few confused seconds before recognition shone through in his eyes.

'Must be the sports gear,' Svinland said. 'I hardly recognised you. Meet my wife.'

Svinland opened a palm in the direction of the woman. 'This is Frølich. The man I talked about. The investigator.'

'But we've met before,' Frølich said, shaking her hand.

She didn't answer.

Svinland looked from him to his wife, taken aback. 'Met before?'

Her hand was limp and her eyes were puzzled. 'We met outside Fredrik Andersen's house,' he said. 'I told you I was waiting for him. You were coming out.'

'Oh, yes,' she said, freeing her hand.

Svinland looked at his spouse, who looked back. 'When was that?' he asked, still taken aback.

His spouse didn't answer. Frølich didn't feel it was his call. The question hadn't been directed at him.

The young man and Frank Frølich were now spectators of something it was hard to describe in words. All he could think was that he must have said something wrong. The woman grabbed the trolley and pushed it ahead of her, away from this stand-off. The husband let her go, then took his crutch and hobbled after her. Leaving behind Frank Frølich and the young man, who made an apologetic gesture and followed the couple.

Frank watched them go until he got the point that not one of them was going to come back. Then he spun round and went back to the freezer counter, thinking that whatever an elderly couple had unspoken between them was their business. He picked up a couple of frozen pizzas and grabbed a six-pack of beer on his way to the cash desk. Here he paid and then went out.

74

It was evening when Matilde phoned.

He apologised for the empty fridge and promised that next time she would be able to have a proper breakfast in his flat, too. Matilde didn't answer. She was unusually taciturn.

In the end, he asked her straight out: 'What's eating you?'

Well, she was wondering if he could take a few days off.

He considered the suggestion. A couple of days off? Nothing would please him more, he concluded. He could escape from crazy bastards carrying baseball bats. He could queue in Rome at some tourist site or go to the mountains. Go to a spa in Budapest or some other exotic place. The wad of notes he had been given by Snorre Norheim gave him the freedom to forget work for a few days.

'Think I can,' he said. 'I'm free and can do as I like. What's your plan?'

She wanted to go to Tingvoll.

He consulted his geographical knowledge. Nothing. 'Where's Tingvoll?'

'Vestland, between Ålesund and Trondheim.'

'What do you want to do there?'

'I've just found out I have a brother.'

He heard what she said, but couldn't quite digest it.

'Congratulations.' That was the best he could manage.

She giggled. 'Wild, isn't it? He's my half-brother. He and I have the same father. You're the first person I've told. I got a letter today. He's written that he's my brother. He also says he contacted our father a few years ago.'

'That's fantastic. Getting a brother when you're thirty-four.'

'He traced me. He does genealogy. And I can take time off in lieu. I fancy going there. Are you up for a trip?'

'Perhaps we can go via Ulsteinvik?'

'Of course. What are you going to do in Ulsteinvik?'

'It's this *Sea Breeze* story. There's a woman who lives in Ulsteinvik I'd like to talk to, but she rings off when I call.'

He got up at the usual time and went to the window to check if there were any strangers around with malevolent intentions. Everything can become a habit.

There were gaps in the lines of parked cars. The pathway behind them seemed deserted. He fixed his gaze on one of the newly planted trees alongside the path to register, if possible, any sudden movements in his peripheral vision. But he saw only the postman pulling his trolley.

He tore himself away, brewed a cup of coffee and sipped it while packing the essentials in a rucksack. Thinking how wonderful it would be not to give a damn about anything. But he did. He put the memory stick containing the police documents in the rucksack. And packed his laptop. Then he stood by the window wondering what else to take with him so that he didn't lose his grip on his assignments while he was away.

He was by the window when Matilde reversed up in front of the block of flats and hooted her horn – like in a film. He also felt as if he were in a film when, a few minutes later, he dumped his rucksack onto the rear seat beside Petter, who lifted a paw to attract his attention.

Matilde was excited. She was both looking forward to this and dreading it, she said, as they drove through Bryns Tunnel towards Alnabru. There was the sense of freedom you had when setting out on a journey without making any plans for your return. The destination was quite another issue though: family she had never known about and – not least – the prospect of finding out more. What had made her decide to visit them was that her brother wrote that he had contacted their father.

'A letter appears in the post box and it opens a whole new world, a new life. At first I thought someone was taking the piss. But then I saw the family tree in the letter and checked with my mother, and she says it's correct. The man who fathered this guy is my father, too. His name's Simon.'

'Your father?'

'No. My half-brother. The man who wrote the letter. He's a few years older than me.'

'Does he know you're coming?'

'No.'

'Shouldn't you ring to make sure he's at home?'

'No. I don't want to ring. I want to see him when he speaks.'

'What if he isn't at home?'

She glanced at him. 'Try to be a little positive. I have a brother. I can meet my brother and then I might meet my father, too.'

She stretched her arm back to Petter and picked up a pile of CDs, which she handed to Frank. 'You'll have to be the DJ.'

She poked a cigarette in the corner of her mouth and pressed down on the car lighter. A red varnished nail uppermost.

Frank chose blindly from the pile. *Trespass* by Genesis, and soon the voice of Peter Gabriel filled the speakers.

✳

They had been driving for three quarters of an hour when Matilde's phone rang. She lowered the music and put the phone to her ear. After putting it down she had a worried expression on her face.

'Who was it?'

'Guri's aunt. The funeral's on Thursday.'

He fell quiet and so did she. It wasn't going to be a long holiday.

'Do you want to turn back?' he said.

She shook her head. 'Do you?'

'No.'

Matilde turned up the music and put her foot on the accelerator.

<h1 style="text-align:center">2</h1>

When he checked his wristwatch, a little later, he noticed a rattling sound in the casing. He turned down the music. Loosened his watch strap, shook it and listened.

'What's up?' she said.

'There's a weird sound in my watch. There's something loose.'

'But is it working?'

'Yes. What's more, it's accurate.'

She grinned. 'A screw loose in all that sophisticated machinery? Sooner or later the watch's bound to stop.'

*

They decided to drive on the western side of Lake Mjøsa. So they left the motorway at Minnesund, but stopped out of courtesy to let a line of veteran cars leave the petrol station. Matilde, who prided herself on her knowledge, reeled off the makes and models as the vehicles turned onto the road in front of them.

'An A-model Ford, perhaps from around 1930, a Mercedes 300 Adenauer from the mid-fifties, an E-class 280 convertible – the stiff design tells you it's from around 1980; the low-slung job is a Corvette Stingray from the mid-seventies; notice the change to the Volvo saloon from the sixties, and that one, that's cool, a Mercury 1949.'

'David Lindley sings a blues number about it,' he said.

'I've got that CD here,' she said, putting the car in gear, but braked when a last veteran wanted to come out and join the others. It was a Citroën HY van from the late forties.

It looked like a bulldog struggling to keep up.

Matilde joined the line at the back and grinned. 'There we are. We're like a seventeenth of May procession.'

Frank took the pile of CDs and flicked through until he found David Lindley's *El Rayo-X*. Pressed it into the player.

The first kilometres on the west of the lake felt like driving in Vestland. The road was narrow and winding with sudden cuts in the rock down to the water. North of the Skreifjella ridge the countryside opened up into a flat rural region.

On the way between Lena and Gjøvik Frølich nodded off. When he awoke it was because of a pungent smell. It was Matilde steering the car with her knees while varnishing her nails.

'Check out the White Swan,' she shouted, waving her fingers to let the varnish dry. She was right – the paddle steamer *Skibladner* was on its way from Gjøvik northwards.

The veterans bid farewell at the roundabout by Mjøs bridge. Matilde wanted to drive through Østerdalen valley and took a right to the bridge over the lake.

They found the R3 and turned onto it. Almost colliding with a car parked on a bend. Behind the car a man was urinating at the side of the road. He stood with his head bowed as if praying.

It was time to put on a new CD. He took one at random and soon a slow blues was oozing from the speakers.

'Who's singing?'

'Janiva Magness.'

Matilde was hungry. When a roadside inn appeared, she left the road and parked. They went in and sat alone in a sea of spindle-back chairs. The menu informed them that the plat du jour was rissoles, cabbage with white sauce and potatoes. They made do with a couple of bread rolls each. Matilde asked if the Coke was in glass bottles.

No, they had only plastic bottles. Matilde ordered water instead.

'And you?' she asked.

'A beer,' Frølich said.

Afterwards they left the inn and walked down to the river flowing nearby. An idyllic gravel pathway ran alongside the river bank. They followed it under a bridge. When they emerged on the other side, the current slowed. Here the water in the river was still. They left the path and came to a clearing between pine trees where the noise of traffic was only a faint drone far away.

They sat down on the grass and gazed around. He closed his eyes. Her hair tickled his cheek and the sun warmed his neck, as though it was her breathing on him.

'It's hot,' she said.

He opened his eyes and looked at her. 'We're alone.'

'And on holiday,' she said, snuggling closer and fingering his shirt buttons. There was a rustle in the forest. They sat up.

Something white fluttered on the slope above them. Shortly afterwards a bride ran out from between the trees.

3

The bride was holding a bouquet in one hand and raising her dress with the other so as not to trip. She apologised for the disturbance, but she had an appointment with a photographer here.

'Now?'

'In three minutes,' the bride said after consulting a tiny watch on a gold chain around her wrist.

They rearranged their clothing before her entourage arrived. As they drove off, the bride and bridegroom were up to their knees in the water while an apprentice photographer held a white parasol above their heads.

Matilde turned down a less busy route running parallel with the main road. A turn-off appeared, a gravel track leading between the trees.

'After all, we're on holiday.'

The track became tractor ruts leading to a firing range. The convertible swayed like a hammock and the chassis occasionally scraped the ground. A sign said the firing range was private. They drove up to the clubhouse, turned, reversed a few metres and stopped under a birch tree with hanging branches, the leaves almost sweeping against their heads.

This car is a house, he thought, removing his seat belt. It has connections with every part of our lives. When it is scrapped and recycled one day, people's journeys and their forgotten histories, full of life-affirming adventures, will be etched into every single nail that rolls out onto the conveyor belt. In this way our souls will live on in the walls of houses and children's failed carpentry projects.

'What are you thinking about?' she said as she clambered over the console.

'Us and the world.'

He was weighed down by a feeling of shame at having sex in a car in a forest and found it difficult to relax. Not only that, the dog at the back seized every opportunity to lick his ears. However, it was a moment that grew in beauty and strength as the affection they bestowed upon each other produced a special admixture of tenderness and laughter.

Matilde slept with her head on his left shoulder. He sat without moving to avoid waking her, playing with the birch leaves above him and gazing across the valley and the river at the mountain that rose on the opposite side. A nuthatch climbed down the trunk of the birch tree with its head down and tail up. Both he and the dog were watching it.

He reflected on his conversation with Bernt Weddevåg about the fire-stricken ferry. He reflected on Shamal and the colonel who wanted to get in touch with him. These thoughts bothered Frank. Even now, on a trip away from everything, he couldn't quite shrug off the yoke he'd wanted to escape. He could feel a lock of Matilde's hair tickling his neck and tried to deflect his sense of duty and appreciate instead the freedom he now had: the chance to put everyday cares behind him. After many years in the police he had longed for precisely this state of mind. When, late at night, he was dying to go home or simply be somewhere else, but was obliged to be present without knowing what he was really waiting for. Or when lack of sleep made getting through the start of a day as difficult as rowing a boat against the current. How satisfying it had been to say to Matilde on the phone that of course he could go on a trip. There was nothing here to hold him back.

But he wasn't totally free, he reproached himself immediately afterwards. He had mentioned Oda Borgersrud's name when Matilde asked him if he wanted to go with her. He had packed his laptop and his work commitments in his rucksack.

Could he not leave everyday life behind him after all? Or was it the control freak in him that made him want to legitimise the journey to himself, as though a mutinous conscience deep within him still viewed dropping what he was doing as irresponsible? *I'm not leaving everything behind me,* he thought. *I've packed Jørgen Svinland's assignment in my rucksack. Matilde is going to see her brother. I'm going to see Oda Borgersrud.*

∗

Matilde was cold when she woke. She whispered that she didn't want to move because then time would start up again. He reached for her coat on the rear seat and wrapped it around her shoulders.

After a while she began to smile, even though her eyes were closed.

'What is it?'

'My back hurts.'

'So time has started up again?'

She nodded.

4

They passed Rena. Matilde's hair fluttered in the wind and the sun was reflected in her sunglasses. On the stereo there was a song that fitted their surroundings: 'Long Strange Golden Road' by The Waterboys. Matilde told him that her mother's partner also had an old American car, a 1962 Rambler, and that he had just installed a record-player in it.

'An original Norelco Mignon. It plays singles while you're driving, forty-fives, and it doesn't jump. It's absolutely unbelievable. The challenge is to find singles that match the style of the car. Elvis and Jim Reeves and so on, and those discs aren't easy to find.'

When they had reached the village of Stai she asked whether it was alright if they had a little company in the car. He shrugged. He didn't mind and he had an inkling that they were now into her Østerdalen project. She pulled into a bus lay-by, took out her phone and began to text while telling Frank that she knew a guy who lived in Koppang. She informed this Gunnar that she and her 'buddy' were heading for Nordvestland and then he had asked if he could hitch a lift to Dombås.

'Hope he hasn't got a lot of luggage,' Frank said, looking at the back seat. The dog was sitting on the floor, panting, and they had already stowed quite a bit of stuff on the seats.

Soon her phone peeped.

'Gunnar's ready,' she said, throwing her phone into the glove compartment and making a sign. She told him that Gunnar was a musician and she knew him from the time when she tried her luck as a vocalist in a rock band.

'Wow, have you sung in a band?'

'It didn't come to anything. Too much individualism among those guys.'

He leaned back, thinking the road in Østerdalen was made for cruising, with the taiga snow forest and the mighty river as a backdrop. He reached for a cigarette. She kept both hands on the wheel. He poked the filter between Matilde's lips and held her cigarette as she took a drag. The filter was soon smudged with her lipstick.

At Koppang she left the main road and crossed the river Glomma, which formed eddies by the bridge piers.

The guy called Gunnar was waiting for them on a steep hill by Koppangtunet Hotel. He was in his forties, a tall, thin man with a somewhat odd appearance – an already long head was lengthened by a droopy moustache and a much-too-small peaked cap. He was wearing a white shirt and an open, black leather waistcoat over green, *wadmal* trousers secured with braces. On his feet he wore military boots with tightly laced shafts. The footwear made him look like a sculpture on stems. His luggage was an instrument case. He quickly cleared himself a space in the middle of the rear seat and sat down, without treading on the dog.

They drove for a while in embarrassed silence, then Frank Frølich thought he should break the ice. He turned round and asked Gunnar if he was a musician.

5

The passenger leaned forward, planted his elbows on the backs of their seats and said: 'Eh, what?'

Matilde pressed the button that activated the folding soft top. Gunnar had to move his instrument case so that the top slotted into place. And when the silence settled around them and changed the sound of wind and speed to a muted hum, Gunnar said:

'It was wonderful. Jesus, it was wonderful. At that time I was actually doing alright.'

'When was that?'

'When we played together.'

'We rehearsed in a really awful hall in Gamlebyen,' Matilde explained. 'In Fredrikstad.'

'And I was living in Øra. I was living with a dame, Francine. Did you meet her?'

Matilde shook her head.

'She was Canadian and it was, like, just us most of the time. We spoke French and none of my pals did, nor anyone in my family or the block of flats, for that matter. In a way it was the language that bound us together.'

'We practised on Wednesdays,' Matilde explained. 'But we had to give up in the end.'

'Why was that?'

'You tell him,' Matilde said via the mirror to the man in the rear seat.

'I was playing an old Höfner bass,' Gunnar said, 'the same model that Paul McCartney played in The Beatles, and Vidar played a Goldtop, he always did have a load of money, did Vidar, and then there was Leif with his Stratocaster and Matilde on vocals, but I don't know if you caught my drift there: Höfner bass, Fender Stratocaster and a Gibson Les Paul. You're rooted in tradition there. It's the sixties and seventies in a nutshell. But Vidar had a screw loose. In between songs he sat blacking out sentences in the newspaper. "What are you doing?" I asked. "I'm crossing out the sentences I don't like," he said. And then you start wondering. We practised for hours without a drummer. That was also an argument for keeping a low profile, in my opinion. You can't rehearse your self-penned repertoire without knowing how the drums have to sound. In the end, a drummer called Tommy joined us. He had copied the drum kit Keith Moon used on a record The Who released in 1969.'

'The record's called *Tommy*, of course,' Matilde said.

'Right,' Gunnar said. 'Two Premier bass drums, six tom-toms, one snare drum and three floor toms, three cymbals and a hi-hat. It sounded like a stone-crushing plant with a sense of rhythm. The trouble was that you couldn't trust Tommy. He rarely turned up for rehearsals, and then he was hanging around with that woman from somewhere in Gudbrandsdalen, and she was totally off her trolley. I'm not kidding. We could sit there drinking coffee or Coke and then suddenly she'd start howling.'

'Wearing,' Matilde said.

'Tommy died. So that was the end of the band.'

'And you moved to Koppang and I couldn't be bothered anymore.'

The bass player leaned back without responding. Silence enveloped them. All that could be heard was the low, powerful roar of the V-8 as the car floated like a ship through the countryside.

'Can you find a petrol station and stop?' the voice from the rear seat asked. 'I need a leak.'

6

Matilde slowed down and indicated right. 'There's a toilet here,' she said as they drove up the narrow entrance. 'I always stop here when I come this way,' she continued. 'And this time it's a bit special.'

She came to a halt in a car park between the trees. The bass player strolled over to the outside toilet.

Frank followed Matilde down a path between the pines where bare roots clung to rocky ground. Petter ran in front. The dog was jubilant to be able to move at last.

He understood what she meant. Jutulhogget is the closest you can get to the Grand Canyon in Norway. And mindful of the T-bird's relationship with that place, it was undeniably magical to gaze across the immense cleft cut into the rock.

They heard the toilet door close with a bang and Gunnar's footsteps on the gravel as he wandered back to the car and got in.

'He's seen this before,' Matilde said.

'How wide is it?'

'It varies between a hundred and fifty and four hundred metres,' she said. 'The height is between a hundred and two hundred and fifty metres. If I ever commit suicide I'm going to do it here.'

'Did you want to be Thelma or Louise?' he asked.

'Louise,' she said. 'Louise is the strong one. Besides, she loves a cowboy.'

'She lets him down.'

'This isn't a film,' she said, stretching up onto her toes and kissing him on the lips. 'Do you remember The Rubettes? They made a song called "Sugar Baby Love".'

'Remind me how it goes,' he said.

'*Baby, take my advice, if you love someone, don't think twice.*'

He waited for her to go on. She didn't. She was still serious. They walked to the edge. She told him a *jutul*, a giant troll, from Rendalen smashed a hole in the rock to guide the Glomma river through to Rendalen. But at the last minute the Glomsdal *jutul* put a stop to that.

They stretched out on a gently sloping promontory and threw sticks to Petter, who jumped in the air for them, shook his head as though the stick were prey he wanted to kill, then dropped it and waited for the next.

'We have to decide where to sleep,' she said.

He agreed.

'Ålesund,' she said. 'I know someone who lives there. We can sleep over at hers.'

7

After dropping off the bass player at the railway station in Dombås, they drove westwards. The countryside opened up as they passed Lesjaverk. They drove with the sun angling in from the left and a view of the patchwork of humus-rich fields belonging to the farms on both sides of the Rauma, which plummeted in wild cascades on its westerly course. The river was helped down the mountainside by the waterfalls, narrow cataracts that divided into ribbons of water that resembled spilt milk.

Soon the valley tapered and after a while rock face towered up on both sides. They stopped at Trollveggen – the so-called 'troll wall', in the mountain peaks – out of pure curiosity. They walked over to the information boards and studied the climbing routes and a map of the area.

Frank confessed that he had only seen this mountain on TV, the helicopter photos taken by the rescue service that had to salvage dead BASE jumpers caught hanging on the wall.

Matilde said it would be better to throw yourself off without a parachute. 'I don't think you feel it when you hit the ground at that speed. It would be much worse to hang from parachute cords with broken legs and other injuries for hours before you die.'

'I don't think they jump to be killed,' he said.

'They must've thought about it,' Matilde said, pointing to the top. 'You don't jump from up there without having been tempted by the thought of dying.'

They didn't speak for a while. Eventually he noticed she was staring at him. 'What's the matter?' he asked.

'Do you think she's here now?'

'Guri?'

She nodded.

'You mean do I believe her spirit's here?'

'No. Do you believe death isn't the end? Do you believe the dead continue to exist in a reality that is much greater than anything we can absorb?'

'I don't know.'

She smiled, a little dejected. 'No one can know that kind of thing.'

'But you believe it?'

'Music proves it all the time. There are worlds that are much more beautiful than the one we relate to in this life.'

He stood thinking about what she had said. 'So you think she still exists?'

Matilde nodded. 'I don't think death is as stark as it seems to us.'

'Have you seen any signs?'

Matilde nodded. 'I see them all the time.'

8

When they drove into Ålesund it took them a little while to find the house where Nini-Beate and her partner lived. It was at the top of a hill, block-shaped and looked like an arrangement of rectangular steel containers with large windows. It rested on a promontory with a view of the sea.

Matilde said she had known Nini-Beate from the time they both worked in a nail salon in Lillestrøm. Nini-Beate had been much better at it than her; she knew everything about nails and cosmetics and now she ran a blog that provided her with a good income.

'She earns at least as much as her partner, who's a doctor.'

The house canine was a sad-looking, little Tibetan temple dog who answered to the name Doris. Nini-Beate carried Doris in the crook of her arm while Matilde's more experienced best friend sniffed it. Whether the two of them hit it off was hard to say – they occupied opposing corners of the veranda.

Nini-Beate had dyed her hair so blonde it was almost white, she had lip implants and her face was tanned. She walked around in light-blue, faded, torn jeans and a purple knitted jumper that revealed her navel. Her stomach was as nut-brown as her face.

Her partner had to be at least twenty-five years older than her. He appeared to be muscular in a somewhat cramped way, as though he couldn't quite straighten his body. His arms were long. When he moved he seemed to propel his legs by twisting his hips, like a stooped orangutan. His hair was grey and short.

The man's name was Ove Treschow and he showed Frølich around the house while Matilde and Nini-Beate sat on the veranda drinking white wine. Matilde had seen the house before.

The living room was enormous, with a gas fireplace in one corner and large posters on the walls – motif: scantily clad woman at sunset.

'That's Nini-Beate,' Treschow said. 'I do a bit of photography. Just a hobby.'

In the cellar there was a fitness studio with technologically advanced apparatus and a fridge and sunbed. Treschow lay down on a bench with weights and began to do presses.

'Feel at home, do a workout,' he said, discharging intermittent violent pants as the bar rose and fell.

Frank Frølich leaned against the door frame watching him.

After twenty presses his host put the bar on the stand and sat up.

'As I pile on the years I have to keep myself in form,' he said. 'You know, they do have their needs.' He winked. 'Do you want a beer?'

Frank saw no reason to say no.

The host went to the fridge. He took out two bottles of IPA, which he opened with a screwdriver that was on the floor. '*Skål!*'

They drank.

They stood looking at each other.

'So you're a detective?'

He nodded.

'Why does one become a detective?'

Frølich shrugged. 'Because one once worked for the police, stayed there a bit too long and had no skills when one left, other than knowing how to investigate crimes. And you?'

'I'm a doctor. A gynaecologist.'

'Why does one become a gynaecologist?'

'Aesthetics,' the gynaecologist said. 'It's to do with your gaze. Seeing is an art. You say you see a leaf. I ask you what kind of leaf. Is it circular, heart-shaped, elliptical, lobular, jagged, has it got veins, is it green or are there stains of leaf-mould fungus? It's no good just looking. To have a qualitative understanding of the subject, you need to know if you're looking at an oak leaf or a maple leaf, an alder leaf, an aspen leaf or a chestnut leaf. A botanist systematises large parts of his profession according to the shape of the leaf and drawings of the veins. So what has that to do with my job, you might think. Well, the answer is: my gaze focuses on the centre, where we come from, the birthplace, the flesh. The place at which a woman's thighs meet. But it's a gaze that is steeped with expertise. I can see from your expression that you think such an intense interest verges on depravity or perversion. Perhaps it does, perhaps it doesn't. At any rate I can't imagine anything more edifying than studying female genitals. The mystery of the parted lips.'

The gynaecologist put down his bottle, sat on a mat by the wall bars and tucked the tips of his shoes underneath one. Then he did a series of sit-ups.

Finally he lay flat out, gasping for breath.

'There are no finer moments in my profession than undertaking a gynaecological examination,' he said, breathing calmly again. 'When a patient has rested her legs on the stirrups and is lying with them well apart, and she knows I'm looking, and I'm waiting, a little sniff of the nose and I can sense the effect of the wait. Of course, it's different from woman to woman, the smell and the effect of the wait. Some patients come well prepared and perfumed. Many women start to secrete vaginal fluids as I wait. Did you know that I've saved many women from cervical cancer with that tiny fraction of a moment's sniff?'

Frank Frølich shook his head.

'You develop skills in this area. It can be compared with tasting wine. It's the cork, isn't it. You've heard about the smell of corked wine, haven't you? Porn? I've never been interested in seeing others copulate. But show me a woman's crotch when she walks, sits, bends down, not to mention when she does gymnastic exercises, a gymnast doing the splits naked. A psychiatrist I know thinks that what I'm actually doing is searching backwards, he thinks I have a psychotherapeutic problem, that my training, work with and special interest in women's genitals is actually a hunt for the origins of life, a desire to go back to the security of the womb before the world starts making demands on me. We have long discussions about this. He thinks that what I call art history's conspicuous censorship of cunts reflects a normality.'

The gynaecologist stood up.

Frølich took a step back, but hid his reaction by taking a swig of beer.

The gynaecologist donned a pair of boxing gloves hanging on the wall. He began to pound away at a punch bag suspended from the ceiling.

Frølich took another swig, fascinated by the fact that the punch bag didn't move despite all the energy the gynaecologist was investing in his boxing.

At last the gynaecologist was worn out. He stopped and wiped the sweat from his brow with his forearm. 'The fact that Rubens,' he began, but had to rest, wait until he had his breath back. 'The fact that Rubens, Rafael or, for that matter, Titian paint all the details of a face, down to the tiniest wrinkle, while the bit between women's legs is shown without a cleft, without hair and without any detail at all, not so much as a little follicle or a tiny pimple, reflects an unheeded schism of the times. Look at sculptures, look at the works of Rodin, Bernini and Michelangelo; they always have an underdeveloped penis on their sculptures. Imagine it now: they carefully chip the little winkle out of a block of marble, and *nota bene*: the man isn't circumcised. But what do they do with the vagina? Those who aim to copy God by painting or shaping a perfect anatomy, why don't they proceed to the most important bit, the place where God has of necessity to reside, the place from which we all originate? My psychiatrist has formulated a theoretical class approach to this. He asserts the explanation lies in the fact that Michelangelo, Veronese, Tintoretto and all the others were court artists. They never dared risk painting a dick that was bigger than the king's, so the male motif, the penis – regardless of whether it is David, Achilles or Saint Sebastian – is infantile. Whoever they portray is equipped with a small, innocent child's willy. The same applies to women of course, he maintains. The British royal family was, as we know, at times an inbred bunch of deformed cripples. So the beauty of Aphrodite or Helen had to be limited to the face.'

The gynaecologist peeled off his gym gear and went into the adjacent room to shower. Soon Frank heard the murmur of water from inside.

The door opened.

Nini-Beate stood in the doorway. She nodded to her guest, then shouted to her husband: 'Darling!'

'Yes, dear?' came from the shower.

'We haven't got much food in the house. Let's go out to eat.'

9

The gynaecologist led the way this warm summer evening. Frank and Matilde were shown into seats in the back of his Mercedes. They first drove to Fjellstua restaurant in Aksla, where all four of them stood by the railing looking down on Ålesund.

A magenta hemisphere illuminated the sky. The colours shone from the break in the cloud cover. The sky and the buildings were reflected in the surface of the water, which assumed a deeper, reddish-brown hue.

The gynaecologist compared the centre with Manhattan. He claimed that Ålesund's art nouveau style set off the little harbour town below in the same way that the skyscrapers gave an identity to the strip of land between the Hudson and the East River. Once they were back in the car and heading for the town centre, Nini-Beate inserted a CD in the player. A throbbing rock song came from the speakers and Matilde shouted '*No!*' The hosts beamed and looked at Matilde from each of their mirrors.

'It's me,' Matilde told him apologetically. She asked them to switch it off. But the gynaecologist turned it up louder.

Frank liked what he heard. The accompaniment reminded him of The Clash and her voice of Mélanie Pain. 'Cool,' he said. 'Trendy.'

'Don't listen to the lyrics,' Matilde said.

'It's at least four years,' Nini-Beate said, 'since I've done any back-up vocals.'

'Three and a half,' Matilde said.

The gynaecologist turned into a yellow building, a multi-storey car park.

*

Afterwards they strolled along the pavements, two by two, as flashy cars glided by. A wide, low-slung Porsche reminded Frank of a mother goose waddling ahead of a line of stylish Volvos and Opels that had almost sunk down to the tarmac and had spoilers mounted on the back. There were plenty of heads on the rear seats, and hands holding glasses were stuck out of the windows, occasionally a woman's foot with a gold bracelet around the ankle. The slightly older age bracket, women and their escorts, forty, plus or minus, formed queues into venues guarded by muscular men with polished domes. In this throng the gynaecologist was at home. He knew people, stopped and exchanged the odd word with them or patted someone on the shoulder and made a cheery comment. He probably trained with some of the bouncers. As if by magic, all four of them were waved past a queue. A hunk stretched out an arm and accompanied them. Once inside the door the gynaecologist took another initiative. He grabbed a woman dressed in a short, purple skirt and jacket. She tucked a handful of menus under her arm and walked ahead of them on high heels up a staircase to a packed, dimly lit room. At the back, by a window with a view of the harbour there was, strangely enough, a table free. They sat down. Nini-Beate and Matilde by the window, and the gentlemen on the end.

The gynaecologist spoke at length about this restaurant and the town, its history and the importance of fishing in olden times, tourism nowadays, all the famous chefs who had plied their trade in the kitchen here and, not least, the man who was the chef here now. The gynaecologist insisted that the man had been awarded Michelin stars in Oslo. Now it would soon be Ålesund's turn.

Frølich felt like an extra in someone else's fantasy. He was worn out after the drive and didn't quite catch the topics of their small talk, but nodded and alternated between 'oh, yes' and 'mhm' and 'aha'.

The gynaecologist ordered for everyone. Baked halibut, Hasselback potatoes and other stuff, trimmings with French names. The gynaecologist went to town choosing the wine. He ended up with an apparently very special Riesling, a prize vintage that came from a select cellar in Alsace. He held the glass to the light and lectured on the minerals he could taste on different parts of his palate. Frølich would have preferred a beer, but played the role of guest, as expected, accepted the Riesling in the glass and praised it, as expected.

Otherwise, the conversation traversed Swedish waiters and other immigrants, the war in the Middle East, terrorist attacks and what the gynaecologist saw as the more or less successfully staged comedies of life, and hence the world.

The two ladies wanted a dessert and gave a squeal of pleasure when they saw chocolate fondant on the menu. The gynaecologist had a brandy with his coffee. Frank Frølich politely declined. After Nini-Beate had pecked away at the fondant, a thick stripe of chocolate oozing out on to her plate, she leaned forward to Frølich and said in a low voice:

'Rita Torgersen's here.'

'Who's Rita Torgersen?'

'She's an MP in Stortinget, on the justice committee. I know she was involved in a small way with the case.' She glanced over at Matilde. 'The ferry you were talking about.'

'The *Sea Breeze*,' Matilde said.

'I'll ask her over,' the gynaecologist said. 'I know Rita. She's a patient.'

10

Frank wanted to protest, but the gynaecologist was already up and winding his way between tables. He stopped, bent at the hip, stood with his upper body at right angles and whispered something in the ear of a woman sitting at a table closer to the stairs. She was in her early forties and wore a cream-coloured dress, white gloves and an equally cream-coloured hat on her head. She stood up. The gynaecologist held his hands around her waist and guided her to the table.

'Here, take my chair,' he said.

The woman sat down. A wave of perfume wafted across the table.

Nine-Beate gasped. 'Bright Crystal. That's top of my list!'

Rita Torgersen shook her head. 'Troi L'impératrice. I take turns. Well, you may be right,' she said, reading Nini-Beate's sceptical eyes. 'It could be Versace this evening.'

The head waitress came with an extra chair for the gynaecologist, who sat at the end of the table and introduced everyone.

'What would you like?' he said to Rita Torgersen.

'Nothing, my kind friend,' she said. 'I have to be quick.' Then she settled her eyes on Frølich: 'I hear you're an investigator and knew Fredrik Andersen.'

Frank Frølich nodded.

'So what do you think?' she said.

'About what?'

'About the murder of Andersen.'

Nini-Beate broke in. 'He's investigating to see if there are any links with the *Sea Breeze* catastrophe.'

Rita Torgersen looked at him without saying a word.

Frølich felt a need to explain. 'Andersen wrote a book.'

'I know,' she said. 'I knew Fredrik.'

'So what do *you* think?' Frølich asked.

A waiter came, poured wine and removed the empty plates from the table.

Rita Torgersen rested her forearms on the table cloth and leaned forward. 'I think Fredrik realised he was tilting at windmills and took the consequences. The Norwegian public will forget the *Sea Breeze*. Why can I say that? Well, the catastrophe took place in 1988. The years pass. Criticism rains down on the police. There are no fewer than four calls for a new investigation. Every single time the call is rejected, in a classically arrogant way. Conspiracy theories abound. Rumours abound that the fire was a giant insurance scam and so on. The police and the DPP have to take all this criticism for years unabated. Then comes the twenty-second of July 2011 – one solitary right-wing terrorist manages to blow up the government quarter, then shoots down sixty-nine youths on Utøya, the police powerless to do anything to stop it. They are seen to be a collection of incapable boneheads. And then, after all this humiliation, along comes Fredrik with his book. He rattles on – once again – about how incompetent the Norwegian police can be. The *Sea Breeze*. Arson and murder. One hundred and fifty-nine people killed and an investigation that didn't bear scrutiny. A police force that accuses one of the victims of being behind the mass murder, without a scrap of evidence. In other words, Fredrik succeeded once again in dragging the police through the mire. You can understand that the main actors in the police were furious. It was obvious what would happen when the police were finally ordered to investigate the case afresh.'

'What did you think would happen?'

'They would tell all and sundry that they had *not* failed when the crime took place.'

This answer surprised him. He hadn't expected that an important politician would be so outspoken in her assessment of the police role in this case.

'And Stortinget appointed a committee to investigate,' he said.

'Yes, and I know the committee struggled to find candidates for
the inquiry. In the end they managed to round up some public
employees and a few from the civil service. Not even my grandmother's dog would've trusted such a gang of system-loyal toadies.
The chairman alone is a huge joke. I know him. Ole Franzen, a
judge at Nordmøre district court.'

She looked at the gynaecologist. 'He's from Kristiansund, so you
know what I mean.'

Frank Frølich didn't understand.

'Ålesund, Molde and Kristiansund,' the gynaecologist explained.
'There's a bit of rivalry between them.'

'Aha.'

'When the committee was finally ready,' Rita Torgersen
continued, 'they got hold of two retired Kripos detectives to report
back. These guys were pals with the officers who'd investigated the
case in 1988 and were also chums with the officers who'd cleared
the force in the following round. These two started their work by
establishing that everything the police had done so far was correct.
The committee ordered reports from experts. But if they were
unlucky and received a report criticising the police version of the
tragedy, they immediately ordered a counter-report – even before
they'd started to tremble in their shoes. So when the committee
finally presented its report, it was fundamentally a carbon copy of
the police's own review. But this carbon copy would be difficult to
serve up without the right garnishes. Everyone knew that. The
committee decided to present the report inside Stortinget. So my
old friend from Kristiansund was able, without fear of contradic-
tion, to refer to the mass murder as an "accident". He proclaimed
physical laws that didn't exist. Newton and Galileo would've been
on their backs, laughing hysterically if they'd heard him. But this
wasn't Newton and Galileo's arena, if you know what I mean. The
Sea Breeze had become political. The Norwegian media didn't see
this as street theatre. They didn't even see an emperor without
clothes; the media saw a clean-shaven gentleman in nice clothes
who spoke in the Norwegian Parliament. The reaction from the

press is bound to be a subject for a research project at some point
in the future. You've heard of self-fulfilling prophecies, I'm sure.
We're talking here about a session that summarised two police investigations and one parliamentary inquiry as well. The prophecy
was simple enough: there in parliament, the conclusion would be
perceived of as the truth, regardless of what was said. So the
collected press would report on the speech as though they had heard
God's voice in the wilderness. This was how the sea tragedy was
downgraded from being a national trauma to a private affair of the
bereaved. The press's summary was that there had been no limit to
the state's exertions to fulfil the wishes and needs of the survivors
and bereaved. And now the cup was full. Even the tabloid leaders
declared that now the survivors and bereaved should shut up and
be happy. No one who observed this could do anything about it –
Fredrik Andersen included. He realised the general public could
live without the case of the *Sea Breeze* being resolved, in the same
way that the USA had accepted the unsolved murder of Kennedy
and Sweden was fine with the unsolved murder of Olof Palme.'

Frank Frølich was still impressed. Nevertheless he had to ask:
'But where are you in all this?'

'Me?'

Frølich nodded. 'You have your analysis. You're a politician. You
have power. What are you doing about this case?'

'Nothing.'

He remained quiet.

'As you yourself said, I'm a politician. I've come to the same realisation as Fredrik Andersen. Screaming and shouting about the *Sea
Breeze* is a lost cause now. If you've been cheeky enough to tape
this conversation, there's no point. When I leave this table, I'll have
forgotten I met you. This evening doesn't exist in my memory any
longer.' She looked up, in mock confusion: 'What, me? Don't
know him from Adam, guv.'

Matilde grinned.

Frank felt a need for more clarity though. He said: 'You say this
is a lost cause now. When will something happen?'

'I don't know. Something may happen. Something will happen. You just have to wait.'

'You want to wait, but you don't know what you're waiting for, do you?'

'At school you might've learnt what Bismarck said: "Anyone who sees how sausages and politics are made will never have a good night's sleep again." My experience is a little different. Politics is to a large extent all about timing – waiting for the right time and the right place.'

Frølich wasn't quite as impressed as before. 'It's perhaps not so surprising that Andersen realised that the battle was lost,' he said, 'when those sitting with real power and an understanding of the case take that attitude.'

Rita Torgersen glanced over her shoulder.

Frølich raised both eyebrows.

'I was just wondering who you were talking to,' she said.

Matilde grinned.

'There are those who believe that Fredrik Andersen was killed because of the book he wrote about the *Sea Breeze*,' Frølich said.

She shook her head. 'That's rubbish anyhow.'

'Why are you so sure of that?'

'Today the *Sea Breeze* can best be compared with the trial in Kafka's world or the inheritance running through *Bleak House* by Dickens. You almost need a degree in economics and marine engineering to keep the distinct threads apart. What Fredrik Andersen wrote or didn't write about the *Sea Breeze* is of absolutely no significance.'

She got up. 'Please excuse me,' she said. 'But I have a date and he's waiting.'

The gynaecologist stood up at once. He grabbed her arm and gave her a hug that could only be characterised as warm.

'Of course, Rita.'

He stayed on his feet and watched her for a few seconds admiringly. 'Fantastic woman,' the gynaecologist said. 'Fantastic patient.'

11

He woke up early the next morning and looked straight into the face of Nini-Beate. Her face was four times bigger than the previous evening. She smiled with tense jaw muscles and had both nipples pierced. He closed his eyes and opened them again – reassured. She was on a poster he hadn't noticed when they went to bed the night before.

He lay back and thought about the conversation with Rita Torgersen, the Stortinget politician who insisted that the *Sea Breeze* was a lost cause.

What would Jørgen Svinland be able to achieve, he thought, if he was able to locate Fredrik Andersen's mysterious eyewitness – Ole Berg. What difference would one eyewitness report make, one way or the other? Would it create a stir at all?

If it turned out that Oda Borgersrud was indeed the mysterious Ole Berg, and if he managed to get the woman to talk, so what?

There's no so what, he thought immediately afterwards. *You've taken on a job for Jørgen Svinland. The job is to locate a person. You have to find her, clarify whether she might be Andersen's source and then write a report. The job stops there.*

Or would it?

He wasn't ready to answer that question at this juncture.

*

He let Matilde sleep. Fetched his rucksack and opened the laptop he had brought with him. Sat on the sofa with it on his knees. Googled the judge Rita Torgersen had mentioned.

There were lots of hits. But it was interesting that many of the hits were recent and referred to the *Sea Breeze*.

He set about isolating the older hits. There were barely any. An early hit was a photograph of a family meeting in Surnadal. It was a picture of a big group of people in a farmyard. Several of them were wearing national dress. Another hit was a ten-year-old public document. It concerned Ole Franzen's appointment to the post of judge. There was a hit from Facebook that was just as old. The local community wished him luck with his new job. There was also, more recently, an open letter in the press in which the judge informed local politicians that there was a danger of queues forming at the law court. In other words, Frank Frølich calculated, feeling that he had drawn on his deepest prejudices: Ole Franzen had come from nowhere. He was a judge with an unmerited promotion brought in to lead a parliamentary inquiry. The *Sea Breeze* had placed Ole Franzen at the centre of the media frenzy for one day – the one day when the committee published its report. However, there were hundreds of hits about this one occasion. Photographs of the judge, Ole Franzen, who read the committee's conclusions in Stortinget, and various newspapers' reports of the review. In Norway, Denmark and Sweden.

Could it be so simple?

A state-employed drudge is appointed in a government meeting. He sees his golden chance. Swims with the tide. Cheers on the strongest, and afterwards waits like an obedient poodle for a titbit from the bosses.

Could it *really* be so simple?

Frank Frølich had worked for the police himself. He knew the organisational structure inside out, for better or worse. He had no problems with prejudging this case. The committee's servile attitude could actually be ascribed to arse-licking and good old-fashioned cowardice. An obvious question was whether it was conceivable that an unknown judge, with no career to speak of, with no profile, could be promoted and stand in the breach to reprimand firstly Oslo Police District – the biggest and the most influential in the whole country – and secondly Norway's DPP – the judge's most senior boss and possible model – in a public report. Conceivable? Feasible?

Irrespective of whether the committee's servility was down to cowardice or partisan obedience, the system, which the committee had tried to satisfy, hadn't yet rewarded the chairman. Franzen was still a judge in Nordmøre.

Had he perhaps had time to turn bitter?

Frank continued to search. It turned out that the Nordmøre law court was in Kristiansund. That wasn't far away. It would be possible to pay him a call now that he was up here.

But it wasn't long until Guri's funeral. If he wanted to visit the judge he would have to be quick. Could he fit in a call today?

12

He lifted his head from the screen. Glanced at Matilde, who was still sound asleep. Why was he so preoccupied by this? Why not just accept that the judge was sitting on the key to what happened that night in 1988?

He pondered the question. Was there an answer? At least there were photographs. The ones he had seen at Bernt Weddevåg's. A man weighing ninety kilos burned down to nothing. A woman with a shrunken skull and charred body in a cabin where there hadn't been a single flame.

The Gordian knot in this case was the extreme injuries suffered by the victims. The investigators had deftly skirted the issue of the inexplicable devastation. Could this kind of inquiry be deemed satisfactory?

If he was going to talk to the judge, he had better be well prepared.

But was he primarily interested in satisfying his own curiosity or making progress with his work? He didn't know. Nor was he sure he wanted to know the answer to his question.

At any rate it wouldn't hurt to read up a bit more.

He went through his rucksack, looking for the memory stick containing Andersen's research material. Plugged in his laptop and began to scour the documents.

*

Matilde woke up an hour later.

He rubbed his eyes and packed away his laptop.

Matilde went to the veranda door, let Petter out and stood

looking at the sky and the sea. She established that the good weather was over.

And she was right. The clouds were thick and grey and were shifting towards an ominously black band on the horizon.

They set the table for breakfast. They had the kitchen to themselves, brewed coffee and ate rolled oats with kefir as they stared across the sea and spoke in low voices so as not to wake their hosts.

'We said goodbye to them last night, didn't we,' Matilde said. 'Besides, they like to sleep in when they're on holiday. Who doesn't?'

The dogs wanted to be fed. Petter was obedient and lay on the floor, waiting. Doris was more demanding. She started barking.

Frank picked up Doris in his hand and gently tossed her out onto the veranda. She turned around and stood in front of the glass door with a shocked expression in her eyes.

He filled the Thermos with coffee.

It had just turned nine when they cruised out of Ålesund, heading for the ferry terminal at Vestnes. Matilde left the folding top on and the first raindrops pitter-pattered on the windscreen. This was a trip when the windscreen wipers would provide the music for the day.

They were in a silent, pensive mood, both of them.

'What are you thinking about?'

'What the politician woman we met yesterday said. What are you thinking about?'

'My new brother.'

From a distance they could see the ferry waiting with open doors as they drove along the E39 to the quay. By the time they arrived, the boat had left. But they were at the front of the queue and would get a place on the next one.

Matilde seemed tense. She said: 'I'm dreading this.'

Frank said that was understandable.

'Will you come in with me?'

That was up to her.

She asked him what he thought was best.

'As you've asked, I think I'd meet him alone first,' he said. 'Anything can happen. But it's an important moment and actually quite private. I guess you'll sense if you want to have someone around you or not. But it'll be a bit late if I'm already with you. It'll be much easier alone at first. You can just open the door and wave me in if you need to. If you feel it really is best to stay alone with your brother, you can relax and leave me outside.'

'What will you do if I decide I don't need you?'

'The judge Rita Torgersen was talking about lives in Kristiansund. He's the chairman of the parliamentary committee. It's not far from Tingvoll.'

Matilde rolled down the side-window and sat smoking as the ferry glided in. The ticket man came over, a middle-aged guy wearing a green reflective vest and a sou'wester on his head. He had braided his beard in such a way that it tapered and stuck out from his chin. While they were waiting for the payment terminal to work he studied the convertible. He said he was a member of NRKK – the Nordmøre and Romsdal veteran car club – and had a sixty-eight Mustang GT, the same model Steve McQueen drives in *Bullitt*.

Matilde didn't answer. Usually she would have been keen to contribute to this kind of conversation. They had seen the film together twice and both of them liked the car chases in and out of San Francisco. But now she was staring into the distance without saying a word.

The ticket man said he also had a 1966 VW Beetle cabriolet, which he used for driving bridal couples to church. He added that he hired himself out as a chauffeur and wore a dinner jacket, before a ring of the ferry bell hurried him on to the next car in the queue.

13

Above them the clouds were beginning to open.

After they had driven on board, the sun came out. They left Petter in the car and went up onto the top deck. Below them a

tourist coach rolled onto the ferry at the last minute. An army of
Japanese tourists flocked around the T-bird and took selfies
alongside it. Scenes like this used to put Matilde in a good mood.
Now her chin was set and she seemed tense.

'Shall I drive afterwards?' he asked.

'Why?'

'You seem to have a lot on your mind.'

'No. It's fine.'

The ferry set off. They went into the saloon and bought a griddle
cake each.

He poured himself a cup of coffee from the flask by the cash
desk. The coffee was black and bitter. He surveyed the passengers
around him. The coffee-drinkers were the older guard. They were
laughing and gulping down coffee as if it were spring water.

The ferry put to at Molde. They drove on to Tingvoll. Matilde
was becoming more and more nervous. Frank found a map on his
mobile and gave instructions as best he could.

They passed the blue sign announcing their arrival in Tingvoll
and branched off shortly afterwards by a shop. From here they
carried on along a narrow road with a view of the fjord. Cars, a
horse trailer and a number of caravans were parked along the verge.

'There,' he said, pointing.

Matilde seemed quite stiff as she stopped the car below a grey,
prefabricated house with a veranda above a high cellar wall. A lawn
with no plants stretched from the lower side of the house down to
the cutting towards the road where thistles, mugwort and other
weeds grew.

'This is where he lives,' said Matilde, as though she had to
convince herself. 'It's the right number,' she continued in the same
flat tone. 'Sure you don't want to come in?'

He looked up at the sky, which was now quite blue and cloud-
free. 'I'll wait until you've decided. If you can manage on your own,
I'll go to Kristiansund. It'll take fifty minutes each way. That would
mean you would have to put up with your family for three hours
max.'

She nodded. 'If it's too much, I'll go for a walk with the dog.'

She got out. The dog jumped after her. They walked side by side across the lawn.

Matilde was nervous, that was clear to see. And who wouldn't be, he thought, as he watched the slight figure crossing the grass to the front door.

She rang the bell.

It took time. She turned to him and seemed more dispirited and anxious than ever.

Then the door opened. She turned round and walked in. He prepared for the wait. But was soon woken by a sharp whistle. He looked up. Matilde was on the veranda and waving him to go.

14

Driving this T-bird was like sitting in an armchair and steering a boat. The bonnet was like a ship's bow, a long way off, and after setting off he caught himself wishing the narrow road alongside the fjord was one-way. It wasn't. He first met a tractor pulling a trailer, then a car with a caravan. These incidents were baptisms of fire. By the time he swung out onto the main road he felt as at home with the car as he had as a passenger.

John Fogerty was on the stereo. Fogerty was a working man, a guy in a flannel shirt and jeans with a career full of adversity, a guy it was easy to root for and identify with.

The worst part of the route was a five-kilometre stretch in a tunnel beneath Kvernesfjord between the islands of Bergsøya and Flatsetøya. Fogerty sang 'Lodi' while Frank tried not to get claustrophobia – and consoled himself with the fact that the drive was faster than the ferry.

What bothered him most was the uncertainty about this whole venture. He didn't know what he hoped to achieve by talking to the judge. This short trip was a long way from the assignment Jørgen Svinland had given him.

But it wouldn't stop with finding Fredrik Andersen's mysterious source, he thought by way of an excuse. It was about gaining the necessary perspective over something much bigger. Something that concerned him personally to a great degree. *Two people are dead. They were killed and someone is after you. In this chaos the Sea Breeze tragedy has a role to play. You owe it to yourself to find out what that role is.*

The courthouse in Kristiansund was in the same building as the police station, a square block by the shore of Storsundet with a view of the marina and a hotel on the other side.

He went in, with the clammy feeling he always had when there was a chance he might bump into ex-colleagues. He knew it was irrational, but it was tied to a deep sense of shame. He had been the subject of gossip in Oslo. Now he was five hundred kilometres away. But the police could be like some teachers. They moved around the national network. So there was a probability that he would meet ex-colleagues here. However, the probability calculation was proved wrong. He walked into the courthouse without meeting a single colleague.

He stood in front of the information board, searching for the name of the judge. At that moment a man came running down the stairs. He rounded Frølich and disappeared down the corridor, his jacket flying. Could that be Franzen? There was a certain similarity. The man was bald and he wore a dark suit and was obviously in a hurry.

A teenage boy was at the reception desk. He was passing the time playing an internet game on a tablet. The boy looked up. His fringe fell over his eyes and in a movement worthy of a diva he tossed it back. It stayed in place nicely.

Frølich asked after Franzen.

The receptionist put the tablet on his lap and rang the intercom. Another toss of the head. 'He isn't answering.'

The receptionist put down the phone and went back to his computer game.

Should he give up so easily? After all, he had driven quite a few kilometres to speak to the judge. He could wait, and was about to inform the receptionist that he would, when the man in a hurry returned. Now he was carrying a paper plate with a waffle on it. On top there was a blob of cream with some red jam.

'Franzen,' the receptionist said.

The man stopped with one foot on the lowest step of the staircase.

'Someone asking after you,' the receptionist said.

Franzen, foot poised, looked from the waffle to Frølich and back. The plate bearing the waffle was the man's main focus at this moment.

'I'll be brief,' Frølich said.

Franzen asked him what he wanted.

Frølich tried to suggest a need for discretion with an eloquent glance at the boy and back again.

Franzen gave a sigh that came from the heart. 'My office.'

15

He followed the judge up the stairs. The shadow at the back of his head and above his ears showed that the judge shaved his head to cover up his increasing hair loss.

Inside Franzen's office there was a bare desk, apart from a photograph of himself and one of the committee he had chaired, all wearing broad smiles for the photographer.

Franzen placed the plate on the blotting pad. 'Had to be out of the blocks quickly,' he explained. 'It's waffles day today and they're popular.'

He rubbed his hands. 'In ten minutes the bowl in the canteen will be empty.'

'Don't mind me. It looks good.'

Franzen smiled stiffly. 'What's this about?'

Frank Frølich introduced himself. Private investigator, working for the surviving relatives of Fredrik Andersen.

Franzen couldn't wait. He tore off one of the waffle hearts, dipped it in the jam and cream and put all of it in his mouth.

'A writer who died recently.'

The man chewed and swallowed. 'I know Andersen.'

Frølich felt the time was right to ask the judge if he had chaired the parliamentary committee investigating the *Sea Breeze*.

Franzen grimaced as he swallowed. 'Yes,' he said at length, and after a cough to make his voice carry. He seemed genuinely surprised by the banality of the question. He gazed down at the plate, considered another waffle heart, but refrained. Instead, he said that the committee was authorised to examine how far Stortinget had been fully informed of the case.

Frølich nodded. He had read up on that. 'Fredrik Andersen wrote a book about the catastrophe, as you know.'

The judge did know and nodded. He eyed the waffle again, succumbed and took another heart. Bit more cream this time. He chewed.

'And you – the committee, that is – concluded that everything was fine and dandy the night fire broke out on the boat,' Frølich said, knowing his words had come out wrong.

He tried to be more explicit: 'I mean, the fire broke out of its own accord, people died as victims of unfortunate circumstances and nothing mysterious happened on board before the boat was ablaze or while the wreck was being towed later?'

The shape of Franzen's masticating jaws changed as he listened. This was an irritated judge. He swallowed, coughed and swallowed again, then he spoke up.

'You use different words from those I would've chosen, but essentially that is correct.'

'You didn't discuss the extent of the victims' injuries?'

'We discussed those that were relevant to discuss.'

Frølich raised both eyebrows, but the judge considered it unnecessary to add anything.

'Weren't the injuries relevant to the committee?'

Franzen took a deep breath. But no response was forthcoming.

'Surely there's little chance of discovering what happened if you don't thoroughly examine the deceased?'

Frølich paused. But the judge had nothing to add.

'You had three expert reports concerning the fire.'

'That's correct,' Franzen said, pushing the waffle hearts to the side.

Frølich had his full attention.

'You had one report commissioned by the DPP. This was carried out by the same two investigators who studied the fire in 1988.'

Franzen nodded.

'So they investigated themselves?'

'Those are your words.'

'You commissioned an independent report afterwards. This report slammed the first. The new one concluded that someone carried out sabotage while the ferry was being towed.'

'Sounds as if you've read up on the case,' Franzen said.

'But then you commissioned a third, which forms the basis of the committee's review.'

'That's correct.'

'Why?'

'Because we were stuck with two reports that contradicted each other.'

'So you regarded the two reports as of equal value? You didn't have any doubts about the first?'

'Why should we have?'

'The writers of the report were, as I said, investigating themselves.'

Franzen didn't answer. He contented himself with a shake of the head.

'As I told you, I'm working for Fredrik Andersen's relatives,' Frølich said. 'They maintain that the writers of the third report are unqualified to comment on ships or fires on ships.'

'I find that hard to credit,' Franzen said.

'I did, too, so I went to the trouble of checking the company's areas of expertise on their website. You can do the same yourself. The company has its own portal for its competencies. I'm not lying.'

Franzen looked from him to the waffle hearts and back again.

'What could be the reason for your decision to base the committee's conclusions on a report from individuals who do not have the expertise required to pen this report?'

Frank thought: *I should have been a journalist.*

'The question is tendentious, and I see no reason to reply to tendentious questions.'

'This company's report is dated the twenty-fifth of May. You presented the committee's findings a week later, on the first of June. The findings cover two hundred and fifty pages. Was all this written in six days?'

'Of course not.'

'So how was it possible to write such a comprehensive account based on a report that was only a week old?'

'The committee worked for many months and we took a stance on much more than sabotage claims in our findings.'

'Yes, but the reason the committee was appointed was that certain facts had come to light that suggested certain crew members had sabotaged the firefighting efforts and lit new fires. And when your committee rejected this, you based your rejection on a report that came out a week before the press conference.'

'We based our findings on the best picture of events.'

'How's that possible?'

'How is what possible?'

'How's it possible for a report to give the best picture of events when the authors don't have the necessary expertise?'

Franzen gritted his teeth. When he did finally open his mouth it was to pose a question:

'What is the mandate of your investigation?'

'Mandate?'

'Are you preparing an application for the case to be reopened on behalf of the survivors and bereaved?'

Frølich refrained from answering that question. He had no remit beyond finding a person who may not exist. He saw no reason to tell the judge that.

Franzen angrily pulled the waffle plate closer.

'If so, it's a waste of time,' he said. 'There's no point. The police investigated the matter again after orders from the DPP. An enormous amount of resources was used to satisfy the survivors and the bereaved.'

He folded the last waffle hearts into a thick sponge cake with jam and cream oozing out from the sides. He took a mouthful. Smacked his lips and chewed. He was an efficient eater. Allowing nothing to go to waste, not the jam and not the cream. But his jaws had to work on the goodies. And while he was chewing, he clearly felt the need to defend himself. He wiped his mouth with the back of his hand and – still chomping – said:

'The police shelved the case for the second time after extensive work, which went on for months.' He swallowed. 'Stortinget commissioned the Franzen committee, which also formulated its conclusions based on a thorough report with several thousand pages of enclosures. To take on the job you're doing is cynical, brainless and almost dishonest.'

He took another mouthful. Leaned over the plate as the pink mixture of jam and cream dripped from the waffle.

Frølich watched the man finish eating. He had to smile.

'What's so funny?' Franzen said, holding his fingers in the air and looking for something to wipe them on.

'I don't have any such mandate.'

Franzen fell quiet, somewhat bewildered. Only for a moment though. As he straightened his back he regained his judiciary authority. 'I have a meeting in a few minutes.'

16

Frank Frølich understood. He nodded. 'Good luck,' he said, turning his back on the man and leaving.

Everyone seems to be agreed in this case, he thought on his way out of the building. Rita Torgersen was right. The press, the police and the investigators were playing on the same team. They had scaled down the catastrophe to a private matter, one which only concerned the survivors and the bereaved. And the same three authorities – the press, the police and the investigators – were sick to death of these survivors and bereaved.

How could this go so wrong? he thought, and could feel himself getting angry on Jørgen Svinland's behalf.

But that was definitely a waste of time, it struck him at once. *You are starting to feel some sympathy for Jørgen Svinland. It is pointless.* Fredrik Andersen finished with the *Sea Breeze* when he wrote his book. The day before he was murdered he was with Sheyma Bashur and Guri Sekkelsten. The reason for his murder probably had nothing to do with this old ferry tragedy. *Your assignment on this trip is to talk to Oda Borgersrud. Jørgen Svinland is paying you to find her and talk to her. Do your job.*

17

Tingvoll church turned out to be a towering twelfth-century stone structure set imposingly in the countryside behind a wall with a gate. Matilde was sitting on the wall beside the gate when he arrived. She was holding Petter on the lead. She and the church complemented each other. It was an attractive church. He got out of the car.

They stood with smiles on their faces.

'Come on,' he said. 'Tell me.'

'He's forty-six, twelve years older than me. He's a musician. In real life he's been a welder at a shipyard, but he got COPD three years ago. Then he stopped smoking, but now he's on sick leave. He's divorced and has a daughter of eight who lives with her mother. He lives alone and has a cat called Tormod. Even Petter and the cat liked each other.'

'I infer you got on?'

'Great guy. He's a guitarist with a lot of jazz in his record collection. Biggest one I've ever seen. But when it comes to rock and pop I think he likes Elton John, the Eagles and that sort of stuff. Not exactly my style.'

'Did he say if he has any more brothers or sisters?'

'No. It's just us two. He wanted to meet you, but he had to go to Sunndalsøra and pick up his daughter. Do you want to drive?' she said, getting in.

*

They headed south. The wind tousled Matilde's hair as she sat back in her seat, pensive. The sun vanished behind a hill, reappeared and hung above a dip in the terrain, dark red, like the crater of a volcano.

'Did you make any plans?'

'He's coming with his daughter to visit in a few weeks.'

'What did he say about your father?'

'He couldn't say much. They almost met four years ago.'

'Almost?'

'Simon discovered where our father lived. He'd been very discreet. Rang him and said who he was and that he didn't want to bother him or anything. He just wanted to meet up. Said he had a daughter, in other words, our father had a grandchild. It'd been a very nice chat. And Dad had been interested and curious, and then they agreed to meet. This was in Gjøvik.'

Matilde pushed in a CD. *America. A Horse with No Name.*

She opened the glove compartment, rummaged around and took out her raindrop-shaped sunglasses, put them on and searched for the pack of cigarettes that was also there. She put a cigarette in the corner of her mouth. A flick of a sparkwheel told Frank she had ignited the lighter. She held it in front of her, lit up and settled back, rapt in thought.

'Yes, and?' Frank said, keen to know more. 'They met?'

She shook her head. 'He didn't show up. So Simon drove to our father's home, but the flat was empty. He'd moved.'

She smoked in silence behind her sunglasses.

'Where had he moved to?'

'Simon didn't know. Possibly Sweden or Denmark. There's no one living in Norway under his name, anyway.'

Frank sent her a quick glance. Sunglasses, red lips and fluttering hair.

'Gone,' she said. 'Like a badger out of hibernation. Simon thinks he simply upped sticks and left.'

'How do you feel about that?'

She stroked his hand. 'I think I'm going to find him. And maybe I can learn a few detective tricks from you.'

18

It was early evening when they drove into Ulsteinvik.

Now it was Matilde's turn to ask if he wanted to go in alone or not.

He flashed her a smile. 'You're an assistant in my interpretation of this trip. Don't forget, I'll be putting you on my expenses.'

With that he accelerated up the hill. The revs attracted attention the whole way. People who were having barbecues in the good weather stood up and spied over their hedges. At the top there was quite a large camper van wedged between a low house and a carport. He stopped by the camper van. The house was white and single storey with a hipped roof and a veranda extension. The people who lived there were spoiled with a wonderful view over the sea.

They didn't need to ring the bell. A woman in her fifties, wearing a pink tracksuit with light-blue stripes, had heard them and opened the door.

'Oda Borgersrud?'

The woman nodded, a little confused. She had short, curly henna-ed hair, an attractive face and a quizzical expression in her eyes.

'Frank Frølich,' he said. 'We talked on the phone.'

At that moment a jolly-looking man with a grey beard and fringe strolled around the corner. He was also wearing a pink tracksuit with light-blue stripes.

The man said his name was Roger.

Frank Frølich repeated his own name, introduced Matilde and explained that he worked for Fredrik Andersen's relatives.

The couple exchanged glances upon hearing the writer's name. But neither of them made a comment.

Roger invited them around the house onto a large terrace with decorative flowerpots and an eating area. A table was set for two. On the barbecue there was a fish wrapped in aluminium foil. Frank said they could come back later. But Roger replied: 'Under no circumstances.' They didn't often have guests and they had enough fish. This was Vestland.

He took two extra chairs from the terrace shed while Oda Borgersrud announced that she would get some more fish. Roger opened a bottle of beer bearing an exotic label. Matilde was quick to respond: '*You* have it, Frankie. I'll drive.'

'And for you?' Roger asked Matilde. 'A Coke?'

'Is it in a glass bottle?'

'Of course.'

Roger said he was a retired ship's steward and had worked a lot around Newfoundland and the great lakes. He plied between Saint John's and Toronto for many years. He had learned to appreciate the real McCoy over there and never drank Coke from anything except a glass bottle. 'Besides, it's an environmental thing,' he added, taking a bottle from a cooler bag by the veranda door. Then he showed them around the terrace and pointed across the sea to the view:

'What you can see there is Kleven shipyard, and that's the island of Peholmen and that's Nordre and South Kloholmen there, and beyond them Skarveskjeret.'

He explained that he and Oda took a dinghy from Rana Plast, the boat builders, when they went fishing. He also pointed out places to fish with odd-sounding names and mentioned other places further away that were only visible on the clearest days.

Frank Frølich struggled to follow. He was focused on the wife, who arrived with a salmon fillet, which she spiced with herbs and wrapped in foil before putting it on the barbecue. He was almost a hundred per cent sure she was the Ole Berg that Jørgen Svinland and Bernt Weddevåg had talked about. However, he was unsure how to go about his assignment in this situation.

Later, when they were sat around the table eating barbecued pollock, and salmon with barbecued potatoes and steamed root vegetables in butter, it didn't feel natural to bring up the issue, either. All four of them sat chatting as though they had known each other for years. Matilde told them about her new brother in Tingvoll. Roger wanted to know where the man lived. Matilde explained. Roger, with comprehensive knowledge of the local area, asked for details and said that he had been to sea with a guy who lived not so far from the house where Matilde's brother was, so he and Oda must have driven by the house many times. Roger said he and Oda used the camper van as often as they could, to see new places and, if not to see new places, to meet people. They often met other members of the Caravan Club, but in July and August they went on longer trips, generally to southern Europe. Last year they had driven through Germany, over to Luxembourg, from there to Reims in France and south to Provence. They had driven along the whole of the Côte d'Azur, as the French called it, and into Spain, to Seville.

'Did you know the pope lived in Provence?' Oda asked.

Matilde shook her head.

'He did, and that's where the wine comes from: Châteauneuf-du-Pape. I always thought it was a *pappvin*, you know, wine-in-a-box,' she said, 'but it's called after the pope's residence.' She chuckled.

There had been a heat wave and it was almost forty-five degrees at its peak down there.

'Forty-five degrees! In the shade, phew.'

It was only later, when the hostess came through the door with her freshly baked Pavlova adorned with strawberries, raspberries and big American blueberries, that Frølich thought he would have to bring up the subject of the *Sea Breeze,* while there was still time to go into some depth with his questions. He was already onto his third Samuel Adams Boston lager.

He cleared his throat.

The hosts looked at him with new eyes. They knew what was coming and had been waiting.

19

The unexpected silence took him slightly by surprise. Suddenly he could hear voices in conversation on a veranda nearby, through the piercing sound of a neighbour using a Norsaw to cut boards. Renovation work, he thought, and swallowed a gulp of beer before asking the first question.

'Did you receive a visit from Fredrik Andersen not so long ago?'

Oda Borgersrud nodded.

The couple observed him attentively.

'Did Andersen talk to you about a lifeboat?'

She nodded. 'He asked what I'd seen while I was in the cabin.'

Roger took on the role of commentator and explained the context for Matilde in a low voice: 'Oda worked in the duty-free shop, and she was asleep while the terrible fire was raging and only woke up when the boat was being evacuated. But she couldn't get out. She was trapped in her cabin. The corridor was full of smoke and toxic gases.'

'Ugh, how awful,' Matilde said.

'What did you see?' Frølich asked.

'I saw the lifeboats in the water.'

'Did you see the lifeboat that got stuck on the way down?'

'No. I couldn't see any of what was going on above the cabin.'

'Apparently the ropes jammed when the boat was being lowered. For a long time it hung alongside the ferry, and afterwards, when it was in the water, they had trouble freeing the hawser that held the lifeboat to the ship. One of the passengers had to cut the rope with a pocket knife.'

'Terrible business,' Roger said, still in a low voice.

'I couldn't see what was happening above the cabin window,' Oda said. 'But it's true that a lifeboat was hanging at the side of the ship.'

'Those on board the stranded lifeboat say they saw another lifeboat being lowered astern. They say there were only two people in this boat. They were making for the horizon, in other words they were escaping. Did you see that?'

Oda Borgersrud shook her head.

'No?'

'Fredrik Andersen asked that question,' she said. 'He brought with him a report the police had written regarding the number of evacuees. He gave it to me.'

'A report?'

'Yes,' she said. 'A list. I'll get it.'

She went inside.

'Terrible business,' Roger said again.

They were all staring at the veranda door as it opened and Oda came out with some papers in her hand.

Oda sat down and placed a wad of stapled papers on the table.

'It says eight lifeboats were used to rescue people,' she said. 'The last two were never lowered. Yet there were between twenty and thirty survivors who claimed that they'd seen a lifeboat with two uniformed crewmen leaving the damaged ship. But the list of survivors showed that could not be the case.'

'A mystery?'

'Exactly.'

'Did Fredrik Andersen find this out?'

Oda Borgersrud nodded. 'That is, it was me who found this out.'

She looked at her partner, who nodded encouragement.

'The reason Fredrik Andersen came here was that I read his book some time ago. I'd had it lying around for ages – for well over two years, but I couldn't bear the thought of going back over the incident again. When I finally did get round to it, I read about this rumour of a missing lifeboat. I couldn't make any sense of that and emailed him. Then he got in touch.'

She took the sheet from under the list of survivors. It was an A4 photograph of a cruise ship. Its name was the *Sea Breeze*.

'This picture was taken when the ship was a casino in the Caribbean,' she said, pointing. 'These are the lifeboats on the starboard side: numbers one, three, five, seven and nine. There are just as many on the port side. There they're even numbers: two, four, six, eight and ten.'

'I see,' Frølich said.

She pointed. 'This is the lifeboat that got stuck on the way down.'

He nodded.

'Can you see anything special?'

'About the lifeboat?'

'About the lifeboats.'

He had another look. But couldn't see anything. 'No.'

Oda and Roger exchanged glances. Roger smiled.

'He's never been to sea,' Roger said, excusing him.

'What is it that I'm supposed to be able to see?'

'Lifeboat number nine,' she said, pointing to the one astern.

'It's different,' she said. 'This lifeboat has a covering on the front and at the side.'

Frølich leaned forward. She was right. He could see it now. The lifeboat was different. The covering meant it appeared bigger and more robust. 'But so what?'

'When this lifeboat is lowered the passengers in it aren't visible,' Oda Borgersrud said.

'Only the person steering the boat and the person in charge – in other words, those standing up – are seen. So simple. Those people stuck in the lifeboat at the side of the ship thought there were no passengers in boat number nine. That's wrong. They thought the two men in uniforms were alone and escaping. They weren't.'

'Fredrik Andersen came to me to ask what I actually saw. In fact, I saw everything from a slightly different angle.'

'There,' she said, pointing at the photograph of a cabin window almost down by the water line. 'There's my cabin. I saw straight into lifeboat number nine when it was being lowered. I saw that it was full of people. What Andersen wanted to know was what I saw. The lifeboat never disappeared. It had a motor, left the damaged ferry and was picked up by a Russian freighter that had come to help.'

'My God, and you were trapped in the cabin right down there, surrounded by flames and gases,' Matilde said.

Oda Borgersrud nodded. 'It wasn't my turn,' she said. 'God had decided I wasn't going to die. When I thought the end was nigh, he sent down an angel to save me.'

'An angel?'

She nodded. 'He was Swedish and wearing firefighting gear. The most attractive man I've ever met, apart from you, that is,' she said to Roger.

Frank Frølich inhaled deeply.

Everyone focused on him.

'There's another thing I have to ask you.'

'Go ahead,' she said.

'You stayed on board all the time the vessel was being towed. You're an eyewitness.'

She looked back at him. Waiting for the question.

'The big question is whether there were any new fires while you were on board.'

'You're wondering what I saw?'

'I have to admit I am, yes.'

'A short time after I left the cabin all the fires were out. Later I saw raging blazes that burned for hours. After leaving the cabin I stayed on the bridge deck all the time. I didn't go into the ship once I was out. Everything that happened in those hours happened inside the ship. You ask what I believe. I can tell you, hand on heart, that I believe there was someone lighting more fires. This is not speculation on my part. This is just what I'm sincerely convinced went on. But did I see it? At first I saw firemen putting out fires and then running to fight new, unexplained fires for hour after hour. I know the police were mistaken when they accused a dead passenger of being a mass murderer. He and his room-mate died, both of them, only minutes after the first fire broke out. How would he be able to light fires ten, twelve and twenty hours after he'd died? This tells me the police never did a proper job. Don't forget: someone tried to kill me on board that boat. I've struggled with that all these years.'

'She's been to a psychologist,' Roger said in a low voice.

'Yes,' Oda said. 'I've suffered psychologically and I'm not ashamed to say it. But why have I had to struggle? Because the police never found out who tried to kill me. Can you imagine what that's like? Someone wants to kill you, by a miracle you escape and those supposed to ensure law and order couldn't care less about what actually happened? They blame a poor soul who himself was killed. Without a single shred of evidence. All they've done since is let themselves be driven from one entrenched position to another while refusing to admit their mistakes.'

Oda Borgersrud was angry now. Her eyes flashed. 'Is this answer good enough?' she asked in a serrated voice.

'So you didn't actually see anyone committing sabotage,' Frank Frølich established.

Oda Borgersrud didn't answer. She got up and began to clear the table.

20

Before they took their leave, Roger and Matilde sat discussing various routes to Oslo. Matilde wanted to drive across the Valdresflya plateau. She had dreamed of driving this stretch of road many times.

'The R15 to Lake Vågå. From there, Valdresflya to Fagernes and afterwards the E16 through the Begna valley to Hønefoss and on to Oslo. That should take you about seven to eight hours,' Roger said.

Didn't they want to stay any longer? Oda asked. After all, they'd made the long trip up here, and Vestland had so much to offer.

'We have to go to a funeral,' Matilde said.

Oda asked if it was Fredrik Andersen's.

Frank shook his head, in shame. He didn't know when Andersen would be buried. He didn't even know if the funeral had already taken place.

'A friend of mine,' Matilde said. 'She was no older than me.'

'How awful,' Oda said. 'What did she die of?'

Matilde didn't answer.

Oda glanced at Frølich.

'We don't know for sure,' he said. 'They can't agree on what happened or how it happened.'

'That makes it so much worse,' Roger said.

Matilde nodded slowly, in sombre mood. 'I'd rather not talk about it,' she said.

21

The night was theirs. The T-bird floated all alone across the Valdresflya plateau, and the two of them inside watched a herd of reindeer making their way across the rocks like a moving carpet. The summer night was never completely dark and the snow-covered mountain tops in Jotunheimen towered in front of the violet sky. Matilde insisted she had only seen skies like this on paintings in museums before. She stopped in the parking area of Ridderspranget, the fabled 'Knight's Leap', flicked through the pile of music to find something suitable for driving under the stars and found Pat Metheny's *Upojenie*, fast-forwarded to 'Are You Going with Me?' and drove on.

They sat in silence as the music provided the backcloth for their reflection. Frank was thinking about Oda Borgersrud. The meeting with her had convinced him of only one thing: the murder of Fredrik Andersen couldn't have anything to do with the *Sea Breeze*.

As though my opinion on this case was of any interest, he added to himself. He had to stay away from Fredrik Andersen's death and the accompanying speculation. He no longer worked for the police. He was an insignificant person working on insignificant cases, work that only had significance for the poor person who paid to have the job done. Even if occasionally he had felt as though he were swirling in the middle of a vortex after meeting Guri Sekkelsten for the first time, Gunnarstranda was right. He had to keep his nose out of everything that didn't concern him. The Jørgen Svinland assignment was done now, although the result may not be to the client's satisfaction. The person known as Ole Berg had turned out to be a woman. A woman who was unable to confirm a single one of Svinland's suspicions. Svinland would be disappointed. But the truth was a stubborn soul who never took others into consideration. Besides, he still had one unfinished job to do. He had committed himself to finding someone for Snorre Norheim. This someone was fairly certain to be the man Guri had called Shamal. It shouldn't be difficult to find him. Shamal's interest in Frank convinced him that they would meet face to face before long.

He looked out at the violet sky, at the contours of the mountains. Glanced across at Matilde. The light from the dashboard framed her head. Red lipstick, red hair and a visible black strap on her round shoulder. Her profile could have been a motif for a film poster.

She had been waiting for his attention and lowered the music. 'Do you believe in God?' she asked.

'I don't know. Maybe I believe in co-operation with God.'

'What do you mean by that?'

'Perhaps it has something to do with the job I had. Discovering that there's a lot of evil in the world. A lot.'

'I believe in God,' she said. 'Usually,' she added after a pause for thought.

'So you're a bit like me?'

'I suppose so. What about fairness?'

'Do I believe in it?'

She nodded.

'Is it possible to believe in it?'

'Maybe,' she said. 'The English use the word 'justice' as well – something to do with law and order.'

'Wasn't it the Brits who coined the expression "fair play"?' he said.

'Yes, but "fair". That's an adjective.'

'Where are you going with this?'

'I think good existed long before language,' she said.

He remembered that John the Evangelist had had quite a different opinion. But he didn't say so. Her hand found his in the darkness. She squeezed it.

22

In all, it took them a bit more than seven hours to get from Ulsteinvik to Havreveien. After parking the car they took the dog for a walk. The first traffic was on its way to the city centre. There was so little that the clanking of an early tram carried across the noise barriers. They met paper boys on bikes and the odd single-minded jogger, who lurched to the side when Petter showed them some interest.

They got out of bed at two o'clock in the afternoon. When Matilde went for a shower he jumped on his bike to go and buy some eggs, juice, coffee, fresh rolls and something to put on them.

The radio was on low in the background as they had a breakfast that gave them the feeling they were still travelling without a set destination or time frame.

Later he caught the metro to town and his office. He was nervous as he let himself in. The cleaner had done her job. He sat down, rolled the swivel chair back against the wall, pulled out the lowest drawer with the tip of his shoe and rested his foot inside. Then he called Jørgen Svinland.

He answered the telephone only after it had been ringing for a long time.

'Frølich here.'

'Hello,' Svinland said in a measured tone.

'I've met Ole Berg.'

Svinland didn't say anything.

Frank Frølich hesitated. His client's lack of enthusiasm made him unsure. He said:

'Ole Berg turned out to be a woman. She worked on the *Sea Breeze*. Her name's Oda Borgersrud. She doesn't wish to stand as a witness. That's probably why Andersen referred to her under another name. But I'm afraid Oda Borgersrud has nothing new to tell us.'

'I see. I'm still pleased with the work you've done, Frølich. Do I owe you anything?'

'Far from it.'

He went quiet.

Svinland was silence itself.

It was unusual enough that Svinland didn't seem interested in what Oda Borgersrud had to say. But there was also the atmosphere. Something he couldn't quite grasp and didn't particularly appreciate. Svinland's distance made the conversation disagreeable.

'Are you interested in what she had to say?'

Svinland was still silent.

'It's clear that a lifeboat didn't go missing from the *Sea Breeze* as it was being evacuated. The police documented that in 1988 and she could confirm the same. She was an eyewitness and had told Fredrik Andersen that no lifeboat went missing, in other words, no crewmen fled the boat. She has her suspicions, but did not observe any criminal activity while she was on board.'

This was still a monologue. 'Are you there?'

'I'm here,' Svinland said.

'It's a number of weeks now since she met Fredrik Andersen. She lives in a completely different part of the country and hasn't been to Oslo for many months. The meeting between her and Andersen can't have had anything to do with his death.'

Frølich paused.

Svinland stayed silent.

'As far as the advance I received from Andersen is concerned, it's far too much. I can transfer half to your account if you give me the number.'

'No, no. We're happy. Thank you for all your help, Frølich, and good luck with everything.'

Svinland rang off.

Frølich sat staring at the phone in his hand. Svinland had just hung up. As though he were pleased to be rid of him. As though the news he brought him was boring. As though he were a nuisance.

Svinland was the man who had insisted Fredrik Andersen's death was a link in a larger conspiracy and that conversation with Ole Berg, alias Oda Borgersrud, would provide an answer and solve his long crisis. Now he wasn't interested.

Something must have happened. Something Svinland had no desire to let him in on.

Should he ring the man again?

Well, the guy had hired him to carry out an assignment. He had done it. It was fundamental in a profession like his that you don't become personally involved – in the job or with clients.

But he didn't want to keep Andersen's money. He had decided to give half to Jørgen Svinland or Andersen's mother – whatever his erstwhile client might think. But he didn't have an account number for a bank transfer.

Reluctantly, he grasped the phone and tapped in Svinland's number. It rang for a long time.

No one answered.

He put down the phone and wondered about the meeting with the Svinland family at the supermarket a few days before. Something had happened then.

He tried to remember details of the incident. He hadn't said hello to the young man. Svinland had been off before they'd had a chance to be introduced. A man reacts when you say you have met his wife before. Jealousy? No. It had to be something else.

23

The service was supposed to take place in Askim parish hall. Funerals are not occasions on which you want to attract attention. So they took his Mini Cooper. Petter found himself a comfortable spot on the rear seat.

Matilde connected her phone to the car's system. From the speakers came 'Sierra' by Boz Scaggs.

'I called Ivar last night,' she said.

'Ivar?'

'Her brother.'

Frølich turned down the music. He still hadn't told Matilde about his dealings with Guri's brother. He should have done so long ago. But was this the right moment?

'He's in prison for petty theft, isn't he?' he said, feeling like a fraud. After all, he had testified in court.

'He was on a suspended sentence when he was arrested,' Matilde said. 'So he was put in the clink. It's a kind of open prison term. He does some sort of gardening in Bastøy. But now he's been given leave. So he's been able to see to the practical arrangements of the burial. Their parents aren't alive. By the way, I asked him if he'd heard Guri talk about someone called Shamal. He wasn't sure, but said Guri was heavily into her job and asylum seekers. I knew that already, of course. But he also said there was a foreigner who occasionally slept over at hers. He didn't know the guy's name. I asked what he looked like. He was a bit older than her apparently. I tried to visualise the Shamal we met at the refugee centre. But I couldn't give a very good description. Think I was too caught up with Aisha.'

'Shamal had a ring in his ear,' Frank said, and added: 'Were they in a relationship?'

She shrugged. 'Hard to say.'

'But what do you think?'

She glanced over at him, and gave the matter some thought. 'Actually I doubt it.'

'But as he stayed at hers occasionally, doesn't that mean there may have been something between them?'

Matilde ruminated. 'Perhaps. But she didn't say anything about
it.'

'Did she usually confide in you about that kind of stuff?'

Matilde smiled. 'If it was serious I think she'd have said
something, yes. Why are you so curious?'

He didn't answer. It was no business of his who Guri went to
bed with. But there was something about Guri's commitment that
he had reacted to the first time they met. He had a sense that Guri
had had problems setting clear boundaries. As close relationships
between staff and clients were considered unprofessional and
undesired at the centre, she might well have kept quiet about this
one – to everyone. But so what? was his next thought. What
business was it of his?

He looked around. They were driving past a huge field of barley.
A playful gust of wind sent a shadow across the billowing crop.

24

The bright sun bathed the chapel and surrounding land in a
wonderful light. The car park between the parish hall and the
church was full, and the road to the chapel was lined with cars
parked bumper to bumper. There was a gap on the bend to the car
park. He squeezed the Mini Cooper into it. The car was in the
shade of a birch tree. They let the dog stay in the car and rolled
down the windows a fraction before leaving for the chapel.

Matilde knew some of the latecomers heading for the front door.
She waved to them.

In the doorway a man from the funeral parlour was distributing
a booklet with a picture of Guri on horseback on the front cover.

They took one each and went inside. The room was packed to
the rafters. They found a place almost at the very back, with a large
throng of younger people and a variety of foreigners.

Guri must have been as popular at work as she was in her private
life, he thought, and studied the photograph of the blonde on the
horse. She was wearing national costume. The skirt was black and

the waistcoat green damask. Draped over her shoulders was a black shawl embroidered with roses. Her blonde hair hung loose, falling in waves across her shoulders. Her shoes were black with shiny buckles. Her stockings black. The horse was black and muscular and its coat glistened. Guri was smiling in the photograph. She seemed proud, and perhaps a little embarrassed? There was something about the undisguised happiness in her eyes above the slightly embarrassed grimace on her sensitive lips. Perhaps she was thinking that wearing a national costume while riding a horse was a little too much, although she did appear to enjoy being dressed like that. He could understand it. Guri had been an attractive woman. He thought about her. About the moment she went into Oslo Central Station, turned back and waved to him. He remembered the last conversation they'd had on the phone. Such a short time before he found her. He speculated on how it had happened and where. He wondered if she'd had time to be afraid. He wondered if her family asked themselves the same questions. Or if they were reassured by the police statement.

A group of three girls opened the service by singing the beautiful 'Tir n'a Noir'. The priest told the congregation afterwards that Guri had had a happy childhood and she was a thoroughly pure and kind creature, a helper, someone who was always compassionate to others. Someone who would react at once if she came across injustice. Someone who made friends wherever she went, which the big turn-out at the funeral clearly demonstrated. The family had lived not far from Kykkelsrud power station when she was small. It had been a happy time, filled with animals, and Guri had started riding horses at an early age. Her mother and father passed away far too young, in a head-on collision outside Rakkestad during the night of 1st January on their way home after a New Year's party. Guri and her brother had gone to live with their mother's aunt near the Swedish border.

Guri trained as a nurse after school and had done a specialist course in psychiatry later.

It was clear that mentioning suicide was a difficult way for the priest to conclude his speech, as he immediately switched to talking about how hard life could be for some people, about mountains that had to be climbed and how some didn't manage all the hills.

25

The coffin was borne outside and the congregation slowly trooped out. Frank Frølich and Matilde followed the procession, down the steps and to the hearse, which would be driven to the crematorium. Here, behind the hearse, stood a tall, lean figure receiving condolences. Frølich recognised Ivar Sekkelsten from the trial. Now he was intrigued to know whether Guri's brother would recognise him.

Standing there in a black suit with an unfashionable cut, he seemed out of his comfort zone. His hair was as dark as his sister's had been blonde. He had combed it back with wax. He had a sunken chin, which he tried to compensate for with a sparse beard. Even though he wore a helpless expression on his face, Frølich knew he could be a tough nut if the conditions were right.

'That's Ivar, her brother,' Matilde whispered.

It was their turn.

He grasped Ivar Sekkelsten's hand and expressed his condolences. Guri's brother looked at him. His eyes were grey, like his sister's. He continued to look at his face, even after they had stopped shaking hands. Ivar had obviously recognised him.

Matilde fell around Ivar's neck. They hugged each other for a long time.

The hearse drove off with the coffin.

Matilde went to collect the dog, which was panting and dribbling in the hot weather. She held Petter tightly on the lead.

Ivar Sekkelsten shouted from the steps that close relatives were invited to a memorial gathering after the funeral.

'Presumably that's not us,' Matilde said.

They stayed anyway, like most of the other guests, hanging around, doing nothing and waiting, as people often do when they have just been through a deeply gripping experience and don't know what to do.

That was when he felt someone watching him. An elderly woman nodded to him. She was alone, leaning on a rollator frame. She had a circular face adorned with round glasses and wreathed by grey, curly hair.

At that moment Guri's brother forced his way through. He came towards them and asked Matilde if she would like to join the memorial. Matilde nodded.

'My aunt's tired out,' Ivar Sekkelsten said. He looked Frank in the eye. 'You're a private investigator, aren't you?'

Frank had no option but to nod.

'My aunt's wondering if you could drive her home.'

He looked across at the woman with the rollator.

'Happy to,' he said.

26

Guri's aunt was wearing dark trousers and a grey cardigan. She seemed shrunken by age as she walked slowly beside him, pushing the rollator.

Frank struggled to find a topic for conversation, but as he was folding the rollator and putting it into the car boot, he asked if she was the aunt Guri and her brother lived with after the death of their parents.

She nodded. 'I'm actually Guri's mother's aunt. But the children always call me Auntie.'

He opened the passenger door. She got in. He closed the door behind her, turned and saw that Matilde had climbed into the passenger seat of a pick-up. She manoeuvred the dog onto the rear seat, noticed him and waved.

Guri's brother got behind the wheel. They drove off.

He stood for a few seconds watching the pick-up, then got in, too. It felt like standing by a river and watching a valuable possession drift away with the current. Matilde would be told about

his relationship with Guri's brother – by someone else. And he was
the one who had managed to put them both in this humiliating
position.

He sat with his hands on the wheel, still paralysed by the consequences of his own actions.

Eventually he felt his passenger's eyes on him.

'You live in Ørje, don't you?'

Guri's aunt nodded.

He started the engine.

Guri's aunt waved to people still standing by the chapel as they
drove past.

'How well did you know her?' she asked.

'We only met twice.'

He was lost in a reverie as he tried to find his bearings. Finally
discovered a signpost pointing to the motorway and added: 'Lovely
woman. Attractive, decent, committed. Especially in her work.'

He fell quiet and glanced across at her. She was clearly moved:
her eyes were moist, and she was squeezing a handkerchief in one
hand.

They sat in silence until he accelerated onto the motorway.

She rummaged in a little bag, pulled out a cigarette and lit it.

He pressed a button to open the window on her side a few centimetres.

'You're a detective,' she said.

He nodded. 'And you?'

'I used to be an engineer. I've been retired for a long time now.
I built bridges.'

He nodded again. This situation reminded him of his time in
the police. Gunnarstranda chain-smoking in the passenger seat.

'I don't think she took her own life,' she said.

He didn't answer.

'No, I definitely don't think she did,' she said, looking at him.
'You're a detective. You can find out what really happened, can't
you?'

He didn't answer.

'Why does one actually become a detective?'

He shrugged. 'I worked in the force for a long time. Investigating is a job I persuade myself I can do.'

'Why did you join the police?'

He glanced over at her again.

She returned his glance, cigarette bobbing in her mouth.

'It happened quite by chance. I started with law, but stopped when I was accepted at police college. And started there instead.'

'Why did you apply?'

It was a while since he had asked himself the same question. He tried to think. 'Bit of status,' he concluded.

'Only status?'

'And idealism. A vague concept of justice and the value of law and order.'

'A vague concept?'

'Think I got it as a boy, reading books about children who help the police to catch criminals. The Hardy Boys and Bill Bergson, Master Detective.'

He smiled at himself.

'But you don't have your concept of justice any longer?'

He didn't answer. Not wishing to be confronted with this. At least not here and now.

The silence persisted, and he was trying to conjure up a phrase that would restore the harmony when she spoke again:

'So you started in the police; why did you continue?'

He glanced across at her again. 'It can be a rewarding job. Exciting. No two days are the same. Time passes quickly. Why did you become an engineer?'

'You don't like talking about yourself. Maybe that's why you became a cop. You want to know everything about everyone else, but you don't give anything away personally.'

That put him in his place. He had to smile.

'I can tell you why I started to build bridges. Do you want to hear?'

He didn't answer.

'It came about on a boat called MS Hvaler, which in those days plied between Fredrikstad and the Hvaler islands. It happened during the holidays.'

Guri's aunt told him she grew up in Fredrikstad. Once she had a summer job in the Flora kiosk by Kråkerøy bridge. One weekend, travelling to visit her mother and father at their holiday cabin on Nordre Sandøy, she was sitting on the foredeck of a little ferry beside a nice man with a rucksack on his back. They struck up a conversation. The man said his family had had a cabin on Hvaler for many years. His grandfather had built it. He had just been home to fetch some kitchen equipment and do some food shopping. He patted his rucksack, which was very heavy. Then he began to talk about his interest in seagulls. Folk see a white bird and think it's any old gull, he said. But there are more than twenty types of seagull in Norway, he pointed out.

She had asked him if seagulls were migratory birds and he had answered yes and no. As the boat approached the quay where the man would go ashore, he stood up. He put the rucksack on the bench where he had been sitting and tamped his pipe. He put the pipe in the corner of his mouth and said that only the herring gulls travel to and from Norway every summer and autumn. The ferry was approaching land and the passengers pressed forward and queued by the break in the railing where the gangway – a kind of board or broad plank – would be placed on the quay for disembarkation. The man hoisted the rucksack on his back. It was so heavy that he teetered and had to hold the railing so as not to fall backwards. A boy in knee-length shorts stood in the bow and threw a rope ashore as the ferry glided the last few metres alongside the quay. The passengers rushed ashore. The man with the rucksack wobbled as he puffed to keep his pipe lit. Guri's aunt, who was travelling further with the boat, stood at the railing as the man with the rucksack on his back and the pipe in his mouth stepped ashore. He turned his head and waved to her. At that moment he lost his balance and fell into the water.

The water under the wharf was very clear and green. Snail shells grew on the wharf poles, some clusters of seaweed clung to the rock face and the seaweed waved to her in the water as the man with the rucksack broke the surface of the water and sank like a stone. At first she was surprised by how deep the water was so close to land. The man sank in a froth of bubbles and continued to sink and become smaller and smaller. Another man in dark trousers and a white shirt with stripes on the sleeves dived in, clouding the view. He shouted and swam on the surface, and splashed with his arms and legs as passengers pointed, and he ducked his head under the water to see and came up again gasping for air without having seen anything at all. Guri's aunt couldn't understand how the man could have imagined he would be able to grab the man with the heavy rucksack so far down. She had seen a little red-and-black piece of wood floating on the surface under the wharf. It was the man's pipe.

'That's how quickly it can happen,' she said. 'One minute he's there and the next he's gone. Everything is as it was for everyone. Just not for those standing close to the respective person. For us the world stops. But there's nothing we can do. That's the worst about grief, realising that you can't change anything.'

They drove on in silence. The sun was shining from a clear sky, green corn fields stretched across the landscape, and on a grassy mound a tractor lowered the blades of a mower.

'Did the ferry incident take on a special importance for you?'

'If only you knew. When I got to the cabin, I started designing a gangway. The man would have got ashore without any problems if the plank had had a railing. It was the same incident that made me apply to Trondheim and become an engineer. One thing led to another, and since then I've designed bridges, and there have been quite a few of them over the years. But now I wish only that I could've gone instead of Guri.'

He glanced over at her. Again her eyes had welled up.

Silence had them in its grip once more. Until he cleared his throat to ask what had been on his mind since they left the chapel.

'Why did you really want me to drive you?'

'I want to go home. I can't bear memorial gatherings. They're hypocritical.'

'But why me?'

'You'll find out soon enough,' she said, lighting another cigarette. She inhaled and slowly blew out the smoke. 'Why did you stop? Working for the police.'

They had caught up with a semi-trailer and he moved into the left lane. As he did so, they passed a sign saying it was fifteen kilometres to Ørje.

27

She lived in Elveveien, which for some distance ran parallel to the Ørje river. They had to drive past the sluice gate and into a long drive up to a white, chalet-style house.

He parked beside some steps leading up to a modest entrance. He fetched the rollator from the boot. Unfolded it and held it out for her.

'Can you manage from here?'

'I want you to come inside,' she said. 'There's someone who wants to meet you.'

She pushed the rollator up to the entrance, and he followed her. The door opened.

He had seen the man in the doorway before. On a trip in the Oslo fjord and at a refugee centre. It was the man Guri called Shamal.

They stood eyeballing each other. This must have been how it was for Henry Stanley, Frølich thought. When the man he had been searching for was suddenly there.

'So this is where you are,' Frank said to him in Norwegian.

'You'll have to speak English,' Guri's aunt said. She grabbed the stair railing and pulled herself up the first step. 'This is Frank, dear. Would you please put the kettle on? It's time for tea.'

28

'I was at Guri's,' Shamal said. 'The night she died,' he added.

He admits it, Frank Frølich thought, saying nothing. He wanted to hear more.

They were sitting around a white kitchen table, each with a mug of aromatic chai that Shamal had brewed with great earnestness and a large number of spices.

'I waited for her for hours,' Shamal said. 'I watched *House of Cards* while I was waiting. I called her. But she didn't answer. I went to bed quite late. I'd just fallen asleep when my phone rang and woke me. It was Guri. She said I had to leave; I had to get away from the house at once. I said: "Why?" She said: "Promise me you'll do as I say. You have to leave at once. Go to Ørje, to my aunt." She said: "We'll meet there." I said: "How do I get there?" She explained where it was.'

'And what did you do?'

'I did as she said. I got dressed, went out and drove here.'

And which car did you take when you left? Frølich wondered, but first asked: 'Did she say why you had to get away?'

'She said I was in danger. That's all I know. And she was right, of course. She came home and died herself.'

'Why were you there, at Guri's house?'

'The previous day she wasn't at work. She called me. She said she had to talk to me. She told me to go to hers and wait for her there. I said: "Can't you come here?" – to the refugee centre, I meant. She said: "No. Something's happened. I have to talk to you, alone."'

'Something's happened? Did she say what?'

'No.'

'Did you ask?'

'Yes. She didn't answer. She just repeated that I had to go to hers.'

'And how did you get there, to hers?'

'I drove.'

'In what car?'

'It's in the garage,' Guri's aunt said. 'An Opel. It's a miracle it got through the test.'

Right, he thought, turning to Shamal again. 'But she didn't show up?'

'No.'

'Guri was here,' her aunt said. 'She asked if she could stay with me for a few days, and that was fine by me.'

Frank Frølich tried to summarise: 'You're at the refugee centre. Guri doesn't come to work, but calls you and tells you to go to hers so that she can talk to you?'

Shamal nodded.

'You drive there in an Opel. But when you arrive she's not there and she doesn't come home while you're there?'

Shamal shook his head. 'No, the house was empty. I rang her. She didn't answer her phone, so I decided to wait until she came. After all, she'd said she would come.'

'You had a key to the house?'

'The key's on a board inside the porch by the front door. It's always there. I got there at five in the afternoon, then I waited all evening. In the end I went to bed in a room on the first floor where I'd slept before. But then she rang and woke me up. It was night. It may've been two or half past. She asked me where I was. I said: "I'm at yours, as we agreed." She said: "You can't stay there now. You have to go. Right now." I said: "Why do I have to go?" She said: "You're in danger there." I said: "In danger of what?" She said: "I'll tell you, but now you have to trust me. Leave the house at once. Your life's in danger."'

'Did she use those words?'

'Yes,' Shamal said, and repeated them. '"Your life's in danger."'

'Shamal came here,' Guri's aunt said, and added: 'Later that day the priest came to the door and told us that Guri was dead.'

'Why did Guri think you were in danger, do you think?'

Shamal shrugged his shoulders. 'I have no idea.'

Frank Frølich tried to interpret Shamal's eyes and expression. For some reason he didn't trust his answer. He sensed that Shamal knew.

As though Shamal had read his mind, he repeated the shrug and the answer. 'It's true. I have no idea.'

What had he himself been doing while this was going on? Guri had rung him during the night. He had just seen Bjørn Thyness drive off with the refugee girl. Guri had wanted to meet him at hers. She had said she wanted to meet him there because she was going to pick up some fresh clothes. If Shamal was telling the truth, Guri must have been lying. Either she had lied or she had planned something by asking him to go there. If so, it was a plan that went horribly wrong.

'I spoke to the manager at the refugee centre,' he said. 'She said your appeal was rejected and you took flight.'

'I didn't. Guri rang me and told me to go to hers.'

'Why would Guri tell you to go there and then not meet you?'

Again Shamal shrugged his shoulders. 'I don't know.'

'Whose is the Opel you drove?'

'A brother's.'

'Brother?'

'A compatriot. He lives in Oslo.'

'I drove to Guri's that same night,' Frølich said. 'It was me who discovered her body. I got there at about four in the morning. A couple of hours after you say she called you and told you to leave at once. While I was driving there I passed a red Volvo estate. It was her car. The person in the car must've driven from the place where she died.'

'I knew it,' Guri's aunt said, resigned. 'I knew it couldn't have been as the police said.'

'That's why it's so important to identify who drove away in her car,' Frølich said, keeping eye contact with Shamal.

Shamal shook his head. 'I drove my friend's Opel. I did as she instructed on the phone.'

'He woke me up,' Guri's aunt said. 'And he asked me where Guri was when he arrived. It wasn't quite four o'clock.'

'You're sure of the time?'

'Yes, he woke me up, as I said. I was frightened to death. The doorbell rang and it was almost four in the morning.'

'I shouldn't have left,' Shamal said. 'I should've stayed there and waited for her. I could've stopped what happened.'

Frank Frølich calculated. It was over an hour's drive from Guri's house to here. If Shamal had arrived here just before four in the morning, it couldn't have been Shamal who drove Guri's Volvo. Someone else had taken her car. Guri must have first driven back to her house. Alone or with this other person? They must have travelled together. How would this person have got there otherwise? By bus? Not in the middle of the night. But who could it be? Why did she take the killer back with her?

'You have to tell the police this,' he said.

'I can't talk to the police.'

'Why not?'

'As you said, my appeal was turned down. I'll be arrested. I'll be transported to Turkey or Baghdad. I'd rather die here in Norway.'

Frølich couldn't counter such arguments. But the police should act upon Shamal's information. The police regarded Guri's case as suicide. Shamal's statement could change that. The police based their conclusion on Guri already being in the house – without a car. The police thought she killed herself in a bout of depression. Shamal's statement would pull the rug from under that theory. It would also focus the investigation on her car. Shamal confirmed she was on her way home in her own car that night, so *someone* must have driven off in her Volvo later, as he had also told the police.

'But for Guri's sake you have to talk to the police,' he said.

'Guri's dead. She won't be coming back,' Shamal said.

'If you tell the police this, they'll realise she was murdered. They'll reopen the investigation.'

'I'm not talking to the police,' Shamal said. 'I'm talking to you.'

'Me? Why me?'

'Guri trusted you. I trust you.'

Trust? What did that mean? He was reminded of what Gunnarstranda used to say: *I have yet to see a witness visit me voluntarily without a personal agenda.*

Shamal wanted to achieve something by contacting him. But what?

'You were following me on the Oslo ferry,' he said.

29

Shamal cast down his eyes. 'I wanted to talk to you. I thought you might understand what was going on. Why Guri died. But I didn't dare speak when I had the chance.'

Now Shamal was lying. It wasn't a shy man following him that day but one needing to talk.

'How did you find me?'

'We talked about you after you came to the refugee centre. Guri said who you were. What work you did. We found your address online.'

'You followed me from my flat that day?'

Shamal nodded.

'You followed me to the metro, down to City Hall quay, onto the boat, and further, while I talked to people on the islands.'

Shamal nodded again.

'You spent a whole day shadowing me without approaching me?'

Shamal nodded.

'Why that day in particular?'

'What do you mean?'

'Why did you follow me on precisely that day?'

Shamal seemed confused by the question. 'Because I was in Oslo.'

'What about the other days?'

'What do you mean?'

'What other days did you follow me?'

Shamal looked at Guri's aunt as if for help. She shrugged.

Could Shamal have followed him over several days? Of course he had. *Shamal's strange interest in me leads us back to the core of the matter*, he thought. The meeting between Guri, him and Shamal the first time at the refugee centre.

'What's your relationship with Sheyma Bashur?' he asked.

Shamal looked up. His eyes had hardened.

Frank Frølich repeated the question.

'None,' Shamal said. 'I have no relationship with that woman.'

Frank Frølich looked him in the eye. Shamal stared back defiantly.

'But you know who she is,' he said.

Shamal's eyes didn't deviate. But he didn't answer.

In the end, Shamal turned to his hostess and said:

'I'm tired. I have to rest.'

With that, he was off his chair and out of the room.

The other two were left in the slightly unpleasant atmosphere that always arises when someone suddenly departs, leaving the impression they are offended.

'He's a good boy,' she said at length. 'He is that,' she said again, as though to convince herself.

'Why didn't he go to the funeral?'

She shrugged. 'I think he's still afraid for his own safety.'

'Are the police after him?'

'He says so.'

'He should report to the police. He's holding important information.'

'He daren't. Besides, they're not interested in what you call information. They didn't want to talk to me, either. I rang them. I was put through to a woman who said she was investigating the case. I said I was Guri and Ivar's next of kin. I told the police Guri came here and wanted to stay with me because she was afraid and felt threatened. The policewoman thanked me for the information. That was all. They didn't come here. They didn't ask me to make a statement. They're sure she took her own life.'

They fell into silence again.

Eventually he noticed that her shoulders were shaking. He leaned forward. Saw her face. It was distorted. She was crying.

He didn't know how to react. He was alone with a crying elderly woman. All that occurred to him was to reach out and hold her hand in his.

After sitting like this for some long, pain-racked minutes she freed her hand and stood up. With her back to him, she rubbed her face with the back of her hand.

'How do you see this?' he said. 'How do you interpret the police not being interested in investigating?'

She didn't move and didn't answer at once. At length she went to the kitchen table and tore a sheet of paper from the roll. She wiped her eyes and screwed the paper into a ball in her fist.

'She was thirty-three years old. She had all her life in front of her. The person who stole her from us, stole everything from her. But the crime which is as heinous as the murder is that he's being allowed to go unpunished. Can you understand that? I don't wish to hate. I don't wish to despise anyone. But I can't repress these feelings. As much as I want to see her murderer punished, I want the police punished, the DPP, or whatever the bastards call themselves. Morally and legally these people in authority are not one jot better than the person who took her from us.'

He rose to his feet.

She ignored him, left the kitchen and went into the adjacent room. She plumped into a chair and lifted a remote control.

A TV show was starting. A well-known voice said something and canned laughter underlined that what they said was funny.

Frølich made his way to the hall and found his own way out.

30

Before leaving the house, he opened the garage door and peeped in. An ancient, tired-looking Opel Astra was inside. So in this instance Shamal had been telling the truth. He lowered the door, got in his own car and drove off.

He couldn't let go of the conversation with Shamal and tried to visualise what might have happened.

Guri rang Shamal and told him to leave her house at once. So she must have known the killer was going there. Then the killer drove off in her car, so he must have travelled there with her. She must have known who he was. She must also have known how dangerous he was. Nevertheless she went there with him.

But first of all she called him – Frank Frølich – and told him to go to her house. She didn't say anything about this being dangerous. She didn't mention the person she was going there with and she might be afraid of.

Why didn't she?

Had she thought Frank might be able to prevent something happening to her? Or was this person only a danger to Shamal and not to him?

He squeezed the wheel, trying to remember what Guri had said on the phone. She had told him to hurry, but she hadn't given the impression that the place was dangerous.

What she said to Shamal, but not to him, must have been very important though. On the other hand, she must have grossly underestimated the situation, as she ended up being killed herself.

She must have put the kettle on to serve her guest and herself. That suggested she *didn't* fear the man. So she must have considered him a danger to Shamal, but not to her. So why had she been killed? What was the motive?

The killer couldn't have known she had put the kettle on. If he had, he would have turned off the hob before leaving. After all, he'd gone to the trouble of making her death look like suicide.

The killer must have been somewhere else, not in the kitchen. She had come out of the kitchen, into another room, where the killer was. So she didn't say anything to the killer about having put the kettle on.

Then it had happened, but how?

She didn't have any skin under her fingernails. She couldn't have been able to put up much resistance. She had been taken by surprise.

He imagined a shadow with a rope in his hands. Tightening the rope and forcing her body to the floor.

Afterwards he must have carried her to the outbuilding and under the barn ramp. And staged a suicide.

And the police wanted to let all this evil go unpunished.

He had worked himself into a fury. Had to pull in. Found a bus lay-by. Sat looking vacantly into the distance with his hands on the wheel.

It must be possible to do something.

He took his phone. Searched for the number and called Nicolai Smith Falck. The journalist picked up at once.

'This is Frølich. I've got a tip-off.'

'OK.'

The journalist almost sang the little word. He hadn't heard the guy so elated since the accident in Bygdøy.

'It's about Guri Sekkelsten. The case was held to be a suicide and dropped. You asked me what I thought about the police's conclusion. So I reckoned I'd tell you what I saw when I arrived at the crime scene.'

'OK.'

Slightly more measured tone this time.

'I met her car coming in the opposite direction as I approached the house. Someone was leaving the crime scene in her car.'

He paused to give Falck time to make notes. But he couldn't hear the usual sounds of a keyboard. He must be writing with a pen.

'Is that all?' Falck asked.

'She'd put a kettle on the hob. I took it off a few minutes before I found the body. These are two facts the police chose to ignore when they drew their conclusion that she killed herself.'

'Any more?'

'She'd made arrangements with people. Ones she hadn't called off before she died.'

'Is that all?'

'That should be more than enough. Someone about to commit suicide doesn't make arrangements with people for after her death.'

'Who had she made arrangements with?'

'They want to be kept out of this.'

'I don't know, Frølich. All this comes from – and excuse my language – an ex-cop with grubby hands.'

'What do you mean?'

'You were suspended from the force. You're out for revenge.'

'I retired and I'm living well as a freelancer. I want to have as little as possible to do with the police.'

'Nevertheless, the case will be stronger with the names of those she had made arrangements with. I can interview them.'

Frølich was annoyed and had to take a deep breath.

'You can interview your sources. You can interview the man who led the investigation. You can interview the prosecuting authority. You can confront both of them with this information and ask why the case was dropped when several facts suggest she was the victim of a criminal act and not suicide.'

'As you said, these are my sources.'

So what, Frølich thought. *Is this journo a complete idiot?*

'And I'm a freelancer,' Falck continued. 'Anyway, I'll have to sell this case to the desk and the editor. I don't know. I'll take it up with the desk, then let's see how it develops.'

The conversation was over.

His car hadn't changed. The side of the hill to the west hadn't changed. The dim light hadn't changed. Only he had. He was so angry he wanted to smash something.

He looked out at the evening sky and already knew that what he had said would never appear in print.

Nicolai Smith Falck was a typical representative of his profession. Like a goat on its way to new pastures and greater satisfaction, he had no thoughts of anything else.

So what, he thought. *You've always known the man is spineless and pathetic. Concentrate on things you can change.*

31

The matt sheen on the paintwork of Matilde's T-bird glowed as he drove past, looking for a place to park his car. Even though the windows of the flat were dark, he was anxious when he walked in through the building's front door. Checked the post box. Nothing.

Went on to the lift. His anxiety rose with the lift. When he opened his flat door, his diaphragm was hurting.

He entered.

Leaned against the door and felt the silence vibrate. Empty flat. He checked his phone probably for the fifth time since they had parted. What did it mean that she hadn't come to the flat or contacted him?

Why don't you ring her? he asked himself.

I dread the conversation, he answered.

So what should he do now? Go to bed? Out of the question. He was wide awake and his body was in ferment inside.

Almost automatically he sat down in front of the computer. Plugged in Fredrik Andersen's memory stick. Flicked aimlessly through the police documents. He no longer had any sense of why he was doing this or what he was looking for.

The lifeboat story had turned out to be a myth with no basis in reality. The assignment was finished. Jørgen Svinland was no longer interested in whatever he might have to report back on. The only connection he had with the *Sea Breeze* and Svinland was the fact that he intended to pay back some of Andersen's advance.

Nonetheless, he had to write a report. He couldn't be bothered to make a start. Instead he skimmed documents on the memory stick.

He could see how people could get hooked on this case. The amount of material was immense. In addition to the quantity of police interviews, there was quite a number of reports on the ship's fire-prevention facilities and safety standards. Certificates and descriptions documenting the state of the damaged ship before and after it had been towed to harbour. He could see that he would never have a complete overview of the *Sea Breeze* case.

He started to search for names in the material. He wrote 'Bernt Weddevåg' in the search box and got one hit. The name of the retired marine inspector figured in a recently dated report – a police document.

Weddevåg had said he was one of Fredrik Andersen's most

important sources. If that was correct, Andersen must have stored material from Weddevåg in other places than on this stick, which wasn't surprising. As far as he could see, this stick contained nothing that Andersen had written himself. It contained secondary sources and background material, documents from the police, the legal system, the fire service and investigators.

He wrote the name of the first mate, Rolf Myhre, in the search box and got a lot of hits. He opened the last dated file. It was a police interview carried out barely two years ago.

He skim-read the report. Tick-Tock Rolf said in the interview what he had told Frølich.

He clicked back to the first page. Here there was a list of formal items, such as his date of birth, name, permanent address and so on. There was also the name of the policeman who interviewed Myhre: Bjørn Thyness.

He had to read the name again. And sat looking at it. Trying to digest what this might mean. Bjørn Thyness had been in the group who investigated the *Sea Breeze* a second time. There was a link between Bjørn Thyness and Fredrik Andersen. A link as solid and strong as an anchor chain.

So how deeply involved was Gøril's partner in this matter?

He wrote 'Bjørn Thyness' in the search box.

And he got hit upon hit upon hit. Bjørn Thyness had been deeply involved in the investigation. Bjørn had done lots of police interviews. And now Bjørn was working in the immigration unit. Bjørn Thyness had been spying on Fredrik Andersen, who was writing a book about Norwegian asylum and immigration policies. Andersen and Thyness had had almost parallel careers in recent years, in their own areas of course. One a critic; the other the criticised.

Another question followed on naturally from this: Could Thyness have known Guri?

Guri worked with asylum seekers. Bjørn worked with asylum seekers.

32

He pushed his chair back. Staring into the air. Thinking he had to curb his imagination. He didn't know if Guri and Bjørn Thyness had met. He had to stick to what he did know. Which was that Thyness had been spying on Andersen. What was more, Bjørn had to know quite a lot about the *Sea Breeze*. Presumably Thyness knew the case a lot better than Andersen did.

He heard the voice on the phone: *I'll find you.*

Could it have been Bjørn?

He took a deep breath.

The fact was that both the writer Fredrik Andersen and the policeman Bjørn Thyness had knowledge of the tragedy in the Skagerrak. But they had diametrically opposed views on the matter.

He would have liked to be a fly on the wall when the investigation team were working on the aggravated arson case for the second time.

Who had led the discussion?

What arguments had been employed?

Who had articulated the final reasoning behind the police stance on the case?

What was said aloud and what wasn't talked about?

Who had provided the opposition when the views were too defensive or cowardly?

Had anyone protested at all? And, if so, how were the counter-arguments received? What evidence had the police based their arguments on; what evidence had they rejected? Why did the police and Andersen construe the evidence so differently?

Fredrik Andersen's source was Bernt Weddevåg, who had said that the basis for his own investigations regarding the sabotage was formed when he read the fire crews' log.

Perhaps that was the place to start.

He pulled the laptop close again and searched for the log. He had skimmed through the report once before when he found the name Oda Borgersrud. Now he got the document up again and read it in greater detail.

The log covered several pages. The task-force leader went through everything they had done on board the ferry systematically. Starting with the moment the fire teams boarded the *Sea Breeze* from the helicopter in the early morning until they clambered ashore thirty-six hours later.

The task-force leader mentioned conflicts that had arisen between the fire officers and the three crewmen who had been flown back to the damaged vessel to assist them. The task-force leader believed the three men had worked against their best efforts to extinguish the fires. He wrote that the three crewmen disappeared below deck as soon as they came on board – and that there was friction the few times the fire teams met them.

A whole page of the log was devoted to an attempt to extinguish fires in a corridor on deck four, on the starboard side of the ferry, twelve hours after the ship had been evacuated.

The firefighters' leader categorised this conflagration as an oil fire because of the duration and intensity. The problem was simply that the oil fire arose in a corridor within the passenger section, where there shouldn't have been any oil. He thought, however, that he knew where the oil was coming from and indicated a fractured pipe in the rack under the corridor ceiling. The oil must have flowed out through the fracture and therefore someone must have operated a pump to generate the flow.

Frank Frølich sat up straight and tried to remember the phrasing Bernt Weddevåg had used in their conversation. It had to be this scenario Weddevåg had been talking about. Weddevåg thought that this open pipe must have been connected to one of the ship's diesel tanks by someone with malicious intentions. According to Weddevåg, the presence of fossil fuel was the only logical explanation for the blaze's intensity and duration as well as the extent of the damage to those who had been in the corridor. Bearing in mind the photographs of the charred woman and the twenty bits of coal that had once been a human, Frølich was inclined to agree with Weddevåg.

33

He went back to the document index in the memory stick and studied the dating of the files more thoroughly. Several of them were relatively recent. There were new police documents as well as the investigation committee's report. The number of newer items suggested that Fredrik Andersen had followed the case carefully, even after his book had been published. Andersen had, for example, contacted Oda Borgersrud and put paid to the myth of a missing lifeboat.

Frølich clicked on the document containing Bernt Weddevåg's name. It turned out to be quite large. In fact, it was a report on the leader of the fire crew. It was more recent and signed by Bjørn Thyness.

One element of the criticism levelled at the police work done in 1988 had been that the police hadn't interviewed the fire crews. They, after all, had fought the flames for hours, and it was obviously a glaring error that the police hadn't been interested in their observations.

When the police were ordered to investigate the case again the fire crews were finally interviewed by the police, including the task-force leader. The report by Bjørn Thyness was a commentary on this procedure, in which he constructed an argument against the fire officer's statement. Thyness claimed that this officer was *not* a reliable witness.

He had to reread the sentence. It did actually say that: "not reliable".

But why not?

He read on. The reason for the man's alleged unreliability was that he had been in contact with Bernt Weddevåg.

What was this? Bjørn Thyness had assassinated the character of the fire-crew leader. Thyness's report concluded that the police should ignore everything the task-force leader said in interviews.

Frank had to get up and walk around the flat. He walked back and read the text on the screen again. This document, signed by Bjørn Thyness, was possibly the most important on the whole memory stick. The document must have been written to manipulate the investigation.

The case stank. In actual fact the *Sea Breeze* no longer existed. It hadn't been possible for the police – when they carried out the second investigation – to secure new concrete evidence. The boat had been scrapped years before. Speculation about sabotage on board the *Sea Breeze* could therefore be nothing but speculation – unless it could be backed up with tangible evidence, such as eyewitness accounts. The log the fire-crew leader had written in 1988 was a specific, lengthy and comprehensive eyewitness account. He had described in great detail the mystifying oil fires. He had described the tenacious efforts to extinguish blazes where originally no combustible material existed. He had described the protective outfits they wore, which began to burn because of the intense heat. He had described flames that grew in intensity when water was sprayed on them. He had described the protective visors that cracked and broke because of the extreme temperatures. He had described a heat so intense that crews working in shifts could only manage ninety seconds at a time. He had described a fracture in a pipe for which there was no natural explanation. In other words, he had described a blaze that started many hours after they had assumed all the fires were extinguished – an oil blaze in a place where an oil blaze should not have been possible. The task-force leader's log and the eyewitness accounts were the closest one could come to proving that sabotage was carried out while the ferry was being towed.

But if the man who wrote the document could be condemned as 'unreliable' and 'without credibility', both his testimony and the document he had written were of no value to the investigation.

Bjørn Thyness had simply blackened the name of a witness.

The investigation unit – or to be more precise *some* influencers and central decision-makers in the group – must have predetermined the conclusion when they were ordered to review the case. Part of that process is to rubbish any evidence that contradicts the desired conclusion.

Frank had taken part in investigation units many times. He was aware of the dynamics that can arise, the roles that are allocated. Some excel as critics, some as neutral grafters and some as tough decision-makers. And in this instance one man had taken on the job of ensuring an unspoken decision stood – Bjørn Thyness.

Frølich realised that this case had him well and truly hooked. What intrigued him now was how the parliamentary committee viewed the fire crews' observations.

It took him less than a minute to find the committee's report on the stick and open it. Then he searched for the name of the fire-crew leader. The hits came. The parliamentary committee had been sent the slanderous report by the police and they had welcomed it with open arms. There it was in black and white in their report: the fire-crew task-force leader was unreliable. The document Thyness had written was plugged for all it was worth.

Bernt Weddevåg was written off as a conspiracy theorist, and the fire officer had been so influenced by this public enemy that the parliamentary committee – like the police – 'had been forced' to ignore everything he had to say about the fire crews' experiences on board the *Sea Breeze*.

The man's eyewitness account of 1988 wasn't mentioned. The total cremation of the bodies that Frølich had himself observed wasn't discussed. No attempt was made to analyse the injuries to the corpses or compare them with photographs of the fire. The defamatory report penned by Bjørn Thyness was intended to produce verdicts of 'decision not to prosecute/no criminal conduct' – and assign the case to eternal oblivion.

The conclusion reached by Stortinget's inquiry was the closest you could get to an off-the-shelf decision.

34

He got to his feet once again, went to the kitchen and started the coffee machine. Standing by the window, he mused while the coffee brewed. What could Bjørn Thyness have been given as a reward for sabotaging the truth?

Goodwill? At any rate he had gained a promotion. He had risen from being a duty officer at a police station to leading an operational department in the police's immigration unit.

It must have been a bit of a shock for him to be confronted by Fredrik Andersen's writings there as well.

Yet again he harked back to the phone conversation the night he found Guri: *I'll find you. Curb your imagination*, he told himself. What motives would Bjørn Thyness have to cause any harm to innocent people?

The coffee was ready. He poured himself a cup.

Jørgen Svinland was no longer interested in knowing the results of any investigations into the *Sea Breeze*. *Now I'm the one who's hooked*, he thought. *But should I be? What is the next step now? Finding out what role Bjørn Thyness played in this case? Or finding the cause of Svinland's lack of interest?*

Once again he was reminded of the meeting in the supermarket, and gave a jump when there was a ring at the door.

35

The ring echoed in the evening quiet. Matilde, he thought, shooting a hasty glance at the radio clock on the windowsill. It was half past ten. He went to the intercom and lifted the receiver.

'It's me.'

What an anticlimax, he thought, and asked himself: *Have I got the energy for this?*

Too late. He had already pressed the button. He could hear the lock buzz and the front door open.

He opened his front door and stood waiting. A clunk indicated that the lift had set off from the ground floor. He waited until it arrived.

'You make me jump every time I see you,' Gunnarstranda said. 'A beard suits you better.'

Frølich stepped aside, let him in and closed the door. Gunnarstranda seemed worn out. His body was a little stooped and his face more drawn than usual. There were dark bags under his eyes.

'Take a seat. Anything I can offer you?'

'A beer?'

'If I have one.'

He went to the fridge and took a can from the six-pack. When they worked together Gunnarstranda was prone to appearing at all times of the day and night to discuss the case. But the case had never been the excuse.

He looked at the can. Dark lager. Why had he bought dark lager?

Frank went back to the sitting room with the can. 'How are things going?' He passed the can to Gunnarstranda, but continued with his coffee.

Gunnarstranda read the label. 'Tove's got her sister staying with us. She's into her second week now.'

'Is it tiring?'

'She's an evolutionary theorist.'

'So?'

'I don't know any greater fundamentalists than evolutionary theorists. They're more convinced about their beliefs than religious extremists. They claim man evolved first from a fish or some sea animal that came ashore and mutated to apes, which then turned into man, a creature that adapted to land by developing lungs, arms and legs, language and the ability to construct a cuckoo clock – but couldn't grow a coat to acclimatise to its surroundings. However, to avoid disappearing as a species it developed the ability to make clothes from plant fibres. Tove's sister maintains in all seriousness that our hands will change shape and disappear because nowadays we do less physical work than before and accordingly don't need hands.'

'You disagree, I take it.'

'She's unbearable. Every time we end up discussing religion. I ask: Did we develop the ability to believe in gods when we crawled onto land? Is the need to prostrate ourselves before higher powers a biological adaptation to our surroundings? All ethnicities in the world have religious notions. If we're to take the theory of evolution seriously the notion of the divine must not only be a human creation but a part of being human – something that follows evolution.'

'Moving on,' Frølich said. 'What's new in the Fredrik Andersen case?'

Gunnarstranda looked up from the corner of his eye. 'It's one of several cases we're working on.'

'And you're bound by an oath of confidentiality?'

The reply was cheap, but he couldn't resist. Anyway the sarcasm bounced off Gunnarstranda, who raised his can of beer.

'Have you got a glass?'

Frank stood up to get a glass from the kitchen.

'You can start by telling me about your career in the private sector,' Gunnarstranda said behind him.

He found a decent beer glass in the cupboard, handed it over and said quite openly that he was appalled that Police District East could consider Guri Sekkelsten's murder suicide without summoning important witnesses. He knew of some vital witnesses who hadn't been interviewed.

Gunnarstranda yawned.

'You don't care?'

Gunnarstranda shook his head. 'Not one iota.'

The answer annoyed him. 'If it isn't important, what do you care about? Why do you bother looking for the person who killed Fredrik Andersen?'

Gunnarstranda leaned forward, holding the can over the glass. The foam settled on top like a delicious white duvet. He raised his glass. 'A rare delight,' he said, studying the beer's brown colour. 'Imagine, we humans crawled onto land and lost our ability to digest raw meat, but developed the ability to brew dark lager.'

He drank, licked the froth from his lips and put down the glass. 'I do the job because it gives me some hope of personal satisfaction. If I find the killer it means I can still do a job and that everything has a point.'

'Everything?'

'Call it life.'

'Is it exclusively personal?'

'Everything's personal.'

'That attitude is simply naff.'

Gunnarstranda smirked at the choice of the word.

Frølich still couldn't control his annoyance. 'Guri Sekkelsten's murderer walks free because those who have the responsibility to clear up the matter are using their authority to maintain the status quo so that it isn't cleared up.'

'There's no masterplan, Frølich. The way I see it, you're upset because you're personally involved. If you'd been at home and asleep, instead of travelling to her house and taking the kettle off the hob, you wouldn't have cared.'

'So what? The facts don't change because of my presence.'

'The point is only that I can't make myself believe that the injustice you're referring to is the result of a definite plan. I think people actually do the best they can within their own limitations. That also applies to those investigating the death of this Guri. We've talked about it before. If she didn't kill herself what would the motive be for killing her?'

'She must've known too much.'

'About what?'

'The murder of Fredrik Andersen.'

'What was it that she knew?'

'She must've known the identity of the killer.'

'How did she find out who killed Andersen?'

'I don't know.'

Gunnarstranda took a swig of beer. 'Perhaps she went home with the writer the night after the trip to the restaurant,' he said. 'Perhaps she turned in the doorway and met the killer on his way in. Perhaps she was with Andersen and they were seen by someone who couldn't bear the sight of them together. Perhaps, perhaps, perhaps. It's just speculation. As far as the detectives can see, there are no motives for killing this Guri.'

'They'll have to delve deeper.'

'Neither you nor I know how thorough they've been.'

'If you mean what you say, why don't you drop the Andersen murder case? Why don't you just tell the officer in charge the writer took his own life?'

Gunnarstranda studied his glass before straightening up and replying: 'As I just said, I have a personal agenda for my work. Besides, the Andersen case could never be considered suicide, however much I wanted it to be.'

'Why not?'

'Because someone stabbed him thirty-three times in the chest. One might hang oneself from under a barn ramp, text a suicide note or come up with a lot of other odd arrangements, but not even Arnfinn Brede can convince the world that someone would stab themselves thirty-three times in the chest, especially when the last twelve are after death occurred.'

'Someone he let into the house?'

Gunnarstranda shrugged.

'Any signs of a break-in?'

'No. The perpetrator either went in with him or was let in later, or was already in the house waiting for him.'

'Any motive? Burglary?'

'That was what we.thought at first. But then we found a wad of notes, the man's credit card and an IWC Schaffhausen with a black dial in the bin by the fence. The watch belonged to Andersen and costs close on a hundred thousand. So the killer threw the watch and the valuables in the bin. It wasn't a burglary. He wanted it to look like a burglary. And we still don't have a motive.'

'How did he get home? Is there a taxi driver to speak to?'

'We don't know if Andersen took a pirate taxi or if he drove home with the killer, caught the tram or walked. No taxi driver has come forward, and Andersen was known as a man with politically correct views on ecology etc. He cycled or caught the tram or bus. His bike was where it should be. He might've used it or walked home for all we know. And, according to you, he was at a "fancy" restaurant before going home. We haven't been able to trace this so-called fancy restaurant. You wouldn't by any chance remember where this place was?'

Frank shook his head. 'Guri Sekkelsten used the expression "tarted up". It was me who interpreted that to mean upper end.'

Gunnarstranda sipped his beer.

'When I was outside Andersen's house waiting for him to come home that time, I saw that someone was inside. Someone was behind a curtain, looking out. Have you checked to see whether there was a woman shacked up with him?'

Gunnarstranda put down his glass. 'There's no lover and no jealousy in this case, Frølich. There is, however, a young man. Your sighting of Bjørn Thyness outside Andersen's house turned out to be relevant.'

36

Frølich sat up in his chair so quickly that it made Gunnarstranda smile again.

'Bjørn's interest in Andersen seems reliable enough. The immigration unit had discovered that Andersen was in contact with people living in Norway illegally. Fredrik Andersen was helping immigrants with deportation orders by arranging asylum in churches or other illegal residences. The immigration unit also found out that Andersen had an under-age asylum seeker staying with him. An Afghan with a deportation order. The unit had been carrying out surveillance outside his house because they couldn't force their way into Andersen's home and take the boy. They'd been waiting for the kid to go out to buy cigarettes or play with a ball. Then he would've been arrested and taken to Trandum at once.'

'They'd stopped the surveillance?'

'Officially, yes.'

'I saw them carrying out surveillance the day before he was killed.'

'Bjørn says that wasn't surveillance. Bjørn says a few weeks ago the immigration unit had spoken to Andersen about the Afghan living with him. Andersen had come to the conclusion it would be best for the boy to go back to Afghanistan. Don't ask me why. He'd managed to persuade the boy to hand himself in. The boy had applied to the UDI, the directorate of immigration, for financial support to return home. They'd agreed to support him because they'd managed to locate his grandmother in Kabul. In other words, he was going home.'

'But why would Bjørn still be spying on the house if the case was resolved?'

'If I may finish what I was saying…' Gunnarstranda said, irritated. Frølich nodded.

'Fredrik Andersen was stabbed with a knife from his own kitchen, and the boy hasn't been seen since. He hasn't used his plane ticket. Our highest priority is to get hold of this boy. He's eighteen years old, tall and thin and apparently has a "very normal" appearance – that is, normal in the country he comes from. He doesn't speak Norwegian.'

'What's the boy's name?'

'He answers to the name Alan.'

'If the boy stabbed Andersen and fled the place, surely he would have kept the money and the card, wouldn't he?'

'You have a point. The case is a mystery.'

'The boy could've seen what happened.'

'If he was there. But we don't know if he was. You say you saw a curtain twitch. But you also say you saw an elderly woman come out of his house. It could've been her who moved the curtain, couldn't it? Maybe this elderly woman even knows where the boy is.'

Frølich stared at Gunnarstranda. 'Maybe,' he said.

'You still insist you saw her?'

'I know who she is.'

Now it was Gunnarstranda's turn to sit up. 'What's her name?'

'Lise Svinland. She's related to Andersen. She's married to Fredrik Andersen's uncle.'

'How do you know that?'

'I can't tell you.'

'Why not?'

'That wouldn't be right with regard to one of my clients.'

Gunnarstranda smirked again. 'Another one?'

Frank ignored the comment. 'I still don't understand why you're playing down Bjørn's interest in Andersen.'

'I'm not playing down anything. You don't know what we prioritise and what we don't.'

They sat looking at one another. Finally Gunnarstranda lifted his glass and finished the beer. Put down the glass.

Frølich gestured with his hand. 'Another one?'

37

It was close to midnight by the time Gunnarstranda left.

Frank didn't feel tired. He was excited. Matilde was staying shtum and he knew he wouldn't sleep if he went to bed now.

He stood by the window and looked down. He could make out a little of the T-bird bonnet. The broad grille sneered back at him.

Why would a boy Fredrik Andersen took care of kill him? The result of a furious row? Fury because he felt forced to hand himself in to the police? Where would the pressure come from if the boy's application to the UDI for a travel grant had been accepted? And where would the fury come from in the middle of the night? Could Andersen have come home late at night and caught the boy doing something wrong, which started a huge fight?

He had difficulty imagining this: a poor soul receiving help and food, and everything he needed, attacking the man who was helping him. But if he had done it, why throw his valuables in the bin afterwards?

Was the boy witness to what happened or had he been elsewhere? Perhaps someone other than the boy had been waiting for Andersen when he came home? Whoever it was, their presence, or something they did, provoked a violent confrontation.

Bjørn Thyness? He didn't understand why Gunnarstranda chose to ignore Bjørn's interest in Andersen. The man had been keeping the house under surveillance for no official reason.

Or did a specific event take place that night before Andersen returned home?

Fredrik Andersen and Sheyma must have asked Guri about Aisha. Something must have come up in that conversation. Something that scared the wits out of Guri when she heard Andersen had been killed.

Snorre Norheim was a man who attacked people with a baseball bat if they rang his wife. He could have turned up at Andersen's house after the meeting between Andersen, his wife and Guri.

A dark-haired woman had asked after Shamal the day he disappeared from the refugee centre.

Sheyma Bashur. Everything had started with her.

He took out Snorre Norheim's business card. Flicked it between his fingers as he wondered whether to ring. Eventually he made a decision. He did actually have some news to pass onto his client.

He tapped in Norheim's number. The phone rang only twice before he answered.

'Frølich here.'

'One moment.'

He could hear Norheim putting a hand over the phone and talking to someone. He heard a door close.

'Good, Frølich. What have you got for me?'

'I've found the person who used to stay at Guri Sekkelsten's. His name's Shamal. I don't know the surname. He's an illegal immigrant.'

There was a silence at the other end.

'Are you there?'

'I am,' Norheim said. 'Where is this Shamal?'

'He says he can't testify on anything to do with Guri Sekkelsten's death. He left the house before she got there that night. I believe him.'

'Why?'

'Because he has a witness. Shamal doesn't want to hand himself into the police, either, because he would risk being deported. I understand his position. Guri Sekkelsten's death is officially suicide and suspicious circumstances have been ruled out. Shamal's testimony would do nothing to change that. So I consider your assignment completed.'

'Not so fast, Frølich. I want to know where he is.'

'Why?'

'I'd like to talk to him personally.'

'Why?'

'I can't see that that's any of your business.'

'Then I can't help you. Good night.'

'Wait.'

He put the phone to his ear again. 'Yes?'

'It would mean a lot to me to talk to him. Can you bring him along to meet me?'

'You have to be clearer. Why do you want to meet him?'

'I'll tell you when you bring him along.'

Frank Frølich went quiet.

'Have we an agreement, Frølich?'

'No.'

'Why not?'

'When you're ready to tell me why you want to meet him, we might have an agreement.'

Silence.

He counted the seconds. He cleared his throat. 'So we don't have an agreement. Goodbye.'

'Wait.'

'What is it?'

'It's my wife who wants to meet him. They know each other.'

Frølich waited for him to carry on. But he didn't. 'So you have no interest in this?'

'No, but it's very important for Alicia to meet this man.'

'Why?'

'I've already said too much, Frølich. Will you come?'

'Where do you want to meet?'

'Could you bring him to the fortress, in Akershus?'

'Why there?'

'It's discreet.'

'The fortress is a tourist trap. It's not at all discreet.'

'Not if you come now.'

'Now? It's almost midnight. That's out of the question.'

'How much time do you need?'

'Why can't you meet him tomorrow? We can meet in a café.'

'I'd like this to be discreet, Frølich. You have to be present.'

'Who else will be there?'

'It'll just be you, Alicia and Shamal.'

'Not you?'

'We have small children. One of us has to stay here.'

Frank deliberated.

'What's it going to be?'

'I'll see what Shamal's willing to do. It'll take two or three hours. It's quite a drive.'

'That's fine. Alicia will make sure the door at the Kontrasjæret entrance is open. I work there. I'll give her the key. Meet inside the fortress, by the benches on the west-facing wall.'

Frølich looked at his reflection in the window and nodded.

'If Shamal won't do it, you'll hear from me within the hour.'

38

He stood by the window with the phone in his hand. The man who couldn't bear strangers calling his wife was insisting on a meeting between her and Shamal at a deserted place after midnight – the stench reached his nostrils all the way through the ether.

If anyone showed up at Akershus fortress it would be Snorre Norheim. In other words, Norheim was lying.

He went to the Yellow Pages, found Guri Sekkelsten's aunt's number and called her.

She took a long time to answer.

'It's me, Frølich. It was nice to meet you.'

'You too, Frølich.'

'My apologies for calling so late.'

'I never go to bed before two, Frølich. The first two hours after midnight are the best in the whole day.'

'In terms of the light, do you mean?'

'In all ways, Frølich.'

'Can I talk to Shamal?'

'Just a moment.'

He could hear the shuffle of feet. A silence lasted until he could hear lighter footsteps on the stairs.

'Hello.'

'Hello, Shamal.'

'Yes?'

'This is Frank Frølich here. I've found Sheyma.'

Silence.

'Shall we go to see her together?'

The silence persisted. So he repeated the question:

'Shall we go to see her together?'

'OK.'

'Can you get into Oslo? Now?'

'Just say where we're meeting. I'll be there.'

'We're meeting at Akershus Fortress.'

'Why there?'

'We're meeting a man who knows where she is. Sheyma. He'll take us to her.'

'Who is this man?'

'A military man. He works there, at the fortress. He has a key and will open up for us.'

'What's his name?'

Frank Frølich hesitated. He had passed on the name of a client before. That had been an error. This time he wanted to see the effect of the name. He said:

'The man's name is Snorre Norheim.'

'Can you spell it for me?'

Frank regarded his pale face in the window reflection as he spelt the name. 'When can you be in Oslo?'

'In two hours.'

'Akershus Fortress. The entrance at the top of Rådhusgata, in the area known as Kontrasjæret. Do you know where that is?'

'I'll find it.'

'We'll meet there.'

39

He rang off. Went into the bedroom to find a clean jumper. The bag Matilde had taken with her to Tingvoll was still on the floor. Her dress hung over the back of the chair by the window. For a few seconds he stood gazing at her things, thinking it was a good sign they were still here. He went to the cupboard, found a jumper, went into the bathroom and washed his face. Turned and looked at the washing machine. There were clothes in it. He opened the door. Matilde's clothes.

Should he ring her?

Presumably she was waiting for a call, an explanation, apologies, a confession.

This was a dreadful position he had put them both in. That had to be why she wasn't getting in touch. Because she didn't want to initiate the mortification they would both have to go through when she made her accusation. Naturally, she would think he could have done things differently, that he could have avoided this situation without much effort. She was right, of course. But he couldn't be the one to start this humiliation, either; he couldn't bring himself to contact her. Not now.

He set off in his car too early. So he drove aimlessly around the city centre, feeling an old longing: for a life without duty, without responsibility and without a sense of guilt. For a state of being in which getting plastered in some dive and exchanging vacuities with people as pathetic as himself was a matter of course.

He also feared what he might have set in motion by agreeing to this meeting between Norheim and Shamal in the middle of the night. But he couldn't speculate about the outcome. It felt risky. He couldn't even be bothered to try and predict Snorre Norheim's or Shamal's emotional states. He had enough on his plate with his own. He drove through the city centre for perhaps the third time. Stopped at the lights in Dronning Eufemias gate, thinking about Travis Bickle, who took a job as a New York taxi driver to cope with chronic insomnia at night. It was a tempting thought. A lifestyle without obligations. You appear when other people are having breaks. Spend your time transporting strangers from one stage in their lives to another. When he parked in Kongens gate more than two hours had passed. But he didn't see anything of Shamal as he trudged up towards Kontrasjæret. His phone was exhibiting no signs of life. He checked the display. No one had rung.

He waited at the lights, opposite the fountain with the sculpture of Christian IV's glove. A Slavic-looking prostitute jumped out of a car and raised an eyebrow at him. He shook his head.

The lights changed from green to red to green and back again. People drifted past, young people on their way to the next watering hole. It was a summer's night and, despite a light shower, quite warm.

The Slavic-looking woman had positioned herself by the lights between Rådhus gata and Nedre Slottsgate. She was wearing a kind of corset over a mini-skirt and black boots with high heels. They reached up over her knees and reminded him of the fairy tale *Puss in Boots*. She teetered into the street whenever a car passed. Again she turned to him. He left before she had a chance to make any further advances.

As Shamal had decided to absent himself, he would have to go in alone.

Akershus Fortress was immense. There were museums inside, office complexes for the defence staff and cobblestone paths between high walls for the tourists and the fortress kitsch, such as batteries of cannons and places of execution.

He passed Café Skansen and continued down the lawn to

Myntgata. Here he stopped and listened. There was total silence. A low wrought-iron gate to the right was locked. In front, the cobblestone pavement led to the entrance in the fortress wall. The entrance consisted of double wooden doors under an arch. The doors seemed closed and locked. He walked up and discovered that one was ajar. The hinges screamed as he shoved it open and slipped inside.

The air was saturated with damp mist. But the cobblestones here, behind the walls, didn't seem unsafe. He was alone as he continued up the rampart with the batteries of cannons and a view of the west. Here, he stopped to gaze across Piper Bay and the harbour. The light summer night was at its darkest. The office buildings in Aker Brygge were reflected in the harbour waters. In a few hours the day's first trams would be gliding across the City Hall square. A random selection of people, ignorant of the hopes, pain and defeats of others would be passing one another, people who would have their own problems to contend with, who would allow their fellow creatures to go in peace, thereby demonstrating that most of the time humanity is tranquil.

He sat down on a bench, prepared to wait.

Shamal wasn't coming. Nor was Snorre Norheim, nor was his wife.

They weren't co-operating, and he had no idea why, only that there was reason for concern.

After twenty minutes had passed, he was fed up with waiting and walked back to the double wooden doors under the arch. He stopped and pulled at one door. It was locked.

40

He turned away from the door to find another exit. And jumped as a shadow slid out from behind a wall.

'You scared me.'

'Why are you alone?' Snorre Norheim said.

'Why are you here and not your wife?'

Norheim didn't answer.

'I assume Shamal's on his way. We arranged to meet here.'

Norheim still didn't say anything.

'He might be waiting outside. You've got the key. You can open the door and have a look.'

Norheim still didn't say anything.

'What do you want from him?'

Still no response from Norheim. Nor was it possible to read anything in his eyes. The colonel must have locked the door for a particular purpose, he thought. What purpose could that be? Shamal wouldn't be coming in now. But then he understood: no one would be leaving, either. This realisation caused beads of sweat to form.

'Do you know what I think?' Frank said. 'I think it means a hell of a lot for you and your wife to keep her real identity hidden. It meant so much that you killed Fredrik Andersen.'

Norheim looked back as blankly as before.

'And afterwards you killed Guri Sekkelsten because she could testify against you.'

'You're an amateur, Frølich. You don't have the slightest idea what you've let yourself into. You know nothing.'

'I know you served in Basra in 2004. Was that where you met your wife?'

Norheim didn't answer.

'I know she's changed her name and I know there'll be a no-holds-barred response if someone finds out who she really is.'

'You think you know, but you don't have a clue. You're way off the mark.'

The silence was broken by a phone. One of Norheim's pockets rang. He moved, took out the phone, looked at the display and answered.

He backed away a few steps to speak undisturbed. It was a short conversation. He turned to Frølich with the phone in his hand.

'Did you give Shamal my address?'

'No.'

Norheim stuffed the phone in his pocket. 'Did you mention my name?'

'Of course. You wanted to meet him.'

'Idiot. He's found the address. He's outside there now.'

'So what?' Frølich grinned. 'It'll be a meeting between your wife and him. That's what you said. She's the one who wanted to meet him.'

'You bloody cretin,' Norheim whispered. 'You fucking amateur. The man's her brother. He's spent half his life trying to trace her.'

Norheim crouched down to take something from the ground.

Frank recognised the form of the object a little too late. He was about to retreat as Norheim straightened up and rotated his upper body.

He knew it was the baseball bat even if he didn't see it. All he saw was stars in front of his eyes as something very hard hit him in the temple.

41

He lifted his hand and touched the left-hand side of his head with his forefinger. The bump was big and sore.

The ground was damp, but it wasn't rain. The seat of his trousers, however, was wet and the back of his jacket was becoming just as wet. He might have been out for an hour. Or maybe two minutes or just seconds. He had no idea. He staggered to his knees. His head felt like a rusty can. Bits chafed against each other, and it hurt.

He struggled up and tried to collect himself. Slowly sound returned. He could hear the town. A vague drone. The pain increased. He felt faint, but managed to stay on his feet. He swallowed a wave of nausea. Grabbed the handles of the doors. He shook them hard several times. But the doors were still locked. Norheim must have known another way out.

The throbbing in his head was worse.

Should he try to find the other exit?

He looked around. Some steps beside the door led up to the top of the wall. The staircase was closed off with a black chain. He stepped over the chain and took the steps up the wall, which was topped with slate. There were a few metres down to the lawn below. Maybe five or six. He was one metre ninety. Add on half a metre for his arms, he thought. *I'd survive a fall of two metres. Maybe three.*

What was the risk? A broken leg? Anyway, it was too late for regrets now. He was already hanging by his fingers. With the wall pressed against his stomach and face. He made himself as long as he could. And let go. His face scraped against the wall and his jumper was pulled up by the friction.

He fell to the ground.

Which did nothing for the pain in his head. The idea of standing up wasn't exactly tempting. So he lay back on the lawn for a few more seconds, feeling his body to see if anything was broken. The grass was wet. He lifted first one leg and then the other. Rolled onto his side and sat up.

Someone was speaking.

A young couple were standing on the corner of Myntgata with their arms entwined around each other. He got to his feet and staggered towards them. They backed away. He carried on past them, towards Rådhusgata. Trying to focus. Keeping to the pavement. It was difficult. A taxi driver hooted his horn as he tottered into the road. Frank didn't turn around, but rushed on and crossed into Kongens gate, where he had parked his car.

He had to concentrate to prevent seeing double. Unlocked his car with the remote. Opened the door and plumped down on the seat. Checked his appearance in the mirror. It wouldn't inspire much confidence. Wan with a red smear across his forehead and temple. Probably he had concussion. The pain suggested that. Well, the remedy was to stay awake. He should be able to manage that. He put the gear-lever in first and went to pull out, but braked as the sound of a horn resounded inside the car. It was a taxi coming from behind. It swerved and the driver gave him the finger as he passed.

Frank breathed out. Looked in the mirror. All clear.

42

He parked his car under the same tree as on the previous occasion, but this time behind another car: Shamal's old Opel. He switched off the ignition, but sat for a few seconds taking in the house. The lights were lit on the ground floor. The dormer window on the first floor was dark. The front door didn't appear to be closed properly.

The most striking feature of this scene was the car in front of the garage. Frank had seen it before when Alicia Norheim drove the children to school. It was unoccupied, but the headlights were on and the engine was idling.

He opened the door and got out.

Apart from the purr of the engine, there was silence. His shoes crunched on the gravel on the way to the front steps. The wood creaked as he walked up.

He had been wrong. The door wasn't ajar. It had been locked and broken open. The strike plate part of the lock was hanging off and the door frame was splintered where it had been forced. On the mat lay the tool that had been used to break it open: a blue jemmy.

He left the jemmy where it was and pulled the door to. A man's body lay stretched out on the hall floor, on his back. The head was close to the front door. The feet pointed to the door leading into the house. The body was completely motionless.

He crouched down.

Shamal wasn't breathing and his face had lost colour and texture. The glassy eyes told Frank that he was beyond any help.

He had been shot. The entry wound was in his chest.

But there was very little blood. The splinters on the floor were as clean as before.

He glanced at the door leading into the house. It was half open. He stood up. The hall wasn't very spacious. One wall was covered with a kind of in-built wardrobe with clothes hangers and some coats. There were several pairs of shoes on the floor under the coats. Small sizes. Children's shoes, sandals with straps and small rubber boots. There were photographs of the two girls on the wall beside the front door. The glass in the picture frame was smashed. This is where the bullet had terminated its trajectory, in the panel behind the frame, midway between the girls, who had bows in their hair and were laughing at the photographer and showing their milk teeth.

A voice was speaking softly on the radio somewhere deeper in the house. It was a soft voice, a woman's, talking about the weather in northern Norway. Showers were expected over Nordland, north of Bodø, the following day.

He retreated, pushed the front door open with his shoulder and backed down the steps. On the gravel he stood trying to assimilate the whole scene again:

The front door is closed, locked. Shamal breaks it down. He goes in, gets so far and no further. A shot rings out. Hitting Shamal in the chest. He falls.

The dead man was lying on his back in the hall with his head against the front door. A body that told its own story. He fell backwards. He had been on his way in and the person who shot him was in the house.

And here, in front of the garage, was the family car with its headlamps on and the engine running.

Someone had been in a hurry, jammed on the brakes and run up the steps and in.

Snorre Norheim.

When was Shamal shot? Before or after Snorre Norheim drove up?

The colonel had a phone. His wife had said Shamal was outside.

Frølich realised he had quite a lot to tell the police when the time came.

43

After ending the phone conversation he looked up at the front steps again.

If he had been working for the police now, he would have waited for back-up.

But he wasn't. He could follow his own instincts and just be responsible for himself.

He walked towards the steps. *Wait*, he told himself. *Somebody inside has a gun and has already used it once.*

He pulled the door open and entered. He stepped over the body and went to the half-open door. Paused. Pushed the door fully open. A living room with a large dining table and a chandelier on the ceiling revealed themselves.

He went in. The radio voice had stopped. A song was playing. Bobby McFerrin's 'Don't Worry, Be Happy'.

The room had been built at an angle, like a big L. A broad staircase led up to the floor above. Here, behind the corner, was the stereo. Two column speakers each side of a TV.

A suite consisting of a leather sofa and two chairs were situated around a low table. In one chair sat Alicia Norheim. She appeared to have dressed to do some exercise, in a short-sleeved cotton top, tights and pink trainers. She was staring vacantly into the distance.

There was no weapon to be seen.

But he couldn't see her hands. He asked:

'What happened here?'

She turned her head slowly in his direction. Looked at him. 'Who are you?'

'My name's Frank Frølich. We've spoken on the phone.'

She continued to look at him. 'You should wash your face,' she said. 'You're bleeding.'

He wiped his forehead. Felt his headache throbbing. 'Your children?'

She stared back as vacantly as before.

'Where are your children?'

She tossed her head. 'Upstairs. Snorre's with them.'

'Are you alright?'

She shook her head. She reached out an arm. Pressed a button on the stereo. The music stopped.

He ran his eyes over the room. In the window behind her he

could make out a tree outside. The light from a street lamp reflected on the paintwork of his car.

A sound made him turn to the stairs leading to the first floor.

On the lowest step stood Snorre Norheim. The colonel's right arm was hanging down. In it he was holding a gun. It looked like a G17 Frølich himself had used a lot in training.

'Some people always screw up,' Norheim said. 'For example, they come to places they should never have considered setting foot in. You've made life hell for us, Frølich. What I'm wondering now is what we're going to do with you.'

'You and your wife are responsible for your own actions,' Frølich answered, looking at his watch. 'It's three minutes since I called the police ops switchboard. They'll be here shortly. We should spend the time talking. What happened?'

'Talk? To you?'

'You're my client. There's been a murder in your home. You're very probably holding the murder weapon. I'll be a witness in this case regardless of what you do. And you have a few minutes to influence my testimony.'

'Why on earth would I or my wife be interested in that?'

'It always helps to understand,' he answered. 'Insight creates empathy. One of you took a man's life. I believe my version of our disagreement will carry a certain weight.'

Snorre Norheim regarded him for a few seconds as if he were carrion.

'It was me,' Alicia Norheim said. 'I shot Shamal.'

Snorre Norheim interceded on her behalf. 'It was self-defence. Alicia was defending herself and our two children against an intruder,' he continued. 'I usually keep the gun locked up, but since she's felt threatened recently she's had access to the weapons cabinet.'

'You defended yourself against your brother?'

The colonel answered for her. 'She defended herself against a man who for years has sworn he'd kill her. And who forced his way into the house.'

They both looked at Alicia Norheim.

'A long time ago, when you left for Norway, Shamal followed you?'

She nodded.

'Why?'

'This is just snooping. It has nothing to do with what happened here,' Snorre Norheim said. He stuffed the gun into the waistband of his trousers and straightened his belt. 'But by all means. Sooner or later you'll want to know anyway. Alicia left Iraq with Werner, one of my best friends and colleagues. Alicia's father was killed by Saddam many years ago. She and Werner became a couple despite Alicia being promised to an Iraqi widower. The marriage meant a lot to her mother and the rest of the family, economically and socially. The chosen bridegroom was well-off. Alicia and her brothers and sisters would've been lifted out of poverty. But Alicia followed her heart. Werner was the man she loved. Werner helped her flee. They came here to Oslo. They were going to get married when she had her residence permit.'

Norheim walked over to the half-open door where the dead man was still lying across the threshold.

'Don't touch anything,' Frølich said.

'Don't give me orders in my own house, Frølich.'

'It was well-meant advice.'

'Werner died,' Alicia Norheim said.

Snorre Norheim turned back to them. 'Werner just dropped dead,' he said. 'In training. We were playing indoor bandy. It was quite incredible. Werner had survived several years of active service in many of the world's worst conflict zones. Then he comes home and dies in a gym because a blood vessel in his head bursts. In training. The doctors said it was congenital. A defect no one had seen or noticed. He could've died when he was ten.'

Snorre Norheim crossed the room and leaned over his wife. 'Alicia,' he whispered. 'Come on, get up.'

She shook her head.

Norheim turned back to Frølich. 'Werner and Alicia had a year together. I helped with the funeral and the practical side. Language, bureaucracy. All that. We continued to meet after the funeral.'

On the wall, by the staircase to the first floor, hung a clock. The minute hand jumped.

How many minutes had they been talking?

There was no light to be seen through the window. Not a sound to be heard. Alicia sat by the table, still not moving. Frølich said:

'What do you feel now, really?'

'Nothing,' she said. 'That's what's bothering me.'

'Where does the name Alicia come from?'

'Choosing your own name is about choosing your own life. When I came to Norway I wanted to be free. And I wanted to choose who I shared my life with and who I loved.'

Snorre Norheim was moved. He swallowed and knelt down beside her and held her hand.

'So you two got together?'

Alicia nodded. 'We got married a year after Werner died. My family in the village were informed he'd died. I called my mother and told her. But I regretted it afterwards. Werner's death made no difference. Shamal had his mission and didn't give up. The family's honour had to be "cleansed".'

'We knew it was actually possible he might turn up, even though time had passed,' the colonel said, and rose to his feet. 'But we thought we could keep a low profile. Alicia had a new identity. She kept away from groups of people from the Middle East. Everything would've been fine if you hadn't screwed things up.'

Frølich shook his head: 'What would've happened at the fortress if you'd got your way tonight? Did you turn up without a weapon? Had you planned to kill us both?'

Norheim didn't answer.

'It's just my good fortune that I survived the whack you gave me.'

Norheim stayed quiet.

Alicia looked at her husband.

'You said you were only going to talk,' she said.

'I was going to talk to Shamal. But this idiot told Shamal my name.'

He turned to Frølich: 'That's why Shamal came here instead of meeting at the fortress. That's why he broke in when Alicia wouldn't open the door to him. That's why my wife had to defend herself and our children. That's why Shamal's dead. But it could've been much worse. It could've been Alicia lying there now. And you caused all of this, Frølich. Shamal's death is your responsibility, one hundred per cent.'

'If you'd been open with me, I wouldn't have had any reason to tell Shamal anything.'

'No,' Norheim said. 'This happened because of you.'

'I acted on the information I had. Which of you two killed Fredrik Andersen?'

Snorre Norheim regarded him with despair, took a deep breath and shook his head in a patronising manner.

But Frølich wasn't to be side-tracked so easily. 'Guri Sekkelsten was scared out of her wits when she heard Andersen was dead.'

'As I said earlier tonight, Frølich, you're an amateur. Fredrik Andersen was our supporter, one of our best friends. He contacted you at our request.'

'At my request,' Alicia Norheim said. 'I asked him to talk to you because you went to the hotel and asked after me. I realised that Shamal was behind this. He would use you so that you led him to me. I asked Fredrik to visit you and make you see reason. Fredrik got the money from me to pay you. Fredrik said you refused to say anything, but you'd taken the money. So we had hope. But then he was visited by this girl who worked at the refugee centre. She appeared at his office, talking about a sister I'd never had. Then I understood it had gone too far. I understood that I had to talk to her, to find Shamal and confront him before he found me.'

'Again your responsibility,' Snorre Norheim said. 'You told Guri Sekkelsten about Fredrik Andersen. You gave away the name of your client. You broke the most elementary ethical rule.'

'Fredrik was never my client. He placed a few notes on my desk and refused to take them back.'

'Listen to yourself,' Norheim said. 'You're trying to wriggle out of your responsibility like some brat in front of the head teacher.'

Frølich ignored him.

'You and Fredrik Andersen met Guri Sekkelsten the same night,' he said to Alicia Norheim, who nodded.

'I described my brother to her. I saw at once by her reaction that she knew Shamal. But she lied to me and said she had no idea who he was. She refused to say anything. So I said I would hold her responsible for the consequences. We didn't part as friends.'

She looked down.

'Snorre picked me up after the meeting with Fredrik and the woman,' Alicia said. 'We drove home and went to bed, and woke to the news that Fredrik had been killed.'

'Who killed him?'

44

'Shamal did,' Alicia Norheim said. 'I think Guri Sekkelsten told him about Fredrik and Fredrik knew who I was and where I lived. But I still feel guilty because it was me who got Fredrik to contact you. When Fredrik died I realised that I'd have to find Shamal myself and stop him before he did any more damage. I drove to the refugee centre where the girl worked. I went in and asked after him. They confirmed that he lived there, but said he wasn't at work. Then I rang the woman, Guri Sekkelsten. I said I'd been to the refugee centre to meet Shamal, but that he wasn't there. I asked Guri to tell me where Shamal was. Guri said she could take me to him.'

'You went there, to her place?' Frølich asked.

Alicia Norheim shook her head. 'Snorre went instead of me.'

There were now two pairs of eyes boring into Snorre Norheim. He grimaced. 'Yes, I met Guri Sekkelsten. We drove to her place in her car. But by then the bird had flown.'

'And you killed her there?'

'The case has been dropped, Frølich.'

'But why?'

'I have no idea what you're talking about.'

'You strangled her and made it look like suicide.'

'She killed herself,' Snorre Norheim snapped angrily.

'Snorre,' Alicia said. He turned to her. She seemed even paler now.

'It happened after I left her,' her husband said.

'You drove away in her car. I met you as you were leaving.'

'You shut your mouth,' Norheim said, raising his gun. He held the weapon with two hands, arms outstretched. Legs apart. Shooting position.

Frank Frølich focused on three eyes. One black and two light-blue.

Frank was sweating, still dizzy, feeling that his legs could give way at any moment. Snorre Norheim had years of active service behind him. He was a man who was capable of anything. And one person had already lost his life in this house. How crazy could the man be?

'What do you say now, eh?' Norheim said.

'I found her dead that night. I called her phone. You had it and you took the call. You threatened me. Afterwards you visited me because you wanted to get hold of Shamal. So your idea was to use me to lead you to him. You thought about killing me when I rang your wife at the school where she works. But you held back. You preferred to have me lead you to her brother. I was more use to you alive than dead. I still am.'

'I don't think so.'

'You have two small children on the floor above us. What do you think you'll do to them if you pull the trigger now?'

Norheim didn't answer. But he didn't move, either. The gun still pointed at Frølich.

'Snorre,' Alicia Norheim implored.

'He's imagining things,' Norheim repeated. 'Guri Sekkelsten killed herself. The police say the same.'

Behind Norheim, through the window, Frølich could finally see a blue light flashing. But how far away?

'You killed her,' Frølich said.

Two blue and one black eye were still staring at him. 'You're a bigger fool than I thought,' Norheim said.

Frank Frølich blinked sweat from his eyes. His voice failed him, and he cleared his throat.

'The police'll be here soon,' he said. 'My advice is, do this with as little drama as possible. Remember your children.'

'Don't tell me what to do with my children.'

'Put the gun down now and this will all be fine. Alicia can plead self-defence. Shamal forced his way into the house after swearing that he was going to kill her. Her case is meat and drink to lawyers. She'll walk free. But if you pull the trigger now, you won't get away. Then it's you who'll be destroying the lives of those that mean most to you.'

The blue flashing lights were much nearer. Reflecting on the wall beside the window.

Norheim's arm didn't tremble. Frølich couldn't do any more. He closed both eyes and waited.

Nothing happened.

Until they heard wheels crunching on the gravel outside. A car came to a halt. Doors slammed.

'Snorre,' Alicia said again.

Frank Frølich opened his eyes.

Snorre Norheim lowered his weapon. He secured the safety catch, put the gun on the floor and kicked it in the direction of the corpse. It skidded across the floor and lay still by the door.

Frølich forced himself to keep still. As a police officer he would have run to take the gun and confiscate it at once. But he had felt the whole time that the atmosphere was close to boiling over. He didn't move.

A man in a red boiler suit appeared in the doorway. He knelt down over the dead man. He confirmed what Frølich had confirmed himself several minutes before. He cast a glance through the doorway at them. Saw the gun on the floor. Turned to another officer in red behind him. The two of them mumbled something. Both backed out.

Frølich heard a few more cars brake to a halt.

It's not over, he thought. Through the window he could see Gunnarstranda's weary features.

45

A police officer was cordoning off the drive and house-front when, an hour later, Frølich went to get into his car and drive away. His former colleagues seemed too busy to worry whether he was fit to drive or not.

As he was putting a leg in, he heard the front door of the house open.

'Hey!'

He turned to see Snorre Norheim walking over to his car. He stopped. His eyes were cold and the muscles in his jaws knotted.

'See what you've done,' Norheim said in a low growl. 'I have two children who'll lose their mother now for God knows how long. I had to take my children from their beds. They're waking to a house full of strangers. I have to leave here with the girls, now, in the middle of the night to find a hotel. The two of them have to see their home invaded by uniformed police and they have no mother to console them. You'll suffer for this, Frølich.'

'I'm not Guri Sekkelsten,' Frank said. 'You won't have such an easy time with me.'

'I was angry,' Norheim hissed. 'And I had every reason to be. She'd warned Shamal. He wasn't there. He'd done a runner. She sat in the car, lying to my face. She pretended she didn't know that he'd gone. She was that type, the kind that believe they're doing good, but end up creating a hell for others. All I wanted was to tell her the truth. But I was much too angry. And if you ask me whether I have any regrets, I won't give you the answer you want.'

'Why not?'

'Because I'm alone now. I don't know what tomorrow or the future will bring. You and Guri Sekkelsten have put me in this predicament. It's you who bear the responsibility for my being alone with two children. You and I still have a score to settle.'

'I don't believe your version of events.'

'I don't give a damn what you believe or don't believe.'

'You planned it. You didn't let your wife meet Guri that night. You met her instead. When you got to her house and found it empty you realised what you'd done wrong. Guri knew who you were. You realised she might tell Shamal. He would then be able to trace his sister. You killed her to keep her quiet. That's premeditated murder, Norheim. The worst and the most spineless kind.'

'So what?' Snorre Norheim said.

'I'll tell you so what,' Frank said, leaning on the car door. 'You yourself bear the responsibility for the fact that your children will soon be all alone in the world.'

Behind Norheim, the officer with the roll of cordon tape stopped. He straightened up and watched them.

Frank stepped closer to the colonel. 'You'll soon be all alone in the world,' he repeated. 'Because you'll be convicted. You planned it. You'll get the heaviest sentence the law can give. Believe me.'

Snorre Norheim didn't answer. He seemed to digest what Frølich had said, then he spun on his heel, walked to the house, up the steps and inside, without looking back.

46

Driving home, Frank thought about what Alicia Norheim had said. Could she be right? Could it have been Shamal who killed Fredrik Andersen?

Had Guri contacted Shamal after the meeting with Alicia Norheim and told him about the meeting at the restaurant? Had she confronted him with Alicia's description of her brother? Had Shamal gone there, to the writer's house, in the middle of the night to force Andersen to tell him where his sister lived?

Could that be how it happened? Shamal threatening Andersen and finally killing him?

It wasn't unlikely that Shamal had found out about Fredrik Andersen. Guri hadn't discovered Sheyma's real name at the meeting. But she could have contacted Shamal, maybe even before she turned up at the restaurant to see Sheyma and Andersen. She had been so happy at the café bar when he told her the name of the writer. Guri had rung Matilde to pass on the happy news. She could equally well have rung Shamal too, to share the glad tidings – that Sheyma was alive and living in Norway. Then she might have mentioned the name of the writer who knew her.

There was a good chance that Shamal had gone to the writer's house and waited for him that night. The intention must have been to force him to reveal Sheyma's Norwegian name. Andersen had refused and the outcome had been fatal.

But why had Shamal taken the money, the credit cards and the man's watch and put everything in the bin?

Why would he try and disguise the assault as burglary?

Would Shamal have been able to dispose of cash, credit cards and a valuable watch? After all, he was a man who lived from hand to mouth. He didn't have solid ground beneath his feet.

However, it struck him at once that Shamal had been a man with a strong sense of honour. Shamal might have seen Andersen's valuables as dirty, as something he didn't want any part of.

Thirty-three stabs to the chest. That was a frenzy of violence.

The more he thought about it, the surer he became. It must have been Shamal who did it. He could imagine how it had happened:

Fredrik Andersen walks down the street to the wrought-iron gate. A car door opens. Shamal steps out and introduces himself. Andersen tells him to clear off and goes to his front door. Shamal follows him.

Frølich had no wish to follow this line of thought any further.

47

He parked in Våronnveien. The gap he occupied was huge. He got out of his car and realised he had parked in the gap left by the T-bird.

Matilde's car had gone.

She had been here and had left.

In which case, she would have left a message. He hurried to the entrance. Stopped to open the post box, but dropped his keys and bent down for them. Finally he opened the post box.

No letter. No message. But there was something at the bottom. He struggled to pick it up. Managed to get a grip on it. It was a key.

He stood holding the key in his hand. It was to his flat. She had given it back.

The message was loud and clear. No misunderstanding possible.

Inside the flat her bag was gone. The dress draped over the back of the chair had been taken. He went into the bathroom. The clothes in the washing machine had gone.

He had been all in when he drove home. Now it felt as if he had gone without any sleep or rest for weeks.

He went into the bedroom and lay down on the bed fully dressed.

He dreamt about Guri Sekkelsten. She was wearing a traditional costume and sitting on a black horse and talking. But it was impossible to hear what she was saying. He kept trying to get closer to hear the words issuing from her mouth. But the closer he came, the further away she and the horse were. They became smaller and smaller. He began to run towards them. Then all of a sudden they were gone and he opened his eyes.

*

That night he went to a drinking den, but there was no one of a like mind there. He just got drunk. They played Coco Montoya's 'Am I Losing You'. He moved on to the next bar.

Here they were showing a football match on a big screen and after a while he realised that despite having watched for ages he was still unable to work out who was playing. Then he got up, went out and searched for a taxi to take him home.

It was almost midnight when he let himself in, lay down on the sofa and fiddled with the remote control. He dropped it on the floor and left it there. He was lying like this – on the sofa and fighting nausea until he was woken by the phone in his pocket.

Then he registered it was a new day.

It was Matilde.

'Hi,' he said sleepily.

'Are you asleep?'

'Not anymore.'

She didn't answer. He waited. But silence reigned. In the end, he broke it. 'When will we see each other again?'

Her voice was barely audible as she told him she needed a break.

He didn't answer. He had nothing to say. Waited for the accusation.

'You held things back from me. Guri's brother, Ivar, said you testified in court against him. You'd been snooping around his home.'

'It was a job. It wasn't snooping.'

'But you didn't say anything to me, did you.'

'As I said, it was work.'

'But you were there, in their house. You were there searching for stolen goods long before we met. You knew about Ivar all the time.'

'There was nothing I could do about it.'

'But you asked me questions, pretending you didn't know who he was.'

'I felt I had no choice.'

'But it was lies. Bluff. You lied to me.'

'I didn't mean it badly.'

The silence lasted longer this time.

'Will we see each other again?' he asked.

'I don't think so,' Matilde said.

'What are you going to do?'
'Search.'
'What for?'
'My father.'
'I can help you.'
'I don't know.'
'Give it some thought anyway.'
'OK,' she said. 'I'll give it some thought. But don't expect anything. I need a break.'

48

The phone conversation changed nothing. He had already known this for a while. Now it was confirmed. But he didn't want to accept it. He just wanted to get away from the situation, maybe away from himself as well. It was while he was lying there, unable to do anything sensible, that he discovered the key Matilde had put in the post box. It had slid out of his trouser pocket onto the floor. Now the key was on the carpet. He lay staring at it. There was something about a key. Something that had gone over his head. But what?

He closed his eyes. Thinking: key. What do you use a key for? You open something. You lock something.

He opened his eyes again. There was a white object under the chair. He stretched as far as he could. It was too far away and he fell off the sofa.

The object on the floor was Jørgen Svinland's business card. The second he read the name he knew what he had missed. All of a sudden he understood why the attack on Fredrik Andersen had been disguised as a burglary.

He rose to his feet and walked over to the window. He looked out. Good weather. Blue sky. He went to the bathroom and took a shower.

Svinland's address was on the business card. He lived in Oppsal, in a street called Motbakkene.

He donned shorts, jersey and helmet. Fetched the envelope from his desk drawer. Pushed his bike from the hall into the lift.

The sun was a throbbing yellow globe above the mountain ridge as he set off. It was a quarter of an hour's bike ride to Oppsal. He took the footpath past the ice rink and the hill down to Østensjø. He passed flocks of Canada geese and ducks as he rounded the northern end of the lake. Pedalling up Skøyenåsveien, he didn't see much traffic. Just the odd oncoming car. He continued along Østmarkveien to Motbakkene, which turned out to be a narrow, tarmac path between two walls of wire fencing and green vegetation. He pedalled up slowly. Detached houses glittered in the sun. Someone was sitting on a veranda under a gaily coloured parasol.

The yellow house was hidden behind a wall of pine bushes by the fence. Only one window peered out from above the hedge, like a sleepy eye. He stopped a few metres from the entrance. Pushed the bike the last few metres to the gate. Leaned his bike against it and locked it.

He rang the doorbell.

He heard footsteps on the staircase inside. Light, quick footsteps.

The door opened and he was looking into the face of a young man. It was the same person he had seen with the couple in the Manglerud shopping centre a few days ago.

'Hi, Alan,' he said, proffering a hand.

49

The young man didn't answer. He shook hands and bowed, but appeared confused and very nervous.

'I'd like to talk to Svinland,' Frølich said, letting go of Alan's hand. 'Jørgen Svinland.'

'Who is it?' came the sound of Svinland's voice from above.

The young man backed away and held the door open.

Frank Frølich went in and flipped off his shoes.

He followed the young man and removed his sunglasses as they went upstairs.

The staircase led to a comfortably furnished living room. The veranda door was open. The sunlight was filtered through a white gauzy curtain in front of the door.

Svinland was sitting bent over in an armchair. At first, his expression was only curious. But when he saw who was following the boy up the stairs, his lips trembled with fury.

'I thought I'd told you in no uncertain terms...'

'I've come to settle our differences,' Frølich answered. 'I don't like owing people money.'

'What is it, Jørgen?'

The voice came from an adjacent room. It was a kitchen.

All three of them looked towards the open door as Lise Svinland appeared.

She was wearing a red dress with a white apron in front.

Like a grandmother in a cartoon, he thought, and said: 'Nice to see you again.'

She gaped at him without answering.

'This is Frølich,' Jørgen Svinland said. 'He's leaving.'

Svinland raised himself with some exertion. The young man hurried over to him with his crutch. Svinland hooked the crutch onto his arm and supported himself on it.

'Come on,' he said to Frølich, hobbling to the stairs.

'First of all, I'd like to talk to your wife,' he answered, standing his ground.

Svinland turned to him. 'You can talk to me.'

'Wait a moment,' Lise Svinland said.

She and her husband exchanged glances. 'Let me sort this out,' Jørgen Svinland said.

'And I'd like to have a few words with your guest,' Frølich said.

Both spouses looked at Frølich expectantly. He said:

'Alan's at home here. But that's hardly surprising, is it. He's like a son to you now.'

Svinland was still furious. His voice shook when he spoke.

'Don't you get on your high horse with me and sound off on things you know nothing about.'

Frølich unhitched his rucksack, rummaged around inside and passed Svinland the envelope he had once been given by Fredrik Andersen.

'What is it?' Svinland asked.

'Open it and see.'

Svinland held the envelope in one hand and the crutch in the other.

'I hereby regard our differences as over,' Frølich said.

'They were over before you came here.'

'In a relationship the person who finishes it has a certain status. In my opinion, I'm finishing ours.'

'Alright, you've given us the money. Now would you be so kind as to leave.'

'Your nephew, Fredrik Andersen, was killed. Doesn't that mean anything to you anymore?'

'You have no right to speak about things you don't understand.'

Frank Frølich tossed his head. 'Your guest, Alan, lived with Fredrik Andersen until a short time ago.'

Jørgen Svinland chewed his lower lip.

'You didn't know that at first, did you?'

No one said a word.

'Where did you think he came from?'

The answer to this question wasn't forthcoming, either.

'The police want to speak to the boy,' Frølich said.

Now Lise Svinland spoke up. 'Why's that?'

'They think he was in the house when Fredrik was killed.'

A silence hung in the air now.

'When we first met, you'd let yourself out of Fredrik's house. What had you been doing there?'

Lise Svinland didn't answer.

'You were visiting Alan,' Frølich said. 'Was it Fredrik who asked you to see to the boy? Did Fredrik come to you and say: "Pop by; keep an eye on Alan. He's a foreigner here and has no one." Was that how it was? He gave you the key to his house. I saw that for myself. You locked the door when you left. Alan was inside. He had to go back to his country. Fredrik had convinced him that was best.'

'It's not best. It's dangerous to go there. The government strongly advises people not to.'

'Well, I don't know what's best, but according to the police Alan was supposed to leave. He even had a ticket, but he didn't go. Was this what you wanted to talk about with Fredrik that night?'

'Are you insinuating that Alan killed Fredrik?'

'Fredrik Andersen was killed and Alan changed his plans. Why don't we ask Alan right now what happened?'

The young man seemed bewildered. He knew he was being talked about, but he didn't understand what was being said.

'No,' Jørgen Svinland said. 'Let's leave the boy in peace, and you go on your way.'

'You know what happened that night,' Frølich said. 'But when you and I met for the first time, you didn't. You didn't know that your wife had a key to Fredrik's house until I told you. Was that when you found out what happened?'

Frank looked at Lise Svinland. 'You told your husband what happened, isn't that correct?'

Lise Svinland didn't answer.

'You don't have to tell me, of course. But you can't keep it secret, either.'

He showed them his watch. Shook it. There was a clinking noise.

'Something's loose inside,' he said. 'A screw or who knows what? What's certain is that sooner or later the loose part will touch something vital and then the watch will stop. It's just a question of time. It's the same with the boy you've taken in. It's fine now. Perhaps it'll be fine tomorrow and the day after. But sooner or later you'll have to explain. Who is he? Where's he come from? And why's he here? That moment isn't far away. The police could be knocking on your door at any time.'

'Why?'

'Because the police know that your wife visited Fredrik the day before he was murdered. They know she let herself out with her own key, so that she could go back and let herself in whenever she wanted. One of the two of them – Alan, who lived in the house, or your wife – knows what happened to Fredrik, or both do. The police want to find that out.'

Lise Svinland slumped onto a chair. 'He wanted to take Alan from me,' she said.

'Who did?'

'Fredrik wanted to take Alan from me. Fredrik refused to listen. Everything would've been different if he hadn't been so stubborn. Besides, he was drunk and angry. He asked where Alan had gone. I said that from now on he was living with us. I said it was madness to send Alan to Kabul, but Fredrik was upset and angry. You couldn't talk to him. He shouted at me and didn't listen to sense.'

'What was sense?'

'Alan didn't want to go back to his country. He was afraid. He told me. He asked if he could stay with us instead. I said yes. Fredrik was out that night and then Alan moved to our house. I went back to Fredrik's and waited for him so that I could tell him calmly that this was best for everyone. But Fredrik's reaction was all wrong.'

Frølich nodded. 'And when he didn't listen to sense, you used the knife?'

Jørgen Svinland intervened. 'Don't say any more,' he told his wife, then turned to Frølich. 'The main thing is that Fredrik's dead. He's not coming back. You might've seen Lise lock the door as she came out, but what does it matter? The important thing is that life – after thirty years – finally has some meaning. Can you grasp that someone who has her life back doesn't want to die again?'

With difficulty, Lise Svinland rose from her chair. She wrapped her arm around her husband's shoulders. 'There's no point, Jørgen.'

They looked into each other's eyes. 'Yes, there is,' her husband said in a thick voice. 'There is a point.'

She shook her head.

Silence reigned until Frølich cleared his throat and said to her: 'It's best if you hand yourself in. That'll mitigate the sentence.'

She didn't answer.

Frølich turned and went towards the staircase.

Svinland shouted after him: 'You have no proof. It's just what you believe. Can we rely on your discretion?'

Frølich didn't answer. He went downstairs.

'What does your silence cost, Frølich?'

Frølich didn't answer.

'I've got money,' Svinland shouted. 'Just say what you want to keep quiet.'

He slipped into his shoes without a backward glance, left, went to his bike, unlocked it and cycled down the hill.

✳

He cycled with the sun in his face. Considered turning into the forest down by the lake. Decided against it – he couldn't bear the thought of sitting around and moping in his little flat now. Instead he pedalled on to Brynseng and across Ensjø. Then cycled at a leisurely tempo down to Tøyen. A group of bare-chested young men in shorts were throwing a Frisbee to one another on one of the lawns. He stopped for a few seconds, watched them and envied their laughter and energy. He tore himself away and set off again through the small streets in the direction of Enerhaugen. Turned down and past the police station, went onto the pedestrian bridge that led over the railway lines, passed the Barcode buildings and the opera house, then carried on along the harbour promenade by the quays towards the Fish Hall. A number of camper vans had already parked in the queue by the Denmark ferry that was moored there. He kept cycling. It was still a lovely day and he had no idea what to do. On days such as this you should have a partner, he thought, as he passed the hobby fishermen sitting in a line along Akershus quay. An older man in overalls was in the fish-gutting section, hosing down the entrails from the catch. Frank cycled on, past the sailing ships and restaurant boats. He didn't stop until he was on Honnør wharf and could see one of the small ferries gliding across to Hovedøya. Its wake flashed like silver. The silhouette of the boat made him pensive. The man who had been following him on the boat a few days ago was no more. This thought led him to other incidents he felt a need to shake off. He was filled with an urge to start something completely new. The best thing he could do, he realised, the first thing he should do, was to step out of the mire he had been wading through. He dismounted and pushed the bike to one of the benches along the wall. Here, he took out his phone and sat down to dial Gunnarstranda's number.